She ... **man for anything.**

Bree looked over and saw that Charlie was in fact staring. His eyes never leaving her, never wavering.

She was acutely aware that he could have glanced down to the tops of her pushed-up breasts, to her barely covered thighs. If he had he would have noticed the intermittent tremors, the pink skin she felt sure was not just on her cheeks but the tips of her ears.

It was unbearably sexy, that stare, his dark eyes so large, unblinking. As if he could see more than his share, more than she wanted him to.

As every second ticked by, the heat intensified, until she couldn't take it any longer.

'I've got a window in my bedroom," Charlie finally said, his voice—still low and rumbly— moving through her like distant thunder. "I want to take your dress off slowly. Let it fall down your body."

He reached for her. "I've been wondering for hours what's underneath…"

Dear Reader,

My first true love is New York City. It sounds crazy, but I've been mad for Manhattan since the first time I went there as a kid. My father's from New York, so we'd fly out from California regularly. Later on, I had friends who were commuters, spending half their time in NY and the other half in LA. I visited at least once a year, and knew my way around like a native.

So, when I came up with the concept for *It's Trading Men!* (why didn't they have this when I was younger?) I knew it was a New York tale. Ask any single woman who lives and works in the city, and she'll weep as she explains how difficult it is to find the right man in all the hustle and bustle of skyscrapers and subways.

Heroine Bree Kingston is a sweet girl from a tiny town in Ohio who had the guts and gumption to go solo into Manhattan to find her dreams. She never imagined she'd one day end up in the bed of Charlie Winslow, the blogging king of Manhattan, but that's where she finds herself, during Fashion Week, no less! But chemistry this sizzling and a match this perfect was way too good to last, right?

I hope you enjoy the fantasy and fun of CHOOSE ME. Look for more trading card men stories with *Have Me* in May 2012 and *Want Me* in June 2012.

I love hearing from readers and can be reached at joleigh@joleigh.com. And come visit www.blazeauthors.com

Happy reading,

Jo Leigh

CHOOSE ME

BY
JO LEIGH

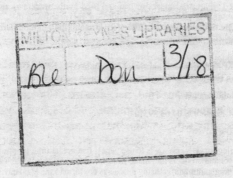

MILLS
BOON

First published in Great Britain 2012
by Mills & Boon, an imprint of Harlequin (UK) Limited,
Eton House, 18-24 Paradise Road, Richmond, Surrey TW9 1SR

© Jolie Kramer 2012

2in1 ISBN: 978 0 263 89370 0

14-0412

Harlequin (UK) policy is to use papers that are natural, renewable and recyclable products and made from wood grown in sustainable forests. The logging and manufacturing processes conform to the legal environmental regulations of the country of origin.

Printed and bound in Spain
by Blackprint CPI, Barcelona

Jo Leigh is from Los Angeles and always thought she'd end up living in Manhattan. So how did she end up in Utah, in a tiny town with a terrible internet connection, being bossed around by a house full of rescued cats and dogs? What the heck, she says, predictability is boring. Jo has written more than forty novels and can be contacted at joleigh@joleigh.com.

To Birgit, for her enthusiasm and support.
And to Debbi & Jill, who rock. Hard.

1

Bree Kingston
Assistant copywriter at *BBDA Manhattan*
Studied Advertising and Fashion at *Case Western University*
Lives in *Manhattan* ❤ Single From *Ohio*
Born on March 22

BREE KINGSTON HAD BEEN IN Manhattan for five months and twelve days. This was her third visit to the St. Mark's Church basement kitchen, where she and sixteen women she barely knew were exchanging ten days' worth of frozen lunches. She'd gotten invited by Lucy Prince, whom Bree had known for four days. Lucy wasn't part of the exchange. Not anymore. She'd moved to Buffalo with her fiancé, thereby freeing up the fold-out ottoman bed that Bree slept on in the one-bedroom apartment she shared with three other girls. Bree's rent was a steal at seven hundred per month. The stove at the apartment had been nonfunctioning for as long as anyone there could remember.

Technically, this was her sixth visit to the kitchen.

She had gotten permission to come to the communal church basement the evenings before the exchanges to prepare her lunches. Sixteen portions of veggie lasagna and medium-heat chili this week packed in small freezer-to-microwave containers, all ready to be handed out during the semimonthly trade.

Although it had sounded odd when she'd first heard about the group, Bree suffered from both of the two major maladies that came with living the Manhattan dream: no decent single men to date and no money.

She'd anticipated both. Since she'd spent most of her twenty-five years planning her escape to The Big Apple, she'd read every article, blog and book about the subject, saved her money like Scrooge as she'd worked her way through college, and even had a decent savings account set aside for emergencies. Bree was in this for the long haul.

Finding the lunch exchange had been a brilliant stroke of luck. Fourteen of the sixteen were also single, worked in the East Village and all of them knew where to find the best happy hours, the cheapest dry cleaning, cell service that actually worked and where not to go on a date, assuming one ever had a date.

Even better, she'd actually made her first real New York friends.

"Attention ladies!" Shannon Fitzgerald, a natural redhead wearing a fantastic knockoff dress Bree had noticed first thing, had needed to shout to get everyone to listen. All of them were standing around a rectangle of tables, their lunches in front of them in neat little stacks. Everyone had brought their own cooler bag with ice packs on the bottom. In a moment, they'd move from pile to pile, an elegant assembly line of working women, all of them under thirty-ish, all of them wearing something dark on this December day. All of them except Bree. She had chosen a yellow-and-black plaid skirt and jacket, emphasis on the yellow, hand-made from her own copycat pattern. Which would have looked very nice on Shannon, now that Bree thought about it.

"Hush," Shannon said, and in a moment, the room fell silent. "Thank you. I have had an idea," she said.

It wasn't just a sentence. Not the way it was said. No, all the words were IN CAPS and **bold**, like a headline. The **IDEA** was going to be good. Exciting. Way more than just a new frozen lunch recipe.

"For those of you who are new—" Shannon nodded toward Bree "—my family owns a printing press. Fitzgerald & Sons on 10th Avenue and North 50th."

Bree had seen the place. It was huge.

"We do trading cards. Mostly sports, but now every-body and their uncle wants them. Artists use them as calling cards, Realtors do the same. They've got them for *Twilight, Harry Potter, The Hunger Games,* and we just finished a ginormous order of official Hip-Hop trading cards."

Shannon paused, looking around the room. Then she smiled. "No one, however, is using trading cards the way they *should* be used—*to trade men*."

Bree blinked, shot a look at her closest friend, Re-becca Thorpe, only to find Rebecca staring back. They raised eyebrows at each other and Bree was grateful all over again that she and Rebecca had clicked at that very first lunch exchange, despite their obvious differ-ences. Bree was from a little town in Ohio and had a huge middle-class family. Rebecca was an attorney, the only child of a snooty New York family and she ran a charity foundation, one of the biggest in the world. Still, within five minutes of meeting, they'd made plans, exchanged digits and by that night they'd been friends on Facebook and LinkedIn and had already talked on the phone for over an hour.

"Intriguing," someone said, and Bree snapped back to the **IDEA** and the drama.

Someone else said, "Go on."

Shannon obliged. "Three weeks ago, I went out on a fix up. My cousin knew this guy who worked with this other guy, and you know the drill. He was great. Really. We met at Monterone—I know, risotto to die for—anyway, he was good-looking, his job was legit, he'd been with someone, but they'd broken up months ago. It was a really nice blind date, one of the best I've been on in ages. But *it* wasn't there." The redhead sighed. "Zero chemistry. I knew it, he knew it. However," she said, only it was **HOWEVER**, "I knew, straightaway, that he and Janice would hit it off like gangbusters."

Every eye turned to Janice. Bree had met her, of course, but she was one of the few Bree hadn't had drinks with. She was a cutie, too. Tall, brunette, great touch with makeup.

Janice grinned. "We've been out three times, and he's fantastic. I can't even believe it." Janice put her hands on the table in front of her and leaned over her frozen chicken enchiladas. "I'm going to meet his mother on Friday."

The whole room said, "Ohhh," in the same key.

"I know," Janice said, standing up again. Back straight, face glowing. As if she'd won not just the spelling bee but aced the math final, as well.

Shannon spoke. "We've all got them, you know. Men who are nice and cute and have steady jobs. Who aren't gay or taken or married and not telling. Combine that with my family's printing press and what you get is…"

This was like a Broadway show, Bree thought. Or the Home Shopping Network. She held her breath, waiting for the reveal, the **IDEA** in all its glory.

Shannon raised her hands. Holding in each one, a card. A beautiful, glossy card. A trading card fit for a Heisman trophy winner, for a Hall of Famer. "On the front," she said, "the picture. Of course." Then she flipped her hands around. "On the back are the important details. The stats that matter."

"Like…" Bree said, surprised she'd spoken aloud.

"First and foremost," Shannon said, "marry, date or one-night stand."

The women nodded. Hugely important. How much pain in life could be eliminated by knowing who was whom. Each had their place. Bree would never be interested in a marry. Probably not a date, although that would depend. But a one-night stand? God, yes. Someone prescreened? It would be perfection. A Manhattan girl's idea of heaven.

"His favorite restaurant," Shannon added, and again, there was a collective "Uh-huh." "Because while I'm a gal who likes the pub down the street, some of you might prefer a little Nobu action. Then there's his passion."

Silence followed this statement, but Shannon milked it, in no rush to explain, though even she had her limits. "You know as well as I do that all of them want to talk about themselves, and usually they want to talk about their thing. No, not *that* thing. I mean, their other main preoccupation. You know, the Yankees, or the stock market, or the iPad or foreign films. If you're into the Mets, you don't want to get stuck with a day trader. Or maybe you do, but, at least, you'll know going in. And finally," she said, taking yet another dramatic pause. "The bottom line. Full disclosure. Snoring might not bother me, but it might bother you. Chemistry is downright fickle. But we all deserve to hear the unmitigated truth. Google can only give you so much, am I right?"

Again, there was silence, but not because anyone was confused. The beauty of the **IDEA** was sinking in, was gelling, was blooming like a rose in winter. As one, the semimonthly St. Mark's frozen lunch exchange began to applaud.

Hot Guys New York Trading Cards was born.

WITH A QUICK GLANCE OUT the window at the snowplow spitting down West 72nd Street, Charlie Winslow pushed his chair across his office to computer number three, the Mac. There were six altogether, each running a different operating system, each rotating views of his *Naked New York* media group. There were setups like this, well not exactly like this, but similar enough, in an apartment in Queens, a bungalow in Los Angeles, a flat in London and an office in Sydney. Then there was the huge old mansion in Delaware where the bulk of his servers were housed.

Naked New York was a gluttonous bitch, needing constant attention. What had begun as a single blog about Manhattan in 2005 had become ten separate blogs generating at last count over two-hundred-million page hits per year, and far more importantly, roughly thirty million per annum in advertising revenue. *NNY* was just like any other conglomerate, only the products manufactured were ideas and opinions, words and tips, photographs and gossip. Ever changing to remain ever pertinent. The revenue stream was one hundred percent advertising, and while Charlie paid a small team of full-time employees and a very large team of contributors, each blog was his baby whether it focused on celebrities, finance, sports, technology, gaming or even the female perspective on life. He trusted his editors, but it was his name on every masthead.

Which had made Charlie a celebrity, at least in the important cities. He liked that part. Hadn't considered it when he wrote up the initial business plan, but there were worse things than getting invited to every major event and having stunning women eager to accompany him to each one. He wasn't in Clooney's league, but Charlie's determination to remain a bachelor had passed from joke to fact to legend in the span of six years.

His phone rang, a call, not a text, and he answered, his Bluetooth gear attached to his ear directly after his morning shower. "Naomi. How are you today, gorgeous?"

"Filled with wonder and delight, as usual," his assistant said, her voice a nasal Brooklynese, her tone as dry as extra brut champagne.

Charlie grinned. "Any changes?"

"Nope. Just don't forget that the tailor is coming by at eleven. Don't make him wait. You did last time, and while you're precious as diamonds to me, his client list would make you tremble."

"You're always so good for my ego." Charlie glanced at his handset to see who wanted to interrupt his call. It was his cousin Rebecca. Odd, she rarely texted on a workday. "Got to run."

Naomi hung up even before Charlie pulled out the phone's keypad.

What's wrong? Has someone died? CW

A moment later, his phone beeped as his screen refreshed.

Everything's fine. I have a treat for you, though.

He sailed across his floor again, this time to check the stats on one of his latest clients. Their ads had been on rotation in five markets, and they were doing well in four.

What kind of treat? CW

A date.

He laughed. His thumbs flew.

Come on, Becca. CW

She was his favorite cousin, which was saying something because he had a ton of them. His parents each had five siblings and they'd all bred like rabbits. Charlie had three siblings of his own, but only one had climbed aboard the baby wagon.

Instead of the beep announcing a return text, his phone rang. Charlie switched to voice.

"Seriously," Rebecca said. "I think you'll get a kick out of her. She's…different. She's new. Brand-new. Still, wears colors, for God's sake. And she's bright, tiny, funny and completely starstruck. She'll swoon over you, and make that head of yours so large you won't be able to fit through your front door."

"Ah, Rebecca. I didn't know you cared. She sounds perfect."

"I'm betting you're not booked for Valentine's day."

He sighed. "Don't be silly. I never plan that far in advance."

"You will this time."

He looked away from his monitor at the sound of her voice. Teasing, as always, but he hadn't missed the dare. He liked a challenge, and Rebecca was clever. Really clever. "Fine."

"I'll be in touch."

"What's her name?"

"Does it matter?"

He inhaled as his hands went to his keyboard. "Nope." Charlie clicked off and two minutes later, he was lost in a conference call, Valentine's Day and intriguing puzzles forgotten.

BREE HAD MADE CHICKPEA veg curry and mac and cheese for her frozen meals, but like everyone else in the big kitchen, she wasn't here for the food.

Today was CARD DAY.

The past few lunch exchange meetings had been more focused on the trading cards than food. Everyone, with one notable exception, had offered up at least two men to the trading card list. They'd brought in pictures, supplied the back copy, agreed that *all* first dates were to be held in very public venues, with the submitter knowing the details and phone numbers involved. Then, Shannon had done mock-ups of the cards, changed them twice until they had a design that worked. The actual printing of the cards hadn't taken that long, but time had stretched like putty since that day in December. Finally, a month and a half later, here it was. There was actually a chance, remote as it might be, that Bree would find a card that had her dream man on the cover, and all he'd want was a night that would blow the lid off this town.

She didn't deserve to find Mr. Right Now, though. Because Bree had brought zero men to the table. Zilch. Nada. She knew some single men at the advertising agency, but she'd never gone out with any of them. Not that she hadn't been asked. But she was planning on moving up in the company as quickly as possible, and didn't want to make any alliances until she'd been there at least a year. She might be from Ohio, but she hadn't just fallen off the turnip truck.

Bree had plans. More specifically, she had a five-year plan. End goal: to become a fashion consultant, author and television personality. The plan was her guiding light, her pathway through the Manhattan madness. One cornerstone of the plan was that under no circumstances was she to get involved with a man. Yes, a girl had needs. She'd been on dates since she'd moved to New York, but only a couple of them had included sex. The earth hadn't moved either time, which meant that the idea of a selection of eligible, vetted, one-night men hadn't been far from her thoughts since December.

Scary thing, being mostly friendless in a city like Manhattan. Thrilling, too. But the men were different than the ones she'd known back home. The rules here seemed to be more…fluid. The stakes higher.

Thank goodness her friendless status had changed as a result of the lunch exchange. Enough, in fact, for her to have been included in the trading card deal even when she hadn't contributed.

Shannon entered the room, and chaos ensued. Frozen meals were abandoned without a backward glance as the women huddled around one empty table. Shannon's penchant for drama made her lift her cardboard box high in the air only to tip it over, covering the table in a cascade of beautiful, practical possibilities, all on 2.5 x 3.5 thick-coated stock, suitable for purse or wallet, as a handy reference, as a focal point for dreams and wishes.

Bree's gaze swept over the puddle of cards, her eyes wide, adrenaline pumping, hoping for someone nice, but not too nice. Someone easy.

Rebecca came up next to her and bumped into her shoulder. Bree glanced at her friend, but only to scowl. When she looked back down at the cards, her breath stilled and for a moment, her heart did, too. There was a single card away from the pile, directly in front of Bree. On it was a picture that sent Bree's heart racing.

It couldn't be. Not possible. The sounds of her friends dimmed behind the whoosh of blood in her ears as she reached with trembling fingers to pick up the card.

Charlie Winslow. *The* Charlie Winslow. It had to be a joke, a trick. He could have anyone. He'd already had practically everyone. Why would he be on offer in the basement at St. Mark's Church?

"I thought you might recognize him."

Bree tore her gaze from the card to look once more at Rebecca. Her friend's smile was as smug as if she'd gotten past the velvet rope at The Pink Elephant, but Bree couldn't hold out for long. She stared again at the trading card, double-checked. Still Charlie Winslow. "How?"

"He's my cousin," Rebecca said.

"Your cousin," Bree repeated.

"Yep. God knows he's single."

"He can have anyone."

Rebecca chuckled. "Yeah, but if all you're eating is

lobster and champagne every night, it's bound to get boring, don't you think?"

Bree shook her head. "Not even a little bit. Although now I understand why you're part of the lunch exchange. We're the tuna fish to your normal caviar, am I right?"

Rebecca dismissed the deduction with a roll of her eyes. "Trust me. He's bored. And he needs a date for Valentine's night."

Bree took a step back, just to keep her balance. "Me? I'm..." She blinked as she stared at the woman she'd thought she knew. They'd gone out for drinks more than a few times, and she and Rebecca had gotten along great. They'd laughed a lot. Rebecca was a couple of years older than Bree, smart as a whip, rich as Croesus, but grounded. Sweet, too. It was one of the mysteries of New York that a woman like her was wanting for dates, but Bree knew that was the truth of it.

"What do you say, Bree? Don't know where he'll take you, but it's bound to be glamorous as all hell."

"I'm from Ohio," Bree said. "I make all my own clothes. Taking the subway is glamorous. He'll get one look at me and fall over laughing."

Rebecca's hand landed on Bree's shoulder. "Don't do that. Come on. That's not you. I wouldn't suggest it if I thought you couldn't hold your own. I've known him my whole life. He's funny. He's smart. You'll like each other. And besides, neither one of you wants more than one night. So what have you got to lose?"

"He's like, the King of Manhattan. What'll I even say?"

"Call him the King of Manhattan. He'll love you forever."

"Don't want forever. But maybe, if people see me with him, even once, they'll remember."

"There'll be pictures," Rebecca said, her focus going back to the pile of cards. "There are always pictures with Charlie."

"What about you?" Bree asked. "See any possibilities in there?"

Rebecca lifted a card. The guy looked yummy, but when she flipped to the back, her expression fell. "One-night stand." She tossed the card back.

"Maybe not," Bree said. "Maybe he only thinks he wants a one-night stand." She kept hold of Charlie's card, knowing if anyone else wanted it, they'd have to pry it out of her cold, dead hand, but picked up the yummy guy's card, as well. "He's a musician. A violinist with the Philharmonic. That's impressive. And he hasn't met you."

Rebecca smiled as she flicked her long tawny hair behind her shoulder. "Are you going to change your mind? Suddenly want marriage and kids from one date with Charlie?"

Bree laughed. "No. Doesn't mean it couldn't happen to someone else."

"Don't worry about me, Kingston. I'll find someone. Let's get you all squared away first. Valentine's night. I'll set it up. Let you know the deets ASAP."

"Oh, God." Bree looked at her outfit. Made on the Singer that shared her closet-cum-bedroom. Hunter-green skirt, lined, with a mod patterned silk blouse, transformed from a thrift store bonanza. Black tights, black heels, a ribbon in her short, short hair. The only thing that had cost any real money were the shoes, and they were secondhand. What if he wanted to go to Pegu Club or 24 Ninth Avenue? Everyone would see instantly that she was a no one from nowhere, wearing nothing that mattered.

"You've got more style in your pinkie than anyone in this room. Than anyone on *Project Runway*. Come on, Bree. This is what you came to New York to do. It's your chance to grab the city by the short hairs. You can do it. I know you can."

Bree straightened her back. "All right. Worst that could happen, I make a complete idiot of myself. I've done that plenty of times. Get Charlie Winslow on the phone. Tell him he's about to meet someone new."

Rebecca laughed. Then she leaned forward just a bit. "You should probably take a breath now, Bree. In fact, maybe we should find a chair. Come on, hon. There's a paper bag right on the counter. That's a girl."

2

Charlie Winslow
Editor in Chief/CEO *Naked New York Media Group*
Studied Business/Marketing at *Harvard University*
Lives in *Manhattan* ❤ Single From *Manhattan*

BREE BLINKED UP AT THE forty-three-story tower at 15 Central Park West, the newest of the luxury, legendary co-op buildings that lined the street across from the park. Just several blocks up were The Dakota, The Majestic and The San Remo. This was quite like being in the center of a very realistic dream. Except that it was freezing. She'd splurged on a taxi even though she'd spent every spare cent on her outfit, using every moment of the trip to talk herself out of a panic attack. The affirmations hadn't been very effective evidently, because even though her date with Charlie Winslow was about to start, she couldn't make her legs move.

She still couldn't believe it. If she hadn't known better, she'd have sworn it was all an elaborate practical joke. Why on earth would Charlie Winslow want to go out with *her?* Of course, she'd asked Rebecca that very question approximately a million times. Bree had gotten a variety of answers, all boiling down to the fact that Rebecca thought the two of them would have a good time.

A good time.

Bree couldn't *move*. Except for her now chattering teeth. The forties era shawl she'd found in Park Slope may have been the perfect accessory, but it did nothing to protect her from the cold. She might as well have worn her gargantuan puffy coat, considering the fact that she was *rooted to the corner of Central Park West and West 72nd Street.*

For God's sake, the most amazing Cinderella night of her life was only moments and a few feet away. She had pictures of this very corner in her New York dream book, the one she'd been compiling for eight years. The only reason Charlie Winslow's photograph hadn't been clipped and pasted was that even her outlandish imagination hadn't been that optimistic.

She had to remember not to call him Charlie Winslow, as if he was a movie star or an historical figure. Bree had practiced. She'd said his first name a hundred times, sometimes laughing, sometimes looking shyly away, coy, sassy, demure, outraged. She was very good at saying *Charlie,* but she couldn't quite help the Winslow part. She'd read so many articles by him and about him, and none of them referred to him as Charlie, or even Mr. Winslow.

She pushed herself forward. If she waited any longer she'd be late, and he'd probably leave without her, which had its merits as then she wouldn't have to endure actually meeting him, but that would defeat the purpose, and dammit, she was brave. She was. She'd gotten on a plane all by herself, knowing absolutely no one in New York, let alone in Manhattan. That took guts.

So did tonight. But she could do it. Because, like her relocation, Charlie Winslow fit perfectly in her five-year plan.

1. Move to New York
2. Get a job in fashion advertising
3. Continue fashion education
4. Find a way into the Inner Circle
5. Become a regular at fashion events
6. ????
7. Publish
8. Success!!!!!!

Look how far she'd come already. She was flying past three directly into four and she'd only been in Manhattan six months! Meeting Charlie Winslow was a piece of cake. The easy part.

Okay, no. That was a total lie. As she headed for the doorman, complete with hat and epaulettes thank you very much, the truth settled like a stone in her stomach. Meeting Charlie Winslow was like meeting the President or Johnny Depp, or Dolce *and* Gabbana.

She would not throw up.

Somehow, the door was opened by the tall man in the cap and gloves, and he smiled at her as he gave her a tiny bow. Then she was inside where it was warm and unbelievably gorgeous. This building wasn't as famous as The Dakota, but it was right up there in the stratosphere of luxury. Her entire apartment could fit into the reception area where she had to sign in. Everyone smiled. The security guard, the other security guard, the woman by the elevator wearing a winter-white suit, whose huge honkin' diamond ring must make it an effort to lift her hand.

No Charlie Winslow in sight.

Bree let out a breath.

"May I announce your arrival?" The security guard sitting behind the beautiful burnished oak desk leaned forward so elegantly it made her think he was desperate to hear who she was going to see. Either that, or he'd almost lost his grip on the automatic weapon hidden above his lap. Just in case she didn't have the right name or something.

"Bree Kingston for Charlie Winslow," she said, and she only had to clear her throat once.

The way the uniformed man's left eyebrow rose meant something. Bree had no idea what. She glanced down to make sure she hadn't dribbled on her dress, but she appeared fine. If nervous. If very, *very* nervous.

The guard picked up a phone, but his hand stilled midway to his console. He nodded, looking past Bree's shoulder.

She turned, holding her breath, praying she wouldn't make a complete ass of herself. And there he was. Just like his pictures, only better.

Tall, though everyone was tall to her, considering that she barely reached five-one. His hair was as perfectly mussed as it was in his photos—dark, cut with such precision that she imagined he woke up looking camera-ready. He wore a black suit with a simple perfectly tailored white shirt beneath, no tie, slim cut, Yves Saint Laurent? Spencer Hart? Or maybe her beloved D&G?

As gorgeous as the trimmings were, it was his face that snagged and kept her staring. Much, much better than his pictures. Big eyes, brown. Very big. A generous mouth, too, but she kept getting snagged on the eyes, and how he looked as if he'd discovered something wonderful and interesting, except he was looking at her. Smiling big-time. At her.

His gaze let hers go as he took his time across the lobby. Not that it went far: a long slow trip down her body, pausing for a moment on her boobs. Not enough of a pause to make her self-conscious. Any more self-conscious.

She'd been scoped out before, sure. But this felt different. Like an audition. Her heart pounded, blood rushed to heat her cheeks, hell, her whole face. Then he was looking in her eyes again, and she exhaled when he seemed even more pleased. Maybe it was an act, probably was, in fact, but it didn't matter because it was only for one night and she'd imagined dozens of expressions on his face, but none of them had been quite this fantastic.

"Bree," he said, his voice low, a cello kind of baritone full of resonance and promise.

"Hi," she said. "Charlie."

He took her hand in his. The one not holding her clutch, the edge of her shawl. "Rebecca told me you were pretty," he said. "She's never in her life made such an understatement."

Bree's blush went four-alarm and she knew it was a crock, but a gorgeous crock, and if he wanted to say things like that to her for the rest of the night, she wouldn't mind in the least. "You're very kind."

"Not really," he said. Still holding on to her hand, he glanced behind her. "George, could you call for the car?"

"It's in place, Mr. Winslow."

"Thank you," he said, then Charlie looked at her again. "Did she tell you where we're going?"

"She wouldn't. She said I'd like it, though."

"I hope so." He led her out, his hand still holding hers until they got to the exit. When the door was pulled open, Charlie put his arm around her shoulders and picked up the pace. Before she knew it, she was sitting in the backseat of a black limousine driven by an honest-to-God chauffeur and Charlie was scooting in on her left.

How was this her life? Her high school graduating class had under two hundred kids. Seven years later, every one of her friends were married, and most of them had at least one kid. And here she was, being whisked off into a mysterious night with one of the most famous men in New York. On Valentine's Day. Holy mother of pearl.

CHARLIE NORMALLY DIDN'T have champagne chilling in the limo. It had only happened twice before, in fact. Once, when his guest had been a Queen. Not the kind from Asbury Park in New Jersey, but a real royal Queen. The other time had been for a friend who'd been crushed by a devastating loss in the love department. A night of drunken weeping and aimless driving had helped pass the time and given her the courage to face the sunrise.

In tonight's case, he'd ordered the Dom Pérignon Rosé Oenothèque for Rebecca's sake. He knew every detail of the evening would be reported to his cousin, and he was determined to impress Rebecca despite her opinion that he was still the same adolescent terror he'd been at thirteen.

But now that he'd actually met Bree, he wasn't sure

Rebecca deserved such an expensive champagne. Bree was pretty, all right. Petite and sweet-looking with an elfin haircut and a nice little body. But as his date? What was Rebecca thinking?

Clearly there was something more to Bree than his first impression would indicate. Rebecca was bright and she knew him very well. Which meant she knew that the women he went for had mile-long legs, wore nothing but the top labels, were on the cover of *Vogue,* never *Home Sewing Monthly.*

Bree was…tiny. She didn't look terrifically young, just compact. Everything diminutive. There was definitely something appealing in her almond-shaped eyes, heart-shaped face, her pale skin and slight overbite. She was Lula Mae before she became Holly Golightly, and where they were headed? She would be a guppy out of water.

He was almost afraid to speak to her, not having the first clue what to say. He was just a vain enough idiot to have loved the way her eyes had widened at meeting him, how she'd trembled, although that could have been from the cold. But that rush could only last so long. Some champagne would help both of them.

She turned from the window as he popped the cork. "I didn't know that was a real thing," she said. "Champagne in a limousine."

"It's decadent and foolish, but then this is Valentine's Day. Besides, we're not driving, so what the hell."

"No, we're not. I should warn you, I'm not much of a drinker."

"We'll have to be judicious with our ordering, then. But how about one drink, to christen the adventure ahead?"

She stared at the crystal flute in his hand. "Yes, thank you. I'd like that."

"There will always be tonic, soda or juice wherever we are, although you'll be surrounded by booze." He filled her glass, careful what with the stop-and-go traffic. "If you tell me what you prefer, I'll make sure you have it."

"I like pineapple juice the best," she said, taking the glass from him with her slender hand, her nails trim and shiny and pale.

"Pineapple it is." He poured himself a glass then sat back, lifting the flute to hers. "To blind dates."

Her smile did nice things to her face. Made it clear she hadn't learned to hold back yet, to equate cynicism with sophistication. He hadn't seen that in a long while. Not up close.

"To extraordinary things," she replied, clicking his glass gently.

The champagne was excellent, perfectly cold and just dry enough. "Tell me about yourself, Bree," he said, leaning back into his corner of the seat. He didn't want to crowd her or make her uncomfortable. They had a big night ahead of them, and as long as she was his date, he truly wanted to show her a good time. Nothing extravagant, naturally. Experience had taught him it was better to stay low-key with new people of any stripe. Since the success of *Naked New York,* he'd had to relearn public navigation.

His celebrity could still be an awkward fit, although nothing like it had been when the business had hit critical mass. He'd set out to make a name, but when he'd first put the blog plan together, he envisioned himself more like a Jason Weisberger of BoingBoing than an Arianna Huffington. Someone whose name would be recognized by people who mattered, but who was not easily recognized in person. Instead, he'd become part of a new phenomena. In Manhattan, more people recognized him than recognized the mayor. Financially, it was the best thing that could have happened. Personally, it had been…interesting and not terrifically pleasant.

Bree turned her lovely green eyes to her glass, watching the bubbles pop and fizz. "I'm a copywriter," she said. "At BBDA. A baby copywriter, which means I'm mostly a gofer and I take a lot of notes, type a lot of memos. But it's good. The people I work with are quick and creative and they aren't out for blood. Well, not more than you'd expect."

"BBDA is a big firm. A number of their clients advertise on my blogs."

Her eyes widened again. "Seventeen of them, at the moment. *Naked New York* is a major focus in the eighteen-to-thirty-four demographic."

The last word had been bitten off, and she pressed her lips together for a second. "Anyway," she said, her voice lower, slower. "I graduated last year with an MBA from Case Western. I'd always wanted to come to New York, so I did."

"Is New York what you thought it would be?"

"Much better. I loved it even before tonight."

He laughed.

"Come on, you have to know how much this evening is blowing the bell curve. You're Charlie Winslow and we're going on a mystery date, and even though I have no idea where, I'm sure it's going to be the most thrilling night of my life."

He couldn't help his wince, although he tried not to. "Most thrilling? That's a tall order."

She lowered her head, frowned a bit, then looked up at him through her long lashes. "Really? This—" she waved at the lush interior of the car, at, he imagined, the night in general "—is insane. It may be your day-to-day, but it's certainly not mine." Bree sat back, sipped the cold champagne. "Rebecca wouldn't tell me. Every time I asked why you'd want to go out with me on Valentine's night, for God's sake, she smiled in that smug way that made me want to pinch her."

He smiled. "You know, I find myself wanting to pinch Rebecca a lot."

"Then you'll understand my frustration when I ask you straight-out, why are we doing this? Why are *you* doing this with *me?* I can't help thinking it might be some awful mean-girl prank. That wherever we're going, there'll be a big spotlight on me when I'm covered in green slime or something. Which would be horrible by the way. In case you need to call ahead."

Okay. She made him laugh. Big point in the plus column. And now that she'd admitted her fear, she seemed more relaxed. Now that he'd noticed, he lingered on the way her simple sleeveless dress showed off the woman more than the garment. He liked that she wore no jewelry. It was a bold choice, but it brought his focus to her neck, which had more appeal than a neck had any right to. There was just something about her skin, the way her chin curved, her elegant clavicle. There was a thought he'd never expected to have.

"Rebecca isn't like that," Bree said, softer now, more to herself than him, and Charlie remembered she'd asked him why he'd pursued the date.

Before he could answer, she added, "I haven't known her for long, so maybe I'm wrong, but my instincts are pretty good, and she stood out right from the start."

Bree used her hand again, not a wave this time, but a flip of the wrist. A tiny wrist, delicate and feminine.

"We went for drinks this one night at Caracas, Rebecca and me and our friend Lilly, who teaches music at this amazingly exclusive prep school, and it started out a little weird, because the three of us only knew each other from the lunch exchange, but then we started talking and we clicked, especially Rebecca and me. When I mentioned how desperately I'd wanted to live in Manhattan, both of them completely got it. How I don't mind paying a fortune to live in the Black Hole of Calcutta with four girls I barely know, and how I can't even afford to go to a movie, let alone have popcorn. They grinned and we toasted each other with sidecars, and I felt as if I was home." Bree blinked and then for some reason her shoulders stiffened again. She cleared her throat. "That may have gotten away from me a little."

And…he liked her. Just like that. No, she wasn't his type, not even close, but he liked the cadence of her speech, the way she talked with her hands, how she was clearly nervous but not cowed. The night changed right then, between Columbus Avenue and West 61st.

Charlie touched her arm. She was warm and soft, and she flinched a bit at the contact, catching herself with a breath and a smile.

"No," he said, "it's not a prank or a trick. Rebecca thought we'd get along. She and I grew up together, were friends through private schools and first dates and proms and way too many horrific holiday celebrations." He shuddered thinking about some of the epic Christmases, the ones where half the family wasn't speaking to the other half, where feuds were conducted across air-kisses and designer wreaths. All that passive-aggressive power brokering over Beluga caviar and shaved truffles. "She knows me as well as anyone. And she's never wanted to set me up before."

"So what does that mean?"

He thought for a second. Excellent question. "I don't know."

Instead of pressing him for his best guess, Bree's head tilted fetchingly. "Where are we going?"

"You don't want to be surprised?"

The way she looked at him made him want to meet her expectations, even though there was no way he could. "I've been stunned since you took my hand."

Stunned? "What were you expecting?"

She shrugged. "Not sure. Something else. I mean, I'm not shocked about the doormen, the limousine or how amazing you smell, because I was secretly hoping for all that. I've never been around celebrities much. I've seen some since I've been here. The obligatory Woody Allen sighting, of course, but there've been others. Quite a few of them, now that I think about it, but they've all seemed, I don't know, extraordinary. In the truest sense of the word. As if the air around them was sparkly, or that even if they looked like they'd thrown on a potato sack and bowling shoes, it was on purpose, but I wasn't cool enough to get it. You're not like that."

"Is that a compliment?"

She nodded. "Yes. It would have been okay if you'd turned out to be a major hipster, although I definitely would have bored you to tears."

Charlie grinned. "Know how many hipsters it takes to screw in a lightbulb?"

She grinned back, leaning in for the punch line. "How many?"

He purposely rolled his eyes. "Some really obscure number you've never even heard of."

Bree laughed. It started out as delicate as her wrist, but ended in an unexpected snort. Her eyes widened and she held her hand up in front of her face, but then she did it again. The snort, not the laugh. And she added a blush that was the most honest thing he'd seen in years.

Okay, Rebecca might deserve more than a sparkling wine. The vote was still out if she'd end up with a '96 Krug Clos D'Ambonnay.

3

BREE KNEW SHE WAS BLUSHING, but there wasn't a single solitary thing she could do about it. From the way Charlie was smiling at her, the problem wasn't going to fix itself anytime soon.

She wished they'd get to wherever they were going. She needed some distance, just for a moment. A bathroom stall would work, a private place where she could squeal and jump and act like a fool and get it out of her system. Because *whoa*. Charlie Winslow plus limo plus champagne plus the fact that his dates always ended with more than a friendly peck on the cheek and she was practically levitating. The whole night, no matter where they ended up, was improbably perfect. Her once in a lifetime.

Someone had reached into her fantasies, reviewed those that were most outlandish and most frequent, decided they weren't grand enough then given her *this*. She wanted to lean over the front seat and ask the driver, a nice-looking guy she'd guess was in his fifties, if he had a video camera, and would he mind filming every second of the rest of the night so she could watch it until her eyes fell out.

She glanced out the window and all her thoughts stuttered to a halt. "This is Lincoln Center," she said, her voice high and tight.

"It is," Charlie said, and while she couldn't take her eyes off the scene in front of her, she could hear the amusement in his voice.

"It's Lincoln Center," she repeated, "and this is *Fashion Week*."

"Right again."

"It was in the blog. This morning. I read it. This is the Mercedes-Benz/Vogue party for Fashion Week."

She wanted to open the window, stick her head out like an overexcited puppy so she could see *everything*. But she might as well paint a sign on her forehead that said *hick*. Still, she couldn't help it if her hands shook, if her breath fogged the window, if she wanted to pinch herself to prove she was really, really here.

"I thought you might have guessed." His voice sounded smiley. Not smirky, though, and she would have thought...

"No." She grinned. "No, really. No. It's too much. Come on. It's...fashion Nirvana. The single event after which I could die happy." She turned, briefly, to gape at him, to verify the smile she'd guessed at. "I've been sewing since I was twelve."

Then she was staring again, at the klieg lights, at the people. Glittering, gorgeous, famous, glamorous people. Her heroes and heroines. In one small clump standing near a police barricade there were three, *THREE,* designers. Designers she adored, well, maybe not *her,* because she was kind of derivative, but still, Bree was going to be in the same room, at the same party as Tommy Hilfiger, as Vivienne Westwood!

She turned again to Charlie, almost spilling her drink. "We are going to the party, right?"

"Yeah, we're going to the party."

"Oh, thank God. That would have been really embarrassing. If we were going to a concert or something."

He laughed in a way that made her shiver and reminded her again that this wasn't a dream. The limo was in a long line of limos, and Bree guessed it would be a while until it was their turn. Which meant that she had a window of alone-time with Charlie. She leaned back in the luxurious leather seat so he was the center of her attention. "I remember reading about this last year. It sounded as if you had a good time."

He nodded. "I did, considering it's part of the job. I think this year will be better." He spoke casually, as if they were talking about stopping at the corner market. As if they knew each other. Casually, but not bored or above it all. This was a typical night for him. A night to look forward to but not to panic over.

Speaking of panic. "We're at Fashion Week, and I'm wearing a homemade dress. My shawl…" It had cost fifty cents at the thrift shop but he didn't have to know *that*. "Oh, God."

He studied her, grinning. She couldn't tell if it was because he thought she looked adorably out of her league or laughably ridiculous. When he leaned forward, Bree wasn't sure what to do until he crooked his finger for her to move in closer. Conspiratorially closer. "The whole point of fashion is originality and talent. Everyone will look at you, at your dress, and wonder who the new designer is. I suggest you milk that till the cow's dry."

She had to laugh, because well… "That's a very nice thing to say." She touched the back of his hand to make sure he knew she wasn't kidding, only the second her hand was on his, she realized how they were mere inches apart. She could feel his breath on her cheek, the warmth of his body sneaking into her own.

That he could think she was capable of pulling off something so outrageous was…awesome. "I'm not sure I could keep a straight face."

"Look bored," he said. "That's the key. Act as if you'd rather be anywhere else on earth, and they'll all think you're the next big thing."

"Bored. I can do bored." She had to lean back a bit because being this close to Charlie was making it hard not to hyperventilate. "Actually, no, I can't, not here. My God, no one's that good an actress. But I can be observant. Which almost looks like bored."

He moved back, too, his smile lingering in the way his eyes crinkled. "Observant can work. Remember, though, that there's no one here you need to be intimidated by. Well, almost. But you probably won't meet them, anyway."

Oh, he was good. This was effortless charm, the true heart of tact and perfect manners. To put her at ease as they inched their way to the Mount Everest of her aspirations? Wonderful, wonderful. But she'd better bring herself down a notch, because at this height, a fall could kill her. "I read an article once," she said, "by a woman whose passion was movies, and she went and got herself a job in the business. She said that in the end it was kind of sad. That what she'd loved were the illusions, the characters, the fantasy. Once she'd looked behind the curtain it was never the same again."

Charlie finished off his champagne and put his flute back in the space next to the ice bucket, slowly, as if he were giving deliberate thought to what she'd said. "I can see that. Most terribly brilliant people I've known are also terribly troubled. Not all of them, but a lot of them."

"I don't think I'll be disappointed. I know it's all illusion. And that's okay with me. I had normal. A whole hell of a lot of normal. It wasn't for me."

"Where was that?" he asked. "Your normal."

"Ohio," she said. "Little tiny town. Great big family. Happy. Well-adjusted. My folks had lots of siblings, I have lots of siblings, everyone else in my family wants to get married, if they aren't already, have a bunch of kids, live within driving distance of the family home. We're a Norman Rockwell relic, with small rebellions and modest dreams. I can't tell you how much I hated it. Not my family, they're great, but that life. Knowing what the day would bring. The Sunday dinners and the baby showers, knowing every person at the Cline's SuperValu and never having to look at the menu at Yoders. I wanted out."

She took in a deep breath of Manhattan limousine air. "I want unpredictability and crowds of people, all of them in a rush. I want to go to clubs and stay out till 4:00 a.m. when I have to be at work at eight and I want to eat things I can't pronounce and I want to have my heart broken by callous men who wear gorgeous suits."

She looked away, feeling foolish. Talk about TMI. It was all nerves, of course, but there was no way not to be nervous given the circumstances. The line of limos, hiding their secret passengers, was still impressive.

"I think you'll be great here," Charlie said, and it occurred to her that the timbre of his voice wasn't the biggest surprise, the kindness was. "They're all divas, and what do divas do best?"

"Get free swag?"

Charlie laughed as he shook his head. "They think about themselves. They'll be far too preoccupied to focus much attention on you. The only reason they'll notice me is because they can use me. So relax. Enjoy it. You'll have a great time."

She was already having the time of her life, and they hadn't left the car, so the possibility of enjoying herself for the rest of the night wasn't out of the question. She wouldn't necessarily trip or spill something down her dress. She'd already decided she would eat nothing that could possibly get stuck in her teeth. And she'd make sure she didn't get drunk.

Charlie leaned forward until he had his driver's attention. "We're going to be at least a few hours, Raymond," he said. "Feel free to leave. I'll give you some warning when it looks like we're ready to go."

"Will do, Mr. Winslow. Thanks."

Bree shook her head. When she'd first come to the city she'd been prepared for mass rudeness, cynicism and impatience from every corner. Hadn't happened. Not that there weren't more than a fair share of asshats in residence, but the proportions had been off. Mostly the people she'd met, whether it was asking for directions or standing on line at Starbucks, had been nice. Pleasant. They could be brusque but they were more than willing to help, even when she hadn't asked. Those were the regular folks, though, not people like Charlie. If television shows about rich New Yorkers were to be believed, he should have been a complete bastard.

Instead, he'd brought her to *Fashion Week*. She'd been a slave to fashion since seventh grade. Her walls had been covered with her collages, a perfect pair of shoes from *Vogue,* with a particular skirt from *W* and a top from *Seventeen.* Of course, there'd been photos of accessories included, affixed with Mod Podge and shellacked so they'd be permanent reminders that she had more than a daydream. She had a goal.

Her love of writing had come later, and the combination? That had been a match made in heaven. Her destiny was set—she'd be a style writer, a trendsetter, a goddess of form and function.

To be here with Charlie was…nope. No words came close to what this felt like.

The man himself shifted in the seat so he could watch her, but also have a clear view through her window. "It's a hell of a culture shock, moving to New York," he said. "A lot of people find nothing but trouble in Manhattan."

"I wouldn't mind finding a little trouble," she said, a blush stealing up her cheeks. She touched her purse, hyperaware of the thong, the toothbrush, the condom and the rest that made up her one-night stand kit. Rebecca hadn't said it outright, but she hadn't needed to. Charlie's bachelor ways were the stuff of legend.

The theme from *Mission Impossible* rang from her purse, scaring the crap out of her.

"I bet I know who that is," he said.

Bree opened her clutch, not wanting him to see her kit, or, heaven forbid, his trading card. She snatched her phone and saw she had a message from Rebecca.

U there yet?

Bree grinned.

!!!!!!!

Knew U 2 wld be gr8

We'll talk tomrw I ❤ u for this!

You're welcome. Knock m dead!

Charlie tried to sneak a peek, and she helped him by turning her screen.

He pulled his own phone out of his jacket pocket. Of course it was something amazing looking. Might have been a BlackBerry, she thought, latest gen at the very least, if not some exotic model not available to the public. Unlike her second-hand first-gen iPhone.

He was amazingly fast with his thumbs. Dexterous. But his texting couldn't hold a candle to how expressive his face was. He grinned in a whole different way than he had a moment ago. None of that sweet, reflective rumination. Now he was the very picture of high amusement, his head tilted to the side, his eyebrows raised in either surprise or delight, possibly both. Or maybe something completely different, but this was the night for believing the best, right?

Before she put her phone back, she turned it so she had his face framed for a quick photo. She'd be damned if she wasn't going home with some physical mementoes from tonight, and no, blisters from her incredibly high heels didn't count.

As she reached to put her cell in her bag, it hit her. Why she was here. Why Rebecca had given her Charlie's card. What the whole deal was.

A favor.

First night out with Rebecca, Bree had spilled her five-year plan all over the conversation. Her dreams, the steps, the obsession. Rebecca hadn't told her she was related to Charlie. Hadn't seemed to be aware of Fashion Week at all. That sneaky…

Which meant Bree had better pull her expectations down another fifty notches. She wasn't really on a *date* with Charlie. She was on a favor. Those two things ended in completely different ways. Favors didn't extend to the bedroom.

Charlie put his phone back in his jacket pocket just as her phone beeped again. "It's going to be crowded in there. I've just sent you my number. If we get separated, text me, and I'll find you."

She had Charlie Winslow's cell phone number. She could be excited about that. It might be a one-off, but so what? Just because it was a favor didn't mean it wasn't the biggest kick of her life.

"You okay?" he asked.

"Fine. Great. Am I likely to lose you?"

"Not if I can help it—ah, we're here."

The door next to Bree opened as Charlie slipped her glass from between her fingers. In yet another spectacular fairy-tale moment, she stepped onto a red carpet. She hadn't flashed anyone, she hadn't tripped and she managed not to let her jaw drop even when flashbulbs popped all around, blinding and thrilling in equal measure.

Charlie took hold of her arm above her elbow, and that was good because she really couldn't see a thing. People around her were shouting, "Over here!" and "Look up!" over and over, and she hadn't anticipated so much noise. Whenever she watched this part on TV it was silent, a voice-over, then a cut to a commercial, but here it was loud and scary and intrusive.

Charlie's hand squeezed gently as he escorted her toward a towering white tent, which she knew was the

Fashion Week venue in Damrosch Park. The area was huge, with runway shows from morning till night, cocktail parties, dining areas, meeting rooms, press rooms.

She'd been here, to Lincoln Center, but on the other side, with the fountain and the Met and the magic staircase. To be here now, when the whole complex was dressed up in its fancy best, when to get inside the tents should have been impossible for a girl like her, was a lot to process.

Thank goodness for Charlie's steadying hand. What world was she in that the most comforting thing around her was Charlie Winslow? She honestly couldn't tell if she was trembling more from the freezing cold or the excitement.

There was so much to look at between flashes of light, she was shocked to step inside. There was a line, and because this was the real world, there were metal detectors to go through. No one seemed to mind, though. Security was tight, and the slower pace as they were herded forward gave her a chance to catch her breath, only to lose it again as she got a load of who she was standing near.

Charlie's breath warmed her neck as he leaned in close. Goose bumps. Everywhere. Down her spine and up her arms. When his voice followed, low and warm, her own breath hitched and her eyes may have rolled up in her head for just a second. Probably in a minute she'd get with the program. She wouldn't feel faint from his touch, or by standing one person away from her favorite designer on earth. The problem was, she couldn't decide what to stare at—the clothes or the designers themselves. Oh, God, there was the model who was on the cover of this month's issue of *Elle,* and good God almighty, that was the star of her favorite CSI, and Bree was so grateful for Charlie's arm.

"You'll never see more food go to waste than you will at this party," Charlie said in that same intimate whisper he'd used in the limo. "I don't think any of these people actually eat. They do chew a lot of gum, though. Ketosis. It's a breath thing, not that you'll ever hear about it in *Vogue* or *W*. People who don't eat may look fantastic on camera, but their breath could kill a buffalo. Be warned."

Bree giggled, and while it was true that everyone in the two long lines snaking into the tent was on the ridiculous side of thin, most of the people she saw were subtly chewing, or standing in such a way as to avoid being breathed upon.

Of course, she thought of her own breath now. She'd barely eaten today, too nervous.

"You're fine," he said, with a minty-scented chuckle. "Don't fret."

She smiled at him as they inched along. "I guess I'm not hiding my small-town roots very well, huh?"

"I don't know what you mean."

She gave him a knowing look. "I'll try harder to appear blasé."

"Don't do that for my sake." Charlie tugged her around even more, until they were facing each other. "I like that this is magical for you."

"I'm a real novelty, huh?"

"Truthfully, yes. But a good one. I want to hear much, much more about your life before New York. I'm a native, and the way I was raised, you'd think there wasn't anything between California and New York. I've never been to Ohio, although I'm reasonably sure

I could point to it on a map. It's at the bottom of Lake Erie, right?"

"Wow, I'm impressed. Yeah."

"And where in Ohio did you grow up?"

She waved her hand at him and turned to check on the line's progress. "You've never heard of it." When she looked back, his smile was a bit crooked. "So that food you mentioned. Passed around on little trays? Buffet? Sit down banquet?"

"The first two," he said. "There will be places to sit, tables all around, and here's a secret. You can completely tell the pecking order by who sits, who stands and where those two things happen."

Her eyes widened at yet another morsel of insider-y goodness. She felt as if he was giving her the ultimate backstage pass, and while she knew a lot of it had to do with manners and even more to do with Rebecca, there was a tiny flare of hope buried deep inside that perhaps he was letting her in because he liked her? A little?

Probably a good idea not to linger on that thought. She needed to be in the moment, enjoying the hell out of what she had. To ask for anything more was tempting fate.

4

CHARLIE COULDN'T TAKE his eyes off Bree. What had Rebecca seen that had made her believe this absurd blind date could work? That it was working was…bizarre. He never would have guessed he would find Bree enchanting.

Hell, that he found anything enchanting stretched credulity.

And yet, watching her reminded him what it was like when he'd had heroes. Though he'd never been as innocently enthralled by glamour as Bree. Given his background, how could he have been? His family was part of xenophobic wealthy New York, the inbred, insane inner circle that made disdain and dismissal an art form. So his heroes had been those outside the fold: sports stars, indie musicians who would never be mainstream, oddball scientists and computer hackers. The last, thank goodness, had actually set in motion key aspects of his life.

"Oh, God," Bree whispered, her hand clasping desperately at his lapel. "That's Mick Jagger."

Charlie followed her gaze a few feet away to where the old warhorse stood, surrounded by his all-but-invisible-to-him entourage. The Rolling Stone hadn't been there a few minutes ago, but there wasn't a person in the tent, hell in the city, that would call him out for cutting in line.

"Huh," Bree said, still staring curiously at the megastar.

"Better get used to that," Charlie said, enjoying himself. The past couple of years, the novelty of his lifestyle had dulled. He rarely considered anything outside of the job. Who to interview, who to keep an eye on, who was ready for a career obit. Filling Bree in was fun. She'd been right. No way she could pass for bored. Not even close. "Almost everyone's shorter than you think," he continued, stepping closer to her. "The men, especially. Not the models, though, they're giraffes, but the actors, the musicians? Most of them are even shorter than I am."

"You're not," Bree said. She turned and laid a smile on him that made him feel like a giant. "*I'm* short. Ridiculously so. It's awful."

"Why awful?"

Her smile changed and the tips of her ears turned pink. "I'm twenty-five, not twelve. Everyone thinks I'm cute. And harmless. Like a baby bunny. I've had people pat me on the head. I mean, come on. Who does that?"

"Not me," he said, holding his hands up and away, mostly because now that she'd said it, he wanted to.

"I want to take his picture," she said, lowering her voice as she stole glances at Jagger.

"So? Take it."

She shook her head. "And that would advance my agenda of being a bored new designer how? I'm already an outsider. I'd like to at least pretend for a bit."

Charlie turned to the person in back of him, some

guy he didn't know, but who looked like he might be a reporter. "We'll be back in a sec, okay?"

The guy nodded, and Charlie kept his grip on Bree's arm as he crossed over to the other line, right smack in the middle of the rock stars' party. "Hey, Mick," he said, holding out his hand. "Charlie Winslow. I'd love to get a photograph with you and my lovely date. Do you mind?"

The man shook Charlie's hand, but only smiled once he set eyes on Bree. Then he couldn't have been nicer. In fact, before they'd been there two minutes, Jagger had his arm around Bree's shoulders and Charlie was taking the photo with her phone.

Bree looked thrilled to her toes even when Jagger copped a surreptitious feel during the photo op. Charlie wasted no time escorting her back to their saved place.

"I have to see," she whispered, pressing buttons on her cell. "My hands are shaking. I'm such a dork."

He took over the delicate operation, and she oohed and aahed at her fantastic luck. She was trembling with excitement and he would never have guessed. When she'd stood with one of the biggest celebrities on the planet, she'd appeared completely cool about the whole affair. Now her eyes hid nothing of her excitement. She grinned widely and clapped her hands together like a kid at the circus. Which, he supposed, she was.

Then they were at the security checkpoint, and there were wands and buckets and well-behaved guards. A short walk across a cold path, and they entered the main tent, the vast pavilion filled with music and chatter and laughter and a hundred different perfumes. Dresses that cost more than cars, faces that had been sculpted to the point of madness, lots of skin, lots of white teeth, and Bree looking like she'd arrived in Wonderland.

Charlie tried not to stare at her as they weaved through the crowd, as some chart topper sang her country tunes and photographs were taken. He sent a waiter for pineapple juice, and when he handed it to Bree, she blinked in utter bemusement.

It was too entertaining to last, because while he was on a date, he was also on assignment, and at least fifty percent of the guests at this shindig wanted their names on his blog tomorrow.

Normally this dance was one he could do in his sleep. Tonight, though, he wanted not just to include Bree, but feature her, make sure she met everyone she recognized. He wanted to see what she'd do, how she'd react. Unexpected. Completely out of character for him and puzzling, but nothing he cared to examine.

He felt drawn to Bree, which hadn't happened in so long he'd almost forgotten it could happen. What was more interesting was that he couldn't pinpoint why. If he had his way, he'd spend more time figuring out the deal with Bree than getting the dirt on the A-listers at the party.

"What's wrong?" After a tour of the immediate area, complete with air kisses, handshakes, posturing and pumped-up drama, they found a spot as far away from the speakers as they could get. Yet even next to the side exits to the powder rooms and private paths, Bree had to shout.

"Nothing. You having a good time?"

"Yes," she said. "Although I'm still in shock. It's overwhelming."

"It is. There are a lot of people wanting attention."

"I see what you mean about the seats," she said as she scooted closer to him.

He slipped his arm around her waist. Interesting, holding someone who was so small. He felt... protective.

"It's as if every chair is a throne, exclusively for the most important kings and queens."

He nodded. "Some of them have a seat for a lifetime, but not many. For most of them, it's a limited run."

"You could sit," she said. "You probably do, don't you?"

"Nope. I work the room. I may be recognizable to some, but my job here is to shine a light on the real celebrities. I'll have to blog this in the morning, and if I don't get it right, I'll get dozens of calls and texts and emails from furious PR people telling me I'm a disgrace and I'll never work in this town again."

A waiter carrying champagne came by, and before Charlie could say anything, Bree touched his hand. "I'd like one, please."

"Sure?"

She nodded. "It's a champagne night."

"You must be starving. I haven't seen you eat a thing."

"I'm too excited to eat. I shook hands with Tim Gunn!"

"I know," he said. "He liked what you were wearing."

"He did not," Bree said, almost spilling her drink. "Why, did he say something?" She closed her eyes. "No, don't answer that. You're being sweet."

"Yeah, but if he'd had a minute to notice, he would have liked your dress. You look stunning."

She sighed. "I didn't expect you," she said. "To be honest, I'm not even sure what to make of you."

"What does that mean?"

"I know I'm not at all what you're used to. Yesterday, I saw a picture of you with Mia Cavendish. Then I saw her on the new Victoria's Secret billboard in Times Square. Rebecca went way above and beyond doing me this favor, but you've made tonight incredible. A dream come true. I don't even…"

He hadn't thought of it in the car, or in line, or after the Jagger incident, but right now, he couldn't think of anything in the world he wanted more than to pull this tiny person into his arms and kiss the daylights out of her.

So he did.

BREE SHOULDN'T HAVE BEEN shocked by his lips, but she froze, stunned more completely than she'd been at being bumped by Jean Paul Gaultier. *Charlie Winslow* was kissing *her.* Softly. Teasing her with the tip of his tongue, waiting for permission to enter.

She obliged.

He turned out to be a gentleman in this respect, as well. No thrusting, no swallowing her whole. Entering slowly, he gave her time to get used to him. To savor. She'd expected champagne but he tasted like mint, although come to think of it, she had no idea what the finish of champagne would taste like.

One flat palm touched her bare shoulder, his other hand pulled her closer, and the tentative portion of the kiss ended, as did all but the most basic of thoughts. He angled his head and settled in for a stay as they explored each other. It didn't take long for her shoulders to relax, to feel comfortable enough to pull back for a breath and a peek, then return for more.

That hand on her shoulder moved across her back warming her wherever it touched. It wasn't cold in the room, not with this many people, but Charlie's touch felt hot, not only his hand, either. The bass from the band made the room vibrate but she was already quivering. Kissing Prince Charming did that to a person.

As if the night wasn't spectacular enough.

She'd never forget this, the song that was playing, how she felt him moan even though she couldn't hear him. It was dizzying, every part of it, and her hope that this was more than just a favor went from not daring to think it to letting the idea take a seat.

He pulled back, not very far. "As much as I'd like to stay right here, I have to work. I'll warn you now, the people we're going to meet won't pay you enough attention. They're working the room, as well."

"I don't mind," she said truthfully. She expected nothing from this crowd. Which couldn't be said about Charlie. She had to stop herself from touching her mouth like a lovesick tween, but God, he had great lips. No matter how she looked at it, there'd been no reason to kiss her, none at all, except he'd wanted to. There went her breath, and any hope of walking on her wobbly knees.

"A room this size, it's going to take a couple of hours. Make sure at some point that you get something to eat. I won't be able to look after you as carefully as I'd like, and we can't have you keeling over from starvation. Grab things when you can, or duck out to the buffet. I'll be holding my cell, so I'll hear if you call, and we'll find each other."

She nodded. "Go. Work. Do your magic. I was always excited to read your Fashion Week blogs. You made me feel as if I was there."

"Really?"

"Well, now that I'm here, not exactly, but more than

enough. Don't tell, but I like your reports better than the ones in *W*."

He grinned. "Now you're just being nice."

"Nope." She crossed her heart. "Mean every word."

"Come on, then. Let's go meet some famous people."

Bree was tempted to pull him in for one more kiss, to make sure it had been real, but didn't dare. Although it was hard not to imagine what it would feel like to walk across the lobby of his building, to go up in that elevator. Before her foolish notions got too carried away, she was reminded, quite spectacularly, of what she was doing now. A boatload of iconic symbols had come to life.

She felt like a Lilliputian in a world of Gullivers with Charlie as her guide. He led her through paths between tables, ice sculptures dripping and corks popping, and always, always the intrusion of cameras. Around the perimeter of the party, the different celebrity gossip shows had staked their territories, and their camera lighting bounced off the white of the tent making the entire arena glow.

They would walk two, maybe three steps, then stop as another celebrity, each one a surprise, approached Charlie. Interestingly, none of the familiar faces looked quite right. They were either better or shorter or skinnier or blonder than they looked in *People* or on TV.

Bree was good with makeup. Really. She'd made a point of learning the correct techniques at a beauty school near her college, but there was an element of magic to the faces that passed by. And the clothes...

She'd browsed through some of the high-end boutiques in Manhattan. D&G, of course, but a few couture houses, as well, showcasing their elegantly crafted suits and dresses, not daring to touch because each button or zip was worth more than everything she owned or would own for years to come. Now she saw those creations in motion, and it was poetry. No way to call it anything other than art. Each designer's style was as individual as a Picasso or a Rembrandt. She felt humbled. And grabby.

Instead of touching the fifty-thousand dollar gown, she snagged some hors d'oeuvres. Prawns and sushi and filet mignon, each with a little napkin and dabs of aioli. If she hadn't been an adult person standing next to famous people she wouldn't have stopped shoving them into her mouth because they were *fantastic*. The champagne was chilled, and she should switch back to pineapple juice because even with the food her edges were sliding toward fuzzy.

She turned to Charlie, only Charlie wasn't there. Not where she'd left him, but that had been before she'd followed the hamachi tray, dammit. She did a complete three-sixty, pausing as she saw clumps of celebrities, and that made her giggle, because certainly clumps wasn't the proper collective. What was? A cavalcade of celebs? A coterie? An ensemble? No, a *superficiality* of celebrities. Ha.

Bree pulled out her cell phone, pulled up Charlie's cell number and typed. *You're not here.*

He could be anywhere, so it wouldn't hurt to meander. Maybe get a small bottle of water. Her cell would vibrate when he texted back, so she could work on her Not From Hicksville Face as she gasped to herself.

Where are you? CW

Standing next to 1 of the Olsen twins. Not sure which 1. Doesn't matter.

Not able to find you via Olsen twin. Something more stationary please? CW

Ah. Stella McCartney holding court.

Perfect. But can't leave quite yet. Ten min. CW

Who are you with? Nvr mind. Ur busy.

Bree lowered her phone, but it dinged.

3 people who want in. 2 who'll get in. 0 fun as U. CW

She flushed with pleasure, even though it was a line, nothing more, and yet she'd never delete that text ever.

❤

The second she pressed Send, Bree panicked. It was a heart. She meant he was being sweet. Not— Oh, crap, he'd probably—

Um. I meant thank U.

☺ CW

She exhaled, still freaked out enough to barely glance at the second Olsen twin. She switched contacts, and texted.

Rebecca, I screwed up.

How?

Sent him ❤

???

SENT HIM ❤!!!!!

No worries. He won't mind.

But—

Hush. Trust me. & smile

The ding from a different text happened. Charlie.

Stay by Stella ETA 2 min CW

Bree decided to believe Rebecca and smile. Then she dialed the grin down from eleven to a reasonable five. Her heart, however, wasn't so cooperative. It was a silly mistake, that's all. Not even a mistake. A ❤ didn't have to mean anything significant. She used it with her friends all the time, and they didn't think she was declaring her undying love.

She was nervous, that's all. The atmosphere, the date itself. The *Olsens*.

And what came next. What *might* come next.

As a sneak peek, the kiss held great promise. She liked Charlie more than she'd expected to, and he'd kissed her, so he didn't find her repulsive or anything, so that was a point in her favor. Truthfully? She was equal parts good-anxious and insanely terrified-anxious about spending time alone with him. But first time—only time—sex with anyone was scary. So much potential for catastrophe. The ❤ was nothing compared to all the things that could go wrong.

She'd had her fair share of errors in the bedroom. The memories of which made her blush. But now was not the time to brood about mistakes made when learning the ins and outs, so to speak, of sex with relative strangers. It was the time to look for Charlie, to appreciate every single moment of being here, in this miraculous room, with a date that made her nipples take note, favor or not.

There were no twins at all around her now, but Ms. McCartney had a very large and enthusiastic crowd around her, and it was easy to see why. Although she couldn't hear the designer, or even see her face very well, the people within ear and eyeshot were smiling. Not the kind of smile that made a person shiver, the kind that erased years and made it fun to eavesdrop. But there was Charlie, and his smile....

God.

That was something. If it was fake, she'd take it, hands down over many other genuine things in life. Somehow, though, she didn't think it was fake. No matter, she grinned back, honest as the day was long. It wasn't that he was the most handsome man she'd ever seen. There were a number here tonight who would look better on a magazine cover. Of course, they were models, so that made sense. Charlie's charm was in the reality of his face. There were lines, small ones, that would have been airbrushed out on a cover, but she liked them. They gave him character and made him look as suave as he was. They were smile lines, which were always a good sign. Especially on the King of Manhattan.

She liked that he was thirty-one. Men in their twenties could have…issues. Fine, no problem, she was in her twenties and could make lists of all the things she wished were different, so no throwing stones, but guys were boys longer than women were girls, that was a fact. Charlie would be a wonderful lover, she imagined as she met him halfway to the dessert spread. That kiss had been an amuse-bouche. The meal would be like heaven.

"You look relatively unscathed," Charlie said. "I'm shocked."

"Why?"

"I'd have thought every straight man in the building would have been all over you."

"Stop."

"Not a line," he said. "I mean it. I'm stunned. I rushed. Although I figured you could take care of yourself."

"Based on?"

"Everything I've seen so far. You and Mick Jagger, for instance." Charlie slipped his hand across her lower back. "What would you like to see next?"

Bree met his gaze. "The view from here is fine."

He sighed, and because there was a momentary pause in the music, she heard it. The live music had stopped a while ago, and now there was recorded stuff—the mix excellent. Of course they'd have a great DJ at a party like this.

"Tell you what. Let's do one more circuit. I promise not to drag it out, no matter who we meet, but you're allowed to linger as long as you like, anywhere you like."

"Wow. That's very generous."

"I'm feeling magnanimous." He nodded toward a waiter. "Pineapple juice? Champagne? Pastry?"

She held up her water. "All set."

He hugged her closer and they began the procession, and she truly did feel like a princess. Her free hand ended up around his back, and somewhere around a very large ice sculpture of Michelangelo's *David* that was a bit worse for wear, her head came to rest on his shoulder. There were a number of places she thought about stopping, because the odds of her seeing these people again were nil, but not even Michael Kors himself was enough to pull her out of the spell of being with Charlie, her one-night-only prince.

5

THE LIMO ARRIVED, AND THANK goodness Charlie knew the driver because all of the limos looked identical, except for the radical fringe who liked their Hummers and their Bentleys stretched and bedazzled. Chivalry wasn't dead, Bree was glad to see, as Charlie stood in the safety position blocking her as she got into the backseat. When he climbed in after, he pulled her close, his arm around her shoulders.

"That was amazing," she said, rubbing her hands together in an attempt to get warmer.

"It was. Everyone came out to play tonight."

"I'm still trying to get it in my head that it happened, that it wasn't a dream."

"Nope. A hell of a lot of the pictures and videos coming out of tonight are for *Naked New York*. I'll make sure you get copies, how's that?"

Bree looked up at him, astonished. "Really? Of everything?"

"Yep. On disk, so you can Photoshop whomever. Just do me a favor and don't publish them. That could get tricky."

"I won't, I swear it. Not the Photoshop part—I'm totally going to do that, and I'm going to save every last nickel until I can get a color printer, but I swear I won't publish. I wouldn't abuse the privilege."

"I'm not worried."

She couldn't stop staring at him. "How can you not be? You don't know me at all. I could be anyone. A competitor. I could work for Perez Hilton or Gawker, and then where would you be?"

"You don't, though. Because Rebecca likes you."

"She barely knows me, either."

"Rebecca has excellent instincts about people. You'll do well to stick with her. Don't tell her I said this, but she's very, very smart. The smartest one in the family, and we've got a couple of federal judges running around, in addition to a bunch of politicians."

"Speaking of, lately I've been seeing all these billboards for Andrew Winslow III. I didn't think of it before, but are you guys related?"

Charlie's expression turned sour. "And so it begins. He's a cousin. Not one I'm fond of. Although, I'm not fond of most of them. Rebecca is the exception."

Interesting, his distaste for his family. So different from her own experience. Sad, too. She didn't know what she'd do without her family's support. Best to get back to the relative he liked. "I'm enjoying the hell out of our friendship so far. Rebecca's ridiculously funny. And she knows the city the way I want to some day. All the little places and the secrets."

"Why New York?" he asked.

"The Chrysler Building started it," she said. "I love art deco, although when I first saw pictures of the building I didn't know what art deco was. Then I discovered fashion, then theater and what was available here, something incredible down every street. I fell for the city long before I stepped foot in it. And yes, thanks to Woody Allen, it came with a score by George Gershwin. I think I must have lived here before in another life. Not that I necessarily believe in reincarnation, but if it's real, then I was here. This is home."

"There's a heartbeat to this place that's either in sync with your rhythm or not. I notice its absence every time I travel. If you're one of the chosen, Manhattan becomes home base and every time you come back, it's as if you can finally breathe again. That's how it is for me, at least."

She smiled at him, as if they shared a secret handshake. She supposed they did. Then she leaned over, her head resting gently on his shoulder. "Thank you, Charlie. Tonight's been one for the books."

Charlie closed his eyes as he pulled her closer. He agreed about the night. It hadn't been easy to leave her while he worked, and when had that happened at one of these things? He couldn't recall.

Not that he didn't like the women he asked out— he did. He liked women of *all* sorts, but he had some strong preferences, he wasn't going to deny it. He wasn't just dating for his own amusement, after all. His image was part of the *Naked New York* brand, and so were the women he was seen with. Some were better than others, some he could talk to, some couldn't string two coherent sentences together, but to a woman they were a type.

Bree wasn't even close.

So far she'd surprised him in almost every respect, though, and as he'd plowed through the glitter, he'd tried to remember the last time surprise had been in the mix. Scandals were par for the course these days, scripted or not. Hell, scandals were the point, whether

they were caused by celebrities or of his own creation.
Parties were only excuses to be seen or heard or pho-
tographed. Everything was grist, and he was both the
wheat and the miller. Surprises? Once in a blue moon.

He wanted to know more about the woman warming
his side, which was also rare, at least in this circum-
stance. He'd always been interested in people. That's
why he started the blog in the first place. Well, that and
wanting to shove his parents' plans for him where the
sun didn't shine. He wanted Bree's details. The minu-
tiae of the life she'd given up to come here, who she
hoped to become. Something to do with fashion, obviously. Was that dress of hers a new design? Meant to
stand out? Charlie might be around high fashion far
more than a normal person should be, but that didn't
mean he was a member of the inner circle. As far as he
could tell, Bree's dress was nice. It showed her shape,
the look of her skin, her curves and the soft skin of her
thighs. He liked it. But was it fashion? No idea.

On the other hand, maybe he didn't want to know
more. He'd hardly be seeing her again, even if she and
Rebecca were friends. Charlie's social calendar was a
function of necessity, not desire, and however much
he liked Bree...what the hell was her last name...she
wasn't on the agenda. Couldn't be. Whatever had mo-
tivated Rebecca to set up this date, it wasn't to fix him
up. He'd known that the moment he'd set eyes on the
girl from Ohio. But he wasn't sorry for the time spent
with her. She'd made his night.

She'd fairly sparkled with how the event had dazzled her. He had to give her credit; she'd handled herself beautifully in the face of many challenges, but even
so, there was no hiding her excitement. It was likely she
didn't realize how she came off. He had the feeling it

might bother her to know that she lit up like a marquee every time she saw someone famous. The ideal fan, in truth. No squealing or flailing or "Oh, my Gods." Just that inner light, the spark in her eyes, the coy and charming way she bit her lower lip when it got to be too much.

He breathed her in, glad the perfumes of the night hadn't swallowed her whole. Another surprise came when he noticed he'd been petting her all during the drive home. Running his hand over her arm. By the time the car stopped, Bree was practically purring and from the look in her eyes, exhausted. Adrenaline drop, probably.

She sat up, looked at the building, then back at him. "So, this is good-night?"

Yes sat on the tip of his tongue. What he said was, "Only if you want it to be."

Her eyebrows lifted, as did the corners of her mouth, but a second later she hesitated and concern took over. "You don't have to. I mean, this was—"

"Do you have to work tomorrow?"

She nodded sadly.

He paused for a single beat. "Do you want to come up, anyway?"

BREE WONDERED IF SHE WAS reading the situation correctly. She inhaled sharply as she remembered his kiss, the way he'd touched her. If this were Ohio, she'd have known exactly what he wanted. In New York? She'd have to take a risk. "I would," she said, hoping she sounded far more confident than she felt. She was going up to his apartment. To his bedroom! Maybe!

Charlie helped her out of the limo, and slid his arm around her shoulders as she thanked the driver. They both nodded at the doorman, but nothing was said as she and Charlie crossed the lobby, his arm draping across her back, his touch warm.

They were quiet during the ride up the elevator. She fit at his side, tucked in neatly. It felt amazing having his arm around her, warming her with gentle friction. She studied him in the mirrored cab, but only got as far as his eyes, staring at hers in return.

They got out on eighteen and the doors opened to a small atrium and the entrance to his home. He pushed open the door and stood aside to let Bree walk in first.

Even after reading *Architectural Digest* for years, watching rich people's lives on reality television, she wasn't prepared for the beauty and elegance of the room she entered. "This is…" she said, heading straight to the windows that made up most of the far wall. The view was spectacular, Central Park in its winter glory, the lights of the city sparkling.

Bree wanted to check out his furniture, the gorgeous art deco design work of the black-and-white floor, the magnificent marble fireplace and the sheer novelty of so much space. But she couldn't stop staring at the city. Eighteen floors up, the breathtaking view covered too much territory to take in, not when there were so many other things to think about. She might or might not have another shot at it, though. What the hell, she could go to any high-rise in Manhattan to see a view, but Charlie was one time only.

Charlie spoke behind her. "Would you like something to drink?"

She turned to him, not sure of much, but she knew she was thirsty. "Tea? If you have any."

His hesitation made her think her request wasn't one

he got often. "I think so," he said. "Give me a minute. Make yourself comfortable."

Charlie dropped his coat on the back of a chair before he disappeared into the kitchen. The tiny glimpse she'd gotten through the swinging door showed a lot of stainless steel and what might have been the edge of a teak cabinet. Strange how when she'd mentioned her love of art deco he hadn't told her they shared the passion. Or maybe the apartment hadn't been his design choice?

The weird thing about her mental tangent into decorating wasn't the coincidence of their taste, but her reaction to Charlie. She was fascinated by him, beyond the obvious. Which begged the question: Would she have agreed to come up if he had been anyone else? Was she honestly as attracted to him as her hormones would have her believe, or was it the *idea* of Charlie Winslow that had her aching to strip him naked and do every naughty thing she could think of to him?

She opened her clutch and sneaked out Charlie's trading card. After a quick check to make sure he wouldn't catch her in the act, she turned the card to the back side.

* His favorite restaurant: *Grand Central Oyster Bar*
* Marry, Date or One-Night Stand: *One Night is his max, but it'll be a fabulous night!*
* His secret passion: *Down deep he's old-fashioned. I know, surprise, huh?*
* Watch out for: *The idiot is obsessed with his work. He needs a break.*
* The bottom line: *Have fun! Just be yourself!*

Bree grinned at the personalized responses Rebecca had inserted. This was one card that wasn't going back into the pile, that was for sure. No, this was Rebecca's gift to Bree, and Bree wasn't going to let her insecurity get in the way of the rest of the magical night.

She flipped the card back to his photo. Objectively, he was a good-looking man. It was well documented, how good-looking Charlie was, in magazines, television and online. But she felt completely drawn to him in a way that wasn't exclusively about looks.

She knew what that felt like. There had been times in college and here in New York that she'd liked a man's looks and just gone for it. Those times had been okay in a hedonistic way, not something she did often. But she had to consider why she was staying, assuming it wasn't just for tea. Was the quick beat of her heart a groupie thing or common, everyday lust or... Did it matter?

The answer was as instantaneous as it was physical. She wanted him in a way that was neither common nor everyday. She'd have wanted him even if he wasn't the King of Manhattan. He'd been a surprise. Nice. Captivating. He'd purposefully shared insider nuggets so she would feel less like an impostor sneaking into the palace. He'd come looking for her, and he'd laughed at her jokes, and he'd kept her warm. That kiss had been...

Well, she'd need to be on her toes tonight, that's all. If they did end up in bed, which was not a sure thing as there seemed to be a whole different world of signals and innuendos she wasn't aware of in this rarefied air of his, but if they did, she'd have to be careful.

How Charlie made her feel, *that* could be dangerous. That was the difference. The other guys, both of them, had been fun in that risky sort of exciting manner when you've taken all the safety precautions so you're not precisely scared, but he was new, and what if he was terrible in bed, or his penis was teeny tiny or he wanted to wear her underpants?

Charlie might have all of those issues, but that wasn't dangerous. The real fear was that she could *like* him. The kind of like that meant nothing but trouble. Liking a guy was not part of the five-year plan. In fact, it was the antithesis of the five-year plan, the one thing that could turn even this unbelievable stroke of magnificent luck into a disaster of epic proportions.

After tucking the card back inside her slim wallet, Bree rested her butt on the arm of a gorgeous white leather couch. She continued to wait, wondering what was taking him so long. As her gaze wandered across the cityscape, she reminded herself about Susan. They'd been college roommates their freshmen year, and they'd hit it off from day one. Susan had decided to go into politics. She'd taken prelaw, had already picked out the three schools she would apply to; in fact, it was Susan who'd shown Bree the wisdom and power of the five-year plan. Susan had been brilliant. Formidable memory along with a quick mind and a powerful presence. It was easy to think of her as a potential senator or even president.

And then Nick had come along.

Susan had fallen slowly. Incrementally. But fallen she had, so hard that it had knocked the plan right out of her. She'd gone on to law school, yes, but at UCLA because of Nick. Yale and Harvard had both come calling, but she'd been in love. Bree had been a bridesmaid at her wedding, and the two of them kept in touch on Facebook, but Susan had a baby now, and she was a stay-at-home mom, which was fine. Of course it was fine. But it wasn't the dream.

If it had only been Susan, Bree wouldn't have given

it too much thought. It wasn't, though. Almost every friend she'd had in high school and the early years of college, every female friend that is, had somehow, someway subverted their dreams because of love. Her experience might be a statistical anomaly, but it was a damn scary one.

Bree had nothing against relationships, but that was for later. She wouldn't even entertain the thought of marriage before thirty, and quite possibly longer than that. Forget a child in her twenties. She wasn't even sure she wanted to have a child at all. Not something she had to worry about at the moment, thank goodness, but liking Charlie? That was a distinct possibility.

Of course, his liking her back was highly improbable. On the level of her winning the lottery. Which was worse in some ways, because even though it was one night, and she had a hint of a crush on him, there was every reason to believe there might be sparks in the bedroom. It would be so very Bree to find herself enamored with Charlie, only to crumble in a fit of pining and lovelorn paralysis for however long it would take to get over it. That would also not be good for the plan.

This having-sex decision was more complicated than she'd thought. Thank goodness she hadn't given in to more champagne.

She wasn't wearing a watch, but Charlie really had been gone a long time. She pushed off the couch and went toward the kitchen, hoping nothing had gone wrong. Two steps later, the door swung open and Charlie came in carrying a silver tray. On it, he'd put a pot, an actual teapot, made of fine china decorated with flowers and vines. There were matching cups, two, and saucers, also two. A little cream pourer, a bowl of sugar lumps, tongs, *TONGS,* lemon slices, a strainer, and she had to get closer to see that the tins were actually different varieties of tea. She looked up at Charlie, and he looked back. It was a…moment.

Part of her wanted to laugh, but a bigger part of her wanted to know *what the hell?*

"Seems I have a tea service," he said, his voice low and wickedly deadpan. "I never knew that. I don't do a lot of cooking, and someone else put my kitchen together. But I thought, why not? I may never be asked for tea again."

"I see—oh, that one isn't tea. That's biscuits?"

"English shortbread cookies," he said. "Fresh, according to the package." He put the tray on the coffee table after she'd scurried to clear off some magazines. "My guess is that my housekeeper is the tea aficionado. She comes in three times a week, and I don't pay attention to her snacking habits. Makes sense, though. She stocks the fridge. The tea set looks like something my mother would own, and expect me to own."

"And here I was thinking a mug and a Lipton's tea bag. But this will do."

"It will, huh?"

Bree nodded. "So many different kinds," she said, busy investigating. There was chamomile, Earl Grey, Darjeeling and one she had never heard of called British Blend. She pointed to it. "Shall I make a pot?"

"Go for it."

She was very glad she'd used loose tea before as she poured the leaves into the hot water, then left it to steep. In her cup, she used the tongs to put in two lumps of sugar, poured in a hint of milk and waited nervously as she realized how close together they were on the couch.

This wasn't like having his arm around her at the

party or even sitting pressed up to him in the limo. A bedroom was now involved, only steps away.

She could take one of two approaches to the next minute: she could bring up the decor and keep wondering what was going to happen until he did something obvious, or she could put on her big girl panties and ask if they were going to share more than tea. "So," she said, "you like art deco."

Charlie glanced up at her, his own sugar lump tonged and hovering above his cup. "Yes. I do."

She barely heard him over the cursing in her head, which was frankly not very nice. She wasn't a wimp and hated to think she was a chicken, but the only way to prove she had cajones was to act like it. "Is the whole place art deco?" she asked, trying to be sexily coy, not creepily stiff. "Your bedroom, for example?"

She winced. She couldn't help it. A fifteen-year-old could have done better.

The sugar fell into the cup with a soft plunk and Charlie smiled. "Perhaps, after tea, you'd like to see it?"

Bree nodded, then busied herself with straining the leaves and pouring. She decided she'd said enough already, but Charlie didn't pitch in to fill the silence. He might have been watching her or gazing out the window; she didn't know because she didn't dare look up. It was enough to will her hands steady and her thoughts calm and composed. Something had happened in the past few seconds; maybe it was how his voice had lowered and how the husky murmur slid over her skin like a warm vibrant promise—she had no idea.

No, he was definitely zeroed in on her, she decided, as the weight of his stare seemed to change the very air around them. She could actually feel him watching, waiting, missing nothing. She set down the pot, picked up her cup and took a sip, barely tasting more than the warmth as the quiet stretched between them. The element of surreality, what with silver tongs and it being two in the morning, made time shimmer and slow. She drank again, the delicate cup insisting she raise her pinkie.

She finally glanced over and saw that Charlie was, in fact, staring. He also lifted his cup to his lips, drank silently, his hand large and his fingers long, his eyes never leaving her, never wavering.

She was acutely aware that he could have glanced down to the tops of her pushed-up breasts, to her barely covered thighs. If he had he would have noticed the intermittent tremors, the pink skin she felt sure was not just on her cheeks but the tips of her ears.

It was unbearably sexy, that stare, his dark eyes so large, unblinking. As if he could see more than she wanted him to.

As every second ticked by, the heat intensified, until she couldn't take it any longer. She blinked. "The tea's good," she said, surprised her voice was steady.

He swiped his bottom lip with the edge of his tongue; barely a swipe really, only enough for the light to catch on the moisture.

"Although I have no idea what makes it a British blend. It tastes like…tea."

He lowered his cup. "I've got a window in my bedroom," he said, his voice—still low and rumbly—moving through her like distant thunder. "I want to take your dress off slowly. Let it fall down your body. I've been wondering for hours what's underneath. I'm guessing black, maybe lace, maybe silk, but definitely black. You'll look incredible standing by that window with the lights of the city as your backdrop."

Bree almost dropped her cup, clumsy and awkward as a surge of wet heat flowed through her. She'd been so together, too. All calm and reasonable and thinking things through. And then he had to go and say *that*.

She was officially in another plane of existence because there was no one in the world as she knew it who could have said those words in that tone with that look in his eyes. If she hadn't known better, she would have thought there was someone sitting behind her, some model or actress or virtually anyone who wasn't Bree Kingston.

"Bree?" His smile was slow, controlled, while she hesitated.

God, why *was* she hesitating? A few more seconds and maybe she could get her legs in working order.

He stood and held out his hand for her. Heart beating flamenco style, head swirling in a cloud of lust and weirdness, she rose without spilling, tripping or making any unfortunate sounds.

Instead of pulling her closer, Charlie stepped into her personal space, then into her. His body touched her from chest to thigh, and he was warm and big and he smelled as if he'd just walked in a forest. Looking up was nothing new, but meeting his gaze so near, feeling his tea-sweet breath caress her lips, that was stunning. As he bent down, her eyes closed at the last possible second, and then, and then...

6

CHARLIE SHIFTED HIS BODY as he kissed her. He'd been getting hard for a while now, since he'd put down that ludicrous tea tray. Bree wasn't his type; there was no question about that, but she was something—

Something.

So small. Not thin, thin was ubiquitous, a thing to get over, not to enjoy. At least the kind of thin he was used to. Bree was diminutive, delicate. How he wanted to hold her completely in his arms, lift her from the floor and carry her off to his bed. More absurd than the tea service because there wasn't a romantic bone in his body and also not enough booze to let his imagination get away from him, and yet, his hands moved down her black dress—which had to go—to cup her hips, her bottom.

Instead of giving in to his urge, he walked backward, pulling her with him. He didn't need to look, not yet. It was a straight line to the hallway, where he would have to make sure to turn them, then another straight shot to his bedroom.

They kissed and walked in their odd shuffling gait. He touched wherever he could, mostly the parts that were bare, and warm, and pebbled with goose bumps. He hoped those were from him, not the temperature. Decided not to ask.

The bedroom was obscenely large for Manhattan, but the building was prewar and the place had been remodeled to make it expansive. He'd put in plush carpet for the pleasure of it, outrageously fine sheets, condoms and water bottles near the California king. Bree broke away from his kiss with a gasp. Not at the luxury of the room, she hadn't looked at it yet, but for breath. To give him a smile.

He nodded toward the wall, all windows, the electronic shades up and hidden to capture the view. "There," he said. "I want you there."

She turned. This gasp wasn't for air. "Oh, it's beautiful."

"It pales." He took her hand and guided her closer to the windows and kissed her again, sneaking his tongue between her lips as his fingers found the zipper pull. He heard nothing but breathing and blood flow, but he followed the zipper with his left hand on her bare back until he reached the end. He touched the strip of elastic that was the line of her thong. The touch was enough to pull him away from the gorgeous heat of her mouth. He needed to see.

The dress fell, puddling at her feet, and it was better than he'd imagined. The thong wasn't black, but red. Dark red, tiny. Seeing it against her pale flesh made his cock harder, his desire intense.

Odd, so odd, this reaction of his. She was pretty, she really was, but she wasn't architecturally beautiful. Perfectly proportioned, yet not so slender she didn't have curves and a little bit of a tummy that made him want to rest his head right there for a week. God, her breasts.

They were mouthwatering, with pale pink areolas and firm little nipples, puckered and waiting.

Bree stepped out of her dress, and oh, that was something. Her in nothing but a ruby thong and high heels. Stunning, delicious…for Christ's sake, the woman was two feet in front him, willing and eager.

He worked his clothes off in a controlled frenzy, flinging things away as he multitasked, toeing off his shoes and socks, moving closer to Bree as he unzipped, hissing as the silk of his boxer briefs brushed against the underside of his aching cock.

He kissed her again, but she was trembling and just chilly enough for him to bow to the nonsensical urge to scoop her up into his arms—she was a featherweight of soft flesh and hitching breaths—and dammit, he should have pulled the bedcovering down. She huffed a laugh as he stood her up, and together they got rid of the extra pillows and pulled down the duvet.

He waited, and when she sat and bent to take off her heels, he made a noise. It wasn't a squeak or a whimper, but it was close on both counts. Bree grinned, rose from the bed. There was a wicked sparkle in those lust-darkened eyes of hers, and when she turned around and went onto all fours on the mattress, Charlie made another noise, but this was a groan that came straight from his balls. She crawled across the bed, her hips swaying in invitation, giving him flashes of red between her thighs.

When she got to the second pillow, she made a show of lying down, grinning at him, flushed and breathing hard as she posed for him. Hands behind her, clutching the teak headboard slats, hair dark against the white pillowcase. Her legs came up, one canted over the other, like a pinup from the forties, like a siren, like a dream.

Miraculously, he didn't come right there and then. He made it onto the bed, took his time but he had to close his eyes before he touched her. Because, God.

When he licked a trail up the inside of her thigh, she trembled on his tongue.

BREE STOPPED BREATHING as Charlie's mouth inched up her thigh. The sexy pose wasn't like her, but then, she wasn't the same Bree tonight. Thank goodness her hands gripped the slats or she'd have floated straight up to the ceiling. She wanted to hurry him, his hot breath teasing her so near the creases where thigh met thong but not quite there.

He'd caught her left ankle in his hand, holding her leg aloft as his other hand smoothed up the front of her right thigh. She watched him, her excitement mounting, but the angle of her head was tricky to maintain with the firm pillow smooshed awkwardly under the top of her back. As much as she wanted to let her head loll back, her eyes close, let out the cry trapped in her throat, she couldn't do anything but stare at him, naked, crouched low on the bed between her knees. So she kept watching, urging him to move up, let that hot breath of his sneak under the silk, let his tongue follow.

Every inhale expanded her chest so her breasts, too small for her long erect nipples, came into her line of sight. When he looked up, he smiled at the same broken view, but from below. Okay, so maybe her breasts weren't *too* small. From how he groaned, never letting his tongue lift from her flesh, he seemed to like them. A lot.

Despite the groan, the stubborn man refused to *move*. "Charlie," she whined as she lifted her hips. What did he need, an engraved invitation?

His low chuckle dialed up her frustration.

"Patience," he whispered, his mouth moving closer to where she needed it. But instead of his tongue, he slipped his nose in that crease, nudging the thong over. He inhaled as if she were a bouquet of roses, and oh, God, he lowered her ankle as his teeth gripped silk. The tug was forceful, but not enough to snap the G-string panties, only to push things to the side, to let her feel a brush of cool air on her naked flesh.

When she let go of the slats, her hands ached. She was sure they were dented from the pressure, but she didn't care. It was necessary to touch him. She was shorter than any one of her friends, but the distance between the top of the bed and Charlie's body seemed to stretch on for miles. Yet she reached him with no strain, touched his dark, soft hair, her fingers tracing his temples.

He moaned, inches away from a different crease. Then that artful tongue of his started exploring and Bree's body arched with the shock of it.

The battle with the awkward pillow was lost in an instant. Her head lolled back, her eyes shut as he licked and sucked and flicked until she had one leg pressing down on his shoulder and a grip on his hair that had to hurt like a mother.

He didn't let up, not when she whimpered, not even when she turned his name into a pitiful plea.

She came with a jolt, another full-body arch and a cry that started low and ended so high only bats could hear it.

Charlie held her through the tremors, kissing his way up to her belly button, to her chest. Soft kisses, hard kisses, some wet and filthy, then chaste and sweet. His teeth scraped her skin, making her gasp, but the licks afterward soothed her into a sigh. When he reached her breasts, he settled in for a while. Bree quivered beneath him, every nibble and suck on her sensitive nipples sparking aftershocks.

She ran her hands across his shoulders as she whispered his name over and over, tugging him up, closer. But the obstinate bastard had other plans. He abandoned her nipple with a long swipe of his tongue and met her gaze, his eyes darker than ever. His lips were wet with her moisture, his smile three steps past sinful.

"You need to reach over there," he said, nodding at his bedside table. "Open that drawer."

"I do, huh?"

His smile widened and she felt his hand sneaking down her tummy. "If you wouldn't mind," he said, and she could have sworn his voice had lowered a full octave.

"Charlie, what are you doing?"

"I'm not finished being in you," he said. "So I'll just amuse myself until you think you might like more than fingers."

"Maybe I've got a thing for fingers."

"That's okay," he said. But he was pushing himself up to kneeling until she could see him. See his very hard, very ready cock.

The hand that wasn't petting her pussy, toying at the very edge of her lips, encircled his erection. It was a handful and he looked like he knew how to use it.

She swallowed and clenched her muscles as he squeezed up his length until just his glans peeked out, a drop of precome beading obscenely.

Bree hated to look away, but it couldn't be helped. She found the condom quickly, opened it with shaky fingers. He did the honors of putting on the rubber—

making a damn show of it—and then he laid himself over her, leaning on his elbow so she wouldn't be squished.

The kiss was salt and sex, his tongue giving her a preview of what was to come. Spreading her open, he rubbed up and down between her labia getting his bearings by feel. All the while, he watched her with dark, hooded eyes.

When he thrust, the cry she'd been holding in caromed off the walls, stole all her air.

Everything from then on was white heat and being filled. Raw and hard, every slap of flesh was followed by a desperate gasp from him, from her.

She came again. Squeezing him, pulling him closer, tighter. Then he froze, his face a mask of intense pleasure.

When he came back from the edge, he kissed her. More than the date, more than the tea, more than anything, the kiss turned everything sideways. Long, slow and deep, it wasn't a thank-you or showing off or like any other après-sex kiss she'd ever had. It was as real as the night sky, and it made her as dizzy as if she'd downed a magnum of champagne.

After, as she gathered in her stolen breath, he fell into a graceless heap beside her.

She still had her heels on.

When he forced himself out of the bed and into the bathroom, she closed her eyes, still dazed and confused. "Happy Valentine's Day, Bree," she said softly so he wouldn't hear. "Whoa."

It was six-forty. Charlie had looked at his alarm clock at six thirty-eight, then at Bree, still sleeping, still with him. All he'd been able to see was part of her bare shoulder and the back of her head. Now he was staring at the ceiling and having a panic attack.

He'd never had one before, but the way his heart was hammering in his chest had to be a sign. As a test, he turned his head to catch a glimpse of her. *Fuck.* What the hell had he done?

The last time he'd felt like this, not quite like this but the closest thing he could remember that had a similar vibe, was at fifteen. His first time. It was at Amy Johnson's house, in her twin canopy bed with her parents two doors down the hall. He'd been crazy about Amy, madly in whatever passes for love at fifteen. The sex had been horrible but he'd gotten off. He couldn't imagine how bad it had been for Amy. He'd felt like the stud king of the world, and even when he fell flat on his face escaping out her bedroom window, he'd considered the night a raging success.

He'd made sure his parents found one of the condoms from the box of Trojans. Their apoplectic fit at the inappropriateness of sex with a girl from that kind of family—she went to public school and her father was a dentist at a clinic—had been the most satisfying development in his life until age sixteen and a half, when he'd discovered the joys of older women and realized how much he had to learn.

Those lessons had been a downright pleasure.

But no one and nothing since Amy had recaptured the out-of-his-mind exhilaration of that maiden voyage. Until last night.

No matter what they'd done, Bree was definitely an innocent. Ah. Okay. Bree reminded him of Amy. Nothing to panic about. His breathing should return to normal soon. Last night had been a rerun of a great night. That's all. His reaction had nothing to do with the nice woman in his bed. He would give her coffee and cab fare, and that would be the end of it.

The sooner the better. She had to get to work, and so did he.

He stilled as she turned over and they touched. His hand, her thigh. It was warm, the place where they came together, and all the progress he'd made in the breathing department went to hell.

Why was he getting hard again? Shit.

He pictured her in that pose, her hands gripping the headboard, her nipples hard as little rocks and those heels. Jesus. She'd smelled like honey and tasted like the ocean, and he hadn't been that hard in years. He bit back a moan as he pictured her face when she'd come. And there was the problem in a nutshell. Or should he say in his nuts.

Forcing his mind to focus, he refused to acknowledge anything below the waist. If he'd been thinking with anything but his dick he would've sent her home last night. As soon as she'd asked for tea. Tea? Seriously? Then he'd made everything worse by getting down the goddamn silver. What was that about?

Screw his hard-on. This was ridiculous. He had work. Last night had been a favor for Rebecca, a nice surprise for him. No denying Bree was fantastic in bed, but that wasn't important. It didn't matter. He didn't need a great lay, he needed A-listers, women who would draw readers to the blogs, gossip fodder. He needed Mia Cavendish and her counterparts, the more photogenic and controversial, the better. He wanted to trend on Twitter, make the headlines on the *New York Post*'s Page Six. He needed ad revenue and infamy.

Bree could get him exactly none of that.

GOOD GOD ALMIGHTY, she was in *so much trouble*.

How was it possible that the best thing about her night as Cinderella had been a one-night stand with the King of Manhattan?

Not the limo, not Charlie's fame, not the stars or the dresses or meeting her design heroes. No. The best thing, the thing that would cripple her if she didn't get a grip *right this minute* was making…sex with Charlie.

She was no blushing virgin and she knew what happened between the sheets. She'd had bad sex and she'd had amazing sex and what had happened with Charlie wasn't even on the same scale.

Falling for Charlie was not acceptable.

She really needed to get out of bed because if he moved the hand against her thigh even a little bit, she couldn't be held accountable for her actions.

Where was her dress? By the window. Somehow, the room wasn't filled with light, which it should have been because the last time she'd looked, there'd been nothing but glass between them and Central Park. Yet, it wasn't dark, either. She hadn't opened her eyes, but there was some kind of pale gold thing happening behind her lids, so…

The lamp that had been on while they'd been…

She inhaled quietly, regrouping. It didn't matter what Charlie was doing. She was in control of her actions and her thoughts. She'd throw back the covers, get out of bed, pull up her dress, slip on her heels and go to the bathroom. She wouldn't have to look at him at all.

Crap. The back of his fingers brushed against her thigh. Just that quickly, her resolve vanished and her body tensed. Things were happening against her will. Nipples hardened. Kegel muscles contracted. Not to mention the thunder of her heart.

It was one time, Kingston. One night. You had cham-pagne. It was like being in a fairy tale. It's not real. Things like this don't happen in the real world. It's over. Stop being a moron and get out.

After a silent count to three, she did it. Tossed covers, pulled up dress, screw the zipper, picked up shoes, darted to the bathroom, slammed the door, breathed.

Cursed herself from here to Sunday because while she was in the nice, safe bathroom, her purse with all her stuff was in the living room.

She sighed and leaned on the door, barely restraining herself from banging her head against the wood until she passed out. Her makeup was already a disaster so crying wasn't out of the question.

What were the odds he had a spare toothbrush in this humongous room? The shower alone was bigger than what she laughingly called a bedroom.

She could wash her face with whatever soap he had, and rinse her mouth with something that would at least hide the morning breath for a while. All she had to do was be somewhat presentable for a cab ride home, then she could start forgetting about Charlie as she hustled to get ready for work.

Coffee. Coffee would help everything. No, *aspirin* and coffee. That's what she needed, and her world would fit neatly back into place.

A knock on the bathroom door made her jump so hard her dress nearly slipped all the way down to the floor. "Um, busy," she said, yanking it up again.

"Yeah," Charlie said, and God, his voice rippled through her like a slow fire. "I thought you might want your pocketbook."

"Oh. Uh. Okay. Yes." She turned, holding up her

dress with one arm as she opened the door an inch. It wasn't quite enough. Another inch, then another, and finally her purse was inside. She snatched it as if it were connected to a mousetrap. "Thanks. Be out in a minute. Don't mind me."

Silence followed. Bree didn't know if he was there or not, but she didn't move. She pressed her ear against the door.

"Okay," he said, making her jump again. "I'll go make coffee."

"Great. Thanks. Sounds great." She winced at her stupid mouth, and reconsidered the whole banging her head against the door thing.

Finally, she turned around, resigned that there wasn't enough aspirin and coffee in the world.

"WHAT'S THIS?" BREE ASKED.

Charlie looked down at the hundred-dollar bill he was holding out to Bree. "Cab fare."

"A hundred? You think I live in Connecticut?"

"Wasn't sure. Look, I'm sorry I can't take you myself, but the blog…"

"It's fine. Really. I've got it," she said as she held up her to-go cup. "Thanks for the coffee."

"You're not going to be late for work?"

"Nope. Not if I get a move on."

She hadn't looked at him. Not once. At least, he didn't think so. He'd been avoiding looking at her, so there was no certainty, but it felt like she hadn't.

If nothing else had told him the night had been a colossal mistake, this morning's awkwardness would have. It was epic. Both of them stumbling, mumbling, embarrassed and basically acting like idiots. The problem was he couldn't tell why she was behaving like he had the plague. He'd thought the night had been great, and the sex had been fantastic. Too good.

Maybe that was just him, though.

Naw. It had been spectacular, and he knew what he was talking about. She was being weird for another reason. He'd like to blame the excessive cab fare move, but the weird dance had started when she'd first gotten out of bed.

She was making her way to the front door, although she didn't simply turn around and walk. She took a few steps back, checked behind her, then moved another couple of steps, and it made him want to kiss her.

Shit.

She had to go. Now.

He surged ahead of her to the door and opened it. "I'm sorry I can't see you—" He stopped before he repeated the whole sentence.

"Of course. And I have…" She was right in front of him now, looking up at him with those green eyes. "Thank you," she said. "It was the best night ever. I'll never forget you. It. The party. Doing…stuff."

Her cheeks had turned a really dark shade of pink, and yep, so did the tips of her ears. The urge to move a few inches, lower his lips to hers once more was stronger than he was prepared to admit.

"I had a great time, too," he said, his voice cracking on the end. "We should…" He stopped himself by biting his tongue. It hurt quite a bit. But he'd almost said they should do it again.

"Well, I'll be off. Down the elevator. To get a taxi." She stepped through the doorway sideways. Almost hiding behind her coffee, only spilling a little.

"Right. Bye."

"Bye."

He went to shut the door as she called for the elevator. Then stopped. It would be rude to shut the door. On the other hand, she looked desperate.

He split it down the middle. Left the door ajar, but walked away. To the kitchen. He didn't breathe until he heard the ding.

Holy crap.

7

BREE SAT IN HER CUBICLE, shuffling papers from one stack to the next. She'd been at the office for two hours and she hadn't accomplished a damn thing. Most of the morning had been spent rehashing last night, analyzing to death every single thing Charlie had done or said. Sneaking peeks at the picture she'd taken, of his trading card.

In the harsh fluorescent lights of BBDA, the events featuring Charlie seemed more like a dream than something that could have happened to her. But there was an ache in her body that wasn't a result of working out at the gym. She'd tensed her arms so hard gripping the headboard that her muscles had burned as she'd showered this morning, and there was that thumbprint bruise on her hip. Plus her memories, of course.

She had no business thinking about him. The night. Him. Really now. It was over. Done. A recollection that should bring her pleasure instead of this sense of loss. How could she have lost something she'd never had? Never could have?

God, the whole morning sucked. Her thoughts had been wild enough before she'd seen that he hadn't posted his blog yet. He should have. His routine was like Old Faithful, like atomic time. Instead, three other people had posted—one fashionista, one celeb tracker and one foodie.

So in addition to obsessing over the fact that sex had been no more than a part of the overall standard package rather than a romantically wonderful moment between the two of them, now she was pretty convinced that she had somehow jinxed Charlie. And she had a headache.

Surprisingly, Rebecca hadn't called yet, which was fine because Bree hadn't figured out how much she wanted to tell her and she wanted to be careful about that conversation, not dead on her feet. In fact, she seriously thought about sneaking in a nap today in place of lunch. She needed sleep more than food.

Her cell dinged and when she saw the name flash, she nearly choked. She clicked on the icon.

How are you feeling? CW

Bree stared at his initials, completely stunned. Why was he texting her? Good manners? Had she accidentally taken something from his apartment? She hit Reply then forced herself to think, not text, not yet.

This was silly. She shook her head as she used her thumbs.

Fine. Thanks.

You get to work okay? CW

On time and everything.

I'm glad. Also lunch? CW

What? Lunch? Was he asking her to lunch? Nope, no, that couldn't be right. Not after this morning. She stared at the gray panel of her cubicle for a moment, then looked once again at her message. She hadn't read it wrong. It simply made no sense.

Now her gaze lifted over the cubicle wall, but all she could see was the top of the heads passing by. There wasn't a single person at BBDA she could pull aside for advice. None of them knew about her date with Charlie. Or really anything about her except that she tended to keep to herself.

She quickly typed *BRB* letting him know she was away from her keyboard, and grabbed the landline. Screw not telling Rebecca about what happened. Bree needed help. Fast. She dialed, praying her friend would answer.

The second Bree heard "hello," she launched. "Last night was the most fabulous night in the history of earth, but this morning was completely weird and now he's…"

"Bree—"

"Oh, God, you're busy. Please don't be busy because I don't even— Wait. He's texting me now, and I don't know what to do."

"Texting you what?"

"He wants me to have lunch with him. Today."

Rebecca laughed. "Then go!"

"We both freaked out this morning. He offered me a hundred dollars."

"What?"

"For a taxi."

"Oh. Then I repeat. Go."

"But—"

"Trust me on this. I know him. Really well. Lunch is huge."

"Huge? Huge isn't good at all. It's over now, right? He doesn't do repeats, and I've got a plan, and it doesn't include liking anyone. Huge can't be the thing that comes next."

"Listen to me," Rebecca said, her tone one she surely must use when she was negotiating with billionaires or friends having panic attacks. "Go to lunch with Charlie. Eat food. Listen to what he has to say. You might be surprised. Then call me after."

Bree touched her hair and her face as her stomach flipped from excitement to dread and back again. Damn, she'd done almost nothing with her hair, and her makeup consisted of mascara. Period. She'd had barely enough time to shower and change, and then she'd had to scramble to make it to the office. "You'd better be right, Rebecca."

"I am. Good luck."

Bree hung up, then got her thumbs in position.

Where? When?

Bistro truck? CW

Um...

Mediterranean CW

Okay.

Sending map. U say when. CW

1?

C U there. CW

Her cell let her know the map had arrived, and the Bistro truck was only a block from her office. She typed the name into her search engine to check out the menu, wanting to be prepared and avoid anything messy. Figured she'd go with the phyllo-wrap veg and the Belgium fries, assuming she could eat anything. Even if meeting him turned out to be a horrible mistake, fries would soothe the wound.

After closing her phone, she stared at the paperwork she had to finish before noon, her vision blurring on the words. He wanted to see her again. Why? *Why?* And why was Rebecca so sure she should go?

New York was confusing.

CHARLIE STOOD ON A CEMENT bench on East 14th Street, searching the lunchtime crowds for Bree. Despite her little black dress last night, he remembered Rebecca's comment about Bree's affection for colors, so he zeroed in on anything that wasn't black clothes, which eliminated around seventy percent of the women. It helped that today was unseasonably warm, so that most of the coats were open.

He turned, not minding the stares he earned. This was Union Square at one in the afternoon. He did what worked. And work it did, because there she was. Her clothes hadn't caught his eye; her hair had, though. It was the same short pixie cut, but today she'd worn a slim pink ribbon complete with bow. It was ridiculous, and it made him grin like an idiot.

As she got closer, he forced his gaze down, not stopping on her face, not yet. No coat. Surprising, but not, because they were only a block from her office and she'd already proven she would rather freeze to death than ruin the ensemble. She'd need another winter in New York until she woke up and smelled the frostbite.

Today she had on a pink-and-green-checked long-sleeved button-down, which should have been ugly as sin, but wasn't. And a skirt, a little bitty one in a completely different shade of green. None of it had any business being on a single person at the same time. Even the flat matte gold shoes were wrong. And fantastic.

Her step faltered as he caught her eye. She smiled, one of those full-on middle American smiles that showed a whole lot of teeth. But as she started walking again that faltered, too. By the time he'd jumped down and met her on the sidewalk, she seemed worried. Or hungry. No. Worried.

"You all right?" he asked.

"Yes," she said, nodding. "Fine, thanks."

He wouldn't press now. First they needed to order. "Hungry?"

"Sure."

He grabbed her hand, and before they took a step toward the line at the big white truck, he kissed her cheek. He'd debated that move all the way over here. It seemed rude not to acknowledge their night together, yet he didn't want to emphasize that aspect of their acquaintance, despite the fact that the memory of her in his bed had been a constant low-grade fever since he'd opened his eyes this morning. It didn't surprise him that she stopped short and looked at him as if he were crazy. It didn't matter. He stood by the kiss decision.

Come on, how could he have resisted? One look at her with her pink bow and that small skirt…

Okay, shit, wrong turn. He breathed deeply the scent of fried foods and city buses, getting his bearings once more. They wouldn't be able to order for at least ten minutes, considering the length of the line, then there would be the food to deal with. Might as well dive in. He kept hold of her as he maneuvered himself close enough to talk without being overheard. "I have a proposition for you."

Her eyebrows rose.

"Last night, at the party, you were great."

"Thanks," she said, with just enough of a lift at the end to make it vaguely a question.

"I spent all morning trying to write the blog. So much time I ended up posting fillers from freelancers so people wouldn't get antsy."

"I know. I saw."

"Ah. Of course." He moved them up a half step in line. "Anyway, the thing was, you kept popping up in my first draft."

"I popped up?" She said it slowly, her forehead now furrowed in confusion.

He didn't normally confuse people. Piss them off, all the time, but clarity wasn't an issue. "I realized that I'd felt as if last night was my first time at Fashion Week. That didn't happen even when I did go for the first time. Seeing through your eyes was…different." He'd almost said exhilarating. True, but too much information. "That's what I wrote about. This morning."

"O…kay," she said.

He was not making his point. "I'm posting my blog late because I wanted to talk to you about it. I want to use your vision, for want of a better word, as the hook for the column. An innocent at Fashion Week. A new perspective."

"I'm not that innocent," she said, her tone brusque and bruised, as if he'd insulted her.

"You're new to the city. You're not jaded yet. Since *Naked New York* excels at jaded, I like the idea of approaching this series from another angle. I won't mock you. In fact, I won't use your name or image if you don't want me to. It'll be my impressions of your impressions. Which I've never done before, so you may or may not be fine with it."

"You already wrote the blog?"

He nodded. "Three different versions. One with you specifically, one with you obliquely, and one that focuses only on my impressions. I can send them to your phone now, if you want to read them."

"I would," she said. "Does it say that I…we…" She flinched briefly, then carried on. "You know, got together…at your place?"

"No. No, that's…no. This isn't about personal stuff. It's about the event. The party."

"Oh," she said, and this time it wasn't equivocal. "Send them, then."

He clicked the necessary buttons as a group of five in front of them suddenly dashed off, which moved him and Bree up to the food truck window. "What'll you have? I'll order while you read."

"Fries. Large."

"Nothing else?"

She thought for a moment, but couldn't imagine eating a whole sandwich. Not while her stomach was in knots. "Tea, two sugars."

He grinned. Couldn't help it. He still couldn't believe he'd actually served her tea on a silver platter. With tongs. Bizarre. But then, everything about last night had been.

He heard the sound of her receiving the documents on her phone, then he turned his attention to the guy behind the counter. He ordered, glanced at Bree, paid, looked again, then moved them to the waiting line where he out-and-out stared. He ignored everything but her body language, her expressions, the speed with which she read the screen. He learned absolutely nothing.

Turning so he could only see her in his peripheral vision, he reminded himself that whatever her response, it would be fine. Even if she went along with his whole scheme, it didn't mean anything. Not personally. This was a work thing. That's it. Maybe they'd have the opportunity to get together again, but that wasn't the point.

Even though the pink ribbon killed him. In fact, the pink ribbon *was* the point. None of the people he hung out with would have put that outfit on, not on a bet. It was an anti-Manhattan look. Those who attended Fashion Week were more afraid of not being cool than they were of being hit by a car. Bree's kind of unabashed adoration was straight from the heart with nothing expected in return.

Her point of view would ring true for the majority of his readers, many far more like her, young people who would never have a chance to go to a gala, never stand next to icons of fashion and film, never be able to afford a scarf from any of the designers, let alone a couture gown. The trick in this approach was the balance. There was a hint of sarcasm, because he was a sarcastic son of a bitch, but he didn't make fun of Bree. It was a fine line, a welcome challenge.

The whole concept could bomb, but he didn't think it would. He had good instincts about his readers, and this felt right.

She'd gripped an edge of her lower lip with a barely visible tooth, white and perfect. The urge to kiss her hit him again, only he didn't want her cheek, but her mouth. Ah, Christ, what was his problem? This was business.

"Hey, you. Blog guy. You gonna move up or what?"

The question had come from a beefy man with a pencil thin mustache. Charlie moved closer to the truck, gentling Bree along with a light touch to her forearm.

She looked at him as she closed her cell phone. Her cheeks blushed a pink that almost matched her ribbon. "Oh," she said.

That wasn't enough information. Out of an over-abundance of the need to appear cool at all times, he didn't push for more. He schooled his expression into one of disinterest, which was the only acceptable stance during a strictly business meeting.

Her head tilted a tad to the right. No blinks now, only a piercing gaze and "Why?"

"Why?" he repeated.

She nodded. "Your blog works perfectly as it is. Obviously. Your numbers are incredible. Why would you want to mess with the format?"

"Mixing things up isn't messing with the format. If it doesn't work, I'll find out quickly and drop the idea. It's not the first time I've tried something new, and it won't be the last."

BREE STARED AT CHARLIE. This lunch was even stranger than she'd expected. And not for any of the reasons she'd anticipated. It most definitely wasn't about the sex. Of course. Because that would have been crazy.

"Whatever your decision," he said. "I need to know quickly."

"Sure. Right. I understand." How could she have forgotten even for a second? From the moment Rebecca had shown her Charlie's trading card, she'd wondered what in the world a man like him would want with a girl like her. It had almost been a relief when she'd finally gotten last night that Rebecca had done her a favor, and in turn, he had done one for Rebecca. Why else would he have taken her out on Valentine's Day? Even so, it had not been a date. He'd been very clear about the fact that it was work. She doubted he was ever truly distracted from his business. That's how he'd become Charlie Winslow in the first place.

So he'd used her. Not maliciously, not at all. He'd found a way to parlay the favor, so good for him. He'd grabbed an opportunity, and by sheer luck, it might give her a spot on his blog. Other people would want to know who she was, how she'd scored a "date" with Charlie. She couldn't have asked for a better shot at her dreams. But she had to be smart about it. Especially smart, given that the girlie part of her brain seemed to want to turn this into a romance. Nothing wrong with romance, but there was a time and a place.

Now that she had leapfrogged into the big time, she had to be more clear than ever about what was in her best interest for the long term, and not be dazzled.

"Look—" he said.

"If you need to have an answer right this minute," she said, "it will have to be no."

Charlie stilled and that air of boredom he'd been wearing like a comfy jacket vanished. He seemed disappointed, but that undoubtedly had more to do with his plans being thwarted than not being able to work with her.

"Don't get me wrong," she said. "I liked it."

It occurred to her that she should have ordered more for lunch. She needed to appear as unaffected by Charlie as possible. "The approach is fresh for *NNY*. A good take on something done to death, and you managed to make me sound as if I'm not totally precious. Although…" She clicked on the most personal section of the blog he'd written and scrolled down a bit.

Here's what Bree said, but not in words:

1. Everyone is tall and beautiful and has better clothes than me. Anyone who looked in any way normal wasn't anyone. Example: Me.
2. People can be really rude, but at the same time, very lovely. Being with Charlie got me the last part. The first part was on the house.
3. Everyone has an iPhone/BlackBerry. And cameras are intrusive even if the whole point is getting your picture taken. Also? I'm really not in Ohio anymore.

"I'm really not in Ohio anymore?" Bree sighed. "Still. You did a nice job."

The way his lips parted, it was clear he hadn't expected her response, especially the way she'd said *nice*. Now if she could just keep it up. She'd imagined being the kind of woman who could go toe-to-toe with the biggest names in Manhattan, and now was her chance.

She'd been in Wonderland last night, and she wouldn't apologize for feeling like Alice. Charlie had captured that perfectly in his blog. But she was back on terra firma now. She knew the score, business was business, and if he was going to use her, then she wanted something in return.

Yes, he was *Charlie Winslow,* and her heart had been beating double time since his first text, but there was a larger picture here, and she'd be an idiot to let it slip through her fingers. Being linked to Charlie was cachet she couldn't ignore. "The blog would be better if you used my pictures. Used me."

"Would it?" A hint of a smile came and went. Good. They were both playing the same game. It was important for her to remember he had years of experience, whereas she had… She had chutzpah. It would have to be enough.

Charlie handed her a plate of fries and a cardboard cup of tea. He'd paid, which was appropriate. He'd called this meeting.

At the thought, she had a twinge of sadness, real regret, and dammit, she had to stop that. The sex had been sex. The two of them were about to talk turkey, and she couldn't afford to be sentimental, not for a moment. It had been great sex. The end. Her imagination could be a wonderful place, but it could hurt her, too.

Luckily, they scored most of a bench. The first Belgian fry was so good it made her moan, which made her blush, but only until she saw the spot of mayo on Charlie's chin. If she were the nice girl her parents had raised her to be, she'd tell him about it. But this was business, and him looking so very human helped.

"What's your concern?" Charlie asked.

"I'm really not as innocent as you've painted me. I understand that's the gimmick, which is fine, but I'd like to have some input. My bosses read *NNY,* our clients, too. It may only be one blog, but it'll have an impact on my career."

He took another bite of his burger, and instead of looking at his mouth, remembering what it had felt like against her own, she concentrated on the mayonnaise dotting his chin.

"I want more than one blog out of this," he said, after he'd swallowed.

Her gaze jumped to his eyes and for a sec she thought that maybe this wasn't *all* about business, but then she remembered.

8

"I'D LIKE TO MAKE THIS part one of a series," Charlie said, as if he was asking her for a fry. "Some of which would feature Fashion Week, but not all. Tonight there's a party at Chelsea Piers. I was hoping you would join me."

Bree didn't choke, but she did cough. Mostly to hide her astonishment, and get herself in check. "What do you mean by series?"

"Wednesday's open, but Thursday night is another Fashion Week party. Friday, there's a premiere. Have you heard about *Courtesan?*"

Had she heard about Courtesan? It was a major motion picture from a major studio starring major movie stars, and she'd wanted to see it since she'd caught the first ad. Inside, she jumped about five feet off the ground. For him, she nodded and took a sip of tea. "I have."

"I've got something else Saturday night but I'm not sure what. Either a perfume party or a book thing. Anyway, I'd need you, tentatively, through Saturday night. Maybe more, possibly less. It all depends on the number of hits, the comment activity. Could that work for you?"

To even pretend she had to think about it was useless. He'd know she was bluffing. "Scheduling wouldn't be the issue. I'd make it work, even if I have to get Rebecca to make my frozen lunches.

"That's the thing Rebecca does at St. Marks, right?"

"How we met."

"She's gonna love this." Now he didn't even try to hide his smile. It was the other Charlie, the charming cousin of her friend, the man who'd kissed her silly.

Bree cleared her throat before meeting his gaze. "What do you mean?"

"She's going to think the series was her idea. She'll be insufferable."

"Ah." Bree popped a fry as she fought against another pang. This one was even more foolish. She'd thought for a second there that Rebecca would love the fact that she and Charlie would continue seeing each other. Ridiculous.

But come on, this was better than dating. Sex for someone like Charlie lasted one night. He couldn't even fake interest the next morning. In the long run, what he was offering was more than her paltry dreams had imagined. He'd just shortened her five-year plan by half. "I still want input."

"It's my blog, Bree. People read it for my take."

"I don't want to come off looking like a fool."

"Is that how you read any of those articles?"

"No."

"We can draw something up, something we can both agree to. If the series works, it will be because people like my take on seeing my world through your eyes. It's

in my best interest to make you relatable and sympa-
thetic."

"Okay. But I think I would be even more relatable if
I write some of the blogs myself."

He winced. "I don't know. My name brings the party
to the yard. Sorry."

"Granted. Doesn't mean there can't be a sidebar.
You've done that before."

Charlie used his napkin, wiping off the mayo by
chance. After a longish pause, he nodded. "No guar-
antees. I'll read what you write, see how it works. I'll
have my attorney draw up something to cover the rest
of the week, but I'd like to post the blog I wrote today.
What do you say?"

She knew she was taking a risk, not signing on the
dotted line, but what the hell. Rebecca would have
something to say if Charlie messed with her, but even
more than that, Bree's gut told her to go for it. She held
out her hand.

The shiver that ran through her body when they
shook was strictly in response to the opportunity. Nothing more.

CHARLIE WALKED BREE TO HER office building, a giant
among giants, blocking out most of the sky. It was
windy in the street, and he put his arm around Bree's
shoulders, pulling her close. He liked keeping her
warm, liked the way her hair tickled his chin.

"Charlie?" She had to raise her voice as they walked,
so he bent his head a little.

"Yes?"

"Assuming the paperwork is fine and we end up
going to…things. What are we going as?"

"Uh, oh. Like last night. Together, but not a couple.

If someone asks, say we're friends. They'll all assume it's more, but that's not a bad thing. People like trying to figure things out, make connections, even if they're false. And gossip pays the bills."

She didn't speak, but she did slow her step.

"Bree?"

She stopped. Charlie turned to face her, not liking the troubled look she wore. "What's wrong?"

"Nothing. It's fine. I want to make sure we understand each other. If we do this, it's a business arrangement."

"Yeah." The way she stared at him didn't make sense. He was handing her a gift here. Sure, he was going to make money from the deal, but she would win, too. He should have asked her what she wanted. From her love of fashion, her work at the advertising agency, it wasn't hard to figure her area of interest, but it was sloppy of him not to get specific.

"I keep my business life and my personal life separate," she said.

It took him a beat too long to make the connection. Not because she was being unreasonable. On the contrary, she was being smart. He wasn't used to it, though. The women who came home with him didn't think of the sex as anything outside of the job. Neither had he, not since he'd started the blog, for God's sake. Bree was not from his world. That was the point.

In fact, she was a romantic. Not simply around the issue of sex, but about designers, New York, glamour, beauty, all of it. Too bad it wouldn't last.

Oddly, he didn't rush to agree with her. He'd assumed they'd sleep together. He'd wanted to. If the series got results, they were looking at a week, maybe two. That would be a long stretch to go without. Especially when she would be with him most every night. In the car, at his place.

"Charlie?"

"Right. No, you're right. Strictly professional. Good thinking."

Her smile wasn't very victorious. In fact, he was tempted to follow her as she backed away from him, just to see her better.

"I'm really late," she said, calling out now, against the wind. "Send me the contract, and I'll take a look at it. And the details about tonight. And, thanks," she said, but the word was carried away as she got swallowed by dozens of people all heading for the same entrance.

He lost her before she went inside. He knew BBDA took up four floors of the skyscraper, could picture where the copywriters sat. But he didn't go after her. He'd see her tonight. He pulled out his cell as he went to the corner to hail a cab. He needed to get the blog update done, call the attorney, make arrangements with the stylist.

After he told the cabbie his address, he looked back at Bree's building. No more nights like last night. Well, damn.

BETWEEN THE PHOTOGRAPHERS blinding her and the constant tweets, Bree barely had time to enjoy the party. It would have been overwhelming regardless. This event was much smaller. Maybe five hundred people?

Put on by one of the most sought-after design celebrities, it was being held at The Lighthouse in Chelsea Piers. The huge room had been decked out in Asian-themed splendor with floating lanterns, Zen gardens artfully placed between tables and paper dragons so large and beautifully decorated they were works of art.

Even the view of the Hudson River from the floor-to-ceiling windows stole her breath, and that was before she met a mind-boggling parade of fashion idols and A, B and C-list stars.

The good and bad news was that Charlie had been even more extraordinary, which she hadn't thought possible. He hadn't left her side, which was wonderful, but what got to her even more was how he'd introduced her to his people. And God, they really were *his people.* He made her sound as if she were the brightest new thing to hit the scene since Lady Gaga. It was totally over-the-top, but, and this went directly into the bad news category, it was totally to support the blog series. *She* wasn't important; the image was important, the mystique, the hip-by-association coupled with her "innocence" to make her a mini celebrity.

The plan was working though because after dinner—which was to die for, and God, how she'd wanted a doggie bag—she'd been approached, over and over.

Not that she hadn't realized before that celebrities were never what they appeared to be. They might feel as if they're old friends, having been on her favorite TV series, or in so many movies she knew. But who they were had no relationship to the person she'd created in her head.

She knew that, and she was fine with it. People had always had icons. It made them feel connected. Twitter, Facebook, *Naked New York,* Perez Hilton, E!, *People.* They were watercoolers, the center of invisible towns where neighbors gathered.

Being one of the chosen, knowing everyone she met, whether they were famous or seeking fame, had already made up a story about who she was, what Charlie saw in her, what would happen next, was bizarre in a way she couldn't have predicted. There was no preparation for this kind of exposure, and the strangeness of it was messing with her sense of time. One minute she was reeling from too many gazes centered on her, the next, she was standing beside a window staring out at the water without having any idea how she'd gotten there.

Charlie had helped. His hand on her arm was a steadying force, his presence, his introductions easing the way. But he was acclimated, and she was still gasping for oxygen.

It didn't help that each time, every time, his touch gave her a frisson of excitement that made her breathless once again. It was ridiculous. She should be over it by now. Knowing this was a business arrangement and nothing more didn't help. The disconnect between her brain and her desire worried her. It was as if she'd been given electric shocks all evening, each one immediately followed by a stab of regret.

"You ready?" he asked, his mouth so close to her ear she could feel his heat. It must have been a shout because the music was blaring all around them, but it felt like a caress.

She nodded, and he slipped his arm around her shoulders as they went from the steamy inside to the icy outdoors. Again, there were enough limos to fill a football field, but there were also dozens of valets, running off to find drivers in what must have been an underground madhouse.

"What did you think?" Charlie asked. "Better? Worse?"

"You tell me," she answered. "You were watching me like a hawk."

He studied her expression, and she was struck yet again by how much she liked his face. It really was absurd how outsize his eyes were. They weren't comic-book large or even unsettlingly out of proportion. They were definitely the first thing one noticed about him.

He raised one dramatic eyebrow. "You liked this one more, despite having to work. I think partly because you knew more about what to expect, and partly because you got to speak to some of your favorite designers."

She smiled even though his conclusion wasn't quite accurate. "You're dead-on. Is that a problem?"

"What do you mean?"

"I'm incrementally not as innocent. By Friday night, I'll be a stone-cold cynic."

Charlie laughed, and there were the lines on his face that made it impossible for her not to touch his jacket, touch him. Why lines? It's not as if they were deep grooves or anything close to it. He was in his early thirties, and they didn't make him look a minute older. Perhaps it was because lines of any kind, even laugh lines, were practically forbidden in this glamorous, youth-obsessed culture. She'd hate it if Charlie had Botoxed his out of existence. His lines made him seem genuine, made him seem attainable. *Seem* being the operative word.

"Trust me on this," he said. "While you're very savvy and not to be underestimated, you're nowhere close to jaded. It won't be as unbelievable to meet famous people in a week or two, but the thrill will still be there."

"Good." She wanted the thrill, at least as it pertained to celebrities. She could do with fewer thrills when it came to Charlie. "Sorry I'm making you leave so early. I imagine you close down these kinds of parties."

"Not at all. I stay until I have enough material, then

head home. I have to get up early to get the blog in on time."

"So the photographers send their pictures before they crash for the night?"

"Yep. I go through them in the morning. I also get the freelance pieces and gossip tidbits. I put together the blog, send everything to my assistant Naomi, and she does her thing until it's online by 10:00 a.m. If you've got a sidebar about tonight, I'll need it by nine."

She nodded, not wanting him to see how his mention of that aspect of the job terrified her. The words would be hers. Not an illusion, not a gimmick. She'd sink or swim based on talent. God, she needed to sit down.

"You okay?"

"I've been meaning to ask. The stylist? What are we aiming for here?" She looked down at the dress she'd worn, one she'd made back in college. It was a pretty green, a shade lighter than her eyes, and it was sleeveless with a purple-and-green bolero jacket. It would have been perfect for a night on the town with Rebecca and friends, but she was outclassed here by ten miles. She figured that was the point. Make her look like the hick she was.

"Ah. You're going to like this part. Glam to the max. Everything from shoes to gowns. The whole shebang, complete with makeup, hair, body airbrushing, everything."

"I don't understand," she said, unsure whether he was joking with her or not.

"Those sidebars? They should be about the entire experience. What it feels like to become a princess, to go to the ball. To be plucked out of obscurity and shot to the stars."

She blinked at him as people pushed forward to

get to their cars. Watched a smile bloom on his face. Wished like hell she could jump into his arms and hug him for yet another incredible surprise.

"And you get to keep all the swag."

She shoved him. Kind of hard. "Do not mess with me, Winslow. I will hurt you if you're lying."

"Not lying. Yours to keep."

Flashbulbs had been popping all night, but suddenly they were in her face, blinding her. Only for a moment, though, then they were gone, like a swarm of locusts with cameras. They'd done their job, however, and kept her from leaping into Charlie's arms.

It was the most diabolical torture. Give her all her dreams with one hand, steal her desire with the other. Rinse. Repeat.

"So, we discussed that you'll be meeting Sveta on Thursday, right? That you're off the hook for tomorrow?"

"Yep," she said, switching gears.

"You should sleep. You'll need it."

"I have to go make frozen lunches tomorrow night. Rebecca's going to be there."

"If I know her, she'll keep you up later than I have. The woman is a slave to details."

Before she hit the sack, she'd go through the pictures she'd taken. Those images were what she needed to focus on, not Charlie. Not his scent, not the resonance of his voice, not this wanting to be close to him.

By the time the series was finished, she'd be over her silly crush. Dammit, she would be.

9

"TASTE THIS AND TELL ME if you think it needs more salt."
Rebecca stood back so that Lilly could try the soup.

She obliged and faked a cough.

"Funny." After elbowing her aside, Rebecca saw her
cousin standing at the door of the St. Mark's basement
kitchen. He wasn't looking at her, or, she imagined, for
her. His gaze was on Bree.

Laughter still clung to the steam that swirled over
the industrial stove. Rebecca was making a giant pot
of split pea soup, Lilly was cooking a Texas chili and
even with those pots and the 350° oven, the basement
remained chilly. It wouldn't be for long, though, not if
what she thought was going to happen happened.

It was difficult to look away from Charlie. He was as
unguarded as she'd ever seen him. As an adult, at least.
There was a keen awareness in his eyes, a concentration that spoke of a hunger that had nothing to do with
pea soup.

One of his hands braced against the door frame, the
other held papers. He looked elegant in his bespoke
coat: dark navy, midcalf, styled perfectly. How Charlie it was.

The man knew what looked good on him, what he could get away with, and what would cause eyebrows to raise. Nothing was unintentional. Not online, in person, in a walk to the corner grocer. Seeing him blatantly wanting Bree was seeing him naked. Not that she had any personal experience with that, but she'd been with Charlie in family situations, private moments of grief, in trouble, in failure, in success, and this was new.

Rebecca grinned at her own brilliance. She was awesome. She'd known he would like Bree. And Bree would like him, but even Rebecca at her most conniving hadn't guessed they would have come so far so fast.

She'd have high-fived herself if she could have, for being just that clever. No one in the family believed Charlie would ever fall. He'd always have women, but never one woman. Not Charlie. His merry-go-round hadn't stopped spinning since puberty, and he got bored so quickly. Nothing could have suited her cousin quite as perfectly as this age of instant gratification. Charlie was born for it, breathed it, worked it. Everything lightning fast, and rest was for the weak and dull.

Bree wasn't dull in the least.

Rebecca turned to her friend. They'd played phone tag all day, then arrived at the kitchen as Lilly had come in, so all Rebecca knew was that Bree had gone with Charlie to a big fancy party last night, a heck of a second date, and she'd written a firsthand account of the party that had been in this morning's blog.

If that wasn't testimony to Rebecca's genius, she didn't know what was.

Things got really interesting when Bree shifted and sighted the man standing in the doorway.

If only the door had been closer to the prep area. It was difficult to know where to look. Bree now was a living demonstration of Modern Woman In Full Lust Mode. Her back straightened, her breath caught, showing off her chest in the most positive light possible. The thrift-store cashmere sweater she wore cupped her boobs perfectly, and Rebecca knew Charlie was having a little heart attack at the view.

Then there was the flush that swept across Bree's cheeks. Good lord, it couldn't have been more artfully painted by Renoir. Her eyes got wide and her lips parted and her pheromones were positively dripping.

The only sounds were the slow gurgle of thick simmering from the stove, the hiss of the radiator. Even Lilly, who'd come tonight for the company and the after-cooking drinks, had caught on that Something Was Happening.

Rebecca turned to Charlie again, and he'd dropped his hand, taking a single step inside the kitchen. He seemed to be fighting a smile. It would start to form at the corners of his lips, then flatten, but a second later the grin would start again.

Back to Bree, and it was like the slowest tennis match ever, the invisible ball staying well within the boundaries, the lobs back and forth languid and electric at the same time.

Rebecca's soup would burn in a minute if she didn't stir the pot. "Charlie," she said. "What's up?"

Rebecca almost laughed at how he jerked at her voice. And when she glanced at Bree, the blush had spread over her cheeks and down her neck, and there was a great deal of blinking.

"I came to show Bree her blog." He held up the papers as if proof had been required.

"Kind of hard for her to see it across the room."

Charlie's grin finally broke free as did his legs. He came inside, crossed the basement to Bree.

"That's Charlie Winslow," Lilly whispered, and Rebecca hadn't heard her approach. Luckily, no one saw Rebecca jump because everybody's gaze was on center stage. Even Lilly's.

"Yes, it is."

"Why is Charlie Winslow in the kitchen? With Bree?"

"Because she's seeing him."

"What?"

The word came out loud. Very loud. Loud enough that it halted the action.

Lilly smiled, gave a little wave. "Lilly Denton. Hey."

"Charlie Winslow," Charlie said. "Hey."

The moment passed. Rebecca dragged Lilly to the stove, Charlie went back to mooning at Bree.

"She's seeing him?" Lilly asked, her voice back down to a stage whisper. "Since when?"

"Not long."

"How do you know this?"

"Obviously you don't read his blog."

"I do, but I've been too busy the past few days." Lilly sneaked another peek. "That'll teach me for putting work first."

"Okay, it's not because of his blog, I know because Charlie's my cousin, and your chili is burning."

Both of them took up spoons, the industrial-size ones, and stirred like the witches in *Macbeth*. "Seriously, what the hell?" Lilly said.

"I set them up."

Lilly, who was something of a mystery to Rebecca, a friend in the making, but guarded, so very guarded, opened her mouth, then must have reconsidered. She did, however, step closer to Rebecca. "Explain. In detail, please. And remember, I have a large spoon in my hand, and I swear to God I'll use it if you keep being cryptic."

"I don't usually set people up," Rebecca replied. "Especially not Charlie because he's got hot-and-cold running women in his life, but he and Bree…they fit."

"Before the trading cards? During? Because if Charlie Winslow was a trading card then I want my money back."

"You didn't pay for anything."

"Rebecca."

"Right. He wasn't a card. Technically."

"I've been out with two trading cards. The first one was a wonderful guy, as long as you were willing to put up with his ardent love for his mother. The second guy's card said he wanted a relationship, but his actions were completely one-night stand."

"I know. My dates haven't been life shattering, either, although I hear Paulie met someone fantastic, and that Tess's one-night stand has turned into three."

"Which still doesn't explain Charlie Winslow," Lilly said, frowning.

"It's complicated, and we'll discuss it more when we go for drinks, but if I'm talking to you, my eavesdropping sucks, so let's keep stirring and shut the hell up."

CHARLIE SWALLOWED, WONDERING for the fiftieth time what he was doing in the basement of a church kitchen fumbling around like a teenager on his first date. Bree was reading the blog pages he'd printed out, and she was kind enough not to mention that he hadn't needed to come see her or print out the pages as the blog would be online first thing in the morning.

He'd asked her to do a little bio piece and tomorrow morning it would run. She'd already given a tease—her first sidebar about the Chelsea Piers party—and it could have ended right there. But blog hits had been up, and she'd gotten more than seven hundred comments on her column. Very encouraging.

So he'd moved forward. Tomorrow morning there would be more pictures of Bree, some from college days, one from here in New York in casual wear. He hoped it would start a dialogue.

His gaze went to Rebecca, whom he caught in mid-smirk, and he touched Bree's arm, interrupting her reading. "I'll be back in a few."

She nodded, and he went over to Rebecca. He smiled at her friend, then turned to his cousin. "A minute? Outside?"

Her eyes narrowed, but she put down her spoon and walked with him to the door. Once they were outside, she shivered at the cold, but didn't go back for her coat. "You can thank me now," she said. "And later. I accept gifts, too. The more expensive the better."

"We're not dating."

"I read *NNY,* you dope," she said.

"You read what I write on *NNY.* And evidently you haven't spoken to your friend since yesterday before lunch."

"That's true. We're going out after the meals are in the freezer."

As Charlie stuck his hands in his pockets, she grimaced. The bastard should have given her his coat. "Why did you set me up with her?" he asked.

"Why did you bring me out here to freeze to death?"

He rolled his eyes dramatically and took off his

coat with a sigh that would have done a Broadway diva proud.

She curled herself into the heavy wool coat, the lining as luxurious as the tailoring. "Because she's your type."

"No, she's not. She's not vaguely my type. Do you even know me?"

"Yeah. I do. And those skeletons you go out with every night are a joke. I imagine you can count the ones you actually like on one hand."

"It doesn't matter if I like them."

"You happen to be one of the only relatives I can stomach," she said, "but Charlie, it's time for you to move on. You're what, thirty-two?"

"Thirty-one."

"Over thirty. You've spent your entire working life giving your parents and our family the finger. It's enough. You need to start living for you, and stop giving them all the power."

He stared at her with his great big eyes, mouth open, as if the cold itself couldn't penetrate his shock. "What the fuck are you talking about, Rebecca?"

"*Naked New York*. Your blog. Not the others, not the legit blogs. Yours. The one that runs every aspect of your life. If you want to call it a life."

"I'm raking in millions."

"You already had millions. Look, I have to get back to the cooking. Do what you have to do, but think about it, okay? What it would be like if your evenings were full of things you actually wanted to do? If you went out with people you actually liked?"

"You're insane. The Winslow foundation has driven you around the bend."

"Yeah, well, maybe. Oh, and remember. Don't screw

with Bree, Charlie. She may want to play in the fashion big league, but she's a really decent person. She's not used to people like us. Tread lightly."

"I told you. We're not dating."

"The way you two look at each other? I give it three days. Four at the most."

"It's freezing, and I'm not listening to you anymore." He brushed past her, and she followed, wondering how such a smart, smart man could be such an idiot.

BREE LOOKED UP FROM the blog page as Charlie came toward her. He looked cold, and she saw why as Rebecca followed him. He'd offered his cousin his coat. Another nice thing, but not in the same league as what she had been reading. "You hardly changed anything," Bree said, when he stood in front of her.

"I didn't need to. You wrote a great piece."

"Wow." She flipped through the few pages, stopped at her New York picture. "Why didn't you say anything about my hair?"

"What?"

"It's all…wrong."

"You look gorgeous," he said. "It was difficult to choose which picture to use. Each one was great."

Okay, there was nice, and *too* nice.

Her suspicion must have shown because he touched her arm, making her look into his eyes. "I'm telling the truth."

She didn't speak for a while. Not that she didn't have a lot to say, but it sounded mushy in her head, inappropriate for what they were now. There were questions, too, about why he'd come in person, what it meant, and why on earth did she keep imagining longing in his gaze when longing couldn't be possible? "I have food in the oven," she said.

"Okay," he said, staring at her, waiting for...?

"After we put everything in containers and in the freezer, we're going for drinks."

"We?"

"Rebecca, Lilly, me. You?"

"That's a big crowd. Maybe we could whittle it down?"

It was tempting; of course she wanted to be alone with him, but that he'd even suggested it made her thoughts even more confused. "We've been missing each other, what with parties and appointments and things. I can understand if you'd rather not join us."

"No. I'd like to."

Well, damn. Why would he want to join them for drinks? Rebecca! That had to be the reason. "Good. You can help us put up the food. It'll go faster."

"Swell," he said, and she smiled at his put-upon tone. "Now that you know I make such great tea, you'll want me in the kitchen forever."

Bree's laugh stuttered, and a flush hit Charlie's face. She walked faster, so fast she had to look over her shoulder to say, "It won't kill you. I promise."

He'd come to a full stop. "I'm taking your word for it," he said, going for humorous, but not succeeding.

She made herself focus on food prep, and not the jumble in her head.

THE BAR WASN'T FLASHY. Most of the patrons were in business wear like Bree and her friends. She'd be willing to wager every last one of them was asking themselves what the hell Charlie Winslow was doing in a less-than-swanky pickup bar on a Wednesday night.

If she read him correctly, he didn't seem to mind. He had hailed their cab, insisted on paying for the short trip, then walked them inside as if this was the next stop on the Fashion Week tour.

The women in the place eyed him with undisguised hunger, the kind of looks that would make a statue blush, and all she could think was *I was with him the other night. Naked.*

She had to stop that *right now.*

They scored a booth in the back, and Charlie scooted in next to her, pressing against her from knee to shoulder. It would have been easier if he'd kept his coat on, but no, it was just him in his close-fitting white shirt, narrow black pants, and his hot body, clenching the muscles in his thighs and his biceps—

"Bree?"

"Hmm?"

"Drink?"

"Ah. Yes. Tequila Sunrise, please. Heavy on the sunrise."

"Got it." Charlie scooted out, and she instantly felt more relaxed. Jeez, didn't the man understand personal space?

Lilly leaned across the table the moment he walked away. The music wasn't deafening but it still made her have to shout. "Oh, my God, Bree, why didn't you tell me you were dating Charlie Winslow?"

"I'm not. Not really."

Lilly gave Rebecca a sharp look before she turned back to Bree. "I don't understand."

"The whole setup is a blog gimmick to get new readers. No big deal."

"Yeah," Lilly said slowly. "Tell it to someone who hasn't seen him look at you."

"Seriously, Lil? Come on. Would a guy like him honestly want to date a girl like me?"

"Yes!"

"Why wouldn't he?"

Bree blinked at her friends. Of course they would say that. What was the alternative? "Yeah, you're right. He could do so much better?" "Anyway," she said, waving off the both of them, "it's great. I get to go to Fashion Week parties, and he's publishing some of my pieces, which will make my bosses sit up and notice. I take a giant step up the ladder to success. Everybody wins, especially me."

Rebecca cleared her throat, and Bree reluctantly met her gaze. She did not seem pleased. "Why is Charlie here tonight?" she asked.

"Blog stuff."

"Since it's written for the internet, wouldn't it have been easier for him to, I don't know, send that stuff to you over the internet?"

Bree opened her mouth, but she had no answer.

EXCEPT FOR THAT WHOLE Psych 101 speech from Rebecca outside the church, Charlie had a great night. The food prep part he could have lived without, although no, that had been great, too. Rebecca was right about one thing—he hardly ever did normal stuff anymore. No grocery stores, no shopping in general, not when it was so easy to get everything delivered or picked up by his housekeeper.

He went to screenings or premieres, not movies. He was sent advance copies of books and films, invitations to parties from New York to Milan, Paris, London, Dubai, L.A. He didn't barhop, and tonight had been the first time in ages he'd had drinks with real people in a regular bar instead of with celebrities behind some form of velvet rope.

He'd liked everything from the music on the juke-box to the raucous laughter from the après-work crowd. He'd been reminded of the old days when he was just starting out with his first blog. The only part that wasn't great tonight had been at the end. Putting Bree in a taxi. Alone. And then hailing a cab for himself.

He consoled himself with the fact that tomorrow would be killer busy for his latest blog contributor. After a full eight hours at her day job, she'd be on the run with the stylist, then they had an art exhibit party to go to, which didn't begin until ten. She'd be lucky to get four hours sleep, and because he was a selfish bas-tard, he'd kept her out too late tonight.

He hadn't wanted it to end. But end it had, as all things did, and in a week, give or take, his time with Bree would be a memory. If it worked out, he'd use her for the odd column, and they'd run into each other at cocktail parties and openings. But he'd move on. That's what he did. What was for the best.

He thought again about what Rebecca had said. That his family felt slapped by what he did for a living was their problem, not his. He'd told them all the way back in high school that he wasn't going to fall into line. The idea of him going into politics had been ridiculous. They should have known that without him having to smear it in their faces. But they'd only seen what they wanted to see.

His answer might have appeared radical to anyone outside the family. Getting arrested in a public scandal his senior year in college was, he'd admit, a dramatic move. But Rebecca, of all people, should have under-stood. He'd done what was necessary. His success had been a matter of skill, planning and yes, luck. Why wouldn't he want to continue to thrive? It would have been nice to be with Bree. He couldn't deny the attraction. But she didn't fit. Not as anything except a temporary gimmick, a sidebar, a tweak on the blog.

And his bed. Good Christ, she'd fit there.

He stared at the window as the cab pulled up to his building. Life was about choices. Some tougher than others. Hell, she was just a girl. He'd learned long ago not to romanticize sex.

10

THE STYLIST, SVETA BREVDA, was tall and manic and thin as a whippet, and she wielded her opinions with an iron fist. The first stop—at *Dior!*—taught Bree to strip quickly, stand straight and keep her mouth shut.

She'd stopped being self-conscious about being naked by store seven. Didn't matter who was in the dressing room. Salespeople. Friends of salespeople, men, women.

For all she knew the pizza delivery guy was standing by the exit, nodding as he studied her slipping into a skintight dress with absolutely nothing beneath it as if he were picking out curtains. But the clothes were…

Bree had lost her adjectives. That's how fantastic the clothes were. And the accessories? Good Lord, she'd died and gone to heaven. Even though the shoes tortured her feet, she couldn't breathe in the two dresses that were honestly a size too small, and she was turned and bent and paraded around like a show pony, but the torture was totally worth it because she got to keep *everything*.

Even the bit where the silver-haired dresser from

Prada stuck his hand down her bodice and lifted her bare breasts. Now *there* was a blog entry.

All this done at the speed of a montage: cabs were hailed seconds before they stepped out doors, clothing selections were made preternaturally and perfectly, and she finally understood the worth of a good stylist.

The only thing missing was Charlie. She kept wanting to tell him things, to see his reaction, to feel his hand on the small of her back, but he was working, and she was, as well. Only this work made her feel like a model—despite the fact that every article of clothing had to be shortened—and like a prom queen. But mostly like someone had made a mistake that would be corrected momentarily.

Charlie wasn't the kind to make mistakes of this magnitude. Yet it would have been better if she could have talked to him. She'd texted in cabs—the only time she'd been able to—but he was in a meeting, so his response would have to wait.

CHARLIE HAD TO WORK TO KEEP his expression mild, to speak as if his parents dropping by wasn't something unwelcome and entirely too coincidental given his talk with Rebecca last night. He'd always liked Rebecca so much. She'd been his ally, his cover, his friend. Her betrayal hit hard and low. Shit.

"We're not here to take up much of your time, Charles," his father said, his gaze scrutinizing the living room. He—both his parents—were busy cataloging every change, the new lamps, the slate that had replaced the bricks around the fireplace. They'd only been to his place a few times over the years. He preferred meeting in neutral territory, although he went to family gatherings, typically one per year, wherever it was being held. He didn't shut his parents out completely.

"You've undoubtedly seen that Andrew is starting his campaign in earnest," his father said, his voice modulated and soft. That had been one of the earliest Winslow lessons. Speak softly. Make them *listen.* "We're very pleased with the endorsements he has now, but the committee is budgeting media advertising, and naturally, your blog group has come up."

So it hadn't been Rebecca. Charlie didn't acknowledge his father's remarks. Another lesson he'd learned at his father's knee. Never give anything away, not in expression, in tone, or in posture.

The Winslows were the quintessential image of subdued elegance. Nothing his parents wore was ostentatious, but everything was meticulously selected to evoke their status. The most expensive watches, Italian handcrafted shoes, tailoring from the finest hands in several countries.

His parents commanded respect, and made everyone who wasn't family feel small and insignificant. Polite to the extreme. They radiated power and privilege.

Christ, what they had tried to do to him. He was sure they wouldn't mention that it should have been his campaign, if only he'd not been so rebellious.

"We would very much like to utilize the family connection in the two most appropriate blogs, *Dollars* and *NYPolitic.*"

"No," Charlie said. "I'm not going to promote the family agenda on my blogs. It's inappropriate, given I think Andrew would be a monumentally bad choice for the senate."

His phone buzzed again, and he took it out of his

pocket to find another text message from Bree. He couldn't read it now.

"We're not asking for a change of editorial direction or for you to give your personal endorsement," his mother said. "Simply space for featured ads. It would mean significant revenue."

He stared at his mother, knowing she was irked that he hadn't offered them drinks. It was only polite, the right thing to do, even for uninvited guests. In her home, nothing of the sort would have ever happened.

He smiled as he looked around. This was his home.

ON MADISON AVENUE, BREE and her posse stopped again, this time for shoes. Or maybe a bag, she wasn't quite sure. It didn't help that Sveta's accent—she was from Belarus—was nearly unintelligible. Bree mostly nodded and tried to keep up and not prostrate herself at the temples of fashion—Versace, Chanel, Anna Sui. Those were the kind of stores that only had a few items artfully displayed in minimalist snobbery. Where excellent champagne was served by stunning hostesses who knew every detail of the design and manufacture of the clothing on display. The music was always… interesting. Nothing you'd hear on Top Ten radio, because you could get *that* at the New Jersey malls.

The price tags made her hyperventilate. And even though the selections for her weren't the top-of-the-top-of-the-line, they were still extravagantly outlandish. Truly, she was in another world, someone else's life. Charlie's world. As she snapped another photograph of herself in a pair of heels that would likely cripple her after five steps, she reminded herself that she was a visitor. A tourist. Nothing more.

CHARLIE'S FATHER STOOD and even he couldn't control the way his rising blood pressure reddened his face. "Andrew is family, Charles. He's a Winslow. We've allowed you to set your own course, have your fun, but this is our legacy you're tampering with. I won't have it."

Charlie moved closer to the door, to the closet where he'd hung their coats. "Huh. It's good to know some things don't change. You continue to hold on to the ludicrous belief that you have any influence over me or my life. It's nice having our own traditions."

"Charles," his mother said, as affronted as his father, but less flushed. "That's enough. We are your parents."

He approached them and held out his mother's coat. "Thanks for dropping by. I hope you had a nice vacation in St. Barts."

She looked at his father who took both coats from Charlie. He didn't quite rip them out of his son's hands. But it was close.

"This will be remembered, Charles," his father said.

"I hope so." Charlie led them to the door. When it was closed behind them, he was still buzzing with anger. He needed to cool down, get Zen about the visit, about the message. He wished Bree were here.

He'd never mentioned his parents to Bree, hadn't asked about hers. They weren't friends. Yeah, he was comfortable with her. Okay, that didn't happen much anymore. But no. He wasn't going to talk to Bree about his parental issues. Jesus.

He pulled out his cell phone, and clicked on the earliest of her text messages. He was grinning by the time he got to his office.

FINALLY, THEY HAD MORE THAN enough clothing to get her through at least a week of parties. The most extravagant was the Marchesa gown for the Courtesan premiere. The evening dress, pinned to fit her body by a bevy of seamstresses, was so out of her league it hurt.

It was almost eight by the time the cab arrived at Charlie's. Sveta didn't need to announce herself. The staff at the front desk nodded respectfully as the doormen helped bring in bag upon bag upon box. Bree rested against the mirrored wall of the elevator, then took a few deep breaths before they entered Charlie's home. Her gaze went immediately to the hallway leading to his bedroom, and the reality of their new arrangement made her ache. Then he stepped into the atrium, and everything else became background noise.

He smiled widely when their eyes met. She shivered as he came closer, knowing he would touch her, and that she was allowed to touch him back, even in front of Sveta and the doormen. Such a mixed blessing. She could touch, but not have.

Bree didn't regret her decision about keeping the relationship out of the bedroom. It was the right decision, the mature way to go. It also completely sucked. "This is too much," she said, as she looked into Charlie's dark eyes. His hands went to her upper arms, and his palms ghosted across her skin down to her wrists and back up again. He kissed her, on the lips, yes, but the moment there was a hint of heat, he backed off. She wondered whom he'd kissed her for. Sveta? The rest of the team? Had to be.

"It's not," he said. "It's part of the gig."

"Charlie, I saw the price tags."

He smiled. "Most everything was free."

"Nothing's free. I know it's barter, but I'm not even famous."

"You will be."

"In a week? I doubt it."

He walked her farther into his apartment as Sveta led the doormen down a hallway, her heels clicking so quickly Bree wondered if it would be rude to suggest a switch to decaf. "You won't be on the cover of *People*," Charlie said, "but you're going to be known in the city, where it matters."

He paused, his palm warm on her skin. When he spoke again, his voice tightened along with his fingers. "You're with a Winslow now, and the Winslows are the very heart of power in this city, didn't you know?"

Bree stopped. She wasn't sure what was going on, but she felt uncomfortable. What had happened during his meeting? He'd brushed aside her questions, told her everything was fine, but that clearly wasn't the case.

"Each item of clothing is going to get a lot of mileage in the blogs," he said, letting her go. His voice had changed back to something less strident, more like Charlie. "In addition to your sidebars, I've got some fashion insiders who'll be plugging them for weeks to come. I guarantee there will be ready-to-wear versions in Macy's by April."

Bree forced a smile even though she knew he was upset, that this last speech was him getting his bearings again. But she had no right to ask him to be honest with her, to tell her a single thing about his private life. "I've already worked up a quick first draft of what it was like to be fitted by a big-league design team."

"Can't wait to see it."

Sveta's clicking heels announced her entry into the living room. "You come dress now."

Bree checked with Charlie.

"It's a media room. Used for these kind of things."

"You style up all your women?"

His lips parted, but Bree hurried to follow Sveta, not wanting to know his answer.

The room itself gave it away, though. There were mirrors, hair and makeup stations, clothing racks. A lot of those racks held men's clothes, but there were women's, as well, all stunning. In a shocking nod to propriety, there was a changing screen in a corner. There were also people. Five people—one of them was a photographer she'd seen at the Mercedes party. His assistant was fussing with lights. Off to the side were giant rolls of backdrops, like bolts of material, ready to be swung into place for any kind of photograph.

There was even a sewing machine in one corner, which Bree longed to check out. It was most probably the Ferrari of sewing machines and would make her so jealous she would weep for a week.

"Change," Sveta said, holding up the purple jacquard V-neck dress they'd picked up from the Victoria Beckham collection.

Bree obeyed, as if she'd dare do anything else. It was a matter of moments to slip out of her office wear into the magnificent cocktail dress, especially because her only undergarment was her own bargain basement thong. Beige on purpose.

The moment she stepped from behind the screen, she was covered in a smock, sat in a chair and set upon by far too many hands touching her hair, her face, her fingernails. The lights made everything more intense, hotter, scarier, and when someone said *open,* she opened her mouth, and someone else tugged her hair so she would bend her neck just so.

Her personal space had never been so invaded. The scent of many breaths and colognes went from cloying to unpleasantly sticky, and if this didn't end soon, she was going to have to do something, stop them somehow.

"Hey."

Charlie's voice cut through, and in two, three heartbeats, those things that had been touching her, brushes, fingers, nail file, eyelash curler, pulled back. Bree sighed with relief, saw that she was gripping the armrests of the makeup chair so tightly with her unpolished hand her knuckles were white.

She watched him in the mirror, felt his hand on her shoulder.

"I didn't even ask," he said. "Have you eaten anything today?"

"I had lunch."

"That was what, eight, nine hours ago?"

"About."

His eyes narrowed in the mirror and he turned to face Sveta. "How long until she's ready?"

"Five minutes. Nails on her left hand. Mascara. Lipstick."

"Hold off on the lipstick. Finish the rest. I imagine you haven't eaten, either. No, don't look at me like that, you have to eat something. There's a spread in the kitchen. Enough for everyone."

Before he looked back at Bree, he squeezed her shoulder and smiled. "It's not drippy stuff, but I'd keep the smock on, anyway. Just in case. We can talk about tonight's shindig while we eat."

She nodded. Calmly. Touched by his consideration. She hadn't realized her panic was hunger. Mostly hunger.

Unable to turn, she was still able to watch him as he went to the men's suit rack, grabbed one from the middle and went out. At the doorway, he turned and winked at her.

Before she could even smile, her hand was grabbed and the camera clicked and clicked and clicked.

THE BEST PART OF THE evening postshow was Bree, but even she hadn't been distracting enough to prevent Charlie from thinking about his parents. He'd put a call in to Rebecca, but it hadn't been returned, and his thoughts just kept circling back to this afternoon. How dare they think he was so spineless he'd cross the line into promoting the Winslow agenda on his blogs. God damn, that pissed him off.

He looked up as a Pyramid Club waiter came by with vodka shots. He'd done it again, let his attention wander, although at this point, there wasn't much more to be seen. Bree was standing against the black brick wall, looking beautiful in her purple dress, in her impossible heels, surrounded by newshounds and fame seekers.

He'd warned her it would happen. This morning's blog insured that Bree was now on the B-list, which could stand for "by association." He had the feeling it wouldn't take her long to stand on her own, though.

Most of the real celebs were huddled outside in the smoking zone, freezing their asses off while they dished about everyone inside, and he should go join them, at least for the few minutes he could put up with the fumes. But Bree was far more enticing.

She held up her glass of pineapple juice, but it was her shining smile that told him he'd made the right choice.

"You enjoying yourself?" he asked after he'd dodged drinks and drunks to get to her.

"Dizzy with it," she said. Shouted. The noise level at these things was going to make him deaf before he was forty.

"It's late. We should go soon."

"Whenever you like."

It wasn't actually that late. Just past midnight. But she had work in the morning, her sidebar to write. And he wanted some time with her where they weren't talking about who to schmooze, who to avoid. He held out his hand.

Cameras flashed as they went toward the exit. It wasn't a surprise that they were stopped several times, but it didn't take long to get the limo.

Once inside, he slid to the corner and waited for her to scoot next to him. Instead, she pressed up against the other door. "You okay?"

"Fine."

"You look…chilly."

"No," she said, tugging down her skirt, avoiding his eyes. "I'm good. Maybe you could call ahead to your building, give them an ETA for a taxi?"

"We'll take you home."

"I have my clothes at your place."

"You're wearing your clothes."

She looked at him. "Right. I forgot."

He moved closer to her, concerned. "What's going on, Bree?"

She folded her hands tightly in her lap. "I was going to ask you the same thing."

"What?"

"You've been jumpy all evening. I admit I haven't seen you at many events, but when I have you've seemed like the most relaxed person in the room. Not tonight. Actually, I felt as though something was off at your place."

He shifted away from her, not one hundred percent comfortable that there was someone else who could read him. There weren't many. Naomi. Rebecca. His college roommate. Charlie liked it that way. It had taken him a long time to cultivate the image he needed for the job, and Bree from Somewhere, Ohio, had already pierced his carefully crafted exterior in more ways than he cared to think about. He considered changing the subject for the rest of the ride home, making it clear she'd crossed a firm boundary.

Instead, he met her gaze. "My folks came by today."

She certainly looked startled by his admission. She wasn't the only one. He barely knew this woman. And yet… "They've wanted me to go into politics," he said. "Ever since I was in high school."

"Really?"

"The Winslows have had political influence through-out the generations. It was time to prepare a new senator from New York. Long-term planners, my family."

"Obviously you weren't enthused about the prospect?"

"No. I wasn't. It didn't matter to them, though. I was taught from an early age that we had an obligation to do public service. That our privileged life meant we had to dedicate ourselves to a larger cause, that what we wanted was immaterial. Which sounds great in theory, noble and philanthropic. But it had more to do with keeping the family in the top tier of society than philanthropy. My destiny was supposed to include law school, the *Harvard Law Review,* a prestigious firm, municipal office, a seat in congress, then the Senate. Carrying the standard of the Winslow heritage."

"Wow, I can't see you as a lawyer. Forget a politician."

His smile was wry. "And what, you've known me for a week? What does that tell you about my family?" He stared out the window for a beat. This true confession business felt as awkward as wearing someone else's clothes. "Not that I don't believe in public service, I do. I take that seriously." He faced her again. "What I didn't want was to live a lie."

"So you decided to become an internet mogul?"

"Sort of," he said, aware his automatic half grin said more than most of his conversations with women he'd slept with. "I didn't expect the blogs would become this big. Not complaining. I was in the right place at the right time. I wanted to be independent."

"It's worked. You are. And quite successfully."

"Yes. It's worked. It'll continue to work." He studied his hands. He was the one who was supposed to unsettle his companions. He was very good at it, and Bree wasn't even trying, so whatever this was, it wasn't a power game. No, he had opened another door for her. Game changers, these exceptions. It made him nervous.

Allowing his parents to rattle him was frankly embarrassing. They didn't for the most part. He'd just been caught off guard, that's all. But telling Bree about it? Jesus.

"So their visit was uncomfortable?"

He reached over and took Bree's hand in his. She was cold, dammit. "It was brief," he said. "I made my point. Have I said how beautiful you look tonight?"

She stared at him, at their hands, then back at him. "Yes, several times. Thank you."

"Am I making you uncomfortable?"

She sighed as she tugged her hand free. "It's not that I don't want to…"

He nodded, leaned back. Incredibly tired all of a sudden. Maybe he was coming down with something.

11

FRIDAY NIGHT CAME ALONG with a tux for the *Courtesan* premiere, and the only reason it was bearable was that Bree was in the media room getting prepped. He would check on her after he was dressed, although this time he'd made sure she'd eaten before Sveta snatched her away.

As he worked on his tie, he thought about the night ahead, pleased that she'd get to walk down a legit red carpet. A dream literally coming true, she'd told him.

The less sleep she got, he'd discovered, the more she revealed about herself. How when she was a little girl she would practice her Academy Award acceptance speech in front of the bathroom mirror, holding a bottle of shampoo or a hairbrush. She would very purposefully *not* thank whoever happened to be annoying her at the moment, which would sometimes be one of her siblings, a teacher, a friend or one of her parents.

It had made him laugh when they were slouched in the backseat of a limo, and it made him grin now. He could picture it so easily. He wondered if she'd always had short hair. Probably, given that she was so small. You wouldn't want to hide any of that face, not with hair, not with too much makeup. Sveta had turned out to be the perfect stylist for Bree. People were taking note.

Her blogs were getting heavy traffic. Unique hits were much higher than with most of his new contributors, which made sense because this approach was fresh. Charlie had never asked one of his companions to post.

Much of the chatter was about the two of them, naturally. Were they? Weren't they? There had been reports of Bree leaving in separate transportation at the end of an evening, and his place had acquired a few more paparazzi hoping to catch her doing the walk of shame in the morning. Speculation without confirmation was exactly what he'd been hoping for.

Bree had turned up on TMZ, PopSugar, Page Six, on almost every single one of his gossip feeds, as well as in the newspaper tabloids.

He slipped on his jacket, glad he'd chosen something so traditional. Beautifully cut, nothing radical. He wanted Bree to shine tonight. He had no idea what Sveta had chosen for her to wear, and he wondered how the stylist was going to top last night's look. Bree had knocked his socks off when she'd made her entrance.

Come to think of it, every time he saw her she got to him. Having her so close, and so damned untouchable probably had something to do with it. Okay, a little interest from his cock, not good for the cut of his suit. Not good in a number of ways. She was off-limits. The statistics didn't lie, and this new deal had increased *NNY*'s unique hits remarkably. It might kill him, but he'd keep to the script. Unfortunately, that meant touching. So much damn touching.

He checked his watch, made sure he had what he

needed in his pockets and then went into the living room. He glanced at the open door in the atrium and wondered why he hadn't taken Bree across to his office. It wasn't that far to the other side of the elevator. Then again, they hadn't had much time for anything but work.

He heard Sveta in the hallway, and swung around in anticipation of Bree's entrance. Damn. She did it again. Like a slap on the back of his head.

She was a vision. So much for not getting excited tonight. He would have to put his cock in a straitjacket to pull that off, and yeah, he did not need to be thinking that when she was walking toward him with a smile that made him forget how to breathe.

Her white-and-purple dress was a structured strapless design that looked like origami. It drew his gaze to her face, then right to the bare stretch of skin from her long neck down to the top of her bust. Her waist looked tiny, her legs slim yet curvy, and with that smile and those smoky eyes, no one would be able to look away.

Jewelry would have been redundant.

"Well?" she said, her shoulders moving in an almost-but-not-quite shrug.

"You're gorgeous. You'll be the most beautiful woman on the red carpet."

Bree blushed, rolled her eyes. Charlie let her think he was talking her up.

He took her hands in his and kissed both cheeks. Very European. All business. Not close to what he wanted. He'd kissed her on the mouth that first night, when he'd barely known her, and now he ached to take her mouth again, to taste her, and not only her lips.

"We have a half hour before we go. Want a drink?"

"Just water," she said. "As excited as I am, I'm so

incredibly tired I'm afraid a sip of booze will have me passed out for the night."

"Can't have that." He nodded at the couch. "Sit. I'll bring you water, then take care of the rest of our group."

"Tell them again how wonderful they are, will you? I did, but I think they think I have to say it. I don't. They're magicians."

How could he not like her? She was the anticelebrity, the cure for New York cynicism, complete with authentic goose bumps and unabashed excitement. But even he could see she hadn't exaggerated about how tired she was. Not that anyone else would notice, but he'd been watching her for days, staring too frequently and too deeply. There was more makeup under her eyes tonight. He wondered if he should cancel tomorrow night's club opening. Bree had to work for a few hours tomorrow morning, but then she planned to sleep for the rest of the afternoon. He doubted that would be enough.

He fetched her water as she made herself comfortable, a feat in that dress, on the couch. Then he conveyed her compliments along with his own to the team and saw them to the door. The limo would be arriving any moment.

He could see Bree's dark hair over the edge of the couch, and he needed to remind her to bring her other shoes for when they got back in the limo. How women walked in those ridiculous heels…

Bree had rested on the leather sofa with one leg curled up under herself. The glass, now empty, tipped at a thirty-degree angle in her hand. She was sound asleep.

After carefully lifting the glass from her fingers, freezing for a moment when she made a little low-pitched sound, he touched her bare shoulder gently. "Bree? Bree, we have to leave now."

She mumbled something and adjusted the side of her face on the back cushion.

He hated that he had to disturb her. He brushed the back of his fingers across her cheek. "Bree," he said as he sat down next to her. He wanted to wake her, not scare her. "I know you're tired, but it's the premiere. Movie stars! Glamour! Lights, cameras, action!"

She tilted. Toward him. He repositioned himself quickly so she would land on the inside of his shoulder, not the bony edge. She slumped against him, the leg that had been tucked under now at a weird angle. While it looked ungainly and not very ladylike, it didn't seem uncomfortable.

It was too easy to shift himself, to wrap his arm around her back, to hold her close, to inhale the smell of her. Slumping turned to snuggling and he sighed as he gave his next move some consideration. Then, with his free hand he pulled out his cell. He had to call Naomi, as he wasn't adept at one-hand texting.

"You in the car?"

Ah, the voice. Car became cah, and he couldn't stop his grin. "No," he whispered.

"What?"

How she'd given that simple word such a swoop gave him equal parts joy and the willies. "We're not gonna make it. Danny can take my place. Catch him quickly, though, 'cause he's not going to be dressed for it."

"Why are you not going? Why are you whispering? Charlie, what have you done? It's something about the girl, isn't it?"

"Shhh," he said, although Naomi's voice over the cell

wasn't going to wake Bree. "She's under the weather. It'll be fine."

"How's it gonna be fine? You've got deadlines. You know how many comments you got today? Over twenty-five hundred. And you're taking sick leave? What the hell, Charlie?"

"It'll work out. Like always."

"Yeah, well, it's me you're talking to, sweetheart, and 'like always' my ass."

"Naomi. Call Danny. I'll send you the copy and photos in the morning."

He disconnected before she gave him additional grief, and put his cell down on the coffee table. Bree hadn't stirred an inch. She'd probably be mad at him for sending someone in their place, and he had no idea what he was going to do about tomorrow's blog pages, but there was no way in hell he was going to wake her. Not now.

She needed to rest. There would be other premieres. He'd spin the story to his advantage. In fact… He had the perfect angle. Take that, Naomi.

He'd have a story for tomorrow, but for tonight, he was keeping Bree to himself.

BREE HEARD A DOG BARK AND while it was a real dog barking, it was a dog once removed. A television dog. But she didn't open her eyes, not yet. She liked this place, the in-between where there was nothing at all unpleasant and no alarm was going to intrude. The subtle, woodsy scent of Charlie made her sigh and smile. He knew how to use cologne, not like some of the guys from work who showered in the stuff. There was always a hint of the man underneath with Charlie, and that was the best part.

She moved a bit, her head at a weird angle and it wasn't her pillow at all, and *oh*. It was dark, very dark. Charlie's window was right there, across from his coffee table and behind his big television. It was late. Wrong. All wrong.

"You're up."

She couldn't exactly see as some of her fake eyelashes were now sticking to her cheek, but she looked up in the general direction of Charlie's voice. "What's going on?" As nice as it felt to be pressed against his chest, she pushed off, up, until her feet were on the ground and she was sitting like a person. "What time is it?"

"A little past nine."

"Nine? p.m.? Oh, God, was the premiere called off? Did something bad happen? Is everyone okay?"

Charlie laughed as he rubbed his shoulder, the one she'd been nestled against. "Everything's fine."

"We were supposed to be at the theater at six."

"You were tired."

"I was…" She peeled the lashes off both eyes and settled them in her palm like two spiders. When she glanced back at Charlie he was still rubbing his arm, shaking it. She must have been sleeping on it the whole time. Hours. He'd undone his bow tie, the top button of his shirt, too. The apartment was darker than it had been because he hadn't turned on more lights. She'd slept through the red carpet. He'd let her. "I don't understand."

"I bet you're starving," he said, as he stood. "I know I am. How does Thai sound? Maybe some Tom Yum soup?"

"Wait." She raised her hand to stop him, but it was

the hand with the eyelashes. "Wait. Explain please. Why are we here? Why was I sleeping?"

"I told you." He turned to leave.

"No, you didn't." She stood up. She might be foggy headed and probably looked like hell, but she was going to get an answer. "Why didn't you wake me?"

He kept walking to the kitchen, his tux jacket swinging loose, and she thought of watching him take it off slowly, seeing those perfectly cut trousers fall.

Her heels clicked on the floor and made her wince with each step. Holy crap, these shoes were the instruments of the devil. Speaking of which, her dress, the architectural wonder of a dress, looked like a badly folded sheet. Sveta was going to kill her. "Charlie!"

He paused. Turned around. Smiled at her. "There'll be other premieres. I promise. I'll make it up to you."

"You don't skip things. You never do. I've read your blog every day forever, and you're always there. Even when you're not, you have a really good excuse. Like natural disasters. Not that your arm was trapped under a sleeping person. So what the hell?"

Charlie sighed. God, he really did look hot in that tux. "Take off your shoes. It hurts just looking at them." He kept walking to the kitchen, and she kept following, the pain in her feet making her blink.

"In fact," he said, not bothering to turn, "just get into something comfortable. We'll eat. You'll have a decent night's rest and so will I. We'll go back to the madness tomorrow."

They were in the kitchen proper and he'd flipped on the lights. It took her eyes a moment to adjust, to see he was holding a handful of delivery menus. Everything felt tilted sideways.

"Thai?" he asked. "Chinese? Pizza? Deli? There's

a terrific Indian place nearby that makes a hell of a chicken tikka masala."

Bree inhaled, noticed that she really needed to brush her teeth, and that she was still completely bewildered by everything that had happened since she woke up. "Whatever," she said, shrugging. "As long as it doesn't have cilantro, I'll like it. I'll be back."

She didn't make it to the media room before she took off the shoes. The dress came off in the hallway entrance. When she reached the racks of clothes, she'd already decided to wear one of the kimono robes because dammit, she wanted to be comfortable even if she did have to dress to go home later. Not a teeny short robe, either, because she didn't want him thinking she wanted *that*. They didn't do *that*. It had been decided.

Besides there was a particularly beautiful long black robe with a crane on the back that felt like heaven over her bare skin and covered her more than her dress had. She didn't even mind that it dragged on the floor. So what if she wasn't an Amazon? She was compact. Efficient. Far more comfortable in airplane seats.

The bathroom was next, and she debated keeping the makeup that had taken such time and effort to apply, but in the end it was just no. It took longer than it should have, but feeling clean and *herself* was worth it.

She looked once more in the mirror and stalled. It made no sense that Charlie hadn't shaken her awake. That they were here instead of Radio City Music Hall. The red carpet was long over now, of course, and that was the important part—not watching the movie. But there was an after party they could have attended.

It was highly unlikely that his excuse that she was "tired" was the real reason they'd stayed in. No, there had to be something bigger in play, but she was too fuzzy-headed to figure it out right now.

What she should do was get dressed, go home and go to sleep so that when she went into the office tomorrow to catch up on her real job, she might have an actual working brain cell or two.

On the other hand, a girl had to eat. That she got to eat with Charlie without a hundred people surrounding them was extraordinary. Unprecedented. They'd been on the run for what felt like months instead of days, seeing each other in snatches and in the blinding light of flashbulbs. The only truly personal moments had been in his bed on Valentine's night—which she wasn't allowed to think about—and last night in the back of the limo. She'd thought about that conversation all day. Not only about how different their worlds were, but how he'd opened up to her. It was as if she'd seen him naked again.

Screw it, she wanted to. Eat with him. Talk to him. Alone.

Her accelerated pulse and the rush of excitement that ran through her body merely thinking about what was next moved her out of the bathroom and into seeing dinner through. It was only her heart at risk, after all. And hadn't she admitted, to him of all people, that she *wanted* her heart broken by callous men who wore gorgeous suits?

12

CHARLIE GRINNED AGAIN. "So you're a black sheep, too?"

Bree swallowed her mouthful of noodles and took a sip of soda before she could answer him. "Oh, yeah. I was supposed to marry Eliot. My high school boyfriend. It was a thing. Big. Tons of teeth gnashing and hand wringing. Comfort food played a big role. In particular, fried chicken."

At the mention, they both ate for a bit in silence, which gave her time to go over what Charlie had told her about his struggles with his family. How was it possible for them not to be proud of his accomplishments? Maybe they were proud, but the family was crappy at communication. Rebecca had said that was an issue between her and her folks, and Charlie's parents were cut from the same cloth. But then again, Charlie was driven. He put the implementation of his goals above everything else. As did Bree. "You know what I can't figure?" she asked.

"What's that?"

"How come you're nice."

"Me? Nice?"

"Very much so. I expected you to be on the conceited side of horrible. You've been great."

He stared at her for a long moment. "Thanks. I'm glad you think so."

"Hmm," she said. "Interesting."

"What?"

"There was absolutely no agreement in that response. To be clear, I meant nice in an Ohio sense. It wasn't a dig."

"Well, then. I appreciate it even more. Nice can go either way around here."

"I gathered. How would you describe yourself?"

"Oh, that's a scary question."

"I'm not frightened."

"I'm not referring to you."

Bree grinned. "Come on. I'm already prejudiced in your favor."

"That's what's got me worried. I like that you think I'm nice."

"But…"

"I'm…focused. Extremely focused."

She ate a bit, trying on the word to see how it fit. "Is that all you are?"

His wince was extravagant for him. "Yeah, I'm pretty sure that's the whole deal."

"You're funny. That's not an opinion. That's fact. You make me laugh a lot."

"Hey, no fair talking about my looks."

"See? Cute. Very cute."

He put down the carton and picked up the beer, but he didn't drink. "What else?"

She almost teased him, but the look in his eyes stopped her. "You're thoughtful. You see who's around you and you don't take advantage of them. I'm not ter-

ribly experienced but I have the feeling that not everyone feeds the makeup and hair crew. Or even notices
the building's security staff."

"That's manners."

Bree shook her head. "Nope. It goes beyond that.
Most people in your position wouldn't give a damn
about anyone around them. It would be easy to be horrible. Expected. But you don't need to be ruthless and
evil to be a powerful presence because you're already
a powerful presence. People get it. You don't have to
shove their faces in it."

"I like that. Not sure I agree, but it's something to
ponder. Of course, I don't want to completely disre-
gard the whole ruthless and evil thing. That has a lot
of appeal."

She gave a quick nod. "Yes. It does."

He drank some more, then reached for the rice container, but as he did so, he managed to move himself
over until they were close enough to touch. The carton
stayed in his hand as he leaned into her.

Bree held her breath. Warning bells went off in the
distance, muted but not silent. "I should call for a taxi,"
she said. "Get home. Take advantage of the night off."

Charlie put the rice down, but his leg, his hip, his side
were pressed warm against her. He smelled like spice
and beer and her eyes closed as she inhaled. "I don't like
beer. To drink. But I really like how it tastes when—"

He waited, not five inches between them, maybe not
even three. "When…?"

"When I do this," she whispered right before their
lips touched.

CHARLIE WANTED TO PULL her into his arms and kiss her
until she cried uncle, but he held himself back, every

muscle in his body on a hair trigger. Her lips were soft against his, brushing, teasing. Her breath came in gentle puffs, scented with galangal and heat, and no matter how fervently he thought *now, now, now,* he let her call it, let her make this decision. What the hell was wrong with him?

The whole night had been one bizarre thing after another. He didn't miss premieres. He didn't sit still for three goddamn hours just so he wouldn't disturb someone's sleep. He wasn't nice. Nice wasn't even a part of the equation, so what was happening? What was he doing?

A touch, fingers, small, cool, delicate on the back of his neck, and he became very aware of his cock. Not for the first time since they'd landed on the couch together. In another bid to make this the weirdest night ever, he'd found himself cycling through stages of hardness. From that first moment she'd leaned into him all sleepy and mumbling, he hadn't been completely soft. Not hard as a rock, either. Which was fine. He'd only touched himself the one time, and that was an adjustment. Even though this whole scenario was as close to an erotic dream as he'd ever had without sleeping.

She tugged his hair, pulled him closer, deepened the kiss. Little licks against his bottom lip, then the top, as if he were ice cream, a caramel apple. His cock filled, pressed against his fly. He should have taken off the tux, but it was too late to worry about that now. Not when she slipped her tongue inside and he tasted her for the first time since the party at Chelsea Piers.

Instantly he realized it was a mistake. A hormone driven error that would come back and bite him in the ass. He'd known better, but had he pulled away? Hell no.

He adjusted his head so they fit together better, then started his own exploration. He was not delicate or tentative. In fact, it was all he could do to stop himself from showing her just how ruthless he could be.

He opened his mouth and claimed her, sucked on her tongue, thrust with his own, and the sound she made, holy god…now he was getting the kind of hard that meant business. With determination and the endgame in sight, he pulled back. "Bedroom?" he asked. Hoped.

She blinked at him. Charlie realized he'd abandoned his beer and taken hold of her upper arms, the silk of the kimono warm beneath his fingers. She was virtually naked under that kimono; he knew that. He could see the push of her hard nipples against the silk. Maybe he'd been hit in the head or something, because this was not his style. This felt reckless, and he hadn't been reckless since his teens.

Her nod let him breathe again. He kissed her once more. It started out thankful and turned desperate with one slick of his tongue against hers.

They stood as they'd been sitting, his hands lifting her up, their mouths working together to remember, relearn, discover.

He had them halfway across the room before they had to take a real breath.

One of Bree's hands was in his hair, the other under his tuxedo jacket on the small of his back, as if they were doing some crazy waltz. "This is a bad idea," she said before she kissed his chin.

"Terrible. We decided." He captured her mouth again, amazed at how she let him guide her, backward, through the space. How, even with the height difference, the important parts matched, like her breasts against his chest and her lips within his reach. He only had to move a single muscle for her to react exactly as she needed to. It *was* a dance, not crazy, just theirs.

"Five years," she said, in a rush of air and half a moan.

"What's five years?" The hallway was coming, so they shifted slightly to the left.

"My plan." Her hand moved down right over his ass as they maneuvered the turn, and he pushed her back into the wall. Her "umph" made him swing her around as he stood straighter, the graceful equilibrium between them going down the drain.

"You okay?"

"Where's the damn bedroom?"

"Close," he said. Speeding them there would have been the smart move. He kissed her instead. The pull was too much, knowing he shouldn't, they shouldn't.

The hand that had been in his hair was now on his chest, rubbing in vague circles.

"What plan?" he said, his voice as husky as a pack-a-day smoker's. "To take over the world? To bring me to my knees? You don't need five years for either."

She laughed, stepped on his toe with her bare foot. It didn't hurt. "I'm going to be a cross between Tim Gunn and Tina Brown," she said, stumbling on the kimono.

If they didn't kill each other before they made it to the bedroom, it would be a miracle. "Good for you. You'll be great."

"Not if I can't say no to you."

He looked at her then, at her darkened eyes filled with a heat that could burn a house down. "You can."

She breathed in, then there was silence. Only his heartbeat loud in his ears.

"Please don't make me," she whispered.

A dark sound came out of his throat as he bent over

and lifted her into his arms. It was ridiculous, something he never did, would never do, but he'd had enough walking, enough of everything but stripping her bare, burying himself inside her for as long as he could, as deeply as he could.

"Charlie," she said, working her arm around his neck. "We're insane."

"I know." The door was there, right there, and it was open. He had her inside in a flash, over the bed in two, but he had to kiss her one more time before he let her go.

She pulled back from the kiss first, but she barely moved. Her breath brushed his face, soft panting, a faint-as-a-whisper tremor.

He lowered her slowly, head on the pillow, the shoulder of the kimono slipping down enough for him to see the crease where her arm pressed next to her side. It made his cock jerk and he wanted her so badly he didn't know what to do.

"It's my turn," she said.

"What?" He pulled his gaze from that patch of heretofore ordinary skin. "Your turn?"

Her normally very sweet smile and her big innocent eyes turned wicked as she looked him over. "Strip for me. Slowly."

He had to grin. She'd said the words like a crime boss, like a vixen. And then she shrugged that partially bared shoulder until the kimono… He could see the edge of her hardened nipple. Only the edge.

BREE BIT HER LOWER LIP hard as Charlie took off his jacket. He'd taken her at her word, so his movements were unhurried, but his technique? Bless his heart, he had no clue how to do a sexy striptease. He kept checking to make sure he wasn't going to trip and he tried to take both arms out of his sleeves at once and that made him cuss, and start again. She didn't want to laugh because, oh, God, he was trying so hard. Her whole body ached with how adorable he was, how the normally smooth, completely controlled internet mogul looked exactly like a seventeen-year-old virgin trying to impress the prom queen. They both relaxed when the jacket hit the floor. She wasn't about to put him through it again with his shirt and trousers.

"Come here," she said, patting the bed. "You needed a fedora for that move. Besides, you're too far away."

"Now look who's being nice," he said as he sat beside her.

Her fingers were working on his buttons. They looked fantastic—it was Armani, after all—but they were small and round and not easy with shaking fingers. By button three, she was tempted to rip the damn shirt open, but she could never abuse quality fashion like that. It would be like shooting Bambi.

Charlie ended up helping, and every time their fingers brushed she gasped. Couldn't help it. Now that he wasn't even trying, his unbuttoned shirt slid off his shoulders as if choreographed, and holy crap, he was half-naked, and so was she.

"This is going to be bad," she said, her perfectly painted fingernails trailing up his beautifully sculpted chest. Somehow, his muscles, his whole body, had been made to her specifications. Enough definition and muscle to be a gorgeous surprise, an ass to die for, and all of it belonging to the same Charlie who'd let her sleep, who made sure she ate, who'd given her a shot at her dreams. "It's everything I want," she went on, "and that never ends well." She finished the sentence with her lips on his chest.

His fingers smoothed through her hair, his inhalation loud in the quiet room. She kissed him again, moving over the warm flesh in front of her, sneaking her free hand to his slacks, only to realize she'd never get him naked like this. He couldn't have picked a more perfect tuxedo for the night. Stunning and sinfully elegant, and yet everything that kept the structure together—buttons, snaps, zippers—were as complicated as menswear could get. She wondered if somehow he'd found boxer briefs that needed a password to come off.

His fingers cupped her chin, and he lifted her up and away from his chest. "We can stop," he said. "I'll have to excuse myself for a few minutes, but we can stop right now."

She nodded, knowing it was the right thing to do, but when he sighed his disappointment, she grabbed for his hand to keep him from going. "There are too many things," she said.

"I'm not—"

"I keep thinking of all the things we didn't do that one time. How we wouldn't get another chance, and I'd never know…" She felt the blush and marveled at her absurd Midwestern shyness.

"Like what?" he asked, leaning over her more closely, his free hand moving to his difficult trousers.

She captured his index finger between her lips. Then she flicked the pad with her tongue before she sucked the digit into her mouth. She tasted him, fluttered her tongue against his flesh, made him understand.

His moan had her squeezing her legs together. She released his finger, but only so he could finish undressing. To say he was eager was an understatement, and he must have worn that tux often to be so adept, but she never blinked as the trousers hit the floor, followed by his sleek black blessedly uncomplicated briefs. Somewhere along the way, he'd toed off his socks, and there he stood. Oh, so hard. His cock painting a wet trail on his stomach as his chest rose and fell in harsh, quick pants.

"You thought about that?" he asked.

She nodded. Ran her hand up between the folds of the kimono, slowing as she traced her bared nipple. "I would really like it if you'd lie down. Soon."

His smile was as erotic as his erection, and both of them together made her squirm. He obliged, not without stealing a kiss that lasted a long, long time. Finally he was spread out next to her, and she could do whatever she liked. Taste, lick, nibble, tease.

She may have said it before, but this time she meant it. No more sex after this, because as she slipped off her panties on her way to straddling Charlie's hips, she realized that it wasn't exactly the smile or the erection or the meals or the clothes. It *was* everything she wanted. *He* was. Charlie. There was no use pretending, not anymore. This was no crush.

HE WAS GOING TO BURST into flames. There'd be nothing left but ash, and it would be worth it. Naked Bree straddling his waist was exactly the last view he wanted. The smile was a bonus, her bending over to kiss him more than a mortal man could take.

The kiss wasn't half as sweet as her grin. In fact, it was kind of a mess, full of tongue and teeth and saliva and his hips lifted her straight up off the bed it was so hot. Her hands on his chest steadied her, but before they had to break for the next breath, her fingers found his nipples. He loved nipple play, but the woman on top gave him two synchronized twitches that forced his head back, his eyes to widen then slam shut and he wasn't even going to try to explain the noise he made.

"This is fun," she said in the most wicked voice ever.

"You're killing me."

"Don't be such a baby. You can take it."

"I'm not used to this kind of insolence," he said, giving her his most imperious stare.

She raised her left eyebrow as she sat up. He only noticed she'd moved her hand around back when she gripped his cock.

He roared up again, thrusting his hips, her, everything, for more. Now. Please.

Then she pumped. Once.

He already knew she weighed next to nothing. He could simply lift her up, reseat her again in a more agreeable position. Because being inside her in the next ten seconds was the most important thing that would ever happen to him, ever, for his whole life, no exceptions.

When she let go he wanted to cry, and would have if he wasn't such a manly man.

Then she scooted back, lifting herself over his cock until she was settled on his thighs, and shit, the view, her bare-naked pussy spread obscenely exactly where he couldn't touch it.

One finger touched the base of his cock and she drew the finger up and up, and his back arched along with it. The crazy thing was, the whole time, he was looking at her, staring into her eyes, and she was laughing. Not out loud, not mean or taunting, just…delighted. Like a kid with the best toy ever. Jesus.

Her mouth opened in a big smile just before she bent over, and engulfed the head of his prick.

His shout came all the way from his balls, and it was everything he could do not to come right then and there.

Game on, he thought. Then he gave up thinking completely.

SHE HAD NO IDEA HOW LONG she'd been on the edge, but it had to have been hours. It was torture, how he'd bring her right there to that place where she held her breath, where she trembled and moaned and prayed, only to pull her over into a quivering mess, and then rev her up again until she couldn't think straight, until she'd pulled the fitted sheet off its corners, until she'd begged herself hoarse.

He came twice.

She lost count.

13

HE COULDN'T POSSIBLY be getting hard again this quickly, especially after a doubleheader, but his body was giving it a hell of a try. Charlie couldn't remember the last time sex had been this…intense. If it ever had.

He liked sex and he liked women, and he had liked some of the women he'd had sex with very much, but this, with Bree, felt different somehow.

He kept staring at her, his pulse quickening as her breasts, the nipples still hard and very pink, rose and fell. While the flush that infused her face and chest was slowly fading, her skin, like his, still glistened with sweat. He needed to get up, get clean. Offer her water, see if she wanted a shower, see if she wanted to go home, although he doubted that. It was crazy late.

His other hand reached over and touched her arm. She turned her head and grinned at him. "That was. Wow."

He grinned back. "Well said."

"I'm surprised I'm speaking English. With real words and stuff."

He laughed, squeezed her arm. "I have to do things," he said.

"Well, you're on your own. I can't move."

He nodded, or at least he thought he nodded.

"Here's what I don't understand," she said.

"Only one thing?"

"Ha. No. I don't understand a gazillion things. Starting with what we were thinking. Not that I'm complaining, mind you. But we did decide not to do this."

"Yeah, well. I blame you."

"What? You can't blame me. It wasn't even my fault."

"It was so. You kissed me."

"You ordered an entire Thai restaurant for dinner."

"You were naked under the robe."

"I had on a thong."

He looked at her again and found she was already staring. "You fell asleep."

"You didn't wake me," she said, only not as quickly. The gleam of laughter fading from her eyes.

"You needed rest," he said, his voice low, soft.

She swallowed, then turned over a little. She wasn't facing him full on, but her body leaned toward him. "You could have gone by yourself."

Whatever he'd thought she was going to say, that wasn't it. Because she was right. He could have. He should have. He could have gone alone. Called any number of women he knew who could have been red carpet ready in a heartbeat if he'd wanted company.

"Why didn't you go alone, Charlie?" she asked.

He pounced on the first answer that came to him. "I didn't want to wake you."

Bree's eyebrows lowered. If she was trying to figure out the hidden meaning in his words, she'd be at it for a long while because there was no meaning. No answer. No explanation. It hadn't occurred to him. Not once in three hours had he entertained the thought of leaving her to sleep so he could do his job.

Shit.

He let go of her arm, flung off his sheet then practically flew off the bed. Naked and really wishing he wasn't, he turned to Bree. "You want some water?"

She blinked, then nodded. "Sure. Thanks."

He got her a bottle from the mini fridge in his closet. When she took it, he headed for the bathroom. After he'd closed the door behind him, he realized he should have said something. Nothing important, just the typical, "Be back in a minute," or something equally mundane. According to Bree, he was supposed to be nice. What he was, in fact, was panicked.

He busied himself with cleaning up, but his thoughts were as scattered as shattered glass. He kept trolling for reasons, for a string of logic that would explain why he was standing in his bathroom washing the come off his dick when he should have been in his office finishing up his notes on the movie premiere and planning his morning blog. Alone. With no Bree in his bed or even in his apartment.

Nothing. It may not have been his idea to stop the sex when they agreed to work together, but he'd agreed. It only made sense. They'd had their one night, and even that had been questionable. It was completely out of character for him to change the rules like this. Something must be wrong with him.

He finished, barely remembering to turn off the spigot, as it occurred to him that because of the blog experiment, he'd been spending almost every night with Bree, which was unusual as hell, and not sleeping with anyone else, which was also bizarre, so, of course, he was off balance.

Okay, so he'd gone without having sex for longer than a week before and he hadn't done anything as stupid as ditch work, but the thing was, even during dry spells, he'd gone out with a variety of women. His batting average, despite the impression he cultivated, was nowhere near one hundred percent. There'd been extended stretches he'd gone without anything but his own hand. But he'd never gone any length of time accompanying the same woman to different events.

He snorted as he grabbed his towel. No cause for alarm. It was probably for the best if he didn't make a habit of this, of Bree, because that could get messy.

He could stop seeing her altogether. Fashion Week was moving on to London. He wasn't covering the show there, but neither was he covering the events at Lincoln Center. Tonight's premiere was only tangentially related, and after the club opening tomorrow night and the perfume party Monday, the town and the blog would move on. There was nothing in the contract that stipulated their working relationship would stop at the end of Fashion Week, although it had been mentioned. It would be simple, a nice, clean break.

Instead of the rush of relief he expected, Charlie paused again, his hand partway to the knob. He opened the door slowly, cautiously, unsure why.

She was in his bed. Sitting up, in fact, her side to him while she faced the window. If someone had been outside looking in, they would have seen her, backlit like a painting. They'd have seen him, too, which should have prompted him to shut the light, if not the door, because he was naked.

But so was Bree. She was naked and lit from behind, and he knew she could see his reflection in the window as he stared at her, as intrigued by the shadows as he was by what the light revealed. His gaze moved down the length of her back to the pillow at the base of her spine. He could see the proof of his fingers in her hair, the dark mark he'd made at the junction of her neck and shoulder. The soft roundness of her breast as it peeked out from under her arm—a suggestion, nothing more. It made him swallow, it made the base of his cock tighten and interest curl deep in his body.

He hated to do it, but he had to turn off the light behind him. The darkness wasn't complete because he'd thought of moments like these when this room had been redesigned. He was a visual man, and had no trouble sleeping when the space was less than inky black.

His image was still reflected, though not as clearly, but she could see him approach the bed, raise his arm, put his hand on her warm shoulder. "Stay?" he asked, his voice as low as the lights.

"I need to be up by eight. Well, eight-ish. I have to go to work in the morning."

"We can do that."

Finally, Bree turned to meet his gaze. "I was so sure you were going to ask me to leave."

"I thought about it."

She nodded.

"But it's late," he said. "And I want you here."

A barely there smile curved her lush lips. "Just this once."

He nodded. "Yeah."

"Good. Fine." She shifted, dislodging his hand. "I need to…" She nodded at the restroom.

He watched her small, perfect body as she climbed out of bed. She didn't reach for the robe, which was a surprise. But she was always surprising him.

The door closed before she turned on the light, and

he felt cheated. This was an irresponsible thing he was doing. Maybe that was the point.

IT WASN'T HER ALARM CLOCK that woke her at a quarter to seven. She wasn't sure what had. It took Bree a moment to remember where she was, and to see she was alone. She hadn't realized she'd wanted to wake up next to him.

The bathroom door was open, no sounds, no lights. She wondered if Charlie was in the apartment at all. It was only seven, so she could technically sleep for another hour or so, but that wasn't going to happen. A shower was, however, but first, she'd have to go fetch her bag, her clothes, shoes. Sadly, she hadn't packed her overnight kit. There weren't supposed to be any overnights. Lesson learned.

She grabbed the kimono and opened the bedroom door. It was quiet and chilly, or maybe the chilly was because she was hurrying across long sections of floor in bare feet. The sheer space of this apartment boggled the mind. She pictured her bedroom/closet and how doing anything was a logistical nightmare. The sewing machine couldn't be up while the bed was; the drawers had to be closed to get the sheets, to get anything on hangers. Most everything else was stored in her suitcases, which weren't particularly big or handy. And here she was darting the length of a football field to grab her bag before she rounded the couch to dash to the media room, never once hearing or seeing the master of the house.

She looked at her work dress and it made her sad. It was her own, of course. Not that it mattered. It was a Saturday morning, hardly anyone would be at her office and whoever was probably wouldn't remember she'd worn the same clothes two days in a row. She couldn't believe she had to go in at all, but between the shopping, the preparations, the parties and writing the blogs, she'd been neglecting her day job. God forbid she got fired. She was beyond lucky to have any kind of job, let alone a great one. At least she'd slept more last night than she had all last week. Which said volumes about how little sleep she'd been getting.

Tempted almost to the breaking point, she left the green DKNY dress that was calling her name on the hanger and fetched the blue shirtdress she'd made in college.

She debated using the en suite bathroom here, or going back to the bedroom. Staying here was too much like work, and she was off until tonight.

She kept her eyes peeled for him, surprised when he wasn't in the bedroom. Maybe not so much surprised as disappointed. Anyway, his shower was an otherworldly experience especially since the water pressure in her building was more or less random spitting. Even so, she didn't linger.

Fresh panties were an issue. She didn't have any, if there were some in the media room, she didn't want to know about it. She'd go without, but in this city? That wasn't a smart move.

What the hell. She went back into Charlie's empty bedroom. Second drawer in, she found what she was looking for. A nice pair of black silk boxer briefs. She'd replace them later.

Once dressed, she checked the mirror carefully, making sure no one would see her secret. It was kind of sexy, wearing something so personal of his. She might even tell him.

Then it was on to patching her makeup and fixing

her hair. It wasn't going to win her any beauty contests, but she'd pass. She left the kimono on the bed and went in search of her host. Or at the very least, a note.

She discovered that Charlie's apartment took up the entire floor. The elevator was situated in an atrium. His office took up most of the previously undiscovered country.

And there he was. Sitting in a giant room with enough computers to launch the shuttle. He wore jeans, which she hadn't even known he owned, and a scrumptious V-neck sweater. He made quite the picture, and not because he was so, so pretty—although that didn't hurt—but because he was in his element. The difference was written in his posture as he typed on his computer, as he sailed across the floor in his chair. She couldn't look away.

When he was at parties, even in the limo before parties, or when he was working with his crew inside the media room, there was never a moment when Bree wasn't aware that Charlie was watching. No. Overseeing. It wasn't super obvious, but she'd felt it, and on a couple of occasions she'd seen others notice. He was always one step removed, above it all.

That was one of the things that made even A-list celebs want his attention. He never gave too much of himself. He held back a small but vital part, the part that judged, evaluated. He was completely charming to everyone, so there was no hint, no clue. His real thoughts and opinions would show up in the next blog, or even worse, wouldn't show up at all.

But he was completely present in his big office. The difference in his attitude couldn't have been clearer. She'd been with this Charlie only twice before—in bed.

She shivered at the memories, still hardly believing any of it had been real.

He hadn't noticed her yet. She wasn't even in the room, just peeking in from the doorway. Bree wondered if it might be better to leave now. He was so wrapped up in the work, he wouldn't care. She shouldn't. Only an idiot would make more of last night than what it was. Tension relief. Nothing personal.

Except for the naked part and the kissing and how she'd felt when he was holding her.

Last night she'd had every ounce of Charlie. His body, his attention, his focus. It had felt like being plugged into the mainframe. Every touch electric and unique—

"You're being ridiculous," Charlie said.

Bree froze, held her breath. His back was to her, how could he—

"Naomi, stop. Just stop right there."

He was on the phone. Not a mind reader.

"Okay, okay. I'll bet you a week's pay there's more traffic today about me missing the premiere than any of the Fashion Week stuff." He laughed. "No, if I win, you have to be nice for a week." Another laugh. "Nice as in pretending to be someone else. Anyone else."

Bree turned to leave. She needed to go, and she could only excuse eavesdropping for so long.

"Naomi, for God's sake, it's the numbers," he said, pushing himself over to another computer. "It's always been the numbers. It's me, remember? When have I ever had another motive? The minute the Bree thing stops paying off, we'll end it. There's nothing else going on, so you can stop with your concern. It's unnecessary."

A spike of ice went through Bree's body, ripping

her heart. None of it had mattered, the conversations she'd had with herself, her determination to be realistic, to focus on business. She'd been an idiot. A fool. The soul-sucking pain told her she'd fallen for him, waltzed right into an illusion, knowing it was an illusion, and she hadn't even realized the fantasy had taken over.

She backed away from the door as quietly as she could on trembling legs. It was weird; she could feel her pupils dilating, feel a chill that had nothing to do with the air around her. But shock was an absurd over-reaction, wasn't it? No matter what was going on in her head, she'd never *believed* Charlie loved her. She hadn't. That he'd liked her, yes. That they clicked? That last night had been mutually extraordinary?

Wrong. Wrong as wrong could be. She was a gimmick. Nothing more. Nothing real. He'd told her up front, and she'd signed a legal document that confirmed it. None of this was Charlie's fault. Hell, she's the one who'd instigated the sex last night. She couldn't even blame him for that.

She had painted herself into this corner. And now that she was there, she had to get herself out. Now. She still had obligations, parties to attend as Charlie's date. He could walk out of his office any minute, and oh, God, if he suspected she had turned into one of *those women,* she'd die a thousand humiliated deaths.

It didn't hit her that she was in the living room until she saw the remains of their dinner on the coffee table. She needed to escape. Get her act together somewhere else. But she'd have to leave a note, something easy and quick.

There was the receipt from the Thai place. A pen in her purse. She scribbled "Thanks for the fun night. See you later!" It was all she could do not to run to the elevator, and even though it made no difference, she pushed the button over and over and over.

Finally, she flung herself into the small mirrored box, grasped the rail with both hands and held herself together. She would have to face the security people, the doorman, get a taxi.

Evidently, she'd learned a few things from Charlie. Like how to smile convincingly, and how to make idle conversation as if nothing whatsoever was wrong.

She even gave the cabdriver her address, and sat back for the ride.

Once she'd cleared Central Park West, she fell apart.

14

CHARLIE WAS ANGRY AFTER disconnecting from Naomi. He wasn't mad at her, not exactly, but she knew better than to keep pressing when he clearly didn't want to be pressed. That the woman kept his life together was an undisputed fact. He could probably survive her loss but even the idea bothered him. Nothing made him more aware of how important his routine was than the thought of his network splintering.

The inner circle—Naomi, the server techs that oversaw the equipment, his blog editors—were like his pulmonary system with Naomi at the heart. Which made it difficult to lie to her.

He'd done it before, mostly for the sake of ease. Trivial matters. That he'd missed the premiere, that he'd been with Bree over such an extended period of time, that he liked her, was not trivial at all.

He'd been staring at his monitor for several minutes without absorbing any data, but rather than getting back to business his eyes closed as the memory of Bree's body beneath him went straight from his brain to his cock.

She was probably still sleeping as it wasn't even eight, let alone eight-ish. The nice thing to do would be to leave her be. The girl was exhausted, and what they'd done last night hadn't helped. Yet he wanted to go to the bedroom right now and do it all over again. What the hell was up with that? They'd agreed, the sex might have been mind-blowing, but it wasn't smart. This was a rookie mistake, allowing his feelings into the mix. He'd end up as just another blogger if he wasn't careful. Someone who used to be someone.

He should wake her. Maybe with a cup of tea?

He pushed himself across the room, calling himself every kind of an idiot. Coffee was the polite thing to do. It was business as usual today. No screwing around. No goddamn tea.

This time, he'd give her a couple of twenties, make sure she took them. Explain to her how it was a write-off. That would get them both back on track.

She had work, they had the club opening tonight, and he had to put a spin on last night's premiere that would bump up the numbers.

As he went toward the kitchen to get her coffee, he saw her note. He picked it up, recognized her handwriting but didn't believe she'd left without saying anything to him. That she'd left a note instead. What the hell... that wasn't like Bree. Had last night been that bad?

Shit, missing the premiere hadn't been like him. Maybe Naomi was right. Maybe he was too messed up to see clearly. He glanced down at her note and the rush of disappointment churning in his gut made him more determined than ever. Bree was a bit player in a long-running play, and he'd better start thinking of her only that way.

THERE WERE SIX OTHER people on her floor at work, which was six too many. Unfortunately she was no longer the invisible new girl. Now she was Charlie Winslow's date. The one whose byline was on the front page of *Naked New York*. She'd wanted to be noticed, and she'd gotten her wish. If she could have, she would have turned around and gone straight back home. But she couldn't put her job at risk. More at risk.

As she sank into her chair, Bree was incredibly grateful for the cubicle walls. She knew she looked like crap with her swollen eyes and her red blotchy skin, but who cared? What difference did it make, now that she understood? The awakening had been inevitable. At least she'd gotten some really good sex out of it, right?

No, she would not cry again. Instead, she took out the preliminary copy for one of their lesser accounts. She blinked back tears and yet one dropped on the word *latte* and the letters in the middle lost their definition, spread and blurred into something that looked like failure.

The copy had been terrible, anyway. She crushed the sheet of paper into a ball and tossed it into the trash bin under her desk. Naturally, she missed. The carpet was a dark, wavy blue that was meant to disguise, meant to trick the eye into thinking it was clean when it wasn't. She didn't bother picking up her mistake.

Her phone buzzed before she could turn to her keyboard. Rebecca, sending a text.

Call me. SOON!

Bree ignored it; the prospect of speaking to Rebecca made her queasy. It wasn't her friend's fault; it wasn't. She had done Bree an unbelievable favor. It was nobody's fault but her own. She'd read the rules, entered the game with her eyes wide-open.

The task of rewriting the copy was too much for her to bear and she considered leaving, going back to her hole-in-the-wall bedroom, cowering under the covers for a while, but couldn't. She'd file now, give herself time to calm down, stop thinking that her life was some kind of tragedy when it wasn't. God, she could be a drama queen.

Poor Bree, getting a chance to meet famous designers and go to all the best parties in New York. How horrible.

Her sigh made the top few pages of her filing stack flutter up like little skirts. She grabbed a handful of reports. Boring as hell, maintenance stuff like expenses, inventory and billable hours, but they had to be sorted before they could be shoved into files, and what happened to the mythical paperless office? They were probably right there next to flying cars and silver unitards for all.

The image of Charlie swooshing across his office in his fancy chair froze her. She blinked it away, but the image lingered, filling her chest with pressure.

The phone, again, and this time it was Lilly.

Can U meet 4 dinner? Or is CW taking U somewhere fab?

The expense reports went on the far corner of her desk, setting the border of the assembly line. There were seven distinct piles, and she put every ounce of her concentration on each item, neatly squaring each stack as she went, the tap tap of the paper against her desk loud in the gray cubicle with the calendar next to the picture of her parents and the clips from newspapers and magazines, all precisely placed with only blue pushpins that matched the carpet and looked good against the gray.

The phone. A text. Again. Only this one…

Hey, Bree. Member me? UR SISTER???? Pick UP. PICKUPPICKUPPICKUPPICKUP. Call me. Beth. Who misses you. Brat.

Bree squeezed her eyes shut so tight she saw stars, little flashes of white that should have been beautiful, should have been fireworks. The pressure in her chest had turned to homesickness so deep it was the Grand Canyon of ache, the Mariana Trench of despair. She wanted to be sitting at the little kitchen table, the one that was for breakfast if all the kids and grandkids weren't there.

She wanted her mother's biscuits with honey from the Iverson's bees, and she wanted thick cut pepper bacon and scrambled eggs, and to hear her father humming tunelessly as he prepared his plate.

She wanted the music that was playing so loud from Beth's room it would shake the rafters, and Willow to be barking like a fiend outside because the chickens weren't behaving, and she wanted to be little again. Safe. Filled with dreams that didn't have thorns.

When Charlie texted, she dropped the papers in her hands.

Missed you this am. Re: tonight. 7 ok? Dinner 1st. Tea? CW

She went to text back, got a blank screen, her thumbs at the ready. But she couldn't do it. All she had to say was okay. Nothing else. Because, of course, she was going to go. She'd signed an agreement. She had a responsibility. It was her *goddamned dream come true*.

She turned off her phone. Just for a while. Until she finished the filing.

CHARLIE TOOK A DRINK FROM the glass of scotch he'd taken from the party and wondered why he hadn't asked for a bottle instead. He looked over at Bree and gave her a smile even though she'd decided, as she'd done on the way to the party, to sit as far away from him as was possible.

In turn, she gave him a pathetic excuse for a smile.

What was going on? She'd texted him once all day, only to tell him she wouldn't be able to make it to dinner. He'd barely seen her as she was getting ready in the media room. He'd wanted to keep things focused, not mention the note or the night before. Her aloof attitude should have played right into his hand, but he hated it. He was still pissed about the stupid note. She could have said something even if they had made a mistake. He didn't like being caught off guard.

Once they'd entered the club, Bree had perked up, charmed everyone she'd spoken to. Had her picture taken, danced with men, women, groups of men. Not him, though. He didn't dance. Everyone knew that.

Of course, people had asked about missing the premiere, and he hadn't answered. Neither had she. The two of them had touched and even kissed, although on the cheek. They'd made sure the crowd believed what he wanted them to. The only fly in that ointment was that the touching and even that nothing kiss had made him hard in his suit, and he'd had to wait outside with the smokers until he'd calmed down.

Whatever the consequences, this bullshit couldn't go on. She wasn't tired; tired was different. Even through the smiles and the gossip and the pictures and the pounding noise she'd seemed dulled, muted. The spark that made her light up a room had been muffled, and that had happened sometime between the best sex of his whole life, and a note on the back of a take-out receipt. Each time he looked at her, he both wanted her, and wanted to know what had happened.

"You're quiet," he said finally, heading into the breach.

She did that thing with her mouth that was supposed to reassure him, but accomplished the opposite. "I worked so much longer than I'd planned, I barely got a nap, and then I woke up in a panic…"

He nodded, but he didn't believe her. "I'm sorry I've been keeping you out so late. We don't have anything going on tomorrow. That's a plus."

"It is," she said, staring at her hands.

"Bree. Did I do something I shouldn't have? I can be an insensitive bastard, I know."

She met his gaze squarely. "No. You did nothing wrong. Not at all. Not one thing. You've been exactly who you said you'd be, and that's great. That's…great."

"Great," he echoed quietly, because that little speech made his gut clench.

"Sorry. You know what? I got a call from home today. Family and stuff. With so little sleep, I suppose I'm not very good company."

For the first time since 8:00 a.m. Charlie relaxed. Not completely, but family crap he understood. God knows, every time he interacted with his family he snapped at everything for hours if not longer. "Anything I can do?"

She shook her head. "Thanks, but no. Nothing anyone

can do, but accept what is. I'll be fine by Monday.
We've got that perfume party, right?"

He nodded. "Yeah. I don't even know how a celebrity begins to find a scent. I sure as hell don't remind
myself of exotic spices or citrus fruit, for God's sake.
And they make millions. Do people really think if they
smell like someone supposedly smells, it makes them
sexier? More likely to become a famous person themselves?"

Bree laughed—the best sound of the night. Even
with the buzzing still in his ears. Finally, it felt right in
the car, if a little cold. She was still very far away.

"You, on the other hand," he said, slipping closer to
her, "would make a wonderful perfume."

She eyed him, and instead of touching her as he'd
planned, he simply lowered his voice. "You smell like
honey and the ocean. The nearer I get, the more pro-
nounced it becomes. It's there no matter what, so either
it's the best perfume ever, or as I suspect, it's just you."

"I don't wear perfume," she said. "And there's no
honey in any cosmetic I own. I'm not even sure what
the ocean smells like."

He shut his eyes as he inhaled. There it was. He was
not making it up. "It's gorgeous," he said. "Like you."

Bree whimpered softly, which made him open his
eyes, smile. But she wasn't looking at him. She was
staring out the window. The feeling of everything being
right again vanished.

"Bree—"

"I'm sorry. It's not you. I promise."

"Okay," he said, uncomfortable that he didn't know
what to do here. "Would you like to come up?"

She stilled, barely even breathed and then shook her
head. "Not tonight, but thank you for the offer."

He shifted slightly, giving her space. Then he picked up his half-empty glass planning to polish it off before they reached his building.

BREE THREW CAUTION TO THE wind when she ordered eggs 'n' apples Benedict on French toast with maple syrup. The others, Rebecca, Shannon and Lilly, gave her approving nods, and even a lift of a Mimosa, then ordered eggs or oatmeal. They were having Sunday brunch at Elephant & Castle, and Bree should have been starving after an hour's wait to get seated. Her hand trembled as she lifted her coffee cup.

"He was nice," Shannon said, and Bree smiled as Shannon flipped her red hair behind her shoulder. Shannon communicated with her body. Her eyes lit up with joy, her disappointment showed in her shoulders and the wry arch of her brow, and when she was angry she jutted her right hip and put her hand on her waist.

In Shannon-speak, the hair lift was more about inevitability than disappointment. A forgone conclusion. Bree didn't have enough hair to copy the move, nor the acceptance. Not yet.

"We should have clicked," Shannon continued, after polishing off her first cocktail. "God knows he was hot. I almost went home with him, but it seemed unfair. To his card, you know? He wants something long-term. Sadly, there were no sparks." She looked around the restaurant, the buzz of the place not intrusive but definitely there. "Is it really only biology? A chemistry project? That doesn't seem fair."

"Well," Lilly said, pulling a trading card from her bag. "Here's mine. No matter what, you'll enjoy the evening. He's a sweet guy, and extremely bright. Money, too."

Shannon took the card, and gave hers to Lilly. "Here's to you and John clicking like crazy."

They both studied their new prospects. Bree sipped her coffee and when her gaze shifted to Rebecca, the woman didn't even pretend she wasn't staring, had obviously been staring.

"What?" Bree said, petulantly enough that she hoped Rebecca would get it.

"What's going on?"

"Nothing. Everything's fine."

Rebecca picked up her Mimosa, but Bree heard her whisper, "liar," before she took a sip.

"Rebecca, please."

"If he's done something horrible, you have to tell me."

"He hasn't."

"Then—"

"It's nothing. I'm telling you. We're fine. We're going to a perfume party tomorrow night. I haven't slept in what feels like years, and I would be in bed now if you horrible people hadn't dragged me out."

"You've been AWOL for too long," Shannon said, "and all we know is what we read on the internet. I have fifty big ones riding on what you and Charlie Winslow were doing instead of attending that premiere."

Bree's face went up in flames, at least that was what it felt like. She traded her coffee for ice water, and willed herself pale. "Nothing of consequence," she said.

The three of them exchanged disbelieving glances and in one more second Bree was going to get her purse and walk out of the restaurant. Quit the lunch exchange group, never look at a trading card again and start checking out airfares to Ohio.

She flushed again, but not because of Shannon's comment. She might have made a mistake allowing her feelings to get out of hand with Charlie, but she was not going to leave the table, or the state. She was not that person, and dammit, it didn't matter how many tears she needed to shed until she got over her heartache, she would not give up. She hadn't come this far only to slink home to Mommy.

"Seriously," she said, sitting up straighter in her chair. "Nothing much happened. Our scheduling was off. Charlie parlayed it into gossip and it worked. We were a blind item in the *Post* today, Page Six. It's all part of the master plan. *NNY* lives for unique hits. It's a whole big mathematical formula that determines how much he can charge for ad space. All relative to individual times a certain person clicks on the blog on any individual computer."

"That's it?" Lilly asked skeptically. "But, you guys are so cute together."

Bree turned from Lilly to Rebecca, meeting their gazes. "We're supposed to look cute together. I'm sorry I'm spoiling it for you guys, but I swear, it's business. In fact, as soon as the numbers dip and I'm no longer useful to the blog, I'll be raiding the trading cards myself."

"You gonna throw Charlie back into the ring?" Shannon asked.

"Believe me. He's not your type. Oh, he's nice and all, but he's not looking to date."

Rebecca tried to stare her down, as if she could make Bree take it back with telepathy. Bree touched her hand. "We'll talk, but not now," she said, low enough that the others couldn't hear, and then there was the food, and that was the distraction she'd needed. She relaxed, confident she'd crossed an important milestone.

Then her phone rang. She almost ignored it. When she did take it out of her purse, she knew before she hit a single button that it was Charlie. Only it wasn't about tomorrow night's perfume extravaganza.

Dinner tonight? Chef's table at Le Bernardin?

Bree saw the name of the top-rated restaurant in the city. The invitation was more than incredible. For her career, for her future, she shouldn't hesitate. There would be pictures and even more gossip when they went out to dinner without an event chaser. But for her sanity, she typed:

Love to. Can't though. Other plans. See you tomorrow!

15

CHARLIE PICKED UP THE PHONE, a smile on his face before he heard the words from the security downstairs. When his cousin's name was announced he flicked an invitation to some bullshit party to the floor as he gave his assent.

Maybe Rebecca dropping by wasn't so bad. It was weird, but not necessarily a terrible thing. She was friends with Bree. Since she rarely visited, she had to be here because of that friendship. Rebecca would know what the deal was, and that would help. Or maybe she'd heard he was going to cancel his reservation at Le Bernardin and she wanted him to take her? Well tough, because he wasn't hungry anymore.

He got up from the dining room table, not bothering to pick up the invite or any of the other accumulated mess. His housekeeper would be back tomorrow. It wasn't until he opened his door that he realized he hadn't put on shoes. Just socks. Black socks. He was in his jeans, and his Yankees T-shirt. He'd laid out clothes for his seven o'clock date, but screw that.

Rebecca, as always, looked as polished as a cultured

pearl. He took her coat and tossed it over the ottoman by the entrance. Heard her indignant huff and ignored it.

"You want coffee? Wine? Vodka?"

"It's two-thirty in the afternoon," she said, her heels clicking behind him as she followed.

"And?"

"Can you even make coffee?"

"You're a riot, Becca."

In the kitchen, she got out the milk while he poured beans into his coffee mill.

When the grinding finished, he put the grounds into the coffeemaker, and stood in front of the counter, with his arms crossed. "So?"

"What have you done, Charlie?"

"About?"

"Don't be obtuse. To Bree."

"I haven't done anything. She's the one who's been…"

"Been what?"

He shrugged, turned to watch as the coffeemaker gurgled. "Quiet. Off. I don't know."

"Want to tell me why you guys missed the red carpet?"

"No."

"Fine. Coffee to go, then. Oh, and congratulations for remaining fourteen no matter how old you actually get. Excellent job. You must be so proud."

"What are you talking about?" He swung around again, in no mood.

"Okay, let's deal with first things first. Do you honestly believe your family needs to advertise in your blogs in order for Andrew to win this election?"

"Yes."

"Then your ego has officially gone off the charts. Their visit to you, Charles, was their version of an olive branch."

"As if I'd endorse that idiot?"

"They weren't asking for an endorsement. You take ad money from all sorts of lunatics. During the presidential campaign, you had both parties shouting each other down constantly. And I know you didn't vote for both."

"So you did set them up. Hell, I gave you more credit than was due."

"What?" she said, taking two steps toward him.

"You actually told them to approach me, didn't you?"

"No. I didn't. I heard about it ex post facto. From Uncle Ford."

"Christ. This family."

"Is your family." She touched his arm. "I don't know what's happened between you and Bree, honestly, but I know she's different. And you—you don't go to your blog correspondents. They come to you. You don't pretend to have a lover for this long. And you sure as heck don't worry if one of your gimmicks is quiet."

He stepped back, dislodging her hand. He took out two mugs and poured for them both. "It's not personal. The numbers are up. They have been since that first night. I suppose I should thank you for that."

"I don't give a damn about your numbers."

He sipped his coffee and it was so hot he scalded the top of his mouth. "That's all I care about."

"Yeah. Right." She got one of his now-famous to-go cups from the cupboard and transferred her coffee, adding some milk before she put on the top. "It's not going to be easy to go back. After Bree, it's going to hit you hard. At least, let's hope so. I think there's a decent man inside you, Charlie. I've known you too long to give up hope."

"Who died and made you Yoda?"

She grinned. "I can dish it out. Probably because I've all but turned into a monk. But you know what? If and when I find someone you think is worth fighting for, I give you my full permission to take no prisoners. You got that?" She stepped right up into his face and looked him in the eyes. "You fight for me, Charlie. Fight dirty. Fight hard. Don't let me be right when I need to be happy." She kissed him on the cheek, took her drink and left him standing in his socks.

By the time he remembered his own mug, it was cold. But he'd made a decision.

CHARLIE CALLED HER at one-ten on Monday. Bree picked up after the second ring.

"Charlie? What's wrong?"

"Nothing. Why?"

"You're not texting."

"Oh," he said. "No, everything's fine. How are you?"

"I'm great. Great."

He winced at that. Two *greats* definitely made something wrong. "Good. Because, you know, there's the perfume gig tonight."

"Right. I was going to text. What time did you want me at your place?"

He swung his chair around and stared out his window. The whole city seemed gray. Despondent. "Seven? Six if you want to eat. We won't be staying late. It's perfume. I promised a friend, or I'd cancel." Charlie waited for her to say something, and when the silence stretched, he had Plan B ready. "You, on the other hand, promised no one. Tonight isn't really a big deal. If you want to pass, that's fine."

"Pass?"

"Yeah. You've had a busy week, and Monday-night parties are always second tier. I'll make something of it in the blog, something that'll keep them talking. If you want."

The silence was broken by her breathing, and he tried to picture where she was. Indoors, as there was no sound of traffic. In her cubicle? A restaurant? He wondered if she had a ribbon in her hair today, and he wished he'd gone to talk to her in person. Her voice wasn't enough.

"That would be great," she said.

"Okay, then. No problem. Get some rest. Catch up on that sleep, because there are a some big doin's going on starting Tuesday." He grimaced, remembering that Tuesday afternoon he'd agreed to walk down the runway for charity, but that wasn't Bree's problem. She'd be at work.

"Okay," she said, in a very small voice. "I'll get some rest. I… Thank you, Charlie. But if you change your mind. If you think it would be better…for the blog for me to be there…"

"Nope. Got it covered. You can read all about it in tomorrow's *NNY*."

She sighed. It sounded sad. He'd given her a lot of thought last night. Fine, he'd missed her. But there was no reason to think this mood was anything other than what she'd said, despite Rebecca's dramatics. Bree was far from home, on her own. She'd been slammed with brutal hours and tons of pressure. Tonight really was a lightweight affair, and while he'd rather be with Bree, he wanted her to take the time she needed to get herself back. He liked her happy. He liked her excited. He liked her.

IT WAS SIX-FIFTEEN ON MONDAY and Bree was in an elevator and it was possible that she'd actually lost her mind between the fifth and sixth floor.

Or maybe this trip was a direct result of not sleeping last night. She'd tried tea, yoga, meditation—that had been a laugh riot—a hot bath, warm milk. Instead of sleeping she'd read a year's worth of *Naked New York* blogs, every article she could find on Google about Charlie and every person he'd ever dated, started a new five-year plan a half-dozen times, and generally been insane. Work had been a circus. If she didn't get fired this week it would be because of divine intervention because she was not earning her salary. No matter what happened next, *that* was going to change. She would need BBDA more than ever after this ill-advised visit.

She hadn't called ahead. George at the front desk hadn't bothered to notify Charlie of her arrival, but he had asked if she'd been feeling okay because she hadn't been there on Sunday. George didn't work on Sunday. So he'd heard from other front desk personnel that she'd missed a night with Charlie. Which meant it wasn't just her—everyone thought Charlie and she were... something they weren't. She wasn't sure if that made her feel better or worse.

As the elevator approached his floor, she had to fight off utter panic because what was she even doing there? She had no idea what she was going to say. She honestly didn't want to go to the perfume party. Bree had never once imagined a world where that would be true.

Anyway, not going to the party felt worse. God help her, she missed him. Knowing everything she knew, she wanted him like an addict wanted crack. The break tonight was supposed to have been used for regaining her energy, refocusing on her goals, making that new five-year plan. Or sleep. Sleep would have been good.

The elevator stopped so smoothly it took her a second to get that she'd arrived. The second the doors whooshed open she panicked, pressed the down button. Twice.

As the doors were about to close, her arm shot out. And wasn't this just the picture of her life. Stuck. Unsure. Afraid to meet her own gaze in the mirror. Terrified to walk forward, unwilling to go back.

She had no plan, and that was the scariest thing of all. But she took those few steps out of the box, ready to face whatever had compelled her to come.

Charlie opened the front door before she knocked. When he saw her, his beautiful brown eyes widened and his smile was so brilliant and so genuine that something inside her changed forever. "Bree," he said with that damn voice of his.

"Hey."

"I thought—"

"I know. I wasn't—"

"Come in. The team isn't here, but we can do this. We can figure this out." He stepped back, his gaze and his smile steady and pleased. "I was just grabbing dinner. Pizza. Cheese and mushroom. I can get something else if you don't like pizza. There's that curry place I told you about—"

"I'm fine. It's fine. Pizza is great." They were standing inside. She was in her coat. Wearing a work dress, boots, nothing special, just clothes because she never imagined she'd get this far.

He was in jeans. A dark purple shirt with rolled-up sleeves. Socks, no shoes. His hair was messy, but not his usual cool messy. One important part was smooshed against his scalp and it made tears bubble and her throat tighten, which made no sense at all.

He came toward her, arms up, as she moved to shrug off her coat but then he hugged her, trapping her arms at her sides. Weird didn't come close to what was happening inside her. Tears on the edge of falling, a flurry of butterflies in her stomach, a blush of epic proportions and the smell of his skin both arousing and comforting.

She felt a little better when she caught him sniffing at her neck. Better still when the stiffness in his body and his stuttering breathing made it clear he felt as awkward as she did.

He stepped back, and oh, God, his blush. It was great. And awful. Because this wasn't what she wanted it to be. It *wasn't*. How could she not get that through her very thick skull?

She let her coat slide to the floor. It was all she could do not to follow it.

CHARLIE WATCHED HER WOBBLE, and he wasn't sure whether to grab her or what.

"Here's the thing," she said, her voice as shaky as her legs.

Charlie got caught by the pink of her cheeks and how she was trembling, and while she wore no ribbons, she did have a butterfly clip pulling back a small section of short, dark hair.

"I know not to mix things up." She tipped forward just a bit. "Business, pleasure. That kind of thing. I know that. You've been nothing but amazing, and you've completely changed my life. My five-year plan? It's fast-forwarded to two, maybe three now, but really, I'm rethinking the whole thing because I—it— I'm different. Because you let me write for you. You gave me carte blanche into the world I'd dreamed of, and dreams that come true become something else. Not bad, just not what I imagined. Which is okay."

She took a steadying breath, and man, she needed it because she'd pretty much said that all in one sentence.

Charlie understood her, though. Despite being swept up in her eyes, in her pink lips and how she flung her right hand to the side when she emphasized a word. He knew he was still smiling. Thought about stopping. Didn't.

"So the problem isn't you," she said. "It's that I broke the one rule. The big rule. The one that can ruin it all. I didn't know I was going to. I sure as hell didn't plan to. I'd made a promise. To myself. That I wouldn't get involved. I wouldn't let myself. Because my friends? My college roommate and all my BFFs from high school? Every one of them fell for a guy and then their dreams…diminished. And, yes, I know one doesn't have to lead to the other, but I know myself, and how I can be obsessive, and that's a great trait when I'm working toward my future, but not so great when it means I'm swallowed whole by love. It's not that I don't think love is good, 'cause it's fine—it's great—but my goals…they're important. I want to prove myself in the world before I settle down. Look at you! You went out and did exactly that. You haven't for a minute let anything or anyone get in your way, and wow, you've done it. You're the most successful man I know, and you didn't become a total sonofabitch doing it, and you have morals and you've been so nice to me, I don't even—"

Good God. Charlie blinked, and his smile cracked. Not completely, but enough. Love? Really? *Love?*

No. No, no, no. That wasn't what was happening here. He liked her. A lot. More than most people. A whole lot. Sex with her was off the charts, and as fantastic as that was, spending time with her was even better, but love?

Not happening. Not on the table. Not open for discussion, so what was she...

He was pretty sure a heart wasn't supposed to beat this fast.

"...but I think it's just because, you know, Cinderella and all," she said, her voice a little slower, her eyes not quite as vibrant. "Although I never expected that kind of happy ending. That's crazy talk. I mean, you're Charlie Winslow. You're the poster guy for living single. I'm the gimmick. Seriously, I know all that. It's fine with me. It's what I signed up for. I had it all planned out, see, how I was going to do this life, this part of my life, and then I went and did something stupid. Not that I'm exactly *in* love, but I'm heading there and if I'm not careful..." She swallowed. "It won't affect you at all. I mean that completely. If it makes you uncomfortable, well, then..."

She pressed her lips together for a second as a flash of hurt crossed her face. Or confusion? "Well, then, I'll just make myself scarce. That's cool. But if you still have the numbers, I'll live up to my agreement. I'll be the best damn gimmick I can be, and I won't embarrass you, I swear. I promise. It's my problem, not yours. Seriously. It's just that you've been so great, and I owed it to you to tell you what was really going on. You really have been great."

It was taking a long time for his brain to catch up to her words, and he might have missed a chunk in there somewhere. He thought she'd said she'd fallen in love? With him? Or maybe she was afraid of falling in love. With him. But she didn't want to because it was against the rules, and he was a poster child, and she was a gimmick. Or Cinderella.

He was pretty sure she'd mentioned it was her problem and not his, but there might be an argument in there about the veracity of that statement. If he gave it some thought, he'd be able to work it out, make sense of what she'd said, was still saying.

"You look terrified," she said. "I'm sorry. Don't be. I won't… I'm not… I'm not like a crazed fangirl or a stalker or anything like that."

She winced, and he'd seen that look before. It got to him, that scrunched-up face. Scrunched and beautiful, and oh, shit.

"Um," she said, softly. "That might have gotten away from me a little."

He had to clear his throat. "Bree, maybe we should go have a bite to eat. You know, slow down. Talk."

The knock on the door didn't register until Bree looked behind him. What the hell? Had the entire staff gone on vacation or something? "Just a sec," he said, then he went to the door.

It swung open and there was Mia Cavendish, in a massively huge faux fur coat, hair and makeup photo-ready and a look of such boredom on her face Charlie thought she might simply melt into a puddle in the atrium.

Mia glanced at Bree, then her wristwatch, then at Charlie. "Am I early? Naomi said to be here no later than six-thirty."

IT WAS LIKE BEING STABBED in the chest. Like an earth-quake. Like a wake-up call. Bree tried to remember how to breathe as she prayed for the earth to swallow her whole, for the strength to move her damn feet before the elevator went back down to the lobby. She was *such* an *idiot*. And a liar, a total, complete liar.

"Naomi?" Charlie asked. "What?"

"For tonight's party," Mia said as she strode into his home as if she lived there. She smiled at Bree, although it was clear she couldn't be bothered. "I think this is what I'm going to wear, but I'm going to check the racks," she said, dropping her coat on an ottoman. "I'd kill for some champagne." She looked at Bree again. "Where's Anna? Oh, she's probably gone. Charlie?"

"Mia, when did you speak to Naomi?"

"This afternoon. Around one-thirty. Why?"

Bree heard them talking, but their voices were muffled. She needed to pick up her coat. Put it on. Get out. Now. Before Charlie noticed her again.

Although, why would he? One of the most beautiful women in the world was standing not five feet away. Tall, willowy, her face impossibly gorgeous—she was the kind of woman who should be with Charlie Winslow.

"Give us a minute, Mia. There's champagne in the fridge."

The model didn't look pleased about it, but she walked off, confident in her insanely high boots.

That got Bree moving. She bent at the knee, as her mother had taught her, to get her coat, and it was cold on her arms, heavy on her shoulders, but it was thick, and when she wrapped her arms around her waist it felt like protection. "I've got to go," she said, looking anywhere but at Charlie.

He came into her peripheral vision, and she stepped aside, quick as she could. "You know what's funny?" she asked while she backed up.

"Bree, wait."

"What's hysterical? I'm from Hicksville. That's the real town I'm from. Hicksville, Ohio. I went to Hicksville High, and nothing on earth has ever been more appropriate than that."

"What?" Charlie blinked at her, looked toward the kitchen, then back. "Wait, this is all going too fast. Don't go. Okay?"

She shook her head. "You've got to get ready. You made a promise, and you can't be skipping things. I've already knocked you out of your routine, and that's bad enough, but they're expecting you. And Mia Cavendish! That's going to raise some eyebrows, right? Wait till Page Six gets a load of you two together. Facebook is going to go nuts."

She hurried away from him, moving sideways, just as she'd done that first morning-after.

"Please," he said. "I don't—"

"It's okay. We'll decide what to do later. I really have to…" And she was out the door, hitting the damn elevator button, and why couldn't he have lived on the first floor? Would it have killed him? She would have been in a taxi already.

The elevator dinged, and she had never been so thankful. She stepped inside just as the door opened behind her, and Charlie walked out.

She found the close-now! button on the first try, and he didn't stick his arm out to stop the doors. Why should he? Charlie Winslow knew exactly where he belonged.

16

CHARLIE WANTED TO BE anywhere but at the Canal Room. The place was packed with the same people he'd seen Saturday night and Thursday night and Wednesday night. The same cameras and reporters and hangers-on made all the same noises. The play repeated endlessly and the only thing that changed was the costumes.

Mia was…somewhere. She'd seemed surprised when he hadn't cozied up after getting out of the car. It hadn't mattered that they'd not uttered a word during the drive, but when the cameras were rolling, there were expectations. Demands. He couldn't have cared less.

The press would say what they wanted to say, then it would be his move, and he'd make a more outrageous statement, and it would continue. Not even chess, but checkers. His thoughts, as he stood nursing a scotch near the rear exit, aside from debating making a run for it, were on the two women who had come to the center stage of his life. Rebecca, who had always been an ally, even when they'd been kids. There was no reason to believe, rationally, that she had changed her allegiance. He'd done nothing to hurt her or embarrass her. They weren't just relatives, they were friends.

Given that, perhaps it was time to consider what she'd been trying to tell him. She had nothing to gain by him reevaluating his relationship to his parents, to his business, to Bree. If he did a complete about-face in all three areas, he and Rebecca would continue on as before.

What was he afraid of? The idea of change? Change was always uncomfortable, and he'd made himself a very comfortable life. Say he was willing to step outside his patterns. Nothing written in stone, so what if he looked at it?

He was under no obligation to do anything his parents asked of him. He hadn't been for years. The life he led was his own. In return, nothing he did or said was going to influence his parents, unless they wanted to be influenced.

He sipped the scotch, felt the burn at the back of his throat. It occurred to him that the race had been over years ago, but Rebecca was right. He'd never stopped running. He'd been incredibly pleased with their horrified response to *Naked New York* and his notoriety. It represented everything they avoided like the plague: common interests, personal exposure, progressive views. Basically anything that wasn't them. He'd kept upping the stakes, they'd kept reacting with shock, with threats, with bribes. Huh. He'd made that little hamster wheel his life's work.

Why, of all the interesting things that were available to a man of his resources, was he still playing this ridiculous game? Movie stars? Fashion? Scandals? It wasn't that he thought all celebrity was nonsense—he didn't. Humans created celebrity culture because they were designed that way. There'd been gossip ever since there'd been speech. Technology only made it more immediate. It was part of the world, but only a tiny part, and when all was said and done, it wasn't a part he particularly valued, outside of the revenue it generated.

He took his glass with him and made his exit. He didn't have his coat, and dammit, it was freezing, but he wasn't willing to go back inside, not now.

He walked down the street, and even at twenty to eleven, there were people in the crosswalks, people talking, lights on, restaurants and bars filled to the rafters. God, he loved this city. The fantastic mess of it. Endlessly fascinating, and he was the luckiest sonofabitch who lived there. Did he even know what to do with this world at his fingertips? If he walked away from *Naked New York* tomorrow, nothing significant would happen. He imagined he would still run the media group. That was fulfilling and he was damn proud of what he'd built. But if he never went to another party, never saw another premiere or opened another club, so what? Manhattan would find another king. He would have to figure out what he wanted to do with himself. His parents could stop being embarrassed by the women he went out with. Shit. He started laughing, out there on the sidewalk, and a couple walking behind him crossed the street in the middle of the road.

Oh, Rebecca was going to be unbearable. No one did smug like Rebecca. But what the hell. He owed her.

Not that he had decided to walk away. Not yet. It was too big a decision to make on a scotch and a confusing night. Besides, he had his team to think about. Transitions, changes, financial repercussions.

Which actually sounded like one hell of a good time.

Shivering, he circled back to the entrance to the club. He had no desire to go in, but he owed it to Mia to tell her she was on her own. So he braved the front door, ignored the strange looks at his reentry. Finding Mia was all he cared about at the moment. Because while leaving the spotlight of *NNY* was a big decision, it wasn't the most important one he needed to consider. Which brought him to the second woman.

If he was going to jump off the cliff without a safety net, he was pretty sure he didn't want to jump alone.

BREE WAS IN THE CLOSET. Her closet. On the ottoman mattress that pretended to be her bed. Her room might have been the size of a toaster oven, but it had a door and no one outside could hear her cry.

Although she wasn't crying at the moment. She was staring at her phone. She'd already decided she wouldn't be on the next plane to Ohio, but she wasn't back in Amazon warrior mode, either. She was sad. About as sad as a person who had so much could be.

That was the kicker. A full-on wallow wasn't possible, not when there were so many people with real problems. The only thing wrong with her life was that the boy didn't like her back. Not the end of the world, not unique, and who was to say Charlie was the great love of her life? Maybe he served a completely different purpose. What if her attraction to him was a test of her fortitude, her commitment to her future? Or a reminder that she had a functioning heart, and that she had to be far more careful with her emotions?

It could have nothing to do with love. He was a fairy-tale kind of guy, and she was human. She'd grown up on Disney movies and romantic notions. Charlie was magic. Of course she'd been swept away.

The problem was in pretending, fabricating, believing he'd been swept away, too.

She picked up her phone, clicked on Contacts and

went through her personal list. She liked Rebecca so much, but she was too close to the ache. Lilly was great, but they hadn't reached the heart-to-heart stage yet.

Bree was too embarrassed to call her Ohio crew. She'd felt so damn superior to them and their tragic mistakes. Talk about falling from the height of her own ego.

No, there was only one place to turn tonight, and that was family. Beth was two years older, and she'd been through a messy breakup before she'd found Max. She was also an amazing listener, and boy did Bree need to talk.

Beth answered after one ring. "Oh, thank God. I know something's wrong. Talk to me already, you insufferable brat."

Bree sniffed twice, and started from the beginning.

CHARLIE STARED INTO THE fireplace. It was late, or to be more accurate, early. He was dog-tired and he needed to sleep, but a lot had happened since he'd come home, and he was still reeling from it.

The moment he'd walked in, he'd headed for the office. The morning blog had been easy. He'd done the real work and built up the party and the fragrance—after all, they were spending big bucks to advertise the scent all over his blogs—and he'd kept the talk of Bree alive. It was surprisingly satisfying to call Mia an old friend. She'd hate that. Especially the old part. But she never stayed mad for long. Of course, he'd had to pump the next few days' worth of events, about the movers and shakers in Manhattan. Then he'd wrapped it up with something…personal.

With all that talk of Bree's goals and dreams, he'd gone back into his archives and reread his original business plan. It had been eye-opening. He'd come so damn far since those days, yet in some ways he'd hardly moved an inch. Right next to the archive file he'd kept copies of the scandal he'd created after being accepted into Harvard law to make sure his family would never consider him for anything of importance.

He'd purposefully gotten himself arrested for drugs. He'd planned it down to the last photograph—no one had been caught with drugs but him, and he'd made damn sure it was so circumstantial he'd never be taken to court. The damage was all in the gossip, in the inferences, in the pictures in the *Post* and the tabloids.

No matter how many attorneys tried to get his trust fund taken away, they hadn't been able to touch a penny.

Yeah. He could probably stop now. Give his folks and his whole family a break. Jesus, he could be an ass. On the other hand, he'd learned from the masters.

So, new plan. Bottom line? He was in a position where he could make a real difference in people's lives. He had money, access, some power. Politics was straight out. Not even a consideration. Creative problem solving? That held a lot of appeal, even if he wasn't sure what that would look like.

Bree by his side?

He stopped breathing as a picture formed, nothing noble or dramatic, just the two of them, lying in bed, in the dark. Naked. And yeah, okay, postcoital. But the fantasy was really about after. About talking. Soft talk in the middle of the night, about whatever. Touching her because he could, and her touching him back.

He thought about that last shot by Rebecca. The thing about fighting to be happy instead of right. Missing the premiere? That had been the easiest decision he'd made in ages. He could still feel the pleasure of having Bree sleeping against him, even with the tingling in his arms. He'd felt more relaxed, happier than he had any reason to be, and why? Not just because he'd put Bree first, but because he'd put himself first, too.

Holy...

Charlie turned away from the fireplace, and walked across the living room to the atrium, then into his office. His computer was still on. He never turned the damn thing off, so it was easy to sit back in his chair and pull up a blank screen.

As his fingers flew across the keyboard he found himself smiling. As the sky lightened over Manhattan, he got closer and closer to the cliff's edge, and there was no net in sight.

BREE HAD LEARNED A LOT in the past week about faking not only a smile, but an attitude, and she was putting her skills to the test as the doorman ushered her into Charlie's building.

"Nice to see you again, Ms. Kingston."

"Thank you, George." She nodded at the other staff in the lobby as she hurried to the elevator. She didn't really breathe until the doors had closed and she was alone. Pressing 18, her finger shook, which was unacceptable. This was business. Charlie already knew the worst about her, so tonight would be nothing but another party, another extraordinary opportunity to learn and network. That's what she'd told her sister, what she'd told herself over and over and over again.

Her shaking hand went back to the buttons and she pressed 17 in the nick of time. The elevator stopped with a whisper-soft bounce and Bree couldn't get out fast enough.

She stood in a hallway. Thank goodness. She hadn't even considered that other floors could be like Charlie's—private residences. No, this was a hall, although from where she stood she could only see two doors.

The carpet was incredibly thick, a rich aubergine, the walls a creamy yellow, and there were several wrought-iron plant stands along the wall with fantastic red gladiolus arrangements. Bree stared for a moment, not thinking about anything but how pretty and elegant it all looked and how in all her years she'd never imagined standing in a hallway like this one. Quiet, sophisticated, beyond classy. It made no sense. Nothing made sense anymore. Most of all the idea that Charlie Winslow could ever, ever want Bree Ellen Kingston, a daughter of Hicksville, Ohio, former member of 4-H, the Girl Scouts and the Aaron Carter fan club. It felt silly, ridiculous, that she'd entertained the notion for a single moment.

She pulled her cell out and clicked on the only text she'd received from Charlie all day.

6? CW

Her response had been the eloquent: K

She pulled up this morning's blog, Charlie's post about the perfume party. The bulk of it was just what it said on the box: who had been there, gossip, bands, more gossip. Barely a word about Mia Cavendish.

But the last paragraph…

Bree read the last paragraph again. Surely this time her heart wouldn't jump, her breath wouldn't catch.

The night could have been improved if the smokers had come inside, but that's nothing new. The upgrades at the Canal Room were minimal, but important. The men's room, the upstairs lounge and the new bartender were all worth a look. I imagine the ladies' bathroom was also better, but I have no confirmation. As for the reason for the party—Jazz and Cocktails perfume looks as sexy as the name, and it smells damn good. Not like the ocean and honey, but still, damn good.

The ocean and honey. God.

No. Nope, getting off at 17 hadn't worked. The hallway hadn't cured her; the moment of clarity hadn't been enough to make her see reason. She was still screwed. But she'd get through the night, because she wasn't thirteen. She'd put on her armor along with her makeup and she would be grateful and attentive and happy.

Okay, grateful and attentive.

She had to wait for the elevator and when she finally stepped inside it was empty. Which was good. She faced herself in the mirror. Back straight, eyes open and expressive, smile—careful, not too much. There. She was ready. Even the kick in the chest when she saw Charlie didn't knock her to her knees.

17

SEEING BREE STEP INTO the atrium stopped Charlie cold. He'd been saying something to Sveta, but he couldn't remember what. It didn't matter. "Hey," he said, holding out his hand to walk Bree into the house. "Rested?"

"Yeah," she said, although she glanced away when she spoke. "Thanks."

"I have some deli in the kitchen. You want to eat before you get ready?"

She made a beeline to the hallway that led to the media room. "No thanks. Not hungry."

Charlie followed, his mood on the downswing as he realized his master scheme for the evening was already going to hell. He could hear the team chattering away as they prepped the room, and he thought about the spread in the kitchen. He'd specifically gotten all the stuff Bree liked from the Carnegie Deli, including the Russian dressing and coleslaw for her corned beef sandwich.

Bree turned the corner, disappeared from view, and he staggered to a stop as it dawned on him that his "master scheme" to sweep Bree off her feet—a whole night that came complete with timetable, great mood lighting and a rather epic soundtrack—had left out only one thing. Bree herself.

Sveta swam in front of him, whipped her hair back in her usual dramatic style, then asked him three rapid-fire questions about tonight's book party.

He blinked at the woman and let her drag him down the hall to where the action was. As he entered the madhouse, he caught a glimpse of Bree in the big makeup mirror. She stared back and her gaze was so full of pain it nearly flattened him.

He'd realized last night that his decision to step away from the hands-on editing of his media group was a huge decision, but *this* leap he was about to make? It wasn't across a murmuring creek, it was across goddamn Niagara Falls. He'd sculpted himself a world that was made entirely of his rules, serving only himself, and every moment of every day was Charlie Winslow-shaped. The only thing he ever compromised on was the blog, but only when he had to, and only when it would serve the greater good—which was also all about his business, so no, he never really compromised at all.

It was good to be the king. And yet, how had he never noticed that it was also incredibly lonely?

Rebecca. She was good; he had to give her credit. She'd said this would happen. That being right only went so far. He wanted more now. More with Bree. With the woman sitting in the center of a whirlwind.

But could he do it? Could he change in the ways he'd need to, to actually be part of a couple? Put her first? A novel concept, and one he'd botched at the starting gate.

He'd been so caught up in the grand gesture that he'd

forgotten that he was about to ask a great deal of this woman. She had her own dreams, her own goals, her wondrous five-year plan. Would she even want what he was proposing? Maybe he should wait, think this through. Acting rashly wasn't in his nature. This was crazy.

He refocused on Bree. She hadn't turned away at all. But she'd done a very good job of masking her pain. Anyone else would have thought that smile was real, that her eyes were bright with excitement and anticipation. But he'd seen her when she was truly happy.

The hell with it. He was going in. "Can I have everyone's attention?"

It didn't take long for the group to settle. "Something's come up. We won't be going to tonight's event, so, if you guys could wrap up what you need to, that would be appreciated."

He knew the whole team would react, but his gaze stayed on Bree's image in the mirror. She looked completely confused, but he wouldn't keep her there long.

"Don't worry," he whispered, then cleared his throat and spoke to the team again. "Don't worry, you'll all get paid for the night's work. There's food in the kitchen. Take it with you. I'll never be able to finish it. Thank you, everyone. Sorry for the inconvenience."

Sveta barely blinked. She started putting the clothes back on the racks, boxing shoes, making sure everything would be in order for the next event. The team followed suit, and since they'd only begun it was a matter of minutes before they were clearing out.

Bree rose from the makeup chair. She grabbed her pocketbook, tugged the bottom of her very-Bree vintage sailor dress. God, she looked sweet. He couldn't help the ache that went from his chest on down. He wanted her to say yes as badly as he'd wanted anything in his life.

Charlie was aware that the team members were staring at him, at Bree, and that they were trying to clear out as quickly as they could. He didn't care.

Bree had her head bowed but her spine straight and tall as she followed the small group. At the door, he caught her hand in his. "I'd like you to stay," he said. "Please."

When they were alone, and they could no longer hear the footfalls of the others, she met his gaze. "What's going on?"

"I had it all planned out," he said. "Like I was writing a play. We'd go to the party, but we wouldn't stay late. I'd convince you to come back here with me. I had a couple of backup plans for that, just in case. It would have been great. Very dramatic." He stared at her, at those amazing green eyes. "But all that really matters right now is how very much I want to kiss you."

"We're not going to the book party because you want to kiss me?"

He smiled. "No," he said, then half winced. "Sort of."

"Oh," she said, as if everything made sense. A second later she shook her head. "I don't get this at all. Charlie, what—"

He kissed her. He couldn't wait another second. Honestly, he didn't want to keep her in suspense—that wouldn't be fair. As soon as he finished this kiss, he'd tell her everything.

Then she kissed him back.

His first response was *thank God*. This was what he'd needed. Bree in his arms, on his lips. The taste of her minty gum and the slide of her tongue made him ache.

"Charlie," she whispered, and it was like a match to kindling, the sound of his name on her lips. He stepped into her. He would have climbed inside her if he could have; instead he walked her back until he had pressed her against the wall, kissing her as if his life depended on it.

With a gasp, her head thunked back, her mouth swollen and damp and irresistible.

He forced himself to slow down. The first brush of his lips was soft, gentle. Tender. But it wasn't enough, and he hauled her up against him, his mouth hard, hungry, desperate, as the kiss deepened into an intense tangle of tongues and teeth that made him groan.

Tearing her mouth free, she gasped for breath as her small hands got busy on the buttons of his shirt. Her eyes were wide and wild as she fumbled and cursed.

"Bree—"

She gave up on his buttons and went for his belt. He groaned, but no.

"Not here," he said roughly, and wrapped his arms tight around her, lifting her straight up, bending slightly until she wrapped her legs above his hips. He wanted to just get them to the bedroom, but as always, he couldn't resist kissing her over and over. He swerved like a drunk, dizzy with the feel of her, with the promise of what was to come.

Somehow, they made it to his room and they stripped. No finesse, no teasing. Simply the need to be naked. Now.

As they stretched out on the bed, he took her hands

in his and guided them above her head as he balanced himself over her body. He looked down into her face and saw a new life.

THERE WAS SO MUCH IN HIS gaze that Bree went still. She was a lost cause, gone, any good sense she had swept away by passion and the awareness of his body. When he whispered her name, the world slowed, the air thrummed with heat and want.

His mouth spread hot, wet kisses down her jaw, along her collarbone. Her breast. His tongue curled around her nipple and he groaned when it beaded for him.

She bucked, and he did it again, reaching for the drawer, grabbing a condom. He protected them both with fingers that actually trembled, and then nestled between her legs. The moon bathed them in soft gray light, so luminous it was enough for her to see the details of his face, although she already knew each feature intimately, and could have sculpted each curve.

"Missed you," he whispered, but his words turned into a moan when he sank into her.

Her eyes closed as he filled her, and her pulse quickened when she pushed up to meet his slow thrust.

They stilled when he could go no farther, their panting breaths loud in the room, but soon it wasn't enough and she pushed up again.

"Move," she said, squeezing his arms, pressing her breasts into his chest.

"God, yes," he said, so softly she barely heard him past the pulse of her heartbeat.

"So good." He cupped her face as he pulled out

slowly, kissing her after a languid swipe of his tongue across her bottom lip.

Her breath stuttered with the shock of his tenderness. She'd been ready for frantic sex. Not this.

He slid his hands to her hips and rocked, going even deeper now, and thinking was all but impossible. Tossing back her head, she gasped his name, and he thrust as if each time would be his last. Again and again, his control driving her wild. She could hear her own heart thundering in her ears, their mingled murmurs and cries, raggedy gasps and low moans. Hers and his.

When his fingers slipped between them, he barely had to touch her. A long moment stretched like a tight-rope in that unbearably sweet limbo just before the crash, and when it came, when her orgasm tore through her like a bolt of lightning, she cried out and clung to him as if he was the only real thing.

He didn't let her go, and he didn't stop. Between her trembling spasms he said her name again and again, and as the pace increased his voice got louder until he filled her so completely she felt him come from the inside.

Finally, he fell beside her, close, and she felt small and tender against his damp body as her gasps slowed. When thought returned as a trickle, everything was perfect and peaceful and nothing else. But the trickle turned into a stream and that brought panic along with clarity.

Oh, God, she'd done it now. Again. She'd made things a million times worse. She should have left while she could have, made a break for it and kept on running. Because they'd made love. The sound of her name in his low voice was imprinted forever. She was a goner.

She rolled away from him and out of the bed, grabbing her dress from the floor. If she was lucky, she could still make a quick getaway and salvage some part of her heart.

His hand on her wrist stopped her.

"I have to go," she said, her voice quivering and her heart pounding.

"No, please. Wait." He tugged. "Please."

She took in a big breath before she faced him. "I appreciate all you've done for me, Charlie, but this was a mistake. You and I both know it. I can't kid myself anymore. Not after this. I have to stop. Full stop. No working parties with you, no writing side-bars, nothing. I've stepped over the line and there's no road back except the one that takes me far away from you."

He sat up, never releasing her wrist. "Bree, please. I promise I won't stop you if you still feel this way after… Ten minutes. That's all I'm asking."

Bree's dress wasn't on, in fact, it just hung from her hand and for a moment she stared at it as if it was something she'd never seen before, but it wasn't her dress that had her blinking. Things were getting mixed-up again, and she was already so far past the line with Charlie she'd lost all her ground rules. There was no getting around it. She had fallen in love with him. Nothing would fix that except time and distance. But ten minutes? She could risk that, right? But only if she wasn't naked.

He let go of her, and then she slipped her dress on. Her panties were puddled by the door, but she could get those in a minute. Now, though, she needed to hear what he had to say.

She sat down on the bed, not close, either. If he touched her, there was a very good chance the tiny bit of backbone she'd found would vanish like smoke. "I'm listening."

He nodded, but then did some maneuvering under the sheet that had become a bundle at the foot of the bed. He dragged out his boxer briefs snagged by his toes, and he smiled with the achievement as he slipped them on.

That little grin didn't help. It was clear that ten minutes was nine minutes and fifty-nine seconds too long. She should have run when she had the chance.

Now that Charlie was really going to tell Bree about the plan, there was more than a hint of panic involved. He sat up, bolstered his back with a hastily arranged pillow, then met her gaze. Might as well just dive into the deep end. "Okay. First, I need to ask you a question. Did you have a good time Friday night? When we missed the premiere?"

Still looking a little dumbstruck, she nodded. "Yeah. Yeah, I did."

"Were you happy?"

A flash of pain was there and gone in a breath. "Yes. Very."

"Me, too."

Bree looked at him as if he was nuts, and he supposed she was right.

"I was really happy that night," he said. "I didn't give a damn about the red carpet or the blog. I wanted to be exactly where I was. With you. I didn't expect that."

"That's…" She floundered for a moment, her hands rising, falling into her lap. "Amazing."

"You can say that again. I haven't felt this way about anyone, not for ages—actually, never. I like you so damn much." It was horrible not to touch her.

Wrong. He abandoned his pillow and swung his legs over, scooting inelegantly until they were sitting side by side, touching. Until he had her hand in his. "I haven't wanted to talk with anyone the way I want to talk with you. Going to parties this week has been a revelation. And working together, well, damn that's been…"

He lost his train of thought as she blinked up at him, her mouth open in what looked more like shock than confusion. Yet when she straightened her shoulders and leaned away from him, he was the one who was confused.

"I'm glad," she said. "I am. And maybe in a while I can come back on board, because what you've given me… But I have to focus on my goals. Especially now that they've changed. I'm not even sure what exactly I want, but I know it's important to keep my eye on the prize, and not let myself get distracted. And sorry, Charlie, but you're the biggest distraction ever."

"No, no. Wait, Bree. Don't decide yet. 'Cause I'm talking about change, too. For the better, I hope. Look, the last thing on earth I'd ever want is to sideline your dreams. I believe in you. You're a talented writer, and you have an eye for detail and fashion. You'll be successful no matter what you decide you want to do, and a big part of what I want to do is support you in any way I can."

She exhaled a big breath. "Okay…"

"I've decided to step down as editor of *NNY.*"

"What?"

He grinned at how loudly the word echoed in the moonlit bedroom. "It's time to take on some new challenges. That don't involve celebrities or supermodels or fashion shows. I have no idea what that'll look like. Just that it won't be what it has been."

"Oh," she said again, and he could practically see her mind struggling to make sense of what he was telling her, rearranging everything she knew about him. Hell, throwing it all out the window.

He brushed her cheek with the tips of his fingers. He wanted her to say yes so badly. "We're good together. We are. We fit. I want to explore that. Together. While we both find out where we belong individually. Because I'm pretty sure I'm in love with you."

BREE THOUGHT ABOUT pinching herself. But when she looked at his eyes she believed him. He loved her.

"Oh, my goodness," she said.

He laughed. "Yeah."

"You love me? Me?"

Charlie nodded. "Not sure I'll be any good at it. You know, first time and all."

She swallowed as she struggled to appear as if she wasn't freaking out. "That's okay. You're pretty good at everything else. I imagine you'll pick it up quickly."

"Thanks," he said.

It was her turn to touch, to run her hand up his arm before she caressed his cheek. That helped a lot. She'd needed grounding and the feel of him was familiar and lovely. "Are you sure about this? Really sure?"

"Oh, yeah. I'm in."

"This is insane. This isn't even a life I could have imagined, and when I was seven I wanted to be a unicorn."

He laughed as he pulled her close, as his lips captured hers and she could taste his grin and his excitement. She was ten feet off the ground, in the arms of the soon-to-be-abdicating King of Manhattan, and the hell with a unicorn. She was Bree, and she wouldn't trade that for the world.

She thought about her friends at the St. Marks lunch exchange, and how they were all so hopeful and scared when they picked up a trading card. She couldn't wait to tell them not to give up. Ever. Anything was possible. Anything.

The Next Day...

Huffpost Entertainment: CHARLIE WINSLOW QUITS!

New York Post: Today in Page Six…No More *Naked New York?*

FACEBOOK

edit profile

Charlie Winslow
Editor in Chief/CEO *Naked New York Media Group*
Studied Business/Marketing at *Harvard University*
Lives in *Manhattan* ❤ In a Relationship

* * * * *

Dear Reader,

While other women might think immediately of romance on certain days, I don't—I think of chocolate. After nearly twenty years together my husband knows that I don't require dinner out or a box of fancy truffles. Though I've sampled Godiva, Ghirardelli, See's, Whitman's and various different other chocolates, nothing tastes as good to me as plain old Hershey's. It's simple, delicious and in that sweet little kiss form? Ah…bliss. And speaking of kisses, the hero in this book certainly knows how to do that well.

Former Ranger Jackson Oak Martin is as big, steady and strong as the tree he's named after. But when being too near a bomb when it explodes renders him partially deaf in one ear, Jack knows that his career in the military is over. When he's recommended for a position at Ranger Security, Jack is unquestionably relieved. But when his first assignment results in forced proximity with pastry chef Mariette Levine and involves catching a "Butter Bandit", Jack can't help but wonder what the hell he's gotten into. Particularly when he becomes obsessed with getting into her…

As always, thanks so much for picking up my books! I am so very thankful for my readers and love hearing from them, so be sure to follow me on Twitter @RhondaRNelson, like me on Facebook and look for upcoming releases and news on my website, ReadRhondaNelson.com.

Happy reading!

Rhonda

THE KEEPER

BY
RHONDA NELSON

First published in Great Britain 2012
by Mills & Boon, an imprint of Harlequin (UK) Limited,
Eton House, 18-24 Paradise Road, Richmond, Surrey TW9 1SR

© Rhonda Nelson 2012

2in1 ISBN: 978 0 263 89370 0

14-0412

Harlequin (UK) policy is to use papers that are natural, renewable and recyclable products and made from wood grown in sustainable forests. The logging and manufacturing processes conform to the legal environmental regulations of the country of origin.

Printed and bound in Spain
by Blackprint CPI, Barcelona

A Waldenbooks bestselling author, two-time RITA®
Award nominee and *RT Book Reviews* Reviewers'
Choice nominee, **Rhonda Nelson** writes hot
romantic comedy for the Blaze® line. With more than
twenty-five published books to her credit and many
more coming down the road, she's thrilled with her
career and enjoys dreaming up her characters and
manipulating the worlds they live in. In addition to a
writing career, she has a husband, two adorable kids,
a black Lab and a beautiful bichon frisé. She and
her family make their chaotic but happy home in a
small town in northern Alabama. She loves to hear
from her readers, so be sure to check her out at www.
readrhondanelson.com.

Prologue

"WHAT ABOUT YOU, OAK?" PFC Heath Johnson asked. "What do you want in a woman?"

Doing a routine sweep through his little portion of Baghdad, Major Jackson Oak Martin was only half listening to his fellow comrades enumerate what qualities their ideal woman would possess. He'd been through this area countless times over the past few months and was familiar with every pile of garbage, every mate-less shoe, every blown-out window. He carefully scanned the area ahead, every sense tingling.

Something had changed.

"Eyes out, guys," Jack told them, slowing down as the hair on the back of his neck prickled uneasily. "I'm pulling a weird vibe."

"Bullshit," PFC Chris Fulmer scoffed, seemingly annoyed and bored, his usual mood. "It's the same old, same old here, Major. Nothing's happened in weeks in this area. I don't know why we can't move on," he continued to predictably complain. He grunted. "Ignorant-ass waste of time, if you ask me." He shot a grin at Johnson and pulled a cocky shrug. "You want to know what *I* want in a woman, Johnson? It's simple enough." He made an obscene gesture.

The group laughed and Jack quickly quieted them, growing increasingly uncomfortable. Dammit, he knew something was different. Could feel it. He looked left, then right, along both sides of the cluttered abandoned street. He scanned the rooftops and windows, the blown-out cars and debris. On the surface everything appeared undisturbed, innocuous even, but every iota of intuition he possessed was telling him that it wasn't, that something—however small—had been altered.

And the small things were just as capable of getting them killed as the big things were.

"You're a shallow bastard, you know that, Fulmer?" Johnson told him.

The young Nebraskan was as wholesome as the farm he'd grown up on, intelligent and wise beyond his years, and had quickly become one of Jack's favorites.

A dreamy expression drifted over Johnson's face. "I just want a woman who can cook. One who knows that potatoes don't come out of a box and are better mashed, with gravy. One who knows how to fry chick—"

A blast to their immediate right cut off the rest of what Johnson was going to say, along with his legs.

Jack felt the power of the detonation roll over his body—a terrible shock of pain to his right ear—and felt himself fly through the air and land hard on his left side. He couldn't catch his breath—it had been knocked out of him—and struggled to force the immediate panic aside. Debris and dust clouded his vision, making his eyes water and sting. He lifted his head, saw Johnson shaking uncontrollably on the ground, part of Fulmer's skull clasped in his own hand, and Wilson and Manning were both bleeding from various parts of their bodies.

Oh, Jesus...

He immediately radioed for help, then, heartsick and terrified, lunged into action, crawling with more speed than grace to Johnson's side.

The boy's big blue eyes were wide with shock, and his mouth worked up and down. He grabbed Jack's sleeve and yanked him down. His ashen lips moved shakily, but no sound emerged.

"Medic's on the way," Jack assured him, tearing bits of fabric from the edge of his jacket to fashion a makeshift tourniquet. So much blood, he thought, working frantically, his hands slippery with it. It was a mortal wound, he knew—he was familiar enough with war to know that—but he had to try, had to help. This was Johnson, dammit, his friend.

Johnson writhed and tried to bat his hands away, but Jack roughly pushed him back down. "I gotta do it," he told him, feeling his insides vibrate with dread. "I know it hurts like a bitch, but just stay strong, buddy." Jack could feel his heart thundering in his chest, the tremor in his fingers, a trickle of something wet and sticky running down his neck.

Before he could attach the second tourniquet, Johnson jerked him around hard, his pale, freck-led face a mask of pain and desperation. He kept talking—seemed to be desperately trying to impart something significant—but his lips only moved. Seemingly frustrated when Jack didn't respond, Johnson tried harder, appearing to scream. He said whatever it was again, gave him another little shake, then fell back against the ground once more. His eyes drifted shut.

Oh, no. No, no, no.

"Johnson," Jack said, grabbing the boy's shoulder. "Stay with me, Johnson. Dammit, don't—"

A hand suddenly landed on his shoulder and Jack whirled and struck out, sending the medic sprawl-ing. A second medic was right behind the first and a helicopter had landed in the street fifty yards from where they were located. Jack watched the blades whirl, belatedly noting the lack of sound. He frowned, his gaze darting from one person to the next, watched their lips move, saw the action and reaction.

Dread ballooned in his belly and his heart began to race even faster as the unhappy truth slammed into him.

PFC Heath Johnson had just uttered his last words…to a man who couldn't hear them.

1

Six months later...

PERHAPS BECAUSE HE WAS now partially deaf in his right ear, former-Ranger Jack Martin was certain he had to have heard his new employers incorrectly. He chuckled uneasily.

"The Butter Bandit?"

Brian Payne—one of the three founding members of the infamous Ranger Security Company—nodded and shot a look at fellow partner Guy McCann. "That's what Guy has dubbed him and, I'm sad to say, it's stuck."

Jamie Flanagan, who rounded out the triumvirate, flashed a what-the-hell sort of grin. "You've got to admit that it has a certain ring to it." He pulled a face. "Besides, other than a few éclairs, cookies and bear claws, butter is the *only* thing this thief is stealing."

How…bizarre, Jack thought. He was most definitely a fan of butter—who didn't like it melting on a pile of pancakes or slathering it over a hot roll? He had fond memories of making it himself with nothing more than a little heavy whipping cream in an old mason jar and shaking it up until his arms were tired, the unmistakable "plop" against the side of the jar, signaling it was done. He'd learned the trick from his grandmother, who'd been more butter obsessed than Paula Deen.

But he couldn't imagine even her *stealing* the stuff. It boggled the mind.

"Have there been any other butter thefts in the area?" Jack asked, trying to get his mind around the idea. Not a question he would have ever anticipated coming out of his mouth, but then again nothing about his recent life was anything he'd anticipated.

Leaving the military before retirement had never been in any plans he'd made—unless it had been in a pine box, which he'd been fully prepared to do—much less moving to anywhere other than Pennyroyal, North Carolina, upon retirement. He'd actually purchased property next to his parents there in his little hometown and had been toying with various house plans for years. Just something else he'd need to rethink at a later date.

At present he was just glad to have a job, to have had an alternative to sitting behind a desk for the rest of his career. The mere idea made him feel claustrophobic, hemmed in. While Jack knew there were many powerful men who did their best work from an office, he was not one of those men. He liked to *move,* needed some sort of physical action to coincide with his strategy.

Of course, sitting still had never been easy for him. Even in kindergarten his poor teacher had had to mark a square—with duct tape, the wonder material—on the floor around his desk to keep him there. If he came out of the "box" without permission, then he lost time on the playground.

While other people might think she was being cruel or unreasonable, Jack knew she'd had good reason. He'd given the poor woman sheer hell, had been virtually incapable of sitting still for any length of time. He could hear her, understand and learn without looking at her—while looking at something else or doing something else, like playing with a toy truck, for instance, he thought with a mental smile—but he hadn't realized until much later that other people didn't learn that way. With maturity had come discipline, but the underlying need to move was always itching just beneath the surface.

Even now.

That's what had made the military so perfect for him. Action, reaction, strategy, purpose. It had been the ideal fit. And while Ranger Security wasn't the military, it was run by former Rangers—men like himself—and, though he fully anticipated an adjustment, he knew he was up to the task. He almost smiled.

Even catching a butter thief, of all things, which was evidently going to be his first assignment for the company.

"No," Guy replied to his question. "No other butter thefts in the area. Mariette's store is the only one that's been targeted. We've canvassed the area just to be sure."

"Under normal circumstances we wouldn't be taking this on at all, but after last night we just can't sit back and do nothing," Payne said, his tone grim. "Mariette's more than a local business owner—she's a good friend, as well." He gestured to the other two men. "She's provided many a cup of coffee, breakfasts and snacks for us over the past three years. She's hosted our kids' birthday parties—"

"For which we are eternally thankful," Jamie added with a significant grimace.

"—and her shop is right here on our block."

In other words, *their* turf, *their* friend.

Jack had actually noticed the little bakery when he first arrived here in Atlanta a week ago. It was a pretty redbrick with whimsical window boxes stuffed with yellow and lavender mums. "Raw Sugar" was written in fancy script from a sign shaped like a three-tiered cake. There'd been a teenage girl with Down syndrome sweeping the walk out in front and she'd looked so happy it had brought a smile to his lips.

"What happened last night?" Jack asked, a bad feeling settling in his gut.

The three men shared a dark look. "Mariette heard a noise and went downstairs to investigate—"

"She lives above the shop," Jamie interjected, pausing to take a pull from his drink.

"—and interrupted the guy. Instead of running like a normal criminal who'd been caught, he picked up a dough roller and hurled it at her." Payne's voice lowered ominously. "It caught her behind the ear and knocked her out cold."

Damn, Jack thought, anger immediately bolting through him. He'd like to take a dough roller to the jackass for throwing it at a woman. No wonder they'd decided to intervene. Even though she'd been assaulted this still wasn't a case that was going to get high priority to an overworked local P.D. His grandfather, father and sister had all worn the uniform, so he should know. He'd thwarted tradition when he'd traded the badge for a pair of dog tags, a fact his father never failed to remind him of when he went home. Good-naturedly, of course, but Jack knew his decision to not follow in the "family business" had stuck in his father's craw.

"Do you have any idea what he's looking for?" Jack asked. "Aside from butter, that is?" There was no way in hell this was just about butter. If that were the case, their thief would be hitting multiple businesses, not just Raw Sugar.

Jamie shook his head and released a mighty sigh. "Not a damned clue."

"That's where you're going to come in," Payne told him. "She needs protection, obviously, but more than that we need to know what this guy's after. You find the motive and you'll resolve the threat."

He certainly couldn't fault that logic. He had no idea where in the hell he was going to start looking for motive—with Mariette, he supposed—but otherwise this didn't seem as though it was going to be too involved and shouldn't interfere with his other... project.

"Because the thief hasn't struck during the day while the shop is open, we're assuming that she's in less danger at that point. We're putting Charlie in under the guise of 'helping out' until Mariette closes, which will free you up to investigate during those hours and then cover protection at night, when he's most likely to strike again."

The mention of his sister, Charlie—who was the first female nonmilitary, non-Ranger employee hired on by the company—brought a smile to his lips. He and his sister had always been tight and, if there were a silver lining at all to his impromptu career change, it was that he'd get to see her on a regular basis. He'd actually moved into his new brother-in-law's former apartment here in the building.

When the idea of coming on board with Ranger Security after the accident had first been mentioned, it was ultimately Jay who had convinced him that it would be the right move. The first look at the "boardroom" with its high-end electronics and toys, pool table and kitchenette—complete with its own candy counter—had been proof enough before anything else had been discussed. Between the unbelievable benefits package—the salary, the hardware, the furnished apartment—and the familiar camaraderie of former battle-worn soldiers, he knew that he'd been lucky to find a place where he felt sure he would eventually feel at home. He grimaced.

At the moment, even home didn't feel like home.

But how could it, really? After what had happened in Baghdad? An image of Johnson's frantic, desperate face loomed large in his mind's eye—the dirt and the blood—and with effort, he forced the vision to recede.

For the moment, anyway. Until he could properly analyze it again. Sheer torture, but it had to be done. He would keep analyzing it for the rest of his life if he had to. He owed the kid no less.

Typically when Jack returned stateside it was to a big party and lots of fanfare. He was the only son and frankly, as the former all-star quarterback for the high-school football team, Pennyroyal's golden boy. He was generally met with a cry of delight, a hearty slap on the back, a little nudge-nudge wink-wink and a free drink.

The tone had been decidedly different this time.

The smiles had been pitying and bittersweet, the slaps on the back held a tinge of regret and finality and, because he'd been wounded, there hadn't been a party.

It was just as well. He hadn't felt like celebrating.

Payne handed him a thin file. He'd already given him a laptop, a Glock, the permit to carry concealed and the keys to his furnished and fully stocked apartment. Brian Payne had thought of everything, but then, that's what one expected out of a man dubbed "the Specialist" by his comrades, Jack thought, surveying the seemingly unflappable former Ranger. His gaze briefly shifted to the other two men.

With a purported genius-level IQ and an equal amount of brawn, Jamie Flanagan had been the ultimate player until he met and married Colonel Carl Garrett's granddaughter, and Guy McCann's ability to skate the fine edge of recklessness and never tip over into stupidity was still locker room lore.

He couldn't be working with finer men. Or *woman,* he belatedly added, knowing his sister wouldn't appreciate the unintended slight.

"Mariette is expecting you," Payne told him. He hesitated and, for whatever reason, that small delay made Jack's belly clench. He glanced at his partners, whose expressions suddenly became mildly humorous, then found Jack's once more. "While she appreciates our help, she's not exactly happy about the way in which we're providing it."

Jack felt his lips slide into a smirk. In other words, she didn't want him to spend the night with her.

In truth, he wasn't exactly looking forward to spending the night at her place, either. He was still having damned nightmares and didn't relish the idea of having to explain himself. Besides, cohabitating with a woman for any reason made his feet itch and triggered the urge to bolt.

Irrational? Probably.

But he'd given it a go with his former college sweetheart and that had ended...disastrously.

Both the relationship and the cohabitation.

Who knew that having only one foot of five in closet space would irritate him to no end? Or that the way she ground her teeth at night would feel like psychological torture? Or that when he'd rebelled against the minimal closet space she'd thrown all of his shit out into the yard and set it on fire with charcoal starter and a flame thrower? Jack frowned.

In retrospect she'd been a little unbalanced—brought a whole new meaning to the phrase "crazy sex"—but the lesson had been learned all the same. He liked his own space. He liked his own bed. He liked making his own rules. As such, he didn't do sleepovers. When the goal was met—typically a little mutually satisfying sex with no strings or expectations—he ultimately retreated to his own place.

And planned to *always* retreat to his own space.

Jack didn't know when he'd made the conscious decision to never marry, but when his mother had concluded her I'm-so-glad-you're-home speech with a succinct nod and a "Now you can settle down and get married," he'd mentally recoiled at the thought.

The reaction had been jarring and, even more so, unexpected.

In all truth, he'd never really given much thought to the idea of marriage. He'd been busy building a career he loved, distilling the values he'd always appreciated—courage, honor, love of country, being a man who didn't just give his word, but kept it, one who followed through and always got the job done. He worked hard on the battlefield and played hard off it.

Life, full *friggin'* throttle, unencumbered by any other ties.

And he'd liked it that way.

He hadn't realized exactly how much until after the accident, when everything in his world had shifted.

Losing Fulmer and Johnson had certainly changed him—death had a way of doing that to a person—and the hearing loss had ultimately cost him a career he'd loved, but he'd be damned before he'd give up the only part of himself he'd managed to hold on to. He was still Jackson Oak Martin and, though this life was a stark departure from the one he left behind, he'd figure out a way to make it work.

Because that's what he did.

And the alternative was simply unacceptable.

And, friend of Ranger Security or not, this Mariette person was just going to have to deal with it because he had a damned butter thief to find.

PAYNE WATCHED THEIR newest recruit leave the boardroom and then turned to his partners and quirked a brow. "That went better than I expected," he said. "A lesser man might have balked at catching a butter bandit."

Guy pushed up from the leather recliner he'd been slouched in and grabbed a pool stick. He carefully lined up his shot and sent the number three into the corner pocket. "He's certainly the most determined man we've ever brought on board, I'll say that." He frowned thoughtfully. "And not twitchy, but…barely contained."

Payne had noted that, as well. Jack Martin didn't shift in his seat, avoid eye contact, tap his fingers or his feet—didn't fidget at all, actually—and yet, like a thoroughbred waiting behind the gate, the energy was there. Banked anticipation. Bridled action.

Having joined Guy, Jamie took a shot at the nine and missed. He swore and absently chalked his cue. "Charlie said that the only thing that made leaving the military bearable for him was the job he knew would be waiting here."

Payne could definitely see where that would be the case and Colonel Carl Garrett had seconded Charlie's opinion. According to the Colonel, before the incident in Baghdad, Jack Martin had been rapidly rising through the ranks, on the verge of lieutenant-colonel status. He was well-favored, determined and dedicated. He was a man who had been in love with his career and, though he could have stayed on in another capacity within the military, he couldn't have continued along the same path.

It said a lot about his character that he was willing to blaze a new one.

"You can barely see the hearing aid," Jamie remarked. "I wouldn't have noticed it at all if I hadn't been looking for it."

The blast that had killed two of his men and injured two others had shattered Jack's eardrum so thoroughly that he'd needed multiple surgeries to repair it. As injuries went, he was damned lucky, but it had to have been an adjustment, all the same.

"Has Charlie found out why he's taking the lip-reading classes yet?" Guy asked.

"No." And he wished their curious, master hacker would leave that well enough alone. Everyone was entitled to a few secrets and, for whatever reason, Payne got the impression that the one Jack was trying to keep was as painful as it was significant.

Charlie digging around in something her brother had decided was private wasn't going to endear her to him if he found out. Of course, Jack probably knew Charlie well enough to know that she couldn't resist a mystery and considered very little privileged information sacred. He almost grinned.

It was part of the reason they'd hired her, after all.

"It doesn't make sense," Jamie chimed in. "He can hear. Why would he need to know how to read lips?"

Payne shrugged. "I'm sure he has his reasons."

Jamie took another pull from his drink and settled a hip against the pool table. "I just hope that Mariette doesn't make things too difficult for him. We're *helping* her, for heaven's sake." He shook his head. "Why is being grateful a concept women struggle with?"

Payne felt his lips twist. "She didn't *ask* for our help."

Jamie blinked. "That's my point exactly. She didn't *have* to ask."

"I don't think it's the help that she objects to, per se," Guy remarked, his lips sliding into a smile. "It's the us not leaving her a choice that's got her back up."

"Charlie said we could have handled it better," Jamie said. He paused thoughtfully and grimaced. "Actually, what she really said is that we were all a bunch of high-handed, knuckle-dragging idiots with the tact of a herd of stampeding elephants. Or something like that."

Payne chuckled. That sounded about right. And he'd never met a woman who liked being told what to do. He frowned thoughtfully.

Mariette certainly wasn't going to be the exception there.

He hoped Jack realized that sooner rather than later.

2

MARIETTE LEVINE WAS IN the process of pulling a red-velvet cupcake from the display case when she heard the bell over the door jingle and saw a pair of impossibly long, jeans-clad legs come into view. They sidled forward in a walk that was so blatantly sexy and loose hipped that she momentarily forgot what she was doing.

A flash of pure sexual heat instantly blazed through her, the sensation so unexpected and shocking she felt her eyes round and her breath catch.

Instead of standing up—which would have been the logical thing to do—for reasons that escaped her, Mariette dropped into a deeper crouch so that she could get a better look at the rest of him. She was *not* hiding, Mariette told herself. She had no reason to hide, even if she would admit to being curiously... alarmed.

How singularly odd.

She had no reason to be alarmed, either, and yet something about the stranger—whose face she hadn't even seen yet—triggered an imminent sense of danger. Not of the axe-murderer variety, but something else…something much more personal. Her racing heart stupidly skipped a beat and her mouth went dry.

Intrigued, her gaze drifted up over his crotch—it had to, dammit, to get to the rest of him—and took a more thorough inventory. He wore an oatmeal-colored cable-knit sweater—oh, how she loved a cable-knit sweater on a man—and a leather bomber jacket that had seen better days. His hands were stuffed into the pockets, his broad shoulders still a bit hunched beneath the cold. He was impossibly… big. Not apish or fat, but tall and lean hipped and muscled in all the right places.

And if his architecture was magnificent, it was nothing compared to the perfect harmony of his face.

Sweet heaven…

High cheekbones, intriguing hollows, an especially angular, squared-off jaw. His nose was perfectly proportioned and straight, his mouth a little wide and over full. Sleek brows winged over a pair of heavy-lidded, sleepy-looking light eyes—either green or blue, she couldn't tell from this distance, though instinct told her blue.

His hair was a pale golden-blond, parted to the side, almost all one length and hung to just above his collar. He exuded confidence, fearlessness and moved with a casual deliberateness that suggested he was a man who was well aware of his own strength and ability. He didn't merely inhabit a space—he *owned* it.

And she wasn't the only one who'd noticed. Several of her patrons had stopped to look at him—mouths hanging open, forks suspended in midair—and a quick look to her right revealed that her helper, Livvie, had gone stock-still.

"Wow," she heard Livvie breathe, her eyes rounded in wonder. "You're *tall*. Like the corn man, but not green."

Charlie Martin Weatherford, her assigned daytime bodyguard working under the guise of helping out, exited the kitchen and her step momentarily faltered, then a brilliant smile bloomed over her mouth. "'Bout time you got here," she said to the mystery man with a good-natured snort of impatience. "You get lost, big brother?"

Big brother? Mariette felt her eyes widen and the original irrational panic that had sent her pulse racing only a minute before was minimal to the arrhythmia that had set in now. This was Charlie's brother? *This* air-breathing Greek god in a bomber jacket was the man who was going to be spending the night with her until this ignorant dairy thief was caught?

Oh, no. *No, no, no...*

She didn't know why oh-no, but she knew it all the same. Could feel some sort of impending doom with every particle of her being.

She'd been right to be alarmed.

It was self-preservation in its purest form. He was disaster with a tight-assed swagger and she knew herself too well to think he'd be anything other than irresistible. Why couldn't he have been the aging-detective type her too-vivid imagination had conjured up? She peered up at him again and resisted the urge to whimper. No paunch, jowls or receding hairline in sight.

Just six and a half feet of pure masculine temptation.

Livvie looked down at her and smiled. "Look at him, Mariette," she said in a stage whisper, her small, almond-shaped blue eyes alight with wonder. "There's a giant in the shop."

Following Livvie's gaze Charlie looked down at her, as well, and her lips twitched with knowing humor, as though she knew exactly why Mariette was hiding.

"He's not a giant, Livvie," Charlie told her, slinging an arm around the younger girl. "He's just a very tall man."

She looked at Mariette, arched a questioning brow and mouthed, "Corn man?"

Very reluctantly, Mariette rose, mentally braced herself and turned to meet Charlie's brother. She could hear her heart thundering in her ears and her mouth had yet to recover any of its lost moisture. A breathless sort of anticipation gripped her as she looked up.

She'd been right, she discovered—his eyes were blue. And not just any shade of blue. *French blue.*

Her favorite, naturally.

Though she was utterly certain the earth hadn't moved, Mariette felt it all the same. The soles of her feet practically vibrated from the imaginary vibration. The entire room, with the exception of the space he occupied, seemed to shimmy and shake. Her lungs went on temporary strike and a hot flush rushed over her skin, as though she'd been hit with an invisible blowtorch from one end of her body to the other. Her toes actually curled in her shoes.

Remarkable.

At twenty-seven, Mariette had met many good-looking men and knew enough about sexual attraction to recognize it. But this was unmistakably different. It wasn't a dawning awareness of an attractive man.

This was a bare-knuckle sucker punch of lust— purely visceral—and undeniably the most potent reaction she'd ever had to a man. It was the sort of attraction that was rhapsodized in lyric and verse, secured the human race, rendered reason and logic useless, made one stupid.

It was the sort that could ruin a person.

But not her, dammit. Geez Lord, hadn't she just learned her lesson? What had Nathanial been if not a warning? Aside from a cheating, dishonest little bastard, anyway? To think that she'd been seriously considering marrying him.

Just like all the other men she'd misjudged—and, lamentably, there'd been many—on the surface Nathaniel had seemed like a perfect catch. He was a successful architect working for a local, prestigious firm. He'd stopped by her shop for three solid months, asking her out every single time he came through the door until she said yes. She'd been flattered and she'd liked the fact that he hadn't been a quitter, that he'd been persistent. She'd thought that, in him, she'd finally found *the one*. A real, stand-up guy who genuinely loved her the same way that her mother always had—*unconditionally.*

In reality he just hadn't been used to anyone telling him no. Come to find out she hadn't been the only person he'd been pursuing relentlessly—there'd been several others.

And when she'd caught him getting blown by the plant-watering girl—whose dirty feet still haunted her—at his office, she'd been shocked, humiliated, angry and hurt. The pain hadn't come just from the betrayal, which had been devastating enough—it had come from not being able to trust her own judgment. With previous guys she'd had an inkling of disquiet, an intuitive niggle of doubt that she'd ultimately ignored. Smooth-talking, greasy Nathaniel had slipped completely under her radar. And he'd had a crooked dick, too, Mariette thought. If nothing else, that should have clued her in.

Note to self: Never trust a man with a crooked dick.

To complicate matters, despite her telling him to go play in traffic, he still hadn't learned to accept no for an answer and continued to drop by in the slower hours and try to convince her to take him back. She mentally snorted.

As if.

Fool me once, shame on you. Fool me twice, shame on me. She might not always get things right, but she was a firm believer in education by experience…and that was one she didn't want to repeat.

Mariette steeled herself against her newest battle of temptation. "Are you in any way related to the Jolly Green Giant, Mr. Martin?" Mariette asked him, determined to get control of herself. He was only a man, after all. A mouthwatering, bone-melting, sigh-inducing, lady-bits-quivering specimen of one, yes.

But still just a man. And those were supposed to be off-limits, at least until she figured out just what it was exactly she wanted in one and how to recognize it.

He chewed the inside of his cheek as if to hide a smile. "Not that I'm aware of, no."

"Sorry, Livvie," Mariette told her with a wince. "He's not a giant."

Livvie looked unconvinced, but beamed up at him regardless. "It's all right," she said, smiling shyly. "I like him anyway."

Seemingly charmed, he extended his hand to her. "I'm Jack," he said. "It's a pleasure to meet you."

Livvie giggled delightedly and fingered the Hello Kitty necklace around her throat. "You're nice." She leaned over to Mariette and whispered loudly in her ear—loud was Livvie's only volume—"He's a gold."

Jack's expression became puzzled, but he didn't question it. Livvie said she saw people in colors and was forever telling Mariette which color various people were. She even kept a small color wheel in her apron pocket so that she could easily locate the right shade. Mariette, she'd said, was a lavender. Charlie, a fuchsia. If memory served, Jack was her first gold. Interesting…

Mariette wasn't surprised that Livvie could so clearly see auras. She was as pure of heart as it was possible to be and Mariette liked to think that the gift had been given to her as a means of protection, a way to recognize the good from the bad, and had even seen the girl retreat away from those whose "color" wasn't right.

Would that her mother had had the same sort of gift.

At any rate, Jack Martin had passed her "Livvie

test" and that said something about him. You could tell a lot about a person by the way they reacted to someone different from themselves and Livvie was about as different from Jack Martin as it was possible to be. She was small and round-faced with the short fingers and lower IQ that marked her as a person with Down syndrome.

The majority of Mariette's customers treated Livvie with the sort of care and respect someone with the purest heart deserved—children, in particular, were drawn to her—and anyone who didn't treat her well wasn't anyone who was welcome in her shop.

Born to a mother with Down's who'd been taken advantage of by a male caregiver, Mariette had a unique connection to the condition and had been employing workers with Down's since she first opened her doors four years ago.

If she'd learned anything from her mother it had been that everyone—no matter how different—wanted to be needed, to be useful, to have a bit of independence. There wasn't a day that went by that she didn't miss her and not a day that went by that she didn't want to hurt the father who'd abused her trusting spirit.

Bastard.

He'd served eighteen months for what he'd done to her mother and then promptly fled the state. Mariette kept tabs on him, though, and directed every new employer to his sex-offender status. She inwardly grinned. He never kept a job for very long. He struggled and, though it might be small of her, she thought it was fitting. He deserved that and a lot worse if you asked her.

The idea that his evil blood actually ran in her veins was something she'd struggled with for years, at times even making her physically ill. But her mother's was there, too, and Mariette liked to think that her mom's especially good blood had somehow canceled out that of her father's. Weird? Yes. But she'd never been destined for normal.

Normal was boring.

Her gaze drifted fondly over her dear helper and she smiled. Livvie had been with her for several months now and was doing remarkably well. She loved manning the case and *adored* sweeping. She helped with the birthday parties and refilled drinks and every tip that went into the jar was hers to keep. Which was just as well since the bulk of her check went to fund her Hello Kitty obsession. Her most recent purchase was the watch that encircled her wrist.

"Can I get you something?" Mariette asked Jack, gesturing to the display case.

He hesitated.

"He has a fondness for carrot cake," Charlie interjected slyly.

Mariette shot him a droll look and selected the

cupcake in question. It had been her aunt's recipe—
and was one of her favorites, as well. Oh, hell. Who
was she kidding? Everything in this shop was her
favorite, otherwise she didn't take the time to make
or stock it. Food was a passionate business and if she
couldn't get excited about it—if it didn't make her
palate sing—then she didn't bother. Better to have
fewer phenomenal items on her menu than dozens
of mediocre ones.

Also something she'd learned from her Aunt
Marianne, who'd not only helped raise her, but had
taught her to bake, as well. Some of her fondest
memories were in the kitchen with her aunt and her
mom, cracking eggs, stirring batter, the scent of vanilla in the air.

She popped the dessert onto a little antique plate
along with a linen napkin and handed it to him. Seconds later Livvie had put a glass of tea in his hand.
She'd added two lemons and a cherry, which told
Mariette just how much Livvie thought of him. She
only put cherries in the drinks of her favorite people.
He nodded approvingly at her and shot her a wink,
making her giggle with pleasure once more.

His blue gaze shifted to Mariette and that direct
regard made her more than a little light-headed. "Is
there somewhere we can talk?" he asked, lifting a
golden brow. "I've got a few questions."

Mariette took a bracing breath and prepared herself for imminent humiliation. She couldn't imag-

ine anything more mortifying than telling this man about her butter problems.

MARIETTE LEVINE WAS NOT at all what he'd expected, Jack thought broodingly as he followed her back to the kitchen. Actually, he hadn't really given any thought to what she might be like, so that wasn't precisely true. But—his gaze drifted over her petite curvy frame, lingering on her especially ripe heart-shaped ass—*this* woman wouldn't have been it.

In the first place, Mariette sounded like an old-fashioned name, so he'd imagined a more mature woman. Oh, hell, who was he kidding? He'd thought she'd be old. Which was ridiculous, really. Not all bakeries were owned by plump grandmas in floral aprons, though for reasons that escaped him that was the image that had leapt immediately to mind.

He estimated this particular baker to be in her mid- to late-twenties. In the second place… Well, there wasn't really a second place, though logic told him there should have been. And a third and a fourth and a fifth, for that matter. Furthermore, he felt as though he should have been warned, but couldn't come up with a logical reason for that, either.

What would they have said? *Oh, by the way, Mariette's young and hot with the most unusual gray eyes you'll ever see? That long mink-colored hair will incite the urge to wrap it around your fist and drag her up against you? And her mouth…* Jack swallowed thickly. A much fuller lower lip, a distinct bow in the upper and a perpetual tilt at the corner that suggested she was always enjoying a private joke. It was sinfully sensual nestled between her pert little nose and small pointy chin.

She wasn't merely pretty or beautiful—though those adjectives would apply, as well—but there was something *more* there. Something much more substantial and compelling, and the bizarre tightening in his chest that had occurred when her gaze had met his had been nothing short of terrifying.

Jack wasn't accustomed to being afraid of anything other than failure, so discovering that a woman could incite the feeling was a bit unsettling.

Honestly, when she'd risen up from behind that counter he couldn't have been more surprised if he'd been hit between the eyes with a two-by-four. He'd damned-near *staggered*.

From a single look.

Like a tsunami running headlong into a hurricane.

If he had any brains at all he'd turn around and leave, Jack thought. He'd walk right back up the block to Ranger Security and tell them that they needed to put someone else on this particular case, to give him another one. But short of a natural disaster metaphor, how in the hell could he explain his reasoning?

How could he tell them that she made his gut

clench and his dick hard? That intuition told him he
was headed into uncharted emotional and sexual territory and, weak as it might sound, he wasn't altogether certain he'd be able to control himself? That
something about her scared the hell out of him? *A
girl?*

How galling.

He couldn't tell them that, dammit. He needed
this job, had to make it work. He couldn't bail on
the first damned assignment.

And as much as he was compelled to flee, there
was an opposite force equally as strong that was
drawing him toward her, intriguing him, transfixing
him, and between the two he was stuck, immobile
and powerless.

Another punch of fear landed in his gut.

Mariette gestured toward a small table, indicating a seat and she took the one opposite. A couple of
women worked at a large stainless-steel table driz-
zling icing over pastries and the scent of yeast and
sugar hung in the air, reminding him of Christmas-
time at home, when his mother made her famous
cinnamon rolls. Every surface gleamed beneath the
large, overhead lights. An old wooden ladder outfit-
ted with metal hooks was suspended from the ceiling and held a variety of pots and tongs of varying
degrees and sizes.

A peg board had been anchored to one long wall
and held dozens of bowls, measuring cups, couplings

and icing tips. Fresh flowers sat in old, blue Mason jars on the back windowsill and yet another board—this one a dry erase with what he could only assume were orders—took up another wall. The space was small—narrow like the building—but had been maximized with state-of-the-art appliances and sheer ingenuity.

He was impressed and said as much. "This is a great setup," he told her.

Seemingly pleased, she smiled and tucked a long strand of hair behind her ear. "It was a lot of trial and error in the beginning, but I think I've finally got everything organized in the most efficient manner."

He took a bite of his cupcake and savored the spices against his tongue. It was moist and flavorful, and the icing was perfect—not too sweet, with just the right cream cheese to sugar ratio. Not everyone got that part right, but she'd mastered it.

"And you live upstairs?"

She nodded, swept an imaginary crumb from the table. "I do. I keep long hours and economically, it just made more sense." A wry grin curled her lips. "I've got one mortgage as opposed to two."

Definitely savvy. Sexy, smart and she could cook, too. He hoped to hell he discovered a flaw soon. A hairy mole or a snorting laugh. Anything to derail this horribly inconvenient attraction.

"And when did you notice that someone was stealing your butter? When did the Butter Bandit first strike?"

Looking adorably mortified, she blushed prettily, a wash of bright pink beneath creamy skin. "Three days ago," she said. "At first I just thought one of the girls—possibly Livvie—had moved it from one part of the walk-in to the other. It's a big space and I keep it well stocked. I only use organic products and everything has to be fresh, otherwise the quality isn't up to par."

He could certainly taste the difference. "But it hadn't been moved?"

She shook her head. "No. And more than half of it had been taken."

"And how much is half?"

She chewed the inside of her cheek, speculating. "Roughly thirty pounds."

Jack felt his eyes widen. *"Thirty pounds?"*

She laughed, the sound husky and melodic. *Definitely not a snorter, then. Damn.*

"I typically use between sixty and seventy pounds of butter a week." She gestured to five-gallon lidded buckets beneath the main work station. "That's flour and sugar. And that smaller fridge against the wall? That one holds nothing but eggs."

Good Lord. He'd had no idea. Of course, since he'd never made any sort of dessert in his life that didn't come out of a box and require that he add only water, why would he?

But thirty pounds of butter? Who in the hell would steal *thirty* pounds of butter? To what purpose? For what possible use?

And they'd come back for more and *attacked* her for it.

"Who supplies your butter?" Jack wanted to know. It seemed like the best place to start. Perhaps there was something special about Mariette's butter. Maybe it was made from goat's milk or only harvested during the full moon. Maybe it was intentional butter, much like that Intentional Chocolate he'd gotten in a care package from his mother last year. Supposedly, it had been infused with good intentions by experienced meditators. Enchanted butter, he thought, tamping down the absurdity of the situation. He'd be damned if he knew.

But it was his job to find out, he reminded himself.

"Jefferson's Dairy just north of Marietta," she told him. "They furnish my eggs and milk, as well."

Jack nodded and pushed up from his chair, determined to get started. The sooner he figured this out the better. Besides, one of the ladies had fired up a mixer and the whine was wreaking hell with his hearing aid. For the most part, the little miracle piece could almost make him forget that he needed it at all, but then a certain sound would set it off and he'd be reminded all over again. For the most part, he'd learned to cope with the "disability"—and knew that he'd gotten off easy in comparison to most other war-sustained injuries—but it was still jarring, none-theless. An instant reminder of what he'd lost, an au-tomatic, haunting flashback to Johnson's desperate face. He gave himself a mental shake, forcing him-self to focus on the task at hand.

The bleeding, bedamned Butter Bandit.

The dairy sounded as good as any place to begin. "I'm sure that Payne has called them already, but I want to go out there and do a little poking around."

She stood, as well. "Of course."

"What time do you close?"

"Six."

He nodded once. "Then I'll be back at six."

A fleeting look of irritation and panic raced across her fine features so fast he was almost in-clined to believe he'd imagined it.

But he hadn't. For whatever reason—insanity, probably—that gave him an irrational burst of plea-sure. The whole misery-loved-company bit? he won-dered. Or was it something else? Was the idea of rattling her cage the way she was rattling his the culprit? He inwardly smiled.

It was fair, if nothing else, Jack decided.

A thought struck. "Did you get any sort of look at the guy at all before he threw the dough roller?"

The mere thought of it—of her being hurt—brought on the instant urge to hit something. Pref-erably the asshole who threw the dough roller at her.

What the hell was wrong with people anyway? Jack thought.

She smiled sadly and shook her head. "He was tall and skinny," she said. "He was wearing a hoodie and it was dark. I—"

"No worries," he told her. "I'll get him."

And when he did he was going to think of new and unusual ways to use that damned dough roller on *him*.

3

BOBBY RAY BISHOP KEPT his head down and his ball cap pulled low as he made his way past Mariette Levine's bakery, but darted a quick look through the shop window all the same. The little slow girl was there, as usual. She never failed to give him a hug when he came by with a delivery—he relished those hugs because they were the only ones he ever got. He hadn't been given a pat on the head, much less a hug, since he was eight, so it had been a shock at first, but a pleasant one. No sign of Mariette, but another woman with shoulder-length dark hair whom he'd never seen before was behind the counter. His heart kicked into a faster rhythm.

A new person working in Mariette's place?

Shit, shit, shit. His hands began to shake. He must have hurt her bad, Bobby Ray thought. Could have even killed her.

He hurried past and rounded the corner, then

leaned against the wall of the next building and pulled long, deep breaths into his seizing lungs. Panic and nausea clawed their way up his throat and his nose poured snot, which he dashed away with the back of his hand. He felt tears burn the backs of his lids and blinked them away, determined not to cry. When had crying ever done him any good anyway? Just earned him a backhand against the face or a knock upside the head.

Or worse.

I ain't raisin' no sissy boy, his father had always said. *You gonna cry, then I'll give you something to cry about.*

And he had.

God help him, what was he going to do? He'd been sleeping in his car for days, moving from one place to another to stay at least a step ahead of Uncle Mackie. He snorted. Uncle Mackie wasn't his real uncle, of course. He probably wasn't anyone's uncle at all, but the name had come up at some point or another and stuck, and now it had the power to make him quiver with fear and practically piss himself.

Bobby Ray had lived in fear most of his life and he was sick to death of it.

Uncle Mackie was a bookie and, after a few ill-advised bets plus interest plus whatever "fee" Mackie decided he owed, Bobby Ray was into him for four grand.

It might as well be a million.

He didn't make enough at the dairy to come anywhere near that amount and didn't have anything of value to sell. At nineteen he had a beat-up fifteen-year-old Buick with a salvage title, and lived in a pay-by-the-week motel room. Better than foster care, which he'd ultimately aged out of, thank God, but certainly not the high life, either.

He wiped his nose on the sleeve of his shirt and looked enviously at passersby with their fancy clothes, smartphones and gold watches. He'd bet none of these people had a clue about how people like him lived. Eating microwave mac and cheese every night for dinner, waiting for an empty dryer with a few minutes left on the timer at the Laundromat so that he could afford clean clothes.

He'd always heard that hard work was supposed to pay off, but all Bobby Ray could see in his future was more hard work and a constant, never-ending struggle. He supposed that's why he'd turned to betting. When one five-dollar bet on the dogs had made him more money than he earned in a month, he'd imagined himself a professional gambler. His lips twisted with bitter humor.

And that was exactly what Uncle Mackie had wanted him to think.

Within two weeks he was down two grand and panicking. Mackie's boys had roughed him up pretty good and had told him the next time they came back they wouldn't be so "gentle."

Bobby Ray had never been a saint and wouldn't pretend otherwise. He'd spent more time kicked out of all the various schools he attended than in them, mostly for fighting. Kids were smarter than people typically gave them credit for and they had a talent for sniffing out the kind that was different from them.

Bobby Ray had always been different.

For starters, his eyes were two different colors. Add the Glasgow smile—twin scars that ran from his ears to the corners of his mouth and made him look as if he was always wearing an unnaturally wide grin—compliments of one of his father's drunken rages, and he'd been an easy target. Life would have been a whole lot easier for him if he'd simply accepted the taunts and moved on, but Bobby Ray had never been able to do that.

He always fought. And he lost more often than he won.

Taking the first coin from Audwin Jefferson had been the most difficult thing Bobby Ray had ever done. Audwin hadn't stared at his scars or his mismatched eyes and hadn't cared if Bobby Ray hadn't graduated high school. He'd looked at him and saw an able-bodied man willing to work and the pride that had come with that knowledge had been damned near indescribable.

He bitterly wished he'd never known about the coins, wished Audwin had never taken the little black pouch out of the drawer and laughingly called it his retirement fund. He'd shown him a variety of different coins—buffalo nickels, Confederate money, various pennies and silver dollars, even a gold piece from Nazi Germany that his grandfather had brought back from WWII.

Sweating with dread and sick to his stomach, Bobby Ray had snatched the first coin his fingers had come in contact with and, feeling more miserable by the minute, had taken it to a pawn shop on the other side of town. The broker had given him a thousand dollars for the coin and Bobby Ray had promptly turned it over to Uncle Mackie, but by that point his debt had quadrupled.

And Uncle Mackie had found another way to earn a buck.

Because he'd become irrationally terrified of getting caught, Bobby Ray had started slipping the coins into the butter molds so that they were never actually on his body and then marking the molds with a small X so he knew where to find them. When he left the dairy to make the deliveries, he'd simply pull over and retrieve the coin, then head directly to the pawn shop and then to Uncle Mackie. Every time he thought he was close to paying off his debt, Mackie would fabricate another "fee" and get him on the hook again.

Because a couple of customers had complained that he was delayed, Bobby Ray had been forced to alter his system and start making his deliveries first. And that's when things had gone wrong. He'd set aside the mold he was certain held the coin, then belatedly discovered at the end of the day that it had somehow gotten swapped with a dud. By process of elimination he'd deduced that his coin had gone into Mariette's shop and he'd been desperately trying to retrieve it ever since.

She'd caught him last night and he'd panicked and picked up the dough roller. He hadn't meant to hit her with it—had only wanted to scare her away so that he could make a run for it—but she'd zigged when she should have zagged and it caught her on the back of the head.

She'd crumpled like a rag doll and he'd nearly been sick with fear. He'd dialed 911 from the shop phone, left the receiver on the kitchen counter and ran for it.

Because he needed to know how she was, Bobby Ray decided that he'd find a pay phone and start calling the local hospitals. The idea that he could have seriously wounded her—or worse—was eating him up inside. How had this happened? he wondered again, feeling the hopelessness close in around him. How had things gotten so completely out of his control? It was only a matter of time before Uncle Mackie turned up at the dairy, Bobby Ray thought.

And Audwin would fire him for sure then.

Dammit, he had to get that coin back. He *had* to.

"LISTEN, MARIETTE, I know that the guys have stomped in and taken over your protection and this case, but they mean well," Charlie told her once the afternoon crowd thinned a bit. "They consider you a friend. In their own weird way they genuinely believe that they're doing what's best for you."

"I know that," Mariette said, feeling trapped and exasperated. With herself more than anyone. "And it's not that I don't appreciate it because I do."

And that was true. She'd never had a father, or even a big brother for that matter, who'd had her back. It was odd having Payne insist on taking care of this problem because she'd always taken care of her own problems. Once she'd gotten over hearing so many orders fired at her regarding *her* house, *her* shop and *her* safety, she'd been able to stop and consider that and she'd found that, high-handedness aside, she rather liked that they wanted to protect her. That they thought enough of her to do that.

She'd just been so rattled this morning after the attack that she hadn't been able to think clearly. Mariette had never been afraid before, especially here in her own space. To find that she was vulnerable had been more than a bit disconcerting. She'd spent three hours in the E.R. and, despite various protests from all sides, had come back to the shop to start work. She'd had to—she wasn't just her own boss, she was also the boss of four employees and she did the bulk of the work.

If something got ruined or didn't turn out right, it had an immediate impact on her bottom line. She couldn't afford to just take off, not with dozens of pastries, cupcakes and cakes to make. Furthermore, if she'd gone upstairs and crawled into bed instead of continuing in her own routine… It felt too much like letting him win.

And that was simply unacceptable.

That said, despite the fact that she was equally dreading and anticipating Jack Martin taking over as her security guard tonight, Mariette had to admit that she was looking forward to being able to turn the watch over to him. She was dead on her feet and she could feel the hooks of exhaustion sinking in and tugging at her from all sides. She had a no-sleep headache on top of the headache the intruder had given her and would like nothing more than a warm cookie, a glass of milk and her bed.

With any luck, she'd be too tired by six o'clock to worry about lusting after Jack Martin.

Somehow, she doubted it.

Merely the thought of him made her nipples tingle and a heavy heat build low in her belly. She'd like to tell herself that the only reason she found him so irresistible was because she'd sworn off men for a while—sort of like the everything-looks-more-delicious-on-a-diet mentality—but she knew better.

Jack Martin was…different.

She'd felt it from the instant he'd walked into her

store. A quickening, an awareness of sorts, that had tripped some sort of internal trigger, made her more conscious of him. She was equally unnerved and transfixed. Not a recipe for contentment.

"This is my brother's first case for Ranger Security," Charlie remarked as she straightened a tablecloth. "Since coming out of the military." There was a strange undertone to her voice that Mariette couldn't readily identify. Sadness, maybe? Regret, definitely.

Intrigued, she turned to look at her. "Oh?"

Charlie bit her lip. "I know that we're not as close as you and Emma Payne are, and I really have no right to ask you this, but…" She hesitated, clearly torn.

"But what, Charlie?" Mariette wanted to know, genuinely curious.

"But could you take it easy on him, please?" she asked, her eyes softening with entreaty. "Don't make Jack pay for Payne's methods. My big brother has been through sheer hell the past six months and he needs to do this. He *needs* to help you. He needs to prove to them—and to himself—that he can."

Wow. Mariette didn't know what she'd expected Charlie to say, but that certainly wasn't anything she would have imagined. Jack had been through hell? What sort of hell? What did she mean by that? Her heart immediately swelled with compassion and a matching lump inexplicably formed in her throat.

She knew from Emma that Payne, Flanagan and McCann had all come out of the military after the death of a good friend and formed their security company. Was that the sort of hell Charlie was referring to? Had Jack lost someone? A friend? Had he been injured? Had he come out because he'd wanted to? Or because he hadn't had a choice?

Ultimately none of those questions were any of her business and yet she found herself desperately wanting to know the answers to them and so much more. It was hard to imagine a man as big and vital and alive as Jack Martin being anything other than formidable.

"His middle name is Oak," Charlie remarked thoughtfully. "Like the tree."

Mariette raised a brow. "That's different."

"It's a family name," she said. "I've always thought of him that way, too. Strong, rooted, weathering the storm, sheltering branches. When he came home he was…different. Not broken," she said quietly. "But definitely bent." She shook herself. "Sorry," she said, blushing slightly. She rolled her eyes. "He'd throttle me if he knew I'd said anything. I just worry."

"Of course you do," Mariette assured her. "He's your brother."

And she'd certainly given Mariette a lot to think about.

A splash of color from the storefront snagged her

attention and she turned in time to see a familiar round face smush against the window pane.

She smiled and nudged Charlie. "You want to see something that'll melt your heart?" she asked her.

Charlie nodded.

She gestured toward the door and then to Livvie. "Watch this."

"Dillon!" Livvie exclaimed, bouncing up and down on the balls of her feet, a smile wreathing her face. Dillon Melster, who also had Down syndrome, was Livvie's absolute favorite person in the entire world, which she would tell you in a heartbeat.

Wearing his traditional red baseball hat and his leather bracelet with the silver spikes, Dillon waved from the door, a big smile on his round face. "Livvie! Guess what?"

Livvie went up on tiptoe and leaned against the counter. "What?"

"I'm going to the 'quarium on Saturday to see the whales and Mom said you could come if you wanted to. Do you want to, Livvie? We'll get ice cream," he told her, as though getting ice cream was the most important part of the trip.

"In a waffle cone?"

"Sure. Or in a bowl."

"I like the waffle cone," Livvie told him. "It's more fun to lick. You can't lick a bowl."

Mariette smothered a grin. Livvie frequently

licked the bowls in the back when there was leftover icing. Evidently, she'd forgotten that.

Dillon's eyes widened and he beamed at her. "I've never thought of that before. You're so smart, Livvie."

Livvie blushed and ducked her head. "I got a new Hello Kitty necklace," she said, pointing proudly to the one around her neck. "See? It's got sparkles."

Dillon leaned forward so that he could get a better look. "Oooh, that's pretty. Where did you get it from?"

"Momma found it on the internet for me," Livvie told him.

Mariette leaned over to Charlie and whispered low. "Livvie's mother finds everything on the internet and if she doesn't find it there, then she hits up the Home Shopping Network or QVC. Her family should buy stock in FedEx," she said, laughing softly. "Try and recover a little of the money she spends."

Charlie grinned. "I can't say anything," she said. "I did almost all of my Christmas shopping online last year."

Mariette had bought a few things, as well, but still preferred being able to actually touch something before she bought it.

Charlie lifted her chin at Dillon and Livvie, a smile on her face. "They're adorable," she said. "They seem quite taken with one another."

She nodded. They were, and something about the pair warmed Mariette's heart. It was so pure, their affection. Uncomplicated.

She looked over and watched as Livvie showed him the newest picture of her cat, Piedmont. He was a fat orange-and-white tabby who, according to Livvie's mother, brought bird-watching to a whole new level and had the patience of a saint when it came to Livvie. She was forever trying to dress him up in her Hello Kitty finery. In this latest picture, she'd pressed a pair of pink heart-shaped sunglasses on his face.

"He's such a good kitty," she heard Livvie tell Dillon. "He sleeps at the end of my bed and keeps my feet warm."

"That's nice," Dillon said with a nod. "You see this?" he asked Livvie, pulling up his sleeve. "Bubba got me some ink."

Both Mariette and Charlie leaned forward so that they could get a look at the ink, as well. Mickey Mouse graced Dillon's forearm.

"Ink," she breathed, suitably impressed. "Do you think he could get me some ink?"

Dillon straightened a bit and grinned at her. "My brother can get anything, Livvie. For reals."

"I want a Hello Kitty ink," she said. "I'll put it on my arm just like you."

He beamed at her. "I knew you would like it. 'Cause you're cool like me."

She laughed delightedly and bounced on tiptoe again. "You want me to get you some tea? I'll put some cherries in there for you."

"Sure. Can I get a cookie, too? The kind with the candy bars in them?"

She nodded. "Yes, you can."

"Livvie, would you like to take your break now?" Mariette asked her and of course she said yes. She always took her break when Dillon came into the store.

Dillon's mom, who'd been talking on her cell phone, ended the call and walked over to the counter. She was a pretty forty-something divorcée who lived and breathed her children. Sadly, her husband hadn't shown the same devotion and had left shortly after Dillon's birth. She'd never remarried and had no plans to do so. For whatever reason, it saddened Mariette.

"The usual?" Mariette asked her.

She nodded and glanced over at Dillon and Livvie, a rueful smile sliding over her lips. "If it was up to him, we'd be here every day. He counts the minutes until he can see her again."

Mariette pulled a cranberry-orange muffin from the case and then poured her a cup of hot tea. She smiled. "He's a sweet boy."

"He is," she said, obviously proud. "And has more kindness and capacity to love than any man I've ever known. The world could learn a lot from my boy," she said.

Mariette watched as Dillon took one of the cherries out of his drink and popped it into Livvie's.

And she wholeheartedly agreed.

4

JEFFERSON'S DAIRY WAS A mom-and-pop organic farm that had lost the mom part six months ago. Audwin Jefferson was coping like many men who'd lost a wife—by throwing himself into the work.

The older gentleman was in need of a haircut and an iron, based on the wrinkled state of his clothes. The office garbage can was filled with cheap TV dinners and snack-cake wrappers, which Jack found particularly odd given the man's line of work. He believed in organic enough to make it and adhere to the strict government codes, but not enough to eat it himself?

He followed Jack's gaze and frowned. "Martha was the cook," he said. "I can fry an egg, but that's the extent of my culinary abilities and, now that I'm doing the books and the bulk of the work by myself, I don't have the time or energy to learn." He speared him with a direct look. "You married?"

Jack cleared his throat. "No, sir. I'm not."

He harrumphed. "Can you cook?"

"Not well," he admitted, feeling as though he were failing some sort of unspoken test.

"Well, if you're not going to marry—and so many of you young fools don't these days—then you'd best learn to cook."

His gaze drifted over a photograph that was sitting on his desk. Him and Martha, Jack imagined. Jefferson's hair was inky black, his shoulders wide and straight. Martha's hand was curled against his chest and she was tucked protectively under his arm. She'd been a beauty—a dark brunette with a great pair of legs.

"That picture was taken in nineteen sixty-four. I was twenty. Martha was seventeen. We were married forty-eight years," he said. His bushy brows tangled together in a frown. "It's funny the things you miss. Bacon frying in the morning. Panty hose hanging over the shower rod. The sound of her singing at the clothesline. She liked show tunes," he muttered, a fond smile on his lips. He looked up at Jack. "We weren't designed to be alone. Male and female," he said. "A matched set. And when you find the right one…" He drifted off. "Well, it's an indescribable happiness. I'm not saying it's all roses and sunshine—there has to be darkness to appreciate the light—but nothing is quite so wonderful as holding the hand of the woman you love."

For whatever reason, it was all Jack could do not to squirm in his seat. Hell, he felt as though he'd been called on the carpet and soundly chastised and yet he knew that wasn't at all what Mr. Jefferson had intended. He was merely mourning his wife and sharing it unashamedly with a stranger. There was honor in that, Jack knew, and had to respect it.

Mr. Jefferson blinked and then seemed to snap to himself. "Sorry," he said, mopping his face with a handkerchief. "Didn't mean to go off on a tangent. What can I help you with?"

Jack hesitated. Where to begin? "I know this is going to sound like a weird question, but have you had anyone steal butter from you recently?"

Jefferson's face went comically blank. "Steal butter?"

"Right," Jack told him, feeling more ridiculous by the minute. "One of your clients, Mariette Levine, has had thirty pounds of butter stolen from her over the past three days. The guy broke in again last night. When Mariette interrupted him, he threw a rolling pin at her and knocked her out cold."

Alarm raced across the older man's features and he leaned forward. "What? Is she all right?"

"She's fine," Jack assured him. "More annoyed than anything else, but we're checking every possible source to try and make some sort of connection. Since you're her supplier, I thought I'd check here first. See if you've had any similar occurrences."

"I haven't," Jefferson told him, a thoughtful expression on his lined face. "Business has run as usual." He frowned. "I just can't imagine why anyone would want to steal her butter. It doesn't make a damned bit of sense."

"Is there anything special or different about the butter that you supply Mariette?"

He shook his head. "Not a thing. I send the same thing to bakeries and restaurants all over the city."

"The packaging is the same, as well?"

"It is. Five-pound loaves."

A movement behind him snagged Jack's attention and he turned to find a young man with a pair of unfortunate scars on each side of his face peering around the doorframe. A blond, short-haired dog with large, alert ears and big brown eyes sat at his heels. "Sorry to interrupt, Mr. Jefferson." His gaze flitted to Jack and then away. "Just wanted to let you know that I was back."

Jefferson nodded and the boy turned to leave, clicking his tongue at the dog. "Come on, Prize. Time to get to work."

"Bobby Ray," Jefferson called, halting him. "Mariette Levine was attacked last night in her shop. Someone's been stealing her butter. Have you noticed anything odd? Seen anyone lurking about around here or her back door?" He looked to Jack. "Bobby Ray is my right-hand man and delivery guy. He's been an incredible help since I lost my Martha."

The younger boy blushed and ducked his head and instinctively reached to pet the dog, who'd nudged up under his hand. "Mariette was attacked?" he said, his voice cracking. He cleared his throat. "Is she all right?"

"She is," Jack told him, watching the kid carefully. He was awfully…twitchy.

"Have you noticed anything out of the ordinary, son?"

The boy thought about it for a minute, then shook his head. "No, sir. But I'm not looking, either. I make my deliveries and head to the next drop."

Jefferson nodded. "That's a good lad. Thanks," he said, dismissing him with a nod. The older man speared Jack with a direct look. "I don't know what's going on, but that boy doesn't have anything to do with it," he said. "He's a good kid that's been dealt a bad hand. Those scars on his face? His dad gave them to him when he was eight."

Jack winced, more than a little shocked. What sort of parent purposely disfigured their own child like that? And those were the scars that could be seen. God only knew about the ones you couldn't.

Jack nodded, accepting the warning for what it was, but didn't intend to completely dismiss the kid. Point of fact, he couldn't afford to dismiss anyone at this stage of the investigation. And while it was entirely possible that he was just the type who got nervous around an unfamiliar adult, he hadn't seemed surprised that Mariette had been hurt and that threw up a red flag.

Jack pushed to his feet and extended his hand. "Thanks so much for your time, Mr. Jefferson."

"Most welcome," he said. "Let me know if there's anything at all I can do."

"If you notice anything out of the ordinary or—"

"I'll call you," Jefferson told him. He winced. "I hate that for Mariette. She's a good girl with a good heart. And next to my Martha, she makes the best pound cake I've ever had. Tell her I'm thinking of her, will you?"

"Of course." Jack made the return trek to his car and noticed that Bobby Ray had retreated to his own car for a smoke break. The dog sat next to the back tire, seemingly guarding the boy. Was Bobby Ray nervous? Jack wondered. Or was this simply a regular occurrence? Either way, he bore watching. Jack made note of the tag and waved on his way out. As soon as he turned onto the main road he dialed the office and asked for Payne.

"What's up?"

"I need you to run a tag for me. I've got a first and middle name, but not a last."

"Sure."

"Bobby Ray. The car is an older model Buick." He reeled off the series of numbers and letters. "He's the delivery boy for Jefferson's Dairy."

"You think he's got something to do with this?"

"It's too early to tell," Jack said. "But he was as nervous as a whore in church when he walked in and found me talking to his boss."

"He could always be in some other sort of trouble."

That was true, Jack knew. Those scars, in addition to being a constant reminder of his father's abuse, had more than likely made him an easy target, as well. And kids could be so damned cruel.

"Jefferson warned me off of him. Said he'd been dealt a rough hand."

Payne whistled low.

"I see you've found him. His father did that. When he was eight."

"*Damn*. Poor kid. His name is Bobby Ray Bishop," he said. "He's nineteen. I'll run a full background check and forward it to you with his address."

"Thanks, Payne. I appreciate it."

"How's Mariette?"

"She's cooperating," Jack told him with less confidence than he actually felt, but when in doubt, bluff, right? "I'm heading back over there now."

Much as it galled him to admit it, he couldn't deny the twinge of trepidation tightening his gut. Him, afraid? Of a little slip of a girl? He'd waded into gunfire, fought his way out of countless battles when death had been a serious concern—and Mariette Levine and her dairy thief were making him nervous?

It was ridiculous, Jack told himself, tapping a thumb against the steering wheel. Utterly stupid. It was this case, his first for Ranger Security, his only in the private sector. That was the root of the problem. A fear of failure, of not knowing the proper rules, nothing more.

And if he managed to sell that line of B.S. to himself, then there was some beach-front property in Oklahoma he needed to look at, as well. Jack snorted.

Sexy woman + small space + overnight stay = hell on earth…squared.

And he knew it.

RESIGNED AND MORE THAN A BIT chastened for being less than grateful when Payne had first told her his security plan, Mariette had decided that she was going to do everything within reason to make Jack comfortable. And frankly, she was just vain enough to want him to, at the very least, like her. Probably that was stupid, but as evidenced by her most recent failed romance, she didn't always make the most intelligent decisions.

That was a thought she'd need to ponder later.

Additionally, whatever hell he'd been through that Charlie had alluded to—her heart gave an involuntary squeeze—would certainly be compounded by staying away from his own place, a fact she should have considered when she was mentally whining about her own inconvenience.

And this particular inconvenience was for *her* safety.

The very least she could do was be gracious about it.

At present Jack and Charlie were briefing each other and, in order to give them a bit of privacy, she'd retreated to her apartment above the shop. Because she spent so little actual time in this space she hadn't had to do much in the way of cleaning it up for company. She'd dressed the spare bed in clean sheets, stocked his bathroom with plenty of linens and had made sure that the batteries in the seldom-used remote control for the television still held a charge.

Because she was still putting the bulk of her disposable income back into the shop, her apartment had been decorated with hand-me-downs from her aunt, thrift-store finds, the occasional antique and do-it-yourself art.

She'd framed some of her favorite old album covers, picked up bits of old wrought iron and beaten-up architectural pieces salvaged from old homes. Her curtains were bits of scrap fabric with hot-glued hems and had been hung with pretty up-holstery tacks that she'd nailed directly into the window frame. It was junk-store chic, she liked to joke, but it was home and she loved it.

He rapped softly at the door and called her name. A line of gooseflesh raced down her back and she sank her teeth into her bottom lip as that same phenomenal need she'd experienced in the shop earlier broadsided her.

And she'd only heard his voice.

"In here," she said, feeling unaccountably nervous. *Geez Lord, Mariette. Get a grip.* She'd actually popped up earlier in the day and put a couple of baking potatoes into the Crock-Pot, an ingenious tip she'd learned from Aunt Marianne. Between her mother and her aunt, she'd been thoroughly educated on all things relevant and domestic. She felt a grin twitch at her lips. The whole how-to-choose-a-good-man lesson had been the only one that hadn't stuck.

Mariette had harvested enough fresh greens from her rooftop greenhouse—another little sanctuary—for a couple of salads and had just put the steaks beneath the broiler when she felt him move into the kitchen. The atmosphere seemed to change, become more charged. The fine hairs on the back of her neck prickled and a tremor raced along her fingers.

"Something smells good," he said, venturing farther into the room. His mere presence considerably lessened the space, made her feel small but, curiously, not claustrophobic. "I hope you didn't go to a lot of trouble."

Mariette smiled drolly. "Then you're different from the rest of your gender," she said, shooting him a look over her shoulder. "In my experience, men like it when women go to a lot of trouble, particularly where it pertains to food."

He chuckled softly. "A really good meal is a gift that most anyone with a brain should appreciate. Is there anything I can do to help?"

She gestured to two empty glasses on the counter. "You could put some ice in those. There's tea in the fridge."

Looking as at-home as it was possible to be for someone who didn't live there, Jack did as she asked. She darted another look over her shoulder at him, and smiled when she realized his head damned near brushed the suspended light fixture. She chuckled under her breath.

"What's funny?" he asked suspiciously. "Don't tell me I've done this wrong. I was always the official drink maker at our house growing up. Charlie set the table, I handled the drinks. I'm a champion tea pourer. I couldn't have possibly screwed this up."

Mariette laughed harder and shook her head. "It's not that," she said, giggling. "I was thinking about Livvie's 'corn man' comment earlier today." She turned the steaks. "Another inch and some green paint and you *could* pass for the Jolly Green Giant."

He sighed dramatically and shook his head. "Out of all the tall men she could have chosen, that's the one I brought to mind. A man in a leaf dress with girlie little booties on his feet?"

She swiveled to look at him. "He's wearing booties? Seriously?"

"This isn't the first time I've been mistaken for the big green guy," Jack told her. "It's always a kid's first frame of reference."

"And what tall man would you rather be mistaken for?" she asked, quirking a brow.

He shrugged magnanimously and took a sip of his tea. "Atlas works."

She felt a choked laugh break loose in her throat. "Atlas?"

"Hey, don't knock him," Jack told her. "It's a big job, holding up the world."

She turned back to the stove and chewed the inside of her cheek. "True," she conceded. "I suppose I'd rather be compared to Atlas than the Jolly Green Giant if I was tall, too."

"Damn straight," he said with a grim nod. "I'd never wear a dress or booties."

"But the loincloth would work for you?" Dammit, she shouldn't have asked that question because she could most assuredly see him being able to rock a loincloth. Her gaze turned inward at the thought and she unwittingly held her breath. *Sleek, sculpted muscle and fine bone structure, his masculine form a bare work of art...*

"I don't know about that," he said with a humble

nod. "But I'd prefer it to the other, that's for damned sure." He shot her a speculative glance and a wicked gleam entered his blue gaze. "I suppose you get mistaken for Julia Child all the time."

"Right," she said with a snort. "Because I'm also six two and we favor so much."

He arched a surprised brow. "Julia Child was six two?"

She nodded. Mariette Levine, gatherer of pointless trivia.

He hummed under his breath, seemingly filing that away. "You don't favor anybody I've ever seen," he said a beat later, his gaze drifting over her face as though trying to figure out what it was exactly that made her so different.

"Thank you," she murmured. Heat spread over her face. "I think."

"It's a compliment," he said. "You weren't at all what I was expecting."

Then that made two of them. Because she'd met most of the men who worked for Ranger Security she should have anticipated a fit, attractive guy—the rest of them certainly were. But none of them tripped her trigger the way this one had. She'd never looked at any one of them and felt her personal mercury hit critical mass in the time it took to draw a breath.

No man ever had, for that matter.

Remember the man hiatus, Mariette? Remember Nathaniel? Remember feeling stupid?

Evidently not.

"Oh?" she remarked, blatantly fishing. "How so?"

"I'd expected you to be older. I like your name—it's very different and it suits you—but it's a bit old-fashioned and, as such, I had this mental image of a plump, gray-haired granny with soft cheeks and laugh lines." He paused and sucked in a long breath, his eyes widening significantly as his gaze once again raked her from head to toe. "You're...not," he finished on a laughing exhale.

Wow.

"Not yet, anyway," she said, feeling feminine delight bloom in her chest and a corresponding tug deep in the heart of her sex. Mercy, that look...

And yes, she knew her name sounded old-fashioned...but that's not where it had come from. She inwardly grinned. Its origins were as unique and singular as her mother had been. And that was saying something.

She plated their steaks so that they could rest, then added the salad and potatoes and moved everything to the table. He pulled her chair out for her—an unexpected gesture she'd admit to enjoying—then took the seat opposite.

Mariette cleared her throat and cut into her baked potato. "My mother named me after her two favorite things," she said, her tone purposely light and matter-of-fact.

He carved off a bit of steak. "Really? What

was that?" He popped the bite into his mouth and groaned appreciatively.

Mariette dropped a large pat of butter into her steaming potato, then looked up and smiled. "My aunt Marianne and Smurfette."

5

JACK CHOKED, HIS EYES watering. He thumped his fist against his sternum and tried to swallow, then gulped down some tea.

Eyes twinkling, she continued to blithely eat her food. "You okay?" she asked, arching an innocent brow.

He cleared his aching throat. "Yes," he wheezed. "Just trying to make my lungs digest some food. Wonder of wonders, they're not designed for that."

She chuckled. "Sorry. I should have let you swallow it first."

"Smurfette?" he all but croaked. "Your mother named you after a little blue cartoon character? Seriously?"

"And my Aunt Marianne," she reminded him.

"That's…interesting," he said with a burst of air, because honestly he couldn't think of anything else to say. He'd heard lots of interesting names over the years and the tales of how they'd come about—hell, he was named after a damned tree—but this one… This one certainly took top billing for ingenuity and definitely fell into the WTF category.

"She had Down's," Mariette said, looking from beneath a sweep of dark lashes, evidently to gauge his reaction.

Oh. *Oh.*

Admittedly, this was a degree more shocking than how she'd gotten her name, but Jack kept his expression neutral. She'd said it without the smallest trace of self-consciousness or inflection. She might have said the sky was blue or "pass the salt." It was a simple, matter-of-fact statement. And it was in the past tense. Though he longed to ask several questions, he chose one he hoped was innocent enough.

He forked up a bite of salad. "What was her name?"

"Marlena."

"Also unusual," he commented, still trying to find footing in this treacherous terrain. "But lovely."

"She was a lovely person," Mariette said, her tone fond and wistful. "We lost her three years ago. Heart failure." She winced. "Sadly, it's all too common among those with the condition."

He swallowed. "I'm sorry."

"She was only seventeen when I was born," she said, continuing in that same flat tone. Her lips twisted into a bitter mockery of a smile. "My father, whom I fondly refer to as Wretched Bastard, was a caregiver at the day facility where she worked."

Oh, Jesus, Jack thought, reeling. He set his fork aside. That sick son of a bitch. Because she was his only point of reference, Livvie immediately sprung to mind and he wondered what sort of man it took to do something like that—something so heinous—to a person so innocent. So purely *good*. He set his jaw so hard he feared it would crack.

He closed his eyes, summoning patience from a higher source, then opened them again. "Please tell me he did time."

She snorted. "Not enough. Eighteen months."

Jack swore hotly.

She cocked her head, shot him a sad smile. "Everyone always assumes that having a mother with Down's had to be hard for me," she said, her gaze tangling with his. "But it was exactly the opposite. My mother was good and kind and loved me with the same sort of devotion any mother ever loved a child. She was the gentlest, sweetest person I've ever known." Her voice hardened. "Having that sort of evil for a father? Knowing that his tainted blood runs in my veins? *That* was the hard part."

He could certainly see where that would be true. Talk about two opposite ends of the spectrum. No wonder she was unlike any person he'd ever met. Her history was definitely more unique than anyone in his experience.

"Sorry," she said, giving her head a small shake. "I just find that it's easier to get that little bit of information out of the way. There are pictures of her—of us—all over the apartment and since you're going to be staying here…" She trailed off. "And it's not something I hide," she added, lifting her chin. "I was proud to be her daughter."

He completely understood. And he had no doubt that her mother was equally proud of her.

She straightened, her posture heralding a subject change. "So what did Mr. Jefferson have to say?"

Though he knew he'd have to review this conversation again at some point later, Jack laughed and wiped his mouth with his napkin. "You mean other than telling me to get married or learn to cook? Not a whole helluva lot actually."

Her pale gray eyes widened significantly and she laughed, the sound unreserved, full and throaty. Sexy. "Get m-married or l-learn to c-cook?" she repeated, still chuckling under her breath. "What did you do to provoke such a lecture?"

"What did *I* do?" he parroted, feigning offense. "*I* didn't do anything. I was merely looking at all the empty TV-dinner trays in his garbage can and that brought on the marriage sermon."

She winced, her gaze softening with sympathy. "Poor Audwin," she said. "I took a meal out there right after Martha died, but I haven't been back since." She paused thoughtfully. "I need to do that," she said. "If nothing else I can start sending a few home-cooked things with Bobby Ray when he brings my delivery by."

Ah. "Speaking of Bobby Ray," Jack said leadingly. "What do you think of him?"

Mariette paused to look at him and, much like Audwin Jefferson, something akin to irritation flashed in her gaze. She lifted her chin a fraction of an inch—he loved that quirk—and the mulish gesture was so reminiscent of his sister he wondered if Charlie had taught it to her already. "I think he's a sweet kid who's had a hardscrabble life and is constantly judged on his appearance rather than who he is underneath those scars." She nodded succinctly. "That's what I think of Bobby Ray. I am absolutely certain he has nothing to do with this."

All righty then. "Retract the claws, please, Mariette," Jack told her placatingly, essaying a grin. *Hey, underdogs, here's your champion*, he thought, admiring her spunk. "I'm not judging him on anything but the way he acted when I saw him at the dairy this afternoon."

She blinked, evidently falling off her soapbox. "How was he acting at the dairy? What do you mean?"

Jack hesitated, trying to pinpoint exactly what it was about the kid's behavior that had signaled a misgiving, set off an alarm. "He was bit squirrely," he said. "Unaccountably nervous."

"You're huge," she said, gesturing with a breezy hand to his body as though it should be obvious. "He was probably terrified of you."

Jack winced and passed a palm over his face to wipe away a smile. "You keep this up and I'm going to get a complex. Jolly Green Giant. Huge." His gaze tangled with hers. "I'm tall, Mariette," he explained with exaggerated patience. "The word you're looking for is *tall*."

Her eyes twinkled with unabashed humor and something else, something almost…sinful and damned sure dangerous. "Right," she said, nodding in concession. "No need to freak out. You're tall." She looked away, her eyes widening significantly, and chewed the corner of her mouth. "And a wee bit sensitive, evidently."

Jack laughed and shook his head. "Smart-ass."

She shrugged unrepentantly. "It's a gift," she quipped. She stood then and began clearing the table. "So, is that what you and Charlie were talking about then? Bobby Ray?"

Jack stood, as well, brought his plate into the kitchen, rinsed it off and loaded it into the dishwasher. She'd paused and was staring at him, seemingly transfixed.

"What?" he asked, perplexed at her expression. "Is there something on my face?"

"Are you married?"

That certainly came out of left field. Hadn't they covered this? In a roundabout way, at least? "No."

"Ever been married?"

"No."

"Then who trained you?"

He blinked. "Come again?"

"You just *got up from the table, rinsed your plate and loaded it into the dishwasher.* That's *learned* behavior. It's not normal to your kind."

He laughed out loud, the sound a bit rusty from disuse. Clearly it had been too long since he'd really laughed. "My kind? What am I? Some sort of foreign species?"

She shot him a speculative glance, one that seemed to peer directly into his brain, and grinned. "I don't know what you are, but you aren't normal, that's for sure."

Well, if lazy assholes who didn't appreciate a meal well enough to help clean up was her normal then he was glad, in this instance, to be *ab*normal. Of course, this line of thought brought on a completely new set of questions, ones he didn't have any right to ask. If he was the exception to the rule, then who had been the guy—or guys, he thought ominously—who'd made it? Who'd been the lazy, ungrateful dickhead who'd set the damned precedent?

He instantly hated him, whoever he was.

Irrational? Most definitely. He cast a brooding glance at Mariette, who was busy dumping the leftover salad into a plastic container. The overhead light cast a golden glow over her dark hair, picking up the rich auburn tones. He loved her hair. It was long and hung in wavy layers that framed her face and curled ever so slightly around her beautiful, full breasts.

Longing knifed through him, cutting him to the quick. Heat raced through his blood and settled in his groin and his fingers itched with the need to touch her, to see if her skin was as soft as it looked. Particularly the smooth line of it that ran over her jaw. He caught her particular scent, something slightly exotic with vanilla undertones.

She wore a long-sleeve, lime-green shirt with her logo emblazoned on the pocket and a pair of jeans that were worn and comfortable looking. They didn't so much hug her frame as caress it, molding around her curves as though they'd been especially designed with her in mind. She'd kicked off her shoes—he'd noticed them by the door when he'd come in—and was padding around in her socked feet.

There was something especially endearing about that, but for the life of him he couldn't have explained why. They were feet, for heaven's sake. And the socks were cute, inasmuch as he imagined socks could be. Hers were white with little black Scottie dogs scattered all over them. The dogs were wearing red bowties.

She paused and her gaze followed his. She wiggled her toes and grinned. "Don't make fun," she said. "Livvie gave them to me."

He leaned a hip against the countertop. "I wasn't going to make fun. I like them."

Her smile widened. "I'll tell her so that she can get you a pair, as well. You never answered my question."

"What question? There's been a question amid all the insults you've hurled in my direction?" he teased.

She ducked her head. "Showing me your sensitive side again, are you?"

Jack took a deep breath. "Honest to God, woman, you—"

Her gaze slid away from his, but he caught the curl of her lips all the same. "I'd asked you if that's what you and Charlie had been talking about," she interrupted. "Bobby Ray?" she prodded.

Oh. Right. "As a matter of fact, yes," he said, reminded of his real purpose here. Flirting, fun as it was proving to be, wasn't it, dammit. "I know that you think that he's not involved in this, but I still believe he bears a little investigation."

Skepticism wrinkled her otherwise smooth brow. "Based on him being 'nervous'?"

"Physical tells are just as significant as verbal ones."

She momentarily stilled, then looked over at him. "What do you mean?"

How odd. If he didn't know any better he'd think

she was the nervous one. But what the hell could she possibly have to hide?

"I mean that sometimes our actions give us away long before our mouths do." His gaze dropped to hers and he had to force it back up. *Exactly like that*, he wanted to say.

She licked her lips and swallowed. More torture. "He could have been nervous for a variety of reasons, couldn't he? Did you talk to anyone else at the dairy? Anyone besides Audwin?"

"No," he admitted. "But I've got a background check running on Bobby Ray and am going to do the same thing with the rest of Mr. Jefferson's employees. If there's a red flag, then I'll find it."

"But not Audwin?" she asked, a smile playing over her lips. "What makes you so certain that it wasn't him who threw the dough roller at me?"

Jack crossed his arms over his chest and studied her for a moment, then came to an interesting conclusion. She was arguing for the simple sport of it. How bizarre that he found that attractive, when he couldn't remember ever liking this sort of conversation before. Of course, he wasn't used to a woman arguing with him. No brag, just fact. They typically agreed with everything he said and fell right into bed with him. He'd always liked that—it was expedient, uncomplicated—but wasn't so sure he would now. She'd...changed things.

Damn.

"You said your attacker was tall and skinny," he told her, determined to prove his point, if for no other reason than to show her that he could. "Audwin is not. He's on the short side with a potbelly, and I'd be willing to bet if I looked in his closet he wouldn't have a sweatshirt much less a hoodie." He shot her a grin. "I am certain, however, that I would find lots of flannel. Furthermore, Audwin is left-handed and based on the way you described what happened, your guy threw with his right hand. Additionally, Audwin's hands are so riddled with arthritis I doubt he could grasp a rolling pin well enough to pick it up, much less throw it at you with any accuracy whatsoever." He pulled a shrug. "Based on those things I was able to rule him out as our possible offender."

She blinked owlishly at him for a moment, evidently absorbing that information. "And you got all of that from what little I said and one meeting with Audwin?"

He nodded. "I did."

She looked insultingly surprised. "Well, I guess you know what you're doing, then."

A dry bark of laughter erupted from his throat before he could stop it. Talk about damning with faint praise. He'd been a friggin' Ranger, dammit. One of the best trained soldiers on the planet. "One would hope."

She had the grace to blush. "I'm sorry," she said. "That didn't come out exactly the way I'd intended.

I'm sure you know what you're doing. It's just that there's really not that much to go on. Payne can't leave you here indefinitely and—"

Jack chuckled and shook his head. "Do you know Brian Payne?"

She frowned. "Well, of course I know him. I've known him for years. He—"

"Then you know that once he's taken something on he's not going to let it go until it's finished." He leveled a look at her. "I'm afraid you're stuck with me until then."

Her eyes rounded and she muttered a curse. "It's not that. I don't mind that you're here, really."

He just stared at her.

"I don't!" she insisted. "I don't like being told what to do and that's how this whole thing was presented—after I'd been knocked unconscious, by the way, so I wasn't really at my best—but I honestly don't mind and I'm genuinely grateful that I have friends who want to protect me." She swallowed. "It means a lot."

A woman who didn't like being told what to do? How novel, Jack thought with a snort. And he supposed having her home and place of business seemingly hijacked after another asshole had broken in and assaulted her would make her feel a bit out of control. He couldn't fault her for that.

He smiled and released a deep breath. "It means a lot to me, as well. This is my first case and if I can't catch a damned Butter Bandit, then I'm in the wrong line of work."

She lifted her shoulders in a weak shrug and grinned wanly. "He's slippery."

"He's an amateur who has gotten lucky," Jack told her, laughing at the bad pun. "I also think he's someone who is familiar with your setup here, otherwise he wouldn't know exactly what he was doing."

She winced. "I'd actually thought about that." She pursed her lips. "I still don't think it's Bobby Ray."

Interestingly enough, she didn't sound nearly as convinced as she had before. He hated to destroy her illusions about the boy, but there was something not right there. Call it a gut instinct, a premonition, a second sense or whatever, but every bit of intuition he possessed told him that the boy was involved somehow.

And Mariette wasn't the only one who was going to be hurt if Bobby Ray was ultimately behind this— Audwin Jefferson would be, as well. The older man had been just as quick—if not quicker—to jump to Bobby Ray's defense.

And if both of them were willing to stick up for him, then they had to see something in him that compelled that sort of response. Audwin seemed like a decent enough judge of character and, no longer than he'd known Mariette, he could tell she wasn't the sort of person who wasted her regard on those who didn't deserve it.

There was much more to this than what met the eye, Jack decided. He just hoped he was able to find out what that was before any more damage was done.

Mariette hid a yawn behind her hand.

"You must be exhausted," Jack told her. "You couldn't have gotten much sleep last night."

"Not of the restful sort, no," she admitted. "I keep early hours. I'm normally in the bakery by 4:00 a.m."

"Four?" Damn. That was early.

"I have a two-day policy," Mariette told him. "If something sits in the case for more than forty-eight hours it goes to various agencies around the city—I don't throw them out. I can't abide the waste. But I like to keep the front stocked with my freshest products. That means all new stuff every other day."

He nodded, impressed. "It seems to be working for you."

"It is," she confirmed, a rather pleased tilt to her ripe little mouth. "But I work hard, so that's only fair, right?"

"Most definitely." His gaze drifted over her face, noting the fatigue weighting her lids. "Why don't you go on to bed, then? I'll keep watch."

"All night?" she asked, evidently alarmed. "But when are you supposed to sleep?"

"I'll sleep," he told her. "I've got to set some alarms for the doors and windows and I'm going to review some stuff that Payne was supposed to forward to me. I'll catnap," he assured her, touched by her concern. He was used to his mother and sister fussing over him, but this was a new experience. Pleasant as it was, he wasn't altogether sure he liked it. "I'm used to long hours."

And he fully expected the ones that loomed in front of him to be some of the longest he'd ever experienced.

The hottest, most interesting woman he'd ever met sleeping in a bed mere feet from him—and she had to be off-limits.

Nothing more than self-preservation told him that.

6

DESPITE THE FACT THAT she was beyond exhausted, Mariette couldn't sleep. Typically, this wasn't a problem. Because she wasn't the sort of person who could leap out of bed and be happy and alert and ready to conquer the day—rah! rah! rah!—she was up at three, coffee in hand by three oh five. She liked to check her email, update the website for the shop and ease gently into her morning, like slipping into a warm bath.

By the time she'd had breakfast, showered and tidied up her apartment she was grounded enough in her own company to be able to face the day. From the moment she went downstairs until after 6:00 p.m., she didn't get a single minute to herself unless it was to go to the bathroom.

And she was open seven days a week. The church crowd always came by on Sunday mornings and, until she got the bulk of her equipment paid for and her mortgage paid off, she didn't anticipate being able to change her hours or take a full day off. She did close at one on Sundays, but ordinarily used that time to try new recipes and perfect others, and if she wasn't doing that, then she was hosting birthday parties, baby showers or bridal teas.

In short, she was always busy—there was always something to do—and, as such, being able to fall asleep was never a problem. Drifting off on the couch on the rare nights she tried to watch a movie or read a book was a more common issue. Maybe that was part of her Problem With Men. Impaired judgment from lack of rest? Mariette gave a mental shrug. In lieu of anything else, she'd take it.

Nathaniel, aka Crooked Dick, had been forever insisting that she take off and leave one of her girls in charge and, while she imagined that seemed like a reasonable request, Mariette had just never been able to do it. She'd put everything she had into her business—building it had to come first. She should have known when he'd made the you-make-cookies-you're-not-saving-the-world comment that he wasn't the guy for her.

Asshole.

She didn't give a damn if she was a Porta-Potty cleaner, she'd still give it her best effort. *Anything worth doing is worth doing right*, Aunt Marianne used to always say.

Interestingly enough, she got the impression that

Jack Martin was the same, adhered to the same standard no matter what he was doing. He seemed just as
concerned with catching her Butter Bandit as he did
with anything else. No doubt those especially keen
observation skills and attention to detail had made
him a fine soldier.

Honestly, it was those very skills that had made
her unaccountably nervous. If he'd seen that much
after a few minutes interviewing Audwin Jefferson
and a passing glance at Bobby Ray, then what had
he noticed about her? What sort of observations had
he made?

She was almost afraid to speculate.

Mariette had never mastered the art of hiding her
feelings. If she was mad, she said so. If she was
happy, she said that, too. Living with her mother,
she'd had to be an excellent communicator and there-
fore never tried to hold anything back or hide. While
her mother might have missed sarcasm and the like,
she was top-notch at reading moods, could pick up
on the tiniest shift in Mariette's demeanor. Even
if she'd been so inclined, there'd been no point in
trying to conceal her feelings.

And until all six and half feet of his splendidly
proportioned frame had come walking through her
door she'd never had to worry about it.

But no one had ever affected her quite so strongly
before in her life. No one had ever made her feel *so
much*. On a physical level, he didn't just flip every

switch, he fried the circuits. *The size of his hands, the breadth of his shoulders. All that mouth-watering muscle.* The hot way he ducked his head and smiled when imparting a small joke, the simple quirk of his lips, the barest hint of a dimple in his cheek…and she became a quivering, all-but-drooling pile of goo.

She released a shaky breath.

And then there was the way he moved. It was one of the sexiest things she believed she'd ever seen. It was this loose-hipped, rolling sort of gait that telegraphed his strength, his confidence, his very badass-ness. There was something uniquely intense about him, a banked sort of energy bubbling just beneath the surface. Still waters might run deep, but Jack Martin was more like a tsunami.

And seeing that kind of power gentle with a smile for a girl like Livvie. Seeing the genuine tenderness in his gaze, his desire to please her…

Now, that was some kind of man. That took strength.

And he was in her living room, Mariette thought, her nipples tingling at the thought. She could hear the low hum of the television, the occasional noise that signaled a shift on the couch, a clink of ice hitting the side of a glass. For whatever reason, she'd imagined having a man stay here with her would feel odd, would pollute her space, even—despite her poor choices, she'd never let a man sleep over before—but Jack seemed to be the exception to that rule.

When she'd come out to tell him good-night after taking her shower, she'd found him staring at a photograph on her mantel, a soft smile on his lips. It was one of her favorites—a candid Aunt Marianne had taken of her and her mother at the beach. She'd been five at the time. They'd had on matching sun hats, sitting toe-to-toe, legs spread-eagle, building a sand castle between them. They'd worn the same identical expression of concentration.

"You were a chubby kid," he'd said, pointing out a fat roll, then had gestured to the painted flames canvas in the hearth where a real fire would have been if the chimney would have worked. "Toasty."

Mariette giggled, remembering, and flopped restlessly onto her back. Glanced at the clock. Three minutes had passed since the last time she'd looked at it. Sheesh. This was ridiculous. He was here so that she *could* go to sleep, so that she could rest without worrying.

How ironic that her very protection would be the thing that would keep her up at night.

She was too tightly wound, too aware of her own body and it had been too long since her last orgasm. And he was too hot and too close and too…everything else.

A low throb built in her sex in time with the steady beat of her heart and her nipples pearled even tighter behind her pajama top. A soft hiss slipped between her lips and she shifted, pressing her legs more tightly together to ease the seemingly unending ache.

If anything, that made it worse.

Mariette rolled her head to look at the clock again and then whimpered softly in frustration. Two minutes since the last time. Shit. She was doomed. There was no way in hell she was going to be able to fall asleep in this sort of state. With a resigned sigh, she pushed up out of bed, slipped her feet into her Betty Boop house shoes and padded quietly into the living room.

Jack smiled when he saw her and pulled one of those small earbuds from his left ear. He'd been looking at something on his laptop screen, but nonchalantly closed the lid when she'd walked in.

Too nonchalantly.

Damn, she hoped he hadn't been watching internet porn. Watching porn while he was supposed to be protecting her would demote him from perfect-guy status and kill her lady-bits-quiver-for-him permanently.

"Is something wrong?" he asked, his brow wrinkling. "Am I keeping you up?"

In a manner of speaking, yes, but she could hardly say that, now, could she? He'd changed into a pair of loose pajama pants, the kind that tied at the waist, and a dark T-shirt. His gun was lying within reach on the end table and seeing it gave her a little shiver of dread. She sincerely hoped he wouldn't need that.

"No," she lied. "I was just thirsty." She pointed awkwardly to the kitchen and, feeling ridiculous, headed in that direction.

Liquor, Mariette thought. Liquor never failed to put her to sleep. She'd never been much of a drinker—preferred to have control of herself at all times—but on the rare occasions she'd indulged she'd ended up quite mellow and sleepy. She poked around in the cabinets, trying not to make too much noise in the process, and then finally located the bourbon she typically used to make praline sauce. Rather than dirty a glass, she just ducked low and tipped the bottle up.

It belatedly occurred to her that she probably looked like an alcoholic sneaking a quick fix, which was of course the moment Jack cleared his throat.

"How rude," he chided from the doorway, an amused smile on his lips. He tsked. "You could have at least offered to share."

CURLED UP IN THE backseat of his car, which he'd parked at a local truck stop, Billy Ray huddled deeper into his coat and tried in vain to keep his teeth from chattering. He'd stayed inside the diner for as long as he could without drawing any suspicion—or getting run off for loitering—then had reluctantly left the cozy warmth for his chilly Buick. He couldn't afford to run the car all night—it would use too much gas—and wished he would have thought to bring a blanket from his motel room.

He was absolutely freezing.

But at least he was alive.

And if Uncle Mackie got ahold of him, he knew he'd be praying for death, so, ultimately, this was the better alternative.

Because he knew Uncle Mackie had someone watching his motel room, he didn't dare go back there—wasn't safe—and now that the big guy was snooping around for Mariette, he couldn't afford to attempt to go after the coin again.

At least not yet.

He'd have to at some point—he wouldn't have a choice—but doing it on the heels of what had happened last night would no doubt be a terrible mistake and he'd made so many of those already...

At least he hadn't seriously injured her, Bobby Ray told himself, still appalled that he'd hit her with that damned dough roller. He liked Mariette. She didn't look at him the way other people did, with suspicion in their eyes and a predisposed inclination to distrust him.

Like Audwin, Mariette never failed to offer him a real smile—he knew the difference, was familiar enough with the other kind to spot the genuine article—and usually insisted that he take some sort of snack with him when he left her shop. He'd cruised by after he'd left work and, to his profound relief, had spotted her in her usual place behind the counter.

Despair closed in on him again and he could feel tears clog the back of his throat. He swallowed them back, forcing them to recede. Bad things always happened when he cried. In fact, he hadn't shed a tear since he was eight years old and his old man had given him this ghastly permanent smile.

He always found it odd that people stared at him—he couldn't bear to look at himself.

He really hated that he'd mucked things up, that he'd made such terrible decisions, that, ultimately, he was stealing from the only people who'd ever made him feel like more than a second-class citizen, but he just didn't see any other way. He either paid Uncle Mackie back or they'd hurt him and Billy Ray was sick to death of being hurt. Of being someone else's punching bag.

If he could only get the coin…

What was it one of his foster mother had always said? *If dreams were horses, then beggars would ride.* He laughed miserably.

That pretty much summed up the state of things, didn't it?

It was hopeless, Bobby Ray thought. There was no way out. And until he got that coin back he had no choice but to take another one.

The mere idea made him sick and his stomach suddenly heaved. He quickly leaned over and emptied it into the floorboard, then wiped a shaky hand over the back of his mouth and fought misery.

As usual, he lost.

JACK FOUND MARIETTE crouched furtively in front of the kitchen counter, bottle tipped back like a seasoned drinker. He enjoyed the blinking, miserable alarm that skittered across her expression the minute he'd caught her.

Eyes wide, her long dark hair hanging in a tangled curtain around her face, she slowly lowered the bottle and winced at the burn. "This is not what it looks like," she said in a low wheeze.

He raised a brow and leaned against the doorjamb. "Oh?"

Rather than get up, she exhaled mightily, settled on her rear end and relaxed against the cabinets. She wore a pair of pale blue flannel pajamas decorated with cupcakes and a to-hell-with-it resigned smile. She lifted her shoulders in a small shrug. "It helps me sleep."

"They make medication for that, you know."

She took another swig, the delicate muscles in her creamy throat working as she swallowed and then hiccupped rather adorably. "This is faster."

He chuckled and shook his head, sincerely hoping that it wasn't his fault that she couldn't sleep. He didn't think that he'd made that much noise, but who knew? He'd actually turned up the volume on his hearing aid so that he wouldn't miss any noise from downstairs and had been watching one of his lip-reading tutorials online to pass some of the time.

He had to do something that was going to require enough of his attention to forget about her being just a room away.

As the night progressed, he'd become more aware of her and less concerned with the consequences.

Not good.

Honestly, when she'd walked into the living room after her shower, her face scrubbed clean, her nose shiny and all that hair pulled up into a wet knot on top of her head… Just remembering made blood race to his groin, made his balls tighten and his dick swell. Unbound breasts, the hint of nipple behind fabric, that generous ass…

Hands down one of the sexiest things he'd ever seen.

And, remarkably, she'd been fully clothed.

At least, on the surface, anyway.

He imagined that the rest of her skin beneath the fluffy floor-length chenille robe she'd been wearing was just as lovely and dewy soft as her face had been. He didn't know what sort of soap she'd used—though he fully intended to investigate that later out of nothing but sheer curiosity—but it had followed her into the living room and had smelled so damned good he'd wanted to slide his nose along her neck and inhale the skin in the hollow of her collarbone. It was something exotic with vanilla undertones, sexy and wholesome and unaccountably mouthwatering.

She was mouthwatering.

And knowing that she was so close—all but breathing the same air—and yet untouchable had been unbelievably torturous. He'd desperately needed a distraction, one that would require a great deal of concentration on his part, so watching the videos had been his first thought.

And they were typically his last, as well.

Jack had come to terms with leaving the military, had even been able to shift the blame off his shoulders because, ultimately, he'd done everything he was supposed to do. War was war and there were times when, even with every precaution in place, people were still going to get hurt, still going to die. Seeing any life cut short was awful—heart wrenching—but he'd had a soft spot for Johnson. The boy had been barely twenty, smart and hardworking with a moral compass that didn't drift the way so many of his contemporaries did. The military had made a man out of him much more quickly than the real world would have done and he'd acclimated well, with grace and wisdom beyond his years. He'd had so much potential and his death, aside from being horrible, was such a waste.

That he'd been desperately trying to share his dying words with Jack—his expression, the fear, the very need that had been written in his panicked eyes—was something that haunted him mercilessly. He could remember *everything* about that encounter down to the last detail, from the specks and smudges of dirt on Johnson's face to the way his mouth moved while he was talking. It wasn't until he went to get his last hearing aid and he'd noticed a teenager at the clinic lip-reading that it occurred to him that he could learn, and once he learned it, he could figure out exactly what it was that Johnson had been trying to tell him.

Once that was done, he could finally close that chapter of his life and move on. Or as much as he imagined he'd ever be able to, anyway. But if it had been important enough that he'd spent his last breath trying to share it with him, Jack knew that this was something that he couldn't simply ignore. He had a duty to the boy to see whatever it was through.

And he would.

His gaze drifted over Mariette once more, her lush little body hugged in warm flannel, her creamy cheeks pinkened from the alcohol and a pang of longing—and something else, something much more significant and harder to define—shot through him. He'd never met anyone quite like her before, who engaged every single part of him the way she did. The desire was legendary, singular even, and more pressing than anything he'd ever experienced…but it was much more than that.

She was much more than that.

She was intriguing, a mystery, an enigma wrapped in cupcake pajamas and vanilla scent. She was hardworking and tenderhearted, creative and smart, loyal to those who earned her favor and quick to champion them if she felt they were threatened.

She was also single, which boggled the mind.

He couldn't believe that no one had snapped her up yet. That some enterprising young professional hadn't dragged her to the altar and impregnated her posthaste. Because he was unnaturally curious about her, Jack had looked at every picture that was on display and noted the distinct absence of a current or even a past significant other. He couldn't imagine that it was anything but her choice. So…why? Had the actions of her father so permanently put her off men that she'd paint them all with the same brush? Or was it something else?

These were things that were none of his business and yet he fully intended to find out the answers to them.

Irrationally, he *needed* to know.

She looked up at him, her pale gray eyes a little less focused than they were previously, and with a slow smile of the mildly impaired, offered him the bottle.

Chuckling under his breath, Jack sidled forward and accepted it, then placed it carefully on the counter. He offered her a hand. "Think you can sleep now?"

She looked at his hand as though it were a foreign object, then back at him, almost balefully. She swallowed hard. "Probably not, but I should try."

With a resigned sigh she grabbed hold and allowed him to help her up. She stood a little too quickly, wobbled, and fell against his chest. She inhaled sharply at the contact—a telling breath, both music and doom to his ears—and looked up at him.

The need he saw there nearly felled him.

She was soft and warm, her unbound breasts pressed against him and her scent tangled around him. He was literally burning up from the inside out and yet he was frozen, couldn't have moved if his life depended on it.

He'd instinctively wrapped an arm around her waist to keep her from falling and, though he knew he should let go, couldn't seem to get his brain to make the required command that would move her away from him, that would disconnect whatever it was that was happening between them. This close he could see little bursts of green radiating from her pupil and a tiny freckle to the bottom left of her eye.

He was hit with the insane urge to taste it.

Need slammed into him, gluing his feet even more firmly to the floor, and his heart decided to abandon traditional beating and move at a skipping, breakneck pace that made him light-headed and breathless. *Him,* breathless? He swallowed a maniacal laugh as he considered the incongruity. This sensation, this phenomenon, was so intense and so singular he didn't know whether to be thrilled or ter-rified.

Her wide-eyed gaze was strangely confused and resigned as it searched his, then darkened and dropped hungrily to his mouth.

He went hard.

She noticed.

She released a fatalistic breath, muttered "Oh, to hell with it," and then went up on tiptoe and pressed her mouth to his.

The shock of it—the sheer perfection—made him stagger against the counter and he pulled her with him. The road to hell might be paved with good intentions, Jack thought, but the heaven along the journey was bound to make up for the eventual des-tination.

Surely they wouldn't fire him over a kiss—just *kissing* their friend, Jack thought dimly, and if they did…

Screw them. It was worth it.

7

HAD SHE NEVER TOUCHED HIM—had he never offered her that beautifully large, masculine-veined hand—Mariette imagined that she might not have behaved so shamelessly. She might not have stumbled into his magnificently muscled frame and, had she never known what it felt like to be held so closely by someone who a) turned her lady business into a sauna, b) made her feel strangely protected and safe and c) had the most kissable mouth she'd ever seen, then she might have been able to summon the required wherewithal to back away from him.

She was supposed to be practicing The Hiatus From Men, after all.

But since Jack Martin did that and oh-so-much more, she'd been doomed to failure.

Depending on how one decided to look at it.

And considering she was too busy trying to see

if she could crawl out of her skin and into his, she wasn't looking at anything at all.

She was relishing the deliberate, wholly thrilling slide of his lips against hers, the taste of his expert tongue as it plunged into her mouth and swept the sensitive recesses with a skilled sort of accuracy that most men never bothered to learn because they were too busy trying to move on to the next base.

Despite the fact that she could feel his *more than substantial* erection nudging high up on her belly and she knew that he was as reluctantly snarled up into this mindless heat between them, Jack had made no impatient move to take things to the next level.

He was feeding at her mouth as though that was all that mattered, as though kissing her fulfilled some sort of precious, deeply seated need. He was allowing this first kiss to be just that—a first kiss. The most anticipated and romanticized milestone for couples throughout time and throughout the world. A first kiss could either doom a budding relationship or make it bloom into something special, but ultimately, a lot rode on that initial contact.

In addition, a woman could tell a lot about a man by the way he kissed. If he was sloppy, drippy or in a hurry, then you could bet that he hadn't worked on his other techniques. A good kisser—a man who knew when to suckle, when to slide and when to slip (and, oh, did Jack ever)—was usually one who'd paid enough heed to the little things to ensure that he was going to give the same sort of thorough attention to every other part of the sexual process.

No doubt Jack Martin was a phenomenal lover.

The mere thought made her entire body quicken with anticipation, made the fine hairs on her arms stand up, her sex slicken with moisture and throb. Her bare breasts felt too heavy behind her shirt, too sensitive and too neglected. Mariette pressed herself more firmly against him, slipped one hand along his jaw, savoring the line of bone and soft skin, then pushed the other hand into his hair and let the silky strands tangle through her fingers.

He tasted like minty toothpaste and sweet tea and his particular scent—something musky and crisp— wrapped around her. He was hot and hard, more physically attractive than any man she'd ever met, and with every purposeful slip of his tongue into her mouth, the more fully she settled into the deep, open vee between his legs. The countertop had to be digging into the small of his back, but if he noticed or cared he never made an objection.

He left off her mouth and slid his nose along her jaw, breathing her in. "Hmmm," he murmured. "I've been thinking about doing that all day."

A shiver ran down her spine and gooseflesh peppered her too-hot skin. He framed her face with his hands, kissed the underside of her cheek. It was tender and sensual and something about it triggered a peculiar feeling in her chest.

It jarred her enough to make her pull away, albeit reluctantly.

She couldn't afford to make another wrong decision and something told her there wouldn't be any coming back from Jack Martin. He'd ruin her heart if he broke it.

She peered up at him and smiled self-consciously. "I think I'd better try to get some sleep now."

He grinned. "That would probably be a good idea."

She didn't move, but looked away, released a sigh and shook her head. "You know I'm not going to be able to look you in the eye in the morning, right?"

"I hope that isn't the case," he said. "You've got the prettiest eyes I've ever seen."

Startled at the compliment, she turned back and her gaze collided with his. Though throwing herself at his mouth and practically scaling his perfect body hadn't made her so much as bat a lash, the simple remark made her blush clear to her hairline. "Thank you," she managed, because it seemed like the right response.

He inclined his head. "Welcome."

Feeling uncharacteristically shaken and unsure, Mariette turned and started to make her way back to her room.

"Mariette?"

She stilled, darting him a look over her shoulder. His golden hair gleamed in the semidarkened room and a rueful smile turned the impossibly sexy lips she'd just been kissing. Atlas, indeed.

"If it makes you feel any better, I would have made the move if you hadn't. The only reason you beat me to the punch was because I was too damned stunned by how much I want you, to react. Even knowing that you're a friend of my new employers and they'd kick my newly hired ass—" though, admittedly, it would take all three of them "—wasn't enough to keep me away from you." He leveled a look at her. "If you'd like to request another agent, then now's the time to do it."

He didn't have to add "Or else you know where this is going to lead," because she knew it. She knew that if he stayed here the ultimate conclusion to this hellish attraction would involve the two of them and a bed…and probably the shower and the wall and the kitchen table, as well.

Those visions obligingly took root in her fertile imagination and the image of his gloriously naked body looming over hers, that sinfully carnal mouth suckling her breast sent a barb of heat directly into her clit, making her resist the urge to squirm.

He pushed off from the counter, grabbed the liquor bottle and took a long pull. "Just let me know what you want to do in the morning and I'll take care of it," he said. "And I'll own it."

Meaning, he'd take the blame and wouldn't leave an iota of it at her doorstep.

He was definitely a different sort of man, Mariette thought. The sort that was going to get her into trouble, no doubt.

But when had that ever stopped her?

JACK WATCHED MARIETTE turn and make her way to her room. He waited, until he was certain she was out of earshot and not going to come back, to swear theatrically but quietly under his breath.

He'd known, hadn't he? He'd known the instant he clapped eyes on her this morning that she was going to prove to be more temptation than he was accustomed to resisting. And now that he'd tasted her, felt that lush, womanly little body bellied up to his? The only way to keep this from reaching its ultimate conclusion was by taking himself out of the equation.

Was he proud of this? Not especially.

Jack had never met the irresistible woman...until now.

He'd had friends' girlfriends and wives hit on him over the years, couldn't go into a bar without a girl making some sort of pass at him. He didn't have to beat the women off with the proverbial stick, but he didn't have to do much to attract them, either. He guessed he was passably handsome, tall and fit, had all of his teeth, didn't live with his mother and was gainfully employed.

All of that certainly put him working ahead of the curve.

But this fatalistic, all-consuming, out-of-his-mind *need* that he felt for Mariette Levine was out of the realm of his experience. It was uncharted territory and he was navigating without a map.

He supposed he could try to lie to himself and insist that he could keep things on a strictly superficial level, but despite the fact that he'd been told he could sell ice to an Inuit, Jack knew better than to try and sell himself this self-righteous, self-serving load of B.S.

He'd known before he'd kissed her that she was going to set him off and now that she had? You couldn't put the bullet back in the gun.

It was *done*.

That's why he was giving her the choice, why he'd given her an out.

It was gallingly pathetic how much he hoped she didn't take it.

Ordinarily he'd be worried that fraternizing with a client would end up getting him fired, but since Charlie and Jay had met on the job—and so had most of the other Ranger Security agents, the three founding members included—he didn't see where he could possibly be kept to a standard none of the rest of them had managed to keep. He didn't imagine that they would necessarily like it—Mariette was a friend, after all—but they weren't hypocrites.

They could hardly fire him over something they'd all done, right?

Right.

If she'd just stayed in that room, he thought, trying to get a handle on himself. But no, she couldn't sleep. Perversely, he wondered how well she was sleeping now. He imagined it couldn't be any better than it was before and almost wished it was worse.

He'd been miserable before, thinking about her being in that room, close but not close enough. Now he was in agony. Because he'd touched her, tasted her, felt her hot little body pressed to his, the reciprocated desire in her kiss, the greedy way she'd slid her hands all over his body.

She wanted him every bit as much as he wanted her. That, at least, was gratifying.

His cell suddenly vibrated at his waist and he checked the display. *Charlie.* He rolled his eyes. Perfect timing, as always.

"Yeah," he answered by way of greeting.

"Bobby Ray lives at a pay-by-the-week motel out on Dearborn," she said.

He frowned. There hadn't been a current address in the file Payne had sent over, only the one of his last foster family who had said they hadn't seen or heard from Bobby Ray in more than a year. "How did you find that out?"

"I used my special skills."

He grinned and chewed the inside of his cheek. "Who did you hack this time?"

"That's for me to gloat about and you to never know," she quipped. "Anyway, I waited for a couple of hours for Bobby Ray to show up and when he didn't I went in and talked to the night manager."

"Was he helpful?"

"He had some interesting information to share, yes. He said that Bobby Ray hadn't been back to his room for the past three days, but that a couple of people had been by looking for him."

Ah. He could only imagine what kind of people. "Did the manager know who they were?"

"No," she said. "I suspect he's lying about that, but short of vaulting across the counter and putting him in a choke hold until he told me the truth, there was nothing I could do about it."

He was genuinely surprised that she hadn't. He chuckled. "What stopped you?"

A beat slid to three and she swore low under her breath.

Jack frowned. "Charlie?"

"I haven't even told Jay yet," she said. "Dammit, I can't believe I just did that."

Told Jay what? Did what? Jack felt his eyes widen and he drew a quick breath. "Oh, my God. Are you—" He knew they'd been trying, but...

"Yes," she said, sounding equally exasperated and overjoyed. "And if you breathe a word of it before I—"

"I won't," he assured her, smiling wonderingly. A bizarre sensation winged through his rapidly expanding chest and he gave his head a little shake, trying to wrap his mind around his sister—his scrappy little *badass* sister—becoming a mother. He swallowed, his eyes inexplicably darting toward Mariette's room. "You'll be a wonderful mother," he told her. "Congratulations, little sister."

"Thank you. You're going to make a great uncle," she said fondly.

Evidently done with the mushy stuff, Charlie cleared her throat, all business once again. "All right, back to Bobby Ray. I think you should spend some time watching his motel tomorrow and see if they come back. The night manager says Bobby Ray's rent is up day after tomorrow and that if he's not there to pay up for another week, he forfeits whatever he has in there. Considering that all he has in this world will fit in that little dingy room, he probably wants it."

He imagined she was right.

"Whoever these guys are have frightened him enough to keep him from coming back. That makes him desperate. And desperate people often act in ways they ordinarily wouldn't."

Another Bobby Ray convert, Jack thought. But he understood. He'd read the kid's files, the ones he was able to get through the legitimate channels and the ones that had required Charlie's specialized skill. His foster care file was three inches thick and read like a horror novel. The permanent record she'd managed to pull from the last school he'd attended hadn't been any better. In fact, both documents had painted a picture of a kid who had never been given a modicum of affection, much less a break.

He'd known about his father giving the boy the scars—he hadn't known that his father had done the same thing to his mother "so that the two would match" and that her cuts had been too deep and had resulted in her death.

"I found something else that was interesting, too," Charlie told him.

His senses went on point. "What was that?"

"I let myself into his room and—"

"You what?" he asked, his voice rising. "Have you lost your damned—"

"Hush," she interrupted. "I found a receipt for a headstone in the bedside drawer," she told him. "It was dated a month ago and was twenty-three hundred dollars."

Damn. Where in the hell had the kid gotten that kind of money? A lottery ticket? He doubted it. Otherwise, why were those men following him? And he certainly wouldn't have made that at the dairy.

"It was for his mother," Charlie confirmed sadly. "There was also a printout from the local hospital. Judging by the leftover pain killers and bandages, Bobby Ray ran into some trouble a few days after he bought the memorial."

Jack frowned. Whatever the boy had gotten into, he was definitely in over his head. No wonder he'd been nervous when Jack had shown up at the dairy. He was probably terrified that he'd been part of the crew who was clearly chasing him.

"I'll watch the place tomorrow," Jack told her. "And I'll go by the hospital and see if I can find out anything about Bobby Ray's visit."

"They're not going to tell you anything," she said. "Confidentiality laws. And their computer systems are much more complicated than you'd—"

Jack merely smiled. "You've got your methods, I've got mine. You let me handle it."

"Whatever," she said in that patronizing you're-wasting-your-time tone of hers.

"And Charlie?"

"Yes?"

He braced himself, because he knew she wasn't going to like what he had to tell her. "You stay away from that motel."

He could feel the blast of her anger before she said a word. "Look here, Jack. I am perfectly capable of taking care of—"

"Stay away," he repeated. "Or I'll have a chat with your husband. And your bosses."

She called him something their mother would certainly object to and then disconnected.

A lead at last, Jack thought.

And he knew beyond a shadow of a doubt it was going to royally piss off and disappoint both Mariette and Audwin.

Unfortunately, it couldn't be helped. And he had a job to do.

The next morning Jack found a Post-it note stuck to his bedroom door. It was a single word note and hadn't been signed.

Stay.

8

MARIETTE WASN'T ALTOGETHER certain what was up with Charlie, but she was pale and sullen and not at all the otherwise happy, chatty person she'd been the day before. Because she could be paranoid with the best of them, Mariette wondered if she'd somehow managed to inadvertently telegraph the fact that she'd been crawling all over Charlie's brother the night before and, possessing just as keen observation skills as her brother, she'd noticed it.

Mariette released a sigh. "Charlie, have I done something wrong?"

Charlie looked up at her and blinked. "What?" She grimaced. "No, no," she said, shaking her head. "I'm sorry. I'm just in a funk this morning." Her lips twisted with a wry smile. "When I was trying to persuade Payne, Jamie and Guy into bringing Jack on board after the accident, I was so busy thinking about how wonderful it would be to have him home and work with him that I'd forgotten what a pain in the ass he can be."

While all of that was very interesting, the thing that intrigued her the most was "after the accident" comment. She winced sympathetically, even though she had no frame of reference for Charlie's predicament.

She was an only child, after all, though she'd always imagined that having a brother or sister would have been nice. She'd had to make do with imaginary friends. She'd had one named Charmin, she remembered, and in her imagination, Charmin had borne a remarkable resemblance to Casper the ghost.

"What accident?" she asked as blithely as possible, considering her level of curiosity.

Charlie muttered a curse, squeezed her eyes shut and then bumped the back of her head against the wall as though to knock a little sense into it. "I am losing my freaking mind."

Well, hell. Mariette wiped down another table. "It's fine," she said. "Sorry I asked."

"No, I'm the one who's sorry," she said, seemingly at a loss. "I keep slipping up. I've never been really good at keeping secrets, but lately I've been a lot worse."

"If it's a secret, you don't have to tell me. Really," she insisted. Naturally, she was dying to know. No doubt because it pertained directly to Jack and any nugget of insight—any key to figuring out what made him tick—was of interest to her.

Charlie cast a furtive glance out the front window, then looked back at Mariette. "It was an IED," she confided in low tones. "He was lucky, ultimately. Two of the men who were with him were not." She winced, her face softening with regret. "One of the boys was only twenty and Jack had talked about him often, seemed to really like him. The boy—Johnson, he called him—lost both of his legs. He bled out and died in Jack's arms."

Mariette's stomach rolled, her heart gave a squeeze and she covered her mouth with her hand. "Oh, no."

"I know," Charlie told her. "I don't know how you move past something like that. How you cope after seeing something so horrible happen to a friend. To anyone, really," she added.

Mariette either, for that matter. Justice was one thing—punishment for a crime, particularly those against children, she could handle. Senseless death was another matter altogether.

And what of Jack and his injuries? Mariette wondered. Granted he looked absolutely perfect to her, but how was it that he was able to walk away from a blast like that without any visible scars? Not that she'd seen all of him yet, but…

The key word there being *yet,* Lord help her.

"Jack's eardrum was shattered so badly that it

took three separate surgeries to repair it," Charlie said, answering her unspoken question. "He wears a hearing aid in his right ear," she said gesturing to her own and Mariette couldn't have been any more surprised. She hadn't noticed it at all.

Charlie's lips quirked in sadness. "That's why he's grown his hair out," she told her. "So that it covers it up." She shook her head. "And it's not vanity. It's the idea that someone might think he's compromised or incapable. You have to understand, Mariette, my brother was our hometown golden boy. All the girls wanted to be *with* him and the guys wanted to be *like* him. He was the star quarterback, the valedictorian of his class, the conquering hero every time he came home." She released a low breath. "Except this last time. People treated him differently, as though he were damaged and no longer deserving of the pedestal they'd put him on. It was heartbreaking to watch, more difficult than anything I would have ever imagined." She glanced up. "Do you know what a soldier hates more than anything?"

Mariette's mind had been quickly processing Charlie's words into images and the resulting pictures were heartbreaking. She blinked, belatedly returning her attention to Charlie.

"No," she said, shaken. "What?"

Charlie's shrug was melancholy. "Being pitied. He gladly made his sacrifice and would do it again and give more. And the people who pity him are the ones who don't get that. That's what's difficult to move past." She sobered, cast another glance out the window. "You can't let on that you know," she said. "He'd throttle me."

Mariette swallowed, nodded her promise. "I won't."

"Had you noticed the hearing aid?" she asked.

"No, I hadn't." And she was relatively certain she'd been breathing quite heavily into that ear at one point last night. She felt a blush stain her cheeks and watched Charlie's eyes sharpen with interest.

"He'd be pleased about that. I hope he's been a good guest," she remarked. "Not using all your hot water or leaving dirty dishes in the sink. That was always a pet peeve of our mother's. Dishes went into the dishwasher, period."

"He's fine," she said, because really what could she say? *Your brother makes me hot and last night I came dangerously close to riding him like a mechanical bull at the fair on my kitchen floor? And, oh, yes, he did put his plate in the dishwasher?*

Er…she didn't think so.

As for tonight, she didn't know what was going to happen, though she had her hopeful suspicions, of course. But when he'd offered to have himself removed from this case and someone else assigned in his place, Mariette had known a blind sense of panic that was completely disproportionate to the occasion. She'd known the instant he made the offer that she was going to refuse, but had been too shocked by her own reaction to address it right then.

Because refusing meant admitting that she wanted him as much as he said he wanted her. It meant she was going blindly into another relationship when she knew better. When she knew that she needed to stop for a while and take stock of what she genuinely wanted out of a man so that she wasn't constantly putting her hopes into the wrong one.

And as much as the idea of telling him not to go terrified her, letting him leave without seeing what this was between them was more frightening.

There was something about him that she knew was different. Better. Wishful thinking? Possibly, because who wanted to be wrong again? But she didn't think so. Jack Martin held a special sort of appeal, a spark that marked him as a true original. Mariette sighed.

Clearly the insane attraction had left her mentally compromised. There could be no other explanation for her utterly shameless, wanton behavior. She blinked, struck with sudden insight. He'd turned her into a tramp, Mariette realized. Was it horrible that she rather liked that?

The bell over the door tinkled, signaling a new customer. "I hope that smile is because you're happy to see me," an amused male voice said.

Mariette's grin capsized and her gaze slid reluctantly to the speaker. "Sorry to disappoint you, but no." She glanced at Charlie. "Would you mind helping him? I have something I need to see to in the back."

Looking equally baffled and intrigued, Charlie nodded and stood. "Of course."

Nathaniel sighed and a muscle flexed in his suddenly tight jaw, making a liar of his smile. "I was hoping to talk to you, Mariette," he said. "You can't give me five minutes?"

She turned and glared at him. "No."

He darted a look at Charlie, then back at Mariette and took a step forward. "Really, Mariette," he hissed. "This has gone on long enough. You know how I feel about you and I know how you feel about me."

She was going to send him the bill when she ground all the enamel off her teeth. "If you knew how I felt about you, Nathaniel, you wouldn't bother coming in here anymore. It is over." She smirked at him. "Say hello to Tiffany for me."

He rolled his eyes. "Oh, for heaven's sake, Mariette, that meant nothing. You know that," he insisted.

"And that's supposed to make it *better?*" she asked, dangerously close to losing her temper. "It's done. Move on," she said, wearying of this conversation. "I have."

His bravado slipped. "What do you mean by that? Moved on how? With who?"

"Would you like a cupcake?" Charlie interrupted cheerfully. "Perhaps a cookie or a croissant?"

He flicked his gaze to her, then located Mariette once again. "This is ridiculous, Mariette. I'll be by at six when you close up and we can talk about this then."

Perhaps Nathanial was the one who needed a hearing aid, Mariette thought. "No, we won't," she said. "You are not welcome here anymore."

Infuriatingly, he shot her an indulgent grin. "We both know you don't mean that. See you at six." And before she could utter another single word, he strolled back out onto the sidewalk.

Charlie's eyes were wide and her mouth hung open in apparent shock. "What the hell was that all about?"

Mariette sighed. "That's my ex," she said. "But, as I'm sure you've noticed, he doesn't seem able to grasp the 'ex' part."

"Perhaps someone should help him," Charlie said, her voice throbbing with anger. "What a self-important, condescending, arrogant little ass. Who's Tiffany?"

Mariette chuckled at Charlie's apt description of her ex. She'd thought some of those same adjectives applied the first time she'd met him, but then he'd just kept asking her out and she let her vanity mistakenly revise her opinion. "The girl I caught gargling his balls the last time I went to see him at his office," she said, her lips curving into a bitterly droll smile.

Charlie's eyes widened. "Damn."

"It was never going to work," Mariette told her. "I was more broken up over my poor judgment than anything else." She shook her head, genuinely baffled. "What in the hell was I thinking?"

"I'll admit I was just wondering that myself," Charlie told her.

Mariette chuckled. "I can't say as I blame you."

"You should mention this to Jack," she said with a succinct nod. "He'd get rid of him for you."

She'd just bet he would. "I can handle him."

"Yes, but why would you when you don't have to?"

"I'll think about it," Mariette said. She'd admit that it would be quite gratifying to see Nathaniel's smug smile vanish at the sight of Jack. No doubt he could do some serious damage to those pricey veneers. She glanced at Charlie. "Have you heard from Jack today?"

"Earlier," she said. "He called to gloat."

This sibling rivalry/affection was quite fascinating. "Oh?"

"He was able to procure some information that I didn't think he'd be able to get." She snorted and rolled her eyes. "He's impossible when he's right."

"Congratulations," Mariette said with an eyeroll of her own. "You've just described the male species."

Charlie chuckled and her gaze turned soft. "They have their redeeming qualities," she said. "Mine actually saved my life. I had no choice but to marry him."

Stunned, Mariette goggled at her. "He saved your life?"

She nodded. "He did. He charged into a burning house, found me and carried me out." Her gaze seemed to turn inward, remembering. "He nearly died trying to save me."

"Wow." Inexplicable envy twisted through her. It must be something to be loved like that. To have someone so determined to protect you that they'd offer themselves up instead. That their own life became insignificant. Her mother would have done that. Even her aunt, Mariette would admit. But she'd never had anyone who wasn't blood related love her like that.

And *that's* what she wanted, Mariette thought with a dawning sense of comprehension. She wanted what Charlie had. That's why she kept trying, kept giving guys who didn't deserve it the benefit of the doubt.

Was she happy with her life? Yes. She had a business she loved and a home of her own. She was proud of her accomplishments. But wanting to be loved—truly, genuinely loved—was something she imagined every person wanted. While other people might think that made her weak, Mariette knew better.

Because at least she was strong enough to admit it.

Charlie laughed softly. "Wow, indeed," she said. "Try trying to win an argument with that sort of ammunition." She rolled her eyes. "I-saved-your-life pretty much trumps everything else."

Mariette imagined so.

Charlie sighed, seemingly wrapped up in her own thoughts. "Jack is actually going to be back a little early today. I've got an errand to run."

Mariette nodded, envious of her new friend. "Thanks for being here, Charlie," she said. "I'm truly grateful. I know that you've probably got more exciting things that you could be doing than babysitting me all day."

"Not at all. I—" She suddenly clasped a hand over her mouth and darted for the bathroom with a garbled "Excuse me."

Five minutes later, her face pale and her hands a little unsteady, she made her way back into the dining room. "I'm sorry. I must have eaten something that didn't agree with me."

"From here?" Mariette asked, alarmed. She was fanatic about expiration dates and making sure that everything was fresh and clean. She immediately started scanning the contents of her display cases, suspicious of everything in there now. She hoped that—

"No, no," Charlie quickly assured her. "Nothing from here."

She'd seen Charlie eating a macaroon earlier. She hoped like hell nothing was amiss with those. Several dozen of those had gone out for a baby shower this morning. The last thing she wanted to do was make the expectant mother and all her friends sick. *Damn*. A note of panic made her belly flip.

"Do you think it was the macaroon?" Mariette asked her, her worried gaze swinging to Charlie's. "I didn't see you eat anything else. Did you eat anything else? I—"

Charlie put a hand on her arm. "Mariette, I promise you nothing from your case has made me ill." Her lips rolled into a smile. "Seriously. You don't have to worry."

Charlie almost looked amused, which, frankly, annoyed the hell out of Mariette. This was her business, her livelihood. "It's just I sent a large order of those out—"

"I'm pregnant," she blurted out. "It's morning sickness, not your macaroons." Her eyes rounded in immediate dismay. "Shit, shit, shit," Charlie lamented, evidently regretting the impulsive outburst. "That's twice now, dammit, and I haven't even told Jay yet." She looked up at her. "See?" she said. "This is what I mean. I'm just spewing it out there—" she gave an airy wave of her hand "—and can't seem to help myself."

Dumbstruck, Mariette felt a grin slide over her lips and her gaze inexplicably dropped to Charlie's still-flat abdomen. "That's because it's harder to keep good news a secret."

A light suddenly gleamed in Charlie's gaze. "You know, you're exactly right."

"You should tell Jay," she said. "Before you tell the mail man or your dry cleaner or a total stranger."

"I know," she said. "But I wanted to make it special. Plan a romantic dinner or something and I haven't come up with anything that's over-the-top spectacular."

Mariette grinned. "The *news* is what's over-the-top spectacular, you little nitwit. How you tell him isn't important—it's the telling him that is." Mariette glanced at her case, then back to Charlie. "But I do have an idea if you're interested in hearing it."

"Of course."

"See those chocolate eggs in the case?"

Charlie gasped and nodded.

"Initially I only made them for Easter, but they were such a hit with the kids I stock them year round. Those have a creamy filling, but I could give you a hollow one and you could—"

"Yes!" Charlie interrupted delighted. "Yes, yes,

yes!" She gave Mariette an impulsive hug. "How quickly can you put it together?"

"I've got some hollow eggs in the back," Mariette told her, pleased that she could help. "You give me what you want put in it and I can have it ready in a couple of minutes."

"I've got the perfect thing," Charlie told her. "I'll call Jay and have him come down." She hugged her again. "Oh, thank you, Mariette. You're brilliant. An egg," she said wonderingly, her eyes gleaming with happiness. "How fitting."

"I'll warn you now," Mariette told her. "I'm going to hide behind the counter so that I can watch his re-action."

Charlie grinned and she practically bounced on the balls of her feet. "I don't care if you hang from the ceiling à la *Mission: Impossible*," she said. "I just can't wait to tell him."

And now neither could she, Mariette thought, smiling, happy to be a part of it. Thrilled though she was, a twinge of unexplainable melancholy pinged her heart. She'd have to think about that later, Mariette thought, annoyed with herself.

These Martin siblings were seriously messing with her head…and possibly with her heart, as well.

9

BINGO, JACK THOUGHT as he watched the two thugs climb out of the older-model navy blue Cadillac. He knew enough about goons to spot one and both of these guys had more brawn than brains. And knowing what he knew now after visiting the hospital, it took every bit of restraint Jack had not to spring out of the car and pummel the living hell out of both of them. Damned bullies. He *hated* bullies.

Unfortunately, until he knew exactly what he was dealing with, he suspected he could make Bobby Ray's situation worse rather than better. His best plan of action at the moment, much as it galled him and went against the grain, was to gather information and find out who they were.

Then pummel the hell out of them.

Harsh? Not in his opinion. After what the pair did to Bobby Ray, they needed the ever-loving hell beaten out of them and he grimly suspected Bobby

Ray had never had a single person ever mete out any justice—or even mercy, for that matter—on his behalf.

But Jack would.

Looking first left and then right, they strolled up to Bobby Ray's door and knocked. They didn't look as though they expected a response, but were merely following orders. The two shared a look and the taller of the two shook his head. They turned then and made their way to the office. They were inside and back out in less than a minute, presumably because the attendant on duty didn't have anything more to tell them than the last time they were here.

Jack snapped a couple of pictures with his cell phone and noted the tag number so that he could find out exactly who they were. Once they were safely out of the parking lot, he went in to pay the attendant a visit, as well.

The kid behind the counter was in goth dress with black eyeliner, black lipstick and unnaturally black hair. Parts of her face were pierced in places he'd never seen and he imagined would be intensely painful.

"Those guys who were just in here," Jack said, jerking his head toward the door. "Do you know who they are?"

She picked up a bottle of black—surprise, surprise—nail polish and shook the bottle. "Don't have a clue," she said, managing to sound massively dis-interested with those four words.

"Have you seen them before?"

She slid the brush over her thumbnail, but didn't bother to look up. "A few times."

Damn, he'd lost a word. This was going nowhere fast. "Were they looking for Bobby Ray?"

"Yep."

Down to one. He exhaled mightily. "Have they left a number or asked for a call if Bobby Ray shows up?"

"Nope."

That was interesting. If his rent was up soon then, like Jack, they had to realize that the boy was going to try and come back for his stuff.

"Those men want to hurt Bobby Ray," he said, taking a gamble that this girl was merely feign-ing disinterest. Her hand had trembled across the second nail and she'd spread paint over the edge of her finger. "They beat the hell out of him with a bar of soap shoved down into a sock about a month ago."

The poor kid. Once he'd explained who he was and why he was interested in knowing exactly what had happened to the boy, the nurse he'd confided in at the hospital had pulled the file, opened it to the correct page and then conveniently left to go see about another patient.

By the time she'd returned, Jack had been gone, but the information he'd seen there had been enough to make him sick to his stomach. A Good Samaritan had brought him in. His back and abdomen had been covered with bruises, the deep-tissue kind that were intensely painful and long to heal. Contrary to popular belief, a sock beating *would* leave bruises and it hurt like a bitch.

A reaction at last. She looked up. "It was them? They're the ones who did that to Bobby Ray?"

Hmm. He took another chance. "Were you the one that took him to the hospital?"

She swallowed, seemingly unsure.

"I don't want to hurt him," he said, hoping she believed the sincerity in his voice. "I want to help him. I don't know what he's gotten himself into, but he clearly isn't able to get out of it alone."

And Jack did want to help him. Regardless of whether or not the boy had anything to do with what was happening to Mariette, he still wanted to figure out what was happening with Bobby Ray and try to make it right.

For whatever reason, because there certainly was no physical resemblance, Bobby Ray reminded him of Johnson. Different boys, different backgrounds, but there was a similar kind of core, an essence of something good. Given the kid's history, Bobby Ray should have been in prison by now. But he wasn't. He was working, supporting himself. Trying. Against all odds and virtually any hope, as far as Jack could see.

That took courage.

And as far as Jack could tell, the first people to ever pay the kid a kindness were Audwin and Mariette—he'd never had anyone who had his back.

Furthermore, if he was involved—and Jack still believed that to be the case—then he suspected Charlie was right, that he was desperate.

The girl was thoughtful, stared at him, more than likely trying to decide if she trusted him or not. "They're coming back tonight," she finally said. "They're going to rent the room next to his."

And wait him out. Shit.

And he'd come back, Jack knew. He'd have to. Everything he owned was in that little room. A precious little by the world's standards, but it was all Bobby Ray had. Obviously, Jack would need to see about protecting it.

So the first order of business was to get the kid's stuff out and eliminate his need to return. "Can you let me into his room? I'll pack up his stuff and make sure that he gets it."

She was shaking her head before he even finished. "Look, I realize that you're probably the lesser of two evils, but I can't just give you access to his room and let you take his things."

"Then I'll pay you to do it," he said. "The most important thing is to keep him from coming back here. They're going to jump him if he does." He paused. "I suspect the first beating was a warning.

This one…" He purposely left the sentence unfinished so that she could complete the thought herself. "You can figure out a way to get it to him after all of this is resolved," he said. "Meet up with him somewhere else, a place of your own choosing."

She nodded. "I'll do that. But you don't have to pay me. I like Bobby Ray." Her direct gaze was a bit unnerving. "He looks beyond the surface of things. Sees what's on the inside and judges that for himself. You'll let him know I've got his stuff?"

Jack nodded, thinking that looking beyond the surface was a lesson everyone—himself included—could stand to learn. "I'll get word to him and tell him to call you. They don't appear to know where he works," Jack told her. "If you do, then keep it to yourself."

She nodded.

"Do you know why they're looking for him?" he asked.

Once again, she hesitated. "I have my suspicions," she said.

He waited, letting her make up her mind.

"I don't know who they are, but I know who they work for," she finally told him. "A guy everyone calls Uncle Mackie. He's a bookie." Her lips twisted bitterly. "And once you're on his hook, you're never off it."

Jack had pretty much worked that out for himself. He'd ruled out any kind of drug-related trouble because, despite being terrified, the kid's eyes had been clear. Furthermore, Audwin wouldn't have tolerated it. Audwin trusted him with the truck, after all, and if the old man suspected the boy was using there was no way in hell he'd let him drive.

He nodded, made sure to look her in the eye. "Thank you."

"Don't let anything happen to him," she told him. "He's a good guy."

Jack thought so, too, but one who'd let a bad decision take him down a road that could get him seriously hurt and put the ones he cared about in equally serious jeopardy.

Hopefully he could prevent that.

"BOBBY RAY, YOU'VE GOT a visitor," Audwin called, poking his dark gray head around the door.

Bobby Ray felt his knees weaken and his stomach roll. Oh, God. They'd found him. He didn't know how, but they had. His mouth went bone-dry. "Who—Who is it?" he asked, terrified to the bone.

"It's Jack Martin, that friend of Mariette's. Said he needs to talk to you."

Not any better, really, Bobby Ray thought miserably. But he didn't think he'd try to hurt him here, anyway. It would look odd if he refused to see him, so he couldn't do that. Feeling only slightly less nauseous, Bobby Ray wiped his sweaty face with the back of sleeve—he'd had to turn his shirt inside out to hide the dirt—and made his way to the front. He found Jack Martin with a booted foot propped up against the fence, looking at some cows. He'd chosen a spot a bit away from the office, Bobby Ray noted, and couldn't decide if that was a good thing or a bad thing.

He twisted the brim of his hat nervously in his hands. "You wanted to see me?"

Jack Martin turned, his eyes assessing. "Those thugs who are chasing you and roughed you up last month are renting the room next to yours tonight and they're not going to leave until you show up."

Shit. Bobby Ray didn't know what was worse— that this man knew his business or having Uncle Mackie's men parked next door to his room, preventing him from returning so that he could get his things. He didn't have much, really, but there were some pictures of his mother that he couldn't bear to part with and a few of himself before the scars. He liked to look at those. To imagine how life might have been different if he'd never gotten them. Though he had plenty of memories before the scars, he'd taken them for granted, had taken being normal—looking normal—for granted, as well. People either stared as if he was an exhibit in a freak show, or wouldn't hold his gaze. It was awful.

"Geneva is collecting your things and getting them out before they return," he continued. "She

said for you to call her and she'd meet you somewhere."

Still reeling, Bobby Ray nodded. "All right." Geez
God, how did he know all of this? Why had he bothered to find out? And what had he said to Geneva to
get her to help him? Geneva was more distrustful of
people than he was, and that was saying something.
He liked her. She was kind and had pretty eyes.

"I work for Ranger Security," Jack told him, answering the bulk of his questions with that one admission. "I'm providing security for Mariette until
the break-ins at her shop are resolved. We have an
agent covering her during the day and I'm there at
night. All night," he added, shooting him a look.
He heaved a sigh. "Look, Bobby Ray, I know that
you're somehow connected to this. I don't know how,
though I think I have a good idea why, but I know it
all the same. Whatever it is that you've gotten yourself into, I can help you get out of it."

Bobby Ray snorted before he could stop himself.
Yeah, right. All he was trying to do was trick him
into confessing and he'd be in cuffs so quick his
head would spin. And once he was behind bars there
would be no getting out. He didn't have money for
bail, no one to call. Once Audwin knew he'd taken
some of his coins, he'd lose his job and the old man's
respect. He'd be disappointed and angry. And Mariette… She'd never forgive him for hitting her.

And why should she, really? It's not as if he deserved her forgiveness. He should probably just give up, Bobby Ray thought. Stop running and let them do their worst. It was only a matter of time before everything blew up, until the whole damned thing came to light.

He'd almost rather be dead.

"You've got people who care about you, Bobby Ray. Whatever it is that you've done, it can't be un-forgivable."

If only that were true, Bobby Ray thought. And he genuinely wished he could believe it. That he could confide what he'd done, why he'd done it and figure out a way to make amends. But that would not re-solve the Uncle Mackie issue and his so-called debt would continue to build. He'd never be free of him.

"How much are you into Uncle Mackie for?"

Bobby Ray looked sharply at him and at the look, Jack Martin merely smiled. "Here's my theory," Jack told him. "I think your first bet made you believe that you'd hit a lucky streak and you thought you'd found a way to make some quick, easy cash." He gestured toward the farm. "This is honorable work, but it's hard and the pay can't be that great because of Audwin's overhead."

Bobby Ray swallowed.

"You weren't so lucky with your next bet, or the next and, ultimately, by the time you knew what had happened, you were in way over your head and Uncle Mackie had you right where he wanted you—

into him and afraid. See, I know Mackie's game," Jack remarked. "Bookies like making easy money, too, and if they can charge exorbitant interest and fees on unpaid debt and then scare you into finding a way—*any way*—to pay it back, then they've got a golden goose, a veritable endless ATM machine. *You*," he said significantly. "It's my suspicion that you've taken something from Audwin and he hasn't figured it out yet. And whatever you've taken, you've hidden in one of the butter loaves. But you lost track of one—the one you needed—and have decided that it's at Mariette's. I think you panicked when she caught you and you threw the rolling pin meaning to scare her away, but not hurt her."

Bobby Ray's heart was pounding so hard he was afraid it was going to race right up his throat.

"Here's my plan," he continued. "When I go back to Mariette's, we're going to take every remaining block of butter in her fridge and melt it down until we find whatever it is you're looking for. And when we do, your jig is up. This is all coming to a close, anyway, Bobby Ray. I can help you," he said. "You go ahead and come clean now and we'll sort all of this out. I'll personally back Uncle Mackie and his goons off you and make sure that, as far as they're concerned, your debt is paid."

For the briefest second Bobby Ray was tempted to do exactly as Jack Martin said. He painted a pretty picture of redemption and escape... But, ultimately,

Bobby Ray knew he was here to do a job and his job wasn't to save his skin—it was to save Mariette's. He might have figured everything out, but he didn't have any proof. And until he had proof, Bobby Ray had time to try and sort things out himself.

When it became clear that Bobby Ray wasn't going to say anything, Jack sighed. "The hard way, then? I figured as much."

He reached into his pocket and handed Bobby Ray a wad of folded bills. Bobby Ray looked down and shock detonated through him. They were hundreds.

"Find somewhere to sleep besides your car," he said. "You look dead on your feet, probably from constantly looking over your shoulder. And pick a motel with laundry and room service. A little sleep, some clean clothes and a decent meal will do you a world of good." He handed him something else. "Here's my card. Call me if you change your mind. My cell is on there. No matter what happens, the offer stands, kid."

He clapped him on the back and then turned and walked away. Bobby Ray stood there for what felt like an eternity looking at the money that had just been put in his hand.

For the first time in his life he genuinely didn't know what to think.

"Why are you doing this?" he hollered to Jack's retreating form.

Jack paused, seemingly looking at something that Bobby Ray couldn't see. "Because it's the right thing to do and I don't think people have always done the right thing by you," he said. He paused. "And you remind me of someone."

10

"HEY, JAY," MARIETTE heard Jack say from her vantage point in the kitchen.

"Jack!" Livvie all but shouted. "Do you like chocolate?" she asked.

"I do," he told her, sounding only marginally startled at the out of the blue question.

"Good, 'cause Mariette made some special ones today, only she wouldn't let me have one. I don't know why. I've been good and only had one cookie."

Before this could deteriorate any further, Mariette hurried forward. "I'm making special ones for you, too, Livvie," she said, slinging an arm around the girl. "Come with me, please." She steered her toward the kitchen. "I've got a special job for you."

Predictably, Livvie's eyes lit up. The word *special* always had that effect on her. It made the car commercials—who were always having "specials"—particularly entertaining for her. Mariette shot Jack a significant look and jerked her head toward the kitchen, silently beckoning him to follow her. She was so glad that he'd gotten back in time to see this.

Looking intrigued at her admittedly odd behavior, Jack followed her around the counter and into the kitchen. "You are going to be so glad that you got here in time," she said, practically bubbling with expectation. She turned to Livvie. "I want you to take these to Charlie and Jay. Jay gets the duck plate, okay?"

Jack frowned. "The duck plate?"

"It's got a duck on it, see?" she said, a little impatiently.

Livvie nodded. "Jay gets the duck plate. Charlie gets the flowers."

"Right. Once you've given them their plates, I want you to come back—right back—to the kitchen. I have another special job for you." She pointed to a tray of un-iced sugar cookies. Icing cookies was one of Livvie's favorite things in the world to do. "You're going to take care of those for me, okay? We'll call them the Livvie Specials."

She clapped delightedly. "Livvie Specials! I like that!"

Mariette knew she would.

"Okay," she said, handing her helper the plates. "Hurry," she said. "Jay gets the duck plate," she repeated.

Smiling delightedly, Livvie took off.

Jack arched a brow. "Want to tell me what's going on? You're acting all…stealthy," he said, looking mildly impressed.

Having practically slung the plates down in front of Jay and Charlie, Livvie came running back into the kitchen and took up her icing bag. She was instantly engrossed. Mariette grabbed Jack's hand and hurried forward. "Do what I do," she said. "And be quiet."

Mariette dropped down into a low crouch and duck-walked to the best position behind the case. She'd purposely shifted things around in the case so that she'd have a better view.

"What the hell?" Jack hissed, his brows climbing nearly to his hairline.

Mariette shot him a warning glance and put her finger to her lips, the international sign for "shush." Once she was in a good position, she motioned for Jack to get closer and whispered, "Watch this."

"This feels wrong," he said. "I—"

"Shut up," she whispered fiercely. Like he'd never spied on anyone before. Honestly. "Trust me."

"I don't care if you're hungry or not," Mariette heard Charlie say. "Mariette made a special treat for the two of us, so just eat it."

He made a face and pushed the plate away. "I'll save it for later," he said. "I'm sure she won't mind."

Oh, yes, she would, Mariette thought.

"That's made with special chocolate," Charlie told

him. "It's supposed to enhance your sexual performance."

Jay went comically still and beside her Jack sniggered.

"I wasn't aware there was a problem," Jay said, darting a nervous look around the deserted dining room.

Charlie popped a bite in her mouth and groaned. "But the best can still be made better," she said, pulling a delicate shrug. "I was just more curious to see if it would work, but if it makes you uncomfortable or you're not into it, then that's fine."

"No, no," Jay said, picking up the little egg. "If eating sexual chocolate will make you happy, then I'm happy to oblige." He bit into it and winced. "What the—" He peered at the egg, then frowned at Charlie. "There's paper in here."

"Oh," Charlie said a little too innocently. "Mine didn't have that. You ought to see what it says." She leaned forward.

Mariette was practically shaking with anticipation, her smile so wide it hurt. She grabbed Jack's hand again and squeezed.

Looking adorably uncertain, Jay withdrew the little piece of paper and opened it up. A puzzled frown moved across his brow while he tried to figure out what he was looking at. Then he sucked in a harsh breath and his gaze shot to Charlie. "Congratulations, Daddy," he said, reading the little note at the bottom of the ultrasound picture. "Is this what— Are you— Are we—"

Tears glistened in Charlie's eyes and, smiling, she nodded.

The chair Jay was sitting on fell to the floor as he vaulted up from the table and swept Charlie up. He lifted her completely off the ground and whirled her around. He was laughing delightedly, an expression of pure joy in his face.

"Put me down," Charlie gasped. "You're going to make us sick." She glanced toward the counter. "You can stop hiding now."

Mariette and Jack popped up from behind the counter and Jay's eyes widened in shock. "Did you know?" he asked.

"Only because she couldn't stop herself from telling it," Mariette told him, laughing, too. What a beautiful moment and she'd been a part of it.

An odd expression on his face, Jack squeezed her hand and murmured a thank-you. "The egg had to be your idea. Brilliant." He walked over to Jay and offered him one of those handshake hugs men did. "Congratulations," he told him. "You'll make a fine father."

Jay nodded and slung an arm around Charlie. "I'm sure she'll have me whipped into shape before the baby is born." He blinked and looked down at her. "When will the baby be born?"

"October," Charlie told him.

"October," he repeated wonderingly. "We're having a baby in October."

Jay cast a fond look at his sister. "Go celebrate this news with your husband," he said. "I'm not leaving again today."

A hopeful light gleamed in Charlie's gaze. "You sure?"

He nodded. "I'm sure."

Charlie shrugged and darted a look at Mariette. "Thank you," she said, her eyes still wet.

"Anytime," Mariette told her.

Charlie snagged her purse, the ultrasound photo and the last bite of chocolate off her plate, then hurried back to Jay's side. She threaded her fingers through his as though her hand in his was the most natural thing in the world.

And it was, for them, Mariette realized.

"Does that chocolate really enhance sexual performance?" she heard Jay ask as they strolled out the door.

Charlie laughed delightedly. "I guess we'll see, won't we?"

Jack waited until they were gone, then turned to look at her. His expression was still on lockdown, but she detected a hint of approval for her part and that little bit of admiration burrowed into her heart and bloomed. "That was a great thing you just did."

Mariette grinned, toed a loose piece of rubber on

the mat behind the counter. "It felt good," she said. "They're so in love."

"I know." He grimaced, shot her a conspiratorial smile. "It's a little sickening, isn't it?"

Mariette felt her eyes round. "No," she said, feigning outrage.

He merely stared at her.

She huffed a breath. "Okay, just a little."

Jack laughed, the sound low and husky. "I knew you were a girl after my own heart."

If she didn't get control of herself, she imagined that was what she was going to be after—his heart. In the meantime, she'd just have to make do with the rest of him. A shudder racked her frame as desire spiked. In an instant she remembered the feel of his lips against her own, the way he tasted against her tongue, the way his skin felt beneath her mouth.

Jack's attention suddenly shifted to his cell phone. He checked the display, frowned and then looked up at her. "Who is Nathaniel, why will he be here at six and why am I supposed to take care of him for you?"

Mariette swore. "I need to check on Livvie," she said and made a beeline for the kitchen. It wouldn't put him off, but it would delay him a minute, anyway.

Damn Charlie. Pregnant or not, Mariette could throttle her. While the idea of having Jack convince Nathaniel to leave her alone satisfied some sort of primal cavewoman revenge gene, she really didn't think it was necessary. Yes, he'd been an ass and yes, it had been humiliating. But she wasn't heartbroken and she could fight her own battles.

She'd been doing it her whole life, hadn't she?

Furthermore, she was grimly afraid she'd like it too much, having Jack Martin in her corner.

And, though there were many pleasures she imagined she and Jack would enjoy, that one was somehow more significant, held more emotional appeal than was strictly good for her.

She'd do well to remember that.

"Mariette," Jack called, immediately falling in behind her. "What's Charlie talking about?"

"Oh, that's lovely," Mariette told Livvie, peering over the girl's shoulder. She gave her a squeeze. "You're doing a great job."

"Mariette," he repeated, less patiently.

She glanced up. "It's nothing," she said, blinking innocently. As if he'd fall for that. "It's not a problem."

"Charlie seems to think he's a problem," he said. He frowned, sighed heavily and pulled his phone from his waist again. "I guess I'll just have to call her and interrupt their romantic celebratory dinner and—"

She snatched the phone out of his hand. He was so shocked it took a moment for him to react. "What the hell—"

"I'll give it back," she said, looking at her hand as though she wasn't sure it belonged to her. "Just don't call her."

"Fine," he said. She handed the phone back to him. "Who is Nathaniel?" Jack asked. He had a terrible suspicion that he wasn't going to like this answer and the black cloud of rage settling on his brain was making it seize up. Ridiculous, he told himself. He shouldn't get this spun out over an ex-boyfriend and yet... He genuinely felt like hitting something.

Livvie made a face. "Nathanial used to be Mariette's boyfriend, but she kicked him to the curb."

Mariette gasped. "Livvie! Who told you such a thing?"

"Dillon," she said, as if it should be obvious. "Dillon didn't like Nathaniel, either. He said he had mean eyes." She put another misshapen heart on another cookie. "I didn't notice his mean eyes, but he was a brown. Not a pretty brown like chocolate. A yucky brown, like mud. Or poop."

Jack felt his lips twitch and his gaze tangled with Mariette's shocked and embarrassed one. "He doesn't sound like I would like him, either, Livvie."

"You wouldn't," Livvie said. "He's not a nice man. He only pretends to be. He's good at fooling people, but the colors don't lie."

Mariette winced and rubbed a finger between her brows, as though staving off a headache. "Livvie, you'd better get your things together. Your mom will be here soon."

Livvie placed a final dot on a cookie with flourish and then smiled down at her handiwork. "There you go, Mariette. Livvie's specials," she announced proudly.

Mariette smiled tiredly and hugged her. "Yes, they are."

Livvie buried her head into Mariette's neck, a glowing smile on her face. "I love you, Mariette."

"I love you, too, sweetheart," she murmured, pressing a kiss to the girl's temple.

He smiled softly, touched at the scene. He'd been seeing a lot of mutually adoring looks lately. Between Mariette and Livvie, Charlie and Jay.

Mariette pulled back and glanced down at the girl. "Livvie, why didn't you tell me about Nathaniel's color? You've never mentioned that before."

"I kept hoping it would change. Sometimes they do," she said. "And Momma told me not to meddle," she added, a frown creasing her otherwise smooth brow. "You aren't mad at me, are you, Mariette?"

"Of course not," she said. "I could never be mad at you," Mariette told her, giving her a squeeze. "You're my special Livvie."

Livvie beamed up at her. "You're my special Mariette." The bell on the front door rang, signaling a customer. "I bet that's Mom," she said. "She's always early."

"Livvie," a feminine voice called.

"Told ya," Livvie announced. "See you tomorrow, Mariette. Bye, Jack!"

Jack told her goodbye and then watched her leave. "Sounds like Livvie is a really good judge of character," he remarked. "You should probably start vetting all your boyfriends through her."

She winced and started cleaning up. He liked the way she moved, determined and purposeful with an economy of movement that was graceful, almost regal. "That's not a bad idea, actually."

"What's this Nathaniel been doing?" He tried not to mangle the words, but, at her sharp look, wasn't altogether sure that he'd succeeded. It was ridiculous how much this was eating him up. Of course, she'd had boyfriends before. She was twenty-seven. She was beautiful. It was completely natural and completely normal.

And yet, the idea of her kissing anyone—touching anyone—the way she was kissing and touching him last night made him want to howl like a wounded animal and break things. He was jealous, Jack realized with a jolt of absolute horror.

Jealous of someone he'd never met, never seen.

All because he'd been someone Mariette had been involved with.

Dread ballooned in his belly. Oh, this was bad, Jack thought. This was very, very bad.

He'd never been jealous of anything or anyone

before, had never had reason to be. If a girl he liked chose another guy—which, to be fair, hadn't happened all that often—then he just moved on and found another one. Girls were girls. If one wasn't interested there was always one who would be.

Mariette wiped down the counter, sweeping cookie crumbs into her hands. Her mink-colored hair had been braided in a long rope that hung down on the side of her neck and curled provocatively around her breast. She wore another long-sleeve T-shirt and another pair of equally figure-flattering jeans. Small pearl studs gleamed from her ears and a gold locket dangled around her neck. He didn't have to open it to know that it would contain a picture of her mother.

A thought struck and he blinked. "Where's your aunt?" he wanted to know. "The one your mother named you after?"

She paused and darted him a strange look. "She's in Florida," she said. "She's retired from the state. She worked thirty years for the Treasury Department." She grinned, seemingly perplexed. "That was a bit random. I thought you were still stuck on Nathaniel."

His mood blackened at the reminder. "I guess the question isn't whether I'm still stuck on Nathaniel," he said, trying hard to sound calm and rational, neither of which he was at the moment. "It's whether or not you're still stuck on him."

She snorted as if the idea repulsed her. "No," she said, shooting him a level look. "I'm not."

Jack nodded once. "Good."

Her lips twitched, probably at his utterly ridiculous behavior. He didn't like being jealous. It made him feel strange, God help him, vulnerable even. It completely unsettled him.

She unsettled him.

Because that thought was too revealing and begged a lot of personal exploration involving feelings and emotions and everything else he'd managed to avoid the bulk of his entire adult life, Jack forced himself to change the subject altogether.

To one he knew she wasn't going to like.

Bobby Ray.

"We need to melt down all your remaining butter," Jack announced.

She started and looked up at him. Her pale gray eyes widened in shock. "What?"

Jack recounted everything he'd learned that day and concluded with his trip to the dairy. "I let him know that Mackie's boys were going to stay at the motel and that the clerk I talked to today was going to see to his things so that he wouldn't lose them. He knows I know there's a connection and he's terrified. I told him that I'd help him, that I'd make sure the debt was considered paid and that I'd back them off him, but he just doesn't trust me enough to let me do it. I'm sure he thinks that if he comes clean I'm going to haul him off to jail."

Mariette leaned against the counter, seemingly deep in thought. A line puckered her brow. "It could have been him," she said. "He's certainly the right height and build."

"He's obviously gotten into something he's not capable of getting out of on his own."

She looked up at him. "And you think that whatever he's taking from Audwin is hidden in the butter?"

Jack shrugged. "It's the only thing that makes sense, Mariette. He has no access to anyone or anything else. He's gotten snarled up with a mean-spirited bookie who's roughed him up once. He's shaking in his boots. So terrified that he won't go home." He passed a hand over his face. "And the kid looks terrible. Pale, drawn and sick. He's dirty, he hasn't bathed. I gave him some money for a room and told him to get his clothes cleaned and have a good meal. Maybe if he has a moment of safety he'll come to his senses."

She glanced up sharply and her expression softened. "You did? You gave him money?"

From the way she was looking at him one would think that he'd managed world peace or something equally impressive. Incredibly, he felt heat rise in his face. "I feel sorry for him," he said. "You were right.

He's a good kid who needs to be shown the better side of humanity. All he's seen is its worst."

Mariette tossed the washcloth in her hand aside, walked over to him, grabbed him by the shirt with both hands and yanked him down. Her smiling lips met his in a kiss that made the hair on his scalp tingle and the sensation moved with startling rapidity all the way down his body, clear to the soles of his feet.

Well, all righty, then.

Should he tell her about the old lady he'd helped across the street, too?

He quickly picked her up and set her on the counter behind him, then moved in between her legs. She wrapped her arms around his neck and her legs around his waist and pushed her sweet tongue into his mouth, inflaming him. She smelled like vanilla and sugar and she was achingly soft where she should be soft and firm where she should be firm. Her hair was cool against the backs of his hands and he fisted them in it the way he'd thought about doing the first time he'd ever seen her.

She left off his mouth and rained kisses down his cheek, along his jaw and down his neck. She sucked a little skin into her mouth and the response that hit his dick meant that she might as well have wrapped her lips around it instead.

He pushed up against her, tugged her shirt from the waistband of her jeans and slipped his hands up the small of her back, tracing the fluted spine with his thumbs.

She shivered and let go a low mewl of pleasure, then scooted even closer to the edge of the counter, putting the heart of her sex against the ridge of his arousal. She squirmed against him and he answered with a determined flex of his hips.

Another little gasp of delight slipped between her lips and he ate it, feasting on her mouth. Seemingly desperate to touch him, as well, she burrowed her hands beneath his sweater and skimmed her fingers along his sides. Her touch was soft and cool, but the havoc it wreaked in his body was anything but.

He was burning up.

So hot for her he should have flames spurting out of the top of his head. His head was ringing so hard he thought he heard bells.

The bell. Shit.

"You've got a customer," he said.

She arched against him again. "I don't care," she breathed against him.

Jack chuckled, gratified. "But you will when they leave." He reluctantly pulled away from her.

"Well, I see you have moved on," a male voice drawled from the doorway. Mariette instantly stiffened and Jack's gaze shifted to the direction of the speaker. He was medium height, medium build, nicely dressed and smug.

Jack instantly hated him.

"Let me guess," Jack said. "This must be Nathaniel."

Mariette glared at the intruder. "I told you not to come back."

His thin nostrils flared. "And I told you that you were being ridiculous."

Jack laughed, though the sound was not humorous. "Now I see what Charlie meant." He pressed a kiss against her forehead. "Excuse me a moment," he said and straightened. The look he sent Nathanial would have made a less-arrogant man quail. But this one was more than arrogant—he was stupid, as well.

Jack strolled forward, smiling all the while. If the idiot had one grain of sense he'd be afraid, since Jack desperately wanted to hit him. He refrained, but it wasn't easy. "She is *not* ridiculous," Jack said, his voice a low lethal growl. "She's *perfect* and she is finished with you." Jack wrapped his hand around the back of Nathaniel's neck, causing the moron to yelp like the little dog he was, then turned him around and hauled him back out the front door, then shoved him onto the sidewalk. "Do not come back," he said. "Ever. You are banned."

Strictly speaking, he didn't have the authority to ban anyone from her shop, but under the circumstances he hoped she wouldn't mind. He turned then and she was standing behind the counter, her eyes wide, her smile wider. She shook her head.

"I'm perfect, am I?"

He'd said it in the heat of the moment, but realized just then that he knew it was true. As far as he was concerned, yes, she was perfect.

And he was doomed.

"Lock that door, would you?" She turned to leave, then shot a look at him over her shoulder. "Then come upstairs. We have some unfinished business to complete."

And with another little smile, she left.

Slay a dragon, get the girl, Jack thought. And this girl was more than worth it.

11

MARIETTE HAD NEVER pegged herself for a woman who needed a grand gesture or one who liked for men to fight over her, or even be willing to fight over her, for that matter.

But watching the thundercloud of supreme displeasure descend over Jack's previously sleepy-looking, sexy countenance had been positively... thrilling.

She should be ashamed of herself, really, but couldn't muster the required humility.

She'd felt his anger rise up—could scarcely believe that Nathanial hadn't noticed it—and when her ex had made the "ridiculous" comment, whatever control Jack had attempted to maintain snapped.

Even his laugh—that little dark chuckle—had been rife with pure, white-hot fury. The atmosphere in the room had changed so much she'd felt the little hairs on the back of her arms rise up.

And Nathaniel—she inwardly shook her head—dumb-ass Nathaniel, didn't have sense enough to retreat. To run. He just stood there. She snickered. Until Jack snatched him up and hauled him forcibly out of her shop and onto the sidewalk.

And Jack had done that for her—because she'd been insulted. Because he thought she was perfect.

It was a caveman tactic to be sure, but she'd *loved* it.

Mariette had no more than unlocked the door when she heard him pounding up the stairs behind her. She turned in time to watch him bend down and toss her over his shoulder.

She squealed and gasped as her feet left the ground. "What are you doing? Put me down!"

He went unerringly to her bedroom and tumbled her onto the bed. "If that's what you want," he said, coming down next to her. His mouth instantly found hers, taking her lips in a deep, breath-stealingly electrifying kiss. She felt it all the way down to her toes, where they curled in the shoes she hadn't had time to take off. She did now, kicking them onto the floor, where they landed with a decided *thump*.

She wrapped her arms more tightly around him, pushing her hands into hair. She loved his hair, the silky way it slipped through her fingers. She caressed the soft skin behind his ear, relished the feel of his hard, long body pressed to hers.

He sucked her bottom lip into his mouth and

groaned low. "You taste so good," he said, kissing her again, making love to her mouth.

Mariette tugged at his sweater until he drew back enough to let her pull it over his head. She cast it aside and then looked greedily at him. Smooth, supple skin, the muscular curve of his shoulder, the flare of muscles at his sides, tapering into a lean, hard waist. Blond hairs whorled over his pecs and a treasure trail arrowed low and beneath the waistband of his jeans.

He was absolutely breathtaking. The best specimen of a man she'd ever seen. She trailed her fingers over his chest, his flesh hot and soft, then bent forward and touched her tongue to a male nipple.

He shuddered. Quaked.

And the power instantly went to her head. She did it again, slipping her fingers along his back, down his spine, then nipped at the ruched tip and he sucked in a hiss between his teeth.

Rather than take that lying down, as it were, Jack immediately relieved her of her shirt. His eyes feasted on her bare flesh, making her feel beautiful and wanted, treasured. She reached up and popped the catch on her bra, opening it for him. He bent forward and nudged one cup aside, then circled the globe with his nose, breathing her in. She could feel his hot breath against her skin, raising gooseflesh as it grazed her aching nipple. A chord of longing tightened in her core, and she arched up against him, desperate and needy.

Her breath came in sharp little puffs that were almost embarrassing they were so loud, but she couldn't seem to help herself. When it came to this level of desire, she was way out of her depth. It was beyond anything she'd ever experienced, ever imagined possible. Every cell in her body was clamoring for him—his taste, his scent, his skin on hers, his skin *in* hers.

His mouth closed over her nipple, snatching the breath from her lungs as he suckled deep, his tongue rasping over the hardened peak.

She turned, trying to get closer to him and slid her hand down his belly until she found the button at his waist. He drew a sharp breath when her fingers brushed against the top of his penis, which had escaped its enclosure, as it were.

Sweet heaven, Mariette thought, as she lowered his zipper and he sprung free into her waiting hand. He moved to the other breast, his own clever fingers expertly undoing her jeans, as well. She lifted up so that he could work the jeans down over her hips, then kicked them aside with more haste than grace.

His hands were suddenly all over her, sliding along her side, over her middle and then into her weeping folds. The first brush of his fingers against her sensitive flesh made her inhale deeply and he took that opportunity to find her mouth once more, eating the sigh that came with the exhalation of gratified air.

He dallied expertly between her legs and she worked the long hard length of him against her palm and all the while her skin burned up and shivered and desire alternately weighted her limbs and made her restless. She felt as though she was going to die if he didn't take her, that she'd die when he did and she just wanted, she just needed...him.

"Please," she whispered brokenly, not ashamed to beg.

He drew back, snagged a condom from his wallet and swiftly rolled it into place, then positioned himself between her thighs. He was huge, much bigger than she'd realized. He nudged high, sliding his thickness along her folds, coating himself in her juices before slipping back and prodding her entrance. He gave a gentle push and she inhaled, desperately wanting him more deeply inside her.

"I don't want to hurt you," he said, his face a mask of tight control.

"I'm not going to break," she said, dragging her legs back and opening more widely for him. She arched up, taking a little more of him in and she watched him set his jaw, the muscles jump in his cheek.

He pushed again, just a little, and stars danced behind her lids. He waited, allowing her to stretch and accommodate his size, then she arched up again, taking a little bit more of him.

Sweat beaded his brow and his forearms were lined with taut, distended veins. Any other man would have plowed right ahead, without a care for whether or not she was hurt, but this one… This one would hurt himself before hurting her. An aching swelled in her chest, a tenderness she'd never experienced before.

Mariette bent forward and kissed his chest, his throat. "Come here," she said, pulling him down closer. She found his mouth, kissed him deeply and felt him relax more fully. She arched again, felt him slide in a little deeper, and then with a deep, resigned sigh he breathed right into her mouth—into her very soul—and he pushed in and filled her up.

Literally.

It was indescribably perfect, the way he felt inside of her.

She tightened around him, sighed once more, and then arched up, savoring every ridge, every vein, the engorged head of his penis. She could feel it all in individual parts when he pushed into her and the sensation was nothing short of exquisite.

Once he was certain that he wasn't going to hurt her, Jack became less hesitant and more determined. Now that he'd invaded her body, he was going to make it submit to his will.

And she would, she knew, all too readily.

He plunged in and out of her, a slow, steady rhythm that stoked a fire that was already blazing out of control. Mariette could feel the first flash of release building in her sex, deep in her womb, and she welcomed that reward, needed it more desperately than she'd ever needed anything before. She arched up against him, meeting him thrust for thrust and tightened her feminine muscles around him.

Jack's breath came in hard little puffs and he angled deeper and higher. Her aching breasts absorbed the force of his thrusts, bouncing on her chest, and her belly felt as if it was going to hit her backbone if she breathed any harder. She wrapped her arms around him, licked a path along his neck and to his shoulder.

He quaked against her, pounded harder. Higher, harder, faster, he plunged in and out of her, his tautened balls hitting her sensitive flesh with every brutal thrust.

The orgasm ultimately hit her without warning.

One minute she'd been savoring him—the way he fit inside of her, the way he looked on top of her, the determined glint in his heavy-lidded eyes.

The next she was flying apart, a long, keening cry tearing from her throat. She spasmed hard around him and every muscle in her body seized up and then released, leaving her feeling melted and sated and unbelievably happy.

MARIETTE'S TIGHT LITTLE BODY fisted around him over
and over, her mouth opening in a cry of gratifying
pleasure, her neck arched as she let the delight swell
through her.

Dark hair against the down comforter, her sinfully carnal mouth carved into a blissed-out smile
that he'd put on her face, her breasts rosy tipped and
pouting…

She was unequivocally the most beautiful woman
he'd ever seen.

Or would ever see again, he knew.

Jack buried himself to the hilt again, absorbing
the absolute glory of her perfect body. She was hot
and soft and tight—so *damned* tight—and he'd been
terrified of hurting her, of making a move that would
result in her pain, but she'd taken him in, inch by
inch, degree by degree until he could feel nothing
but her…and that was all that mattered.

Her soft hands glided over him now, greedy and
slow, as though she couldn't get enough of him,
either, as though she needed him—*this*—as much
as he did. She tightened around him, bent forward
and slid her wicked tongue against his throat again,
along his jaw. He loved her mouth, the feel of it, the
taste of it, the things she did with it. To him.

She drew her legs back, anchoring around his
waist once more and her feet curved around the twin
globes of his ass, urging him on. He heard her gasp,

make another little mewl of satisfaction and felt her contract around him once more.

"Oh, no," she said, thrashing beneath him. "I can't— It's too much— I—" She screamed again, her voice low and hoarse and wilted, into the mattress beneath him. Her tight channel closed around him, once, twice, a third time.

He came hard.

His vision blackened around the edges, his head spun and he shook so hard he was afraid his suddenly weakened limbs wouldn't support him.

Release racked through him, twisting through his body like a sensual tornado of feeling. Pleasure, relief, ecstasy and something else, something altogether more tender, more significant and more terrifying than anything he'd ever felt before. He seated himself as far into her as he could go, letting the last of the tremors run through him, then looked down into her upturned face.

Her eyes were closed, the lashes longer and curlier than he'd realized, her cheeks flushed, lips swollen from his kisses. A soft smile, one of absolute contentment, shaped her sinful mouth. She opened her eyes then and he watched the pupils dilate, adjusting to the light. They weren't merely gray, Jack decided. They were silver. And they had the power to look right through him, to lay him bare and leave him open. Much as the thought sent a dagger of dread into his chest, the thing that scared him the most—made him nearly ill when he thought about it—was the idea of not being able to do this again.

He bent forward and pressed a kiss to her lips, slid a finger reverently down the side of her face.

This girl was going to be the end of him, Jack thought. But if so, he'd come to a better end than most.

12

"THAT'S THE LAST OF IT," Mariette said, coming out of the walk-in fridge.

Wearing only pajama bottoms and a puzzled look, Jack arched a brow. "You're sure?"

She nodded and heaved a sigh. "Yes. You've melted all of my butter. I have no idea how I'm going to bake tomorrow," she said, looking forlornly at all that wasted buttery goodness.

Jack winced, his face a mask of utter perplexity. "I was certain that we'd find it," he said. "I know that he's hidden it here. He didn't even try to deny it, Mariette. He didn't even bother."

Mariette plopped up onto a bar stool and snagged one of Livvie's Specials to munch on. Though they'd ordered takeout and she'd eaten plenty, she was still starving. Her lips curled as her gaze drifted down the masculine slope of Jack's shoulders, the sheer magnificence of his muscled frame.

Of course, she'd no doubt burned a lot of calories this evening. Sex would do that for a girl. And lots of blistering-hot, sweaty, splendid sex would do even more.

Mariette couldn't remember a time when she'd ever—*ever*—had a multiple orgasm. Of course she'd heard about the legendary double O, but it had always escaped her. Quite frankly, she'd never achieved orgasm through sex alone. She'd always required a little more…stimulation. The fact that Jack Martin had made her sing the Hallelujah twice without using any digits or battery-operated devices was nothing short of a sexual miracle for her.

He. Was. Awesome.

And huge. And *straight*. As a friggin' arrow.

Even now, just looking at him, made something warm and hot slither into her belly. Her breasts pebbled behind her nightshirt—she'd forgone the bra—and she felt a twinge of remembered pleasure echo in her womb. She could take him again, Mariette realized. Right here, right now. In fact, she grimly suspected that she would always want him, crave him, even, and the idea was as pleasant as it was disturbing.

She didn't want to need him. She didn't want to need anybody, Mariette thought, because needing led to heartache. Unfortunately, when it came to Jack Martin she didn't think she was going to have a choice. He…just made her feel good. He made her body hum and her heart—an organ that had no business being involved in this, considering that she barely knew him—sing. He was smart and funny and honorable and she didn't give a damn whether the people of Pennyroyal thought their golden boy was tarnished.

If you asked her, he was perfect…too.

When he'd told her tonight that he'd given Bobby Ray the money for a motel room and had offered to help the boy—despite believing that he was guilty of something here—something inside of her had just… snapped. He'd reviewed all of the facts, taken the time to find out what was going on with the kid, and then extended an offer that Mariette was sure the boy had never been given before—mercy.

And when he'd kicked Nathanial out… Well, that had just been icing on the cake.

Jack Martin was unlike any man she'd ever met before and she instinctively knew she'd never meet one better. Irrational, considering her track record? Possibly, but she knew it all the same. He was different. He made her feel different. He made her want to believe that she could have what Jay and Charlie had, the kind of love that didn't ask for anything in return. That just…*was*.

A possessiveness she'd never imagined herself capable of burst through her, momentarily taking her aback. The idea of anyone else touching him—of *him* touching anyone else the way he'd just touched her—made her mind turn black with rage and recoil.

"Are you all right?" Jack asked, a concerned line between his brows. "I'll replace your butter," he said. "I'll call Audwin right now and go get it if you'd like."

Mariette blinked, trying to pull her thoughts together. "That's all right," she said. "If you don't mind if I work for a little while, I'll go ahead and get everything ready for tomorrow." That way she could save a portion of it anyway.

Jack swore. "Aren't you tired?" he asked. "You've been up since three and I was under the impression that you hadn't slept very well."

That was true, she'd admit. After their marathon kissing session in the kitchen she'd been even more wound up than she'd been before she'd gone in there. His fault, she thought, heaving a fatalistic sigh. She imagined lots of things in the near future were going to be his fault. She smiled anyway and hopped down from the chair.

"That's true," she said. "But I find myself strangely energized."

His lips slid into a slow grin. "Really? Sex energizes you?" He shook his head. "Could you be any more perfect?"

"No," Mariette quipped. She dipped a finger in the warm butter and sucked it off her finger, her eyes widening appreciatively. "That's good stuff. Every-thing is better with butter."

She looked over at Jack and his mouth had gone a bit slack. He blinked. Swallowed. "I'm sorry. Could you do that again?"

She laughed. "Men are so visual," she said.

"I know," he told her with a pointed look. "That's why I asked you to do it again."

She pulled a bowl from the rack above her head and started measuring out ingredients. "Don't you have anything to do?" she asked. "A file you should be looking over or something?"

He hopped up on another counter, crossed his arms over his chest and studied her. "No. I know who our culprit is," he said. "I've just got to try to convince him to come clean before anything hap-pens to him."

"Why do you have to wait?" Mariette asked. She dumped a pound of sugar into the bowl. "You know who's harassing him. Go whack 'em or whatever."

He chuckled softly under his breath. "Whack 'em? I'm not a mob boss, Mariette."

She measured the butter and dumped it the bowl, then shoved it under the mixer. "I know that, smart-ass. I just meant do to them what you've already told him you'd do. Make them leave him alone. Once you've done that, then he'll trust you and he won't have any reason to continue doing whatever it is he's doing."

Jack was thoughtful for a moment. "You know," he said after a minute, "that's a good idea."

She shot him a droll smile. "Occasionally, I have them."

He grinned. "I didn't mean it like that. Making Uncle Mackie and his muscle back off of Bobby Ray would certainly take the pressure off, that's for sure." He winced. "I don't know what he's taken from Audwin, but that's probably not going to be anything I can fix."

Mariette added eggs and vanilla into the bowl. "Like me, Audwin has a soft spot for Bobby Ray. Whatever it is that he's done, I think Audwin would ultimately forgive him."

Jack paused, snuck one of Livvie's Specials and chewed thoughtfully. "I think you're probably right. But Bobby Ray isn't used to being given any grace. Convincing him to tell the truth isn't going to be easy."

Mariette started measuring the flour in. "If anyone can do it, I'm sure you can."

He was quiet for so long she turned to look at him. His expression was strange, a mix between wondering and haunted.

Mariette frowned. "Did I say something wrong?" she asked.

He chuckled, cleared his throat. "No," he said. "You said something so right it took me off guard, that's all."

Mariette smiled tentatively. "I have no idea what you mean by that," she said.

"Good," he quipped, passing a hand over his face. "Because I don't understand it, either."

"You seem to be adjusting well," she remarked, hoping that she wasn't crossing some invisible booby-trapped line that was going to blow up in her face.

"To what?"

"Being a civilian," she said. She continued to work, purposely didn't look at him.

"I suppose," he said, casting her a speculative look that made her unaccountably nervous. "What all has Charlie told you?"

Mariette darted him a look. "What makes you think she's told me anything?"

"Please," he said, as though she'd insulted him. "You've met my sister. She's bossy, opinionated and has no brain-to-mouth filter." A dry bark of laughter erupted from his throat. "She's filled your ears full, hasn't she?"

Damn, she should have kept her mouth shut. She had no desire to start a war between brother and sister. "She's sung your praises," she said. "If that's what you mean by filling my ears full."

He swore. "She told you about Baghdad, didn't she? Come clean, Mariette. What else did she say?"

"She said that you were valedictorian of your class, the star quarterback for your high school football team and that girls threw their panties at you when you walked down Main Street."

He guffawed, filched another cookie. "Bullshit."

"Well, I might have interpreted that last part based on her 'town golden boy' comment, but otherwise it's all true." She withdrew a cupcake pan and started popping liners into the cups. "She adores you, you know. She thinks the sun rises and sets on you."

Still smiling, he got up and poured himself a glass of milk. "I know she loves me," he said. "And I love her, too. We've always been close."

Mariette sighed. "I can tell," she said. "I'm envious."

He paused. "I guess family was a little thin for you, wasn't it?"

"Just me, my mother and my aunt. My grandparents died when I was three—car accident. My aunt was so busy taking care of me and my mother that she never married or had children of her own. She's got a boyfriend now," she said, shooting him a smile. "It's cute. They play bingo together and are in the drama club in their retirement village."

"That sounds nice."

"I miss her," Mariette said and could hear the wistfulness in her own voice. "I go down for the holidays, usually."

"What part of Florida?"

"Tampa."

"I've always heard that's a nice area."

"It is. I love the ocean. Breathing it in, tasting the salt in the air."

"I haven't been in years," Jack said, a touch of disbelief in his voice.

Mariette looked up. "Why not?"

Another smile. "No time," he said. He grimaced. "War is hell."

She pulled a cup from the rack and started dipping the batter up. "I guess your family would have objected to you coming to the States and going to the beach instead of home."

"Er, yes," he said. "That would have gone over like a lead balloon."

"You've got time now," she pointed out.

"I do, don't I?"

She shot him another look. "Yes, you do. Being home is going to have its perks."

His gaze drifted over her face, lingered on her lips. "I've found one already."

Holy hell, Mariette thought. That look was hot enough to melt that butter all over again. She released a shuddering breath and made herself turn back to the task at hand. She felt his heat before he touched her and it was all she could do not to lean back and sink into him. And then she wondered what the hell was wrong with her. Why couldn't she lean back and sink into him? He lifted the hair off her neck and pressed a kiss to her nape.

"I love the way you smell, Mariette. It drives me crazy."

She shivered, relaxed more fully against him.

He placed another kiss just behind her ear, his breath fanning against her, then reached around and filled his hands with her breasts, massaged them through the shirt, tweaking her aching nipples. She pressed her rear end against him, arching up and felt him harden, his sex riding high against her rump.

She went boneless, her head becoming too heavy for her neck. "Jack, I—"

He shushed her, dipped a finger into the butter and put it to her mouth. "Suck it, Mariette," he whispered. "I want to feel your lips around me."

Oh, sweet hell.

She opened for him, taking his finger into her mouth.

He groaned into her ear, pressed against her. "Damn, woman, you're killing me."

She slid her tongue along the bottom of his finger, mimicking what she'd do to another part of him. "You asked me to," she said.

He chuckled softly and she turned her head, and found his mouth. The kiss was slow and deep, deliberate and thorough and the need she was certain was never going to leave her boiled up inside so quickly that she wondered if something was wrong with her internal thermometer. It couldn't be good for her to be this hot.

He sucked at her tongue, slid his big hands beneath her nightshirt and palmed her breasts once more. She rubbed her rump against him again, arched like a cat, then turned around, twined her arms around his neck and jumped up, wrapping her legs around his waist.

"Take me over there," she said, indicating the small love seat against the wall. "And then just take me."

AND THEN JUST TAKE ME...

God help him, she was going to be the death of him, Jack thought as he did as she asked. He strode over to the little sofa and tumbled her onto her back.

"Oh, no," she said. "Like this." She nudged him into a sitting position and then straddled him. She dragged her shirt over her head, revealing pert, puckered breasts that begged for his kiss and a pair of panties that were so small they might as well be nonexistent.

He slid his hands over her back, relishing the feel of her and pulled a rosy bud into his mouth, suckling her deeply. She squirmed on top of him, then reached down and freed his shaft from his pajama bottoms and positioned it at her entrance. She slid her wet folds against him in a move so provocative, so bold and so damned wonderful he almost came right then. His eyes widened.

"Mariette, I don't have a condom down here."

"Neither do I," she said. "But I'm clean and protected. You?"

"Clean, yes."

"Works for me." She lifted her hips and slowly anchored herself on top of him, her tight, moist heat closing deliciously around him. She hissed low and slow, her eyes fluttering shut as though he felt too good, as though she needed him as much as he needed her.

She lifted again, sank again. Her ass was ripe and wonderful and he slid his hands over it possessively, fed at her breasts while she rode him. It was slow at first, deliberate and purposeful. But the harder he sucked on her, the harder she rode him and before long her hips were moving faster than he could suck. He squeezed her backside and bucked beneath her.

Her fingers scored his chest as she writhed on top of him, dark hair spilling over her shoulders, brushing her breasts, a thatch of equally dark curls at the apex of her thighs. The gentle flare of her hips, the concave belly, the firm thighs…

She was a goddess, a dream, a present he didn't even know he wanted.

And when she'd blithely told him that if anyone could convince Bobby Ray to do the right thing, then it would be him… Jack didn't know what had happened or why her vote of confidence had meant so much.

But it had.

She didn't doubt him. Believed in him.

He knew that his family still believed in him. Hell, even his fellow soldiers had after the accident. Any one of them would have gone out with him again. But until that moment Jack hadn't realized that he hadn't truly trusted himself, hadn't fully believed that he was still the same man. Still strong, still capable.

Still him.

Until *she'd* believed in him.

She swore and rode him harder, her tight little body closing around him. Her breath came in frantic little puffs, her face flushed pink. She sank her teeth into her bottom lip and then arched back and let go a sound that was so personal, so primal and so uninhibited, it set him off like a Roman candle. The release blasted from the back of his loins, shot through the heart of his dick and spilled into her.

He quaked with the strength of it. Shook.

It was the single most magnificent sensation of his life.

The world receded, time slowed to a crawl and even though he could hear his heart racing in his chest, even that seemed suddenly sluggish.

Jack Martin had been stealing kisses since kindergarten, making it to third base in junior high and had been regularly hitting it out of the park, so to speak, since his freshman year of high school.

He had never, not once, had unprotected sex.

His seed had never seen the inside of a woman. Until now.

He wanted to beat his chest and roar, wanted to scoop her up, haul her upstairs and do it all over again. He wanted to brand her somehow, let the world know that she was his and only his.

She framed his face with her hands, slid her fingers reverently along his jaw. Her gaze was tender and replete and rife with affection and something else...something more significant.

"You've ruined me for other men," she said, releasing a fatalistic sigh. She dropped her forehead against his. "I hope you're happy."

And he was.

13

MARIETTE WATCHED DILLON and Livvie from the doorway of the kitchen and felt a lump inexplicably swell in her throat. Both of their heads were bent low, almost touching, as Dillon hooked Livvie up with the promised ink. They were so sweet, so pure and so completely innocent it made her chest ache with joy.

She cast a glance at Charlie, who looked back at her with tears in her eyes. She laughed quietly and fanned her face. "I'm an emotional wreck," she said. "Bloody hormones."

Livvie laughed at something Dillon said and the boy leaned back in his chair, his chest puffed out, practically preening. He adored Livvie and the sentiment was wholly reciprocated.

Because she suspected she might be on to something like that herself—dare she even hope?—she knew her emotions were riding high on the surface.

And she didn't have any pregnancy hormones to blame, either.

She just had a hot former Army Ranger spending the night with her, bellying up to her back, making her middle go warm and squishy and her heart melt like a popsicle on the Fourth of July.

"What happened to all the butter?" Maggie wanted to know.

Mariette blushed, remembering the bit she'd licked off Jack's finger. She'd never look at butter the same, that was for damned sure.

"There was a problem with it," Mariette said evasively, unable to look anyone in the eye, most definitely Charlie who would know that something was up.

She was too perceptive by half, Mariette thought. And, while she didn't expect Charlie to be too broken up over the fact that Mariette had been sleeping—in the literal sense, as well—with her brother, it was nevertheless a conversation she didn't want to have.

"I need a bit more for the bread," Maggie told her. "Just to brush on the tops before I put the loaves in the oven."

"All right," Mariette told her. "I'll run upstairs and get some from my fridge."

She'd called Audwin this morning and told him she was going to need a delivery this afternoon and he'd promised to send Bobby Ray over later in the day. He'd apologized to Mariette—as though it were somehow his fault—and told her not to hesitate to contact him if she needed him. Dear man. He seemed so lost without Martha. No doubt Bobby Ray had been good company for him.

Mariette snagged all that she had and hurried back downstairs, then handed it over to Maggie. "This should tide us over until Bobby Ray comes by," she said.

Mariette had just made it to the door when Maggie made a disgusted harrumph. "There's something in this," she said.

Mariette whirled around, her heart pounding. "What?" She rushed forward and took the block of butter from Maggie's hands.

"Give me a knife, would you?" she asked.

Maggie handed it over and Mariette carefully cut away the part that housed the object. She set the rest of the block aside and worked on clawing away the remaining butter until she'd managed to see well enough to know what she had.

"A coin," Maggie said, surprised. "It looks like an old one, too." Her gaze met Mariette's. "Guess we know what the Butter Bandit was after."

Yes, she thought. They certainly did. She hollered for Charlie and snagged the phone to call Jack.

JACK HAD SPENT THE BETTER part of the day trying to find Uncle Mackie's goons, but had finally lucked out and found Uncle Mackie himself.

Behind a Porta-Potty, getting blown by a scrawny woman with bad skin.

"Leave," he told her. She scrambled up and darted away.

His sister had given him all the ammunition he needed on Uncle Mackie to bring the fat bastard to heel. Mackie was tall, but soft, with a beer belly, buckteeth—the few that he had, anyway—and mean, shrewd eyes.

It was almost better that he wasn't stupid, Jack thought. Perhaps he'd be smart enough to be scared.

"What the hell do you think you're doing?" he blustered, stowing his limp dick.

"Are you Mackie?" Jack asked. He knew he was, of course, but the man was so fond of the Uncle moniker, Jack knew he'd correct him.

"It's Uncle Mackie," he said.

Jack struck. He slammed his fist into the man's soft belly and when he doubled over, Jack twisted his arm up behind his back so hard that he heard it creak. That was for Bobby Ray, he thought. "You're no uncle of mine," he said, his tone lethal.

"You'd better get off me, boy," he said, breathing hard. "You don't know who you're messing with."

Jack pushed his arm up a little more. "As it happens, I do. You're the one who doesn't know who you're messing with. I'm a former Army Ranger with more skills and kills under my belt than you'd ever believe. I know a thousand different ways to hurt, maim, incapacitate and otherwise make you beg for death, you mean-spirited little bitch. I'm not a street thug, Mackie," Jack told him. "I'm a trained assassin, one of Uncle Sam's finest, and I've got *you*—" he gave him a little shake "—in my cross-hairs. I know that you're a misdemeanor away from a felony charge and my old man and grandfather were both with the Atlanta P.D. long enough to know who to talk to to see that you go away for a long, long time." He paused, could smell the fear on him. "Am I making myself clear?"

"Look, man, I don't want any trouble," he said, immediately backtracking. "What do you want?"

"I want you to absolve Bobby Ray Bishop of any debt and leave him the hell alone. If you or anyone associated with you comes within five miles of him—if I hear a single hair on his head has been touched or harmed in any way—I will come after you. I will hurt you. I will torture you." Jack shoved him to the ground and pulled the soap and sock from his back pocket and slowly assembled his weapon, the same one that had been used on Bobby Ray.

Mackie quailed and tried to scramble away, but Jack kicked him, preventing his escape. He took the sock and swung it hard against the man's back, thinking of poor skinny, scarred-up Bobby Ray with every strike.

Mackie howled with pain.

Jack did it again.

"Sucks when you're the one getting the beating, doesn't it, Mackie?" Jack asked conversationally. He swung again and again and ultimately had to make himself stop because he was enjoying it too much. But this was the only language a man like Mackie understood and Jack was fully capable of speaking it when he had to.

"Call them off," Jack said. "And stay away from Bobby Ray. Consider that *my* warning."

Jack turned and walked away, and left the man whimpering on the ground. It was fitting, he decided. That's what he'd done to Bobby Ray.

He'd just reached the car when his cell vibrated at his waist. He checked the display and smiled when he saw it was Mariette. "Hey," he said, pleasure winging through his chest.

"You were right," she said, her voice grim.

"I usually am, but about what this time?"

"I'd forgotten that I took a couple of loaves of butter upstairs," she said.

Every sense went on point. "And?"

"And I found an old coin in one of the loaves."

She sounded sick. "Mariette, we knew that he'd taken something. This doesn't change anything."

"I know," she said, her voice wobbling. "I was just hoping that you were wrong. If he's been stealing valuable coins from Audwin and selling them, he's never going to be able to pay him back or get the coins back." She swallowed. "Audwin will forgive him, I'm sure. I just don't know if Bobby Ray will ever forgive himself."

Jack had wondered that, as well, but knew that was simply going to have to be a bridge they crossed when they came to it.

"Did you find them?" she asked.

"Not the goons, no," he told her. "But I found Mackie. He and I reached an understanding."

"I'm missing a bar of soap," she said. "Did that have anything to do with your *understanding*?" she asked.

"And if it did?"

"Then, good," she said, surprising him. "He deserved it."

"You're bloodthirsty," he said, impressed. "I like that in a woman."

"And I like justice," she said. "And big, badass men like you who aren't afraid to mete it out when needed. You're a good man, Jack Martin."

He swallowed, his throat suddenly tight. "You're a good woman."

She chuckled. "One more lyric and we'll have a country song."

"Smart-ass," he said, laughing.

"You liked my ass last night," she said.

Indeed he did. Heat pooled in his groin, making him shift behind the wheel. "You're just trying to stir me up, aren't you?"

"*Up* works for me," she said, her voice low, almost foggy.

He swerved off the pavement and a car horn blared. *Shit.*

"Jack?" she said, alarmed.

"Mariette, the time for phone sex is not when I'm behind the wheel of my car on eight-five."

She chuckled. "Right. Sorry."

"You don't sound sorry."

"What does sorry sound like?"

"Repentant?"

She *tsked.* "Don't tell me you have the Catholic-schoolgirl fantasy," she said, her voice wicked.

He chuckled darkly. "I will pay you back," he said. "I promise you, I will."

"Can I choose what sort of punishment I want?"

She was killing him. "I'll be there in a few minutes. I'm hanging up now."

"Oooh, are you going to spank me when you get here?"

"Who are you talking to?" He heard his sister ask.

The line instantly went dead.

Jack guffawed.

BOBBY RAY FINISHED LOADING the truck with the delivery for Mariette and, sick with dread, went to let Audwin know he was leaving.

He was absolutely certain that Jack Martin had found the coin and that it was only a matter of time before the police turned up to take him in. He'd resigned himself to it, even knew he deserved his punishment. He should have never taken anything from Audwin and wished that he could go back and undo it. Audwin had been kind to him and deserved better. Bobby Ray knew he had to be a man about this, had accepted it last night when he'd crawled into the warm bed that Jack Martin had bought for him.

Jack had been right. A good night's sleep, a warm meal and clean clothes had made him feel a lot better. It had given him a chance to clear his head, to come to terms with what he had to do.

When he came back from making this last delivery, he fully intended to tell Audwin what he'd done and then turn himself in. The benefit to serving his time would be that, for the moment anyway, Uncle Mackie wouldn't be able to get to him. Once he got out—he didn't figure they'd keep him in there forever—he'd get as far away from Atlanta as he could. Uncle Mackie was brutal, but ultimately a businessman and pursuing him across the country wouldn't be cost-effective. Had he not been so terrified, that would have occurred to him earlier.

And to be fair, he hadn't wanted to leave Audwin.

Since Martha had passed away, the old man was just as alone and lonely as Bobby Ray had been most of his life. He'd figured they were good for one another and would miss him when he left. He'd miss Prize, too, but the dog would have to stay here.

Bobby Ray could barely feed himself, much less a dog, and Prize deserved better. All of them did.

And a man had to do what a man had to do.

He rounded the corner and watched a familiar car bolt down the driveway, away from the house.

His stomach dropped to his knees and he rushed into the office. "Audwin!"

Bobby Ray ran all over the dairy and even up to the house. It wasn't until he came back to the office that he saw the note in the middle of the desk. "The old man is going to take your punishment until you pay up."

Bobby Ray's knees buckled and he fell to the ground. *No,* he thought. *No, no, no!*

Hands shaking, Bobby Ray reached into his pocket, pulled out a card and dialed the number on the front. Jack Martin answered on the second ring.

"They've taken Audwin," he said, the first tears he'd cried since he was eight years old spilling down his scarred cheeks. "I need your help. I'll do anything," Bobby Ray told him, his voice thick. "Anything you want me to do. Just h-help me," he sobbed.

14

"I DON'T GET IT," Charlie said. "Unless there's some special marking that we're missing this is just an old penny." She looked up at Mariette. "Worth only a penny. Why would Bobby Ray take this?"

Mariette shook her head. "I don't know. Maybe he thought it was worth something. Maybe he knows more about it than we do."

"That's possible," Charlie said. "But I've plugged in all the data from this coin to determine its value and it's worth a penny. If he was expecting some sort of windfall for this, then I'm afraid he's going to be very disappointed."

Charlie's cell suddenly chirped and she checked the display. Her lips curled. "Yes, big brother." Her gaze darted to Mariette. "Yes, she's right here. All right, I will. Keep your panties on." She engaged the speakerphone feature. "There you go," she said. "What's up?"

"Uncle Mackie's goons have Audwin," he said, his tone grim.

Mariette gasped, horrified, and Charlie's eyes rounded and she swore. "Those bastards," she hissed. "What can I do?"

"Charlie, I need every possible address for Mackie and his boys. Even their families. We have to find him quickly."

"I'm on it," Charlie said and quickly set to work, her fingers flying over the keyboard of the laptop.

Mariette's mouth was bone-dry. "You think Mackie ignored your warning?"

"No," he said grimly. "I think this had already been set into motion before I found Mackie. That's what makes this dangerous. He knows that I'm going to come for him, that I'll be gunning for him. And he'll either instruct those morons to dump Audwin off somewhere, or he'll…"

"Or he'll make sure he's never found." The floor shifted beneath her feet.

"How did he find out about the dairy?" Charlie asked without missing a keystroke.

"The goons went through the garbage at the motel looking for Bobby Ray's stuff when he never returned. Geneva, the clerk, didn't pack up Bobby Ray's garbage and evidently there was a check stub from the dairy that had gone into the trash."

"How did you find all of this out?" Mariette wanted to know.

"Bobby Ray called me. He saw them leave and found a note that said Audwin was going to take his punishment until he paid up."

"Where are you headed now?" Charlie asked.

"Back down to the track on the off chance Mackie's still there. Doubtful, I know, but…"

"I'm going to call the office," Charlie said. "And give every available agent an address, Jack. There's too many of them and there's only one of you. Time is of the essence here, so don't argue with me—"

"That's brilliant, Charlie, thanks. Mariette?"

Charlie looked momentarily stunned at her brother's praise, then she smiled wide, went to the landline and called Ranger Security.

"I'm here," she said. "What can I do?"

"I've told Bobby Ray to come down to the shop. He should be there any minute now. I need you to do me a favor."

She swallowed, desperate to have something to do, to have a way to contribute. "Anything."

"He's taken a couple of coins to a pawn shop just outside of Hiram. He's got his tickets, but no money. If you could go pick them up, I'll pay you back. The boy is beside himself, pitiful—" Jack's voice broke. "He's going to pay me back, but in the mean time he needs to be able to give those coins back to Audwin, especially after this. I can't put him through— Do you mind fronting me the—"

"Of course not," she said, a lump swelling in her

throat. Had there ever been a better man? A less self-ish one? Mariette wondered, unbelievably moved by Jack's gesture.

"Tell him I'm texting the list of addresses and where each guy is going," Charlie told her. "I've got seven heading out."

Mariette relayed the information. "I'll get your cell number and text you from my phone so that you'll have mine. Keep me posted, Jack. It's going to be hell not knowing what's going on."

"I will," he said. "Thanks, Mariette."

"Be careful," she said. "It would be terrible if you'd survived Baghdad only to come home and get taken out by a couple of common thugs."

"I'll try not to get whacked," he said, chuckling softly. He swore and she could practically hear his head shaking over the line. "I knew she'd told you about Baghdad."

"Don't be angry at her," she said, crouching low over the phone. "She's proud of you."

"I know that, but she only knows part of the story."

Mariette paused. "Well, when you're ready to share the rest of it then I'm ready to listen."

There was a knock at the back door and Billy Ray poked his head in. His face was wet with tears, his eyes red rimmed, his expression utterly miserable.

"Bobby Ray's here," she said. "Call me when there's news."

"I will."

Mariette disconnected, then stood up and walked over to Bobby Ray. She framed the boy's dear face with her hands and thumbed a tear away, then pressed a kiss to his forehead. "It's going to be all right, Bobby Ray," she said and wrapped her arms around him.

He seemed shocked at first, went completely still as though he wasn't sure what to do—and he probably wasn't, Mariette thought, her heart twisting with agony. God only knew the last time the kid had been properly hugged or shown any sort of affection.

She waited, hoping he'd return the hug and, after the briefest of seconds, she felt him wrap his arms around her, his shoulders shaking with regret. "I'm sorry, Mariette. I'm so, so sorry. I didn't mean to—"

She shushed him, swayed with him back and forth and slid a hand down the back of his head. "It's all right, Bobby Ray. Everybody makes mistakes. You just got into something you couldn't find a way out of on your own. But you've got friends. You've got people who care about you. You can ask for help if you need it. There's no shame in that." She drew back and drew a bracing breath. "Now let's go get those coins back, shall we?"

"It's a lot of money, Mariette." He swallowed, clearly humbled. "I can't believe he's going to do this for me, let me pay him back. Mr. Martin is a good guy, isn't he?"

Mariette smiled up at him. "He's the best."

And as much as it was hard to believe, given how long she'd known him...he unequivocally owned her heart.

How in the hell had that happened?

Hiatus, her ass. She'd gone and fallen in love with him.

JUST AS HE'D FIGURED, Mackie had left the track and gone to ground. Jack had checked in with everyone else and so far none of them had had any luck, either. Payne had checked Goon One's home address, McCann had taken Goon Two's and Jamie had started working the family angle.

It was amazing how many of these men, when faced with any sort of fear or threat, returned to their first form of refuge—behind their mother's skirts. Which was why Jack had decided to take a little trip over to Uncle Mackie's mother's house. The address Charlie had found for the woman was in an affluent neighborhood, one of those gated communities with its own clubhouse and swimming pool.

He circled the block, noting a red sports car tucked all the way in the back, parked at an angle that had practically hidden it from view.

But it was Uncle Mackie's.

The vanity plate read Bet Me.

A slow, lethal smile slid across Jack's lips as he

pulled his truck up far enough to nudge the little car's bumper. The fiberglass gave a gratifying crack.

That felt good.

Nailing that fat bastard to the wall was going to feel better. Evidently hearing the noise, Mackie raced outside, took one look at Jack and darted back into the house like a mole returning to its hole.

Shit. He was going to have to abandon good manners.

He bolted for the door, knocked twice and then let himself inside. A petite woman with gray hair and the straightest backbone Jack had ever seen suddenly blocked his path.

"Can I help you?" she said archly.

"I need to speak to your son, ma'am."

She poked her finger in his chest. "Now you listen here," she said. "I don't allow any of that damned fool betting business in my house. If you've got an issue with my son, then you need to take it up at the track. But it doesn't come here."

"Then he shouldn't," Jack told her. "He's taken an old man hostage and, forgive me, ma'am, but I'm not leaving here without getting the necessary information I need to get him back from your son."

She quailed, then rallied, fire lighting her gaze and she whirled around. "Morris!" she called threateningly.

Morris? Jack heard the front door slam and took off. Mackie had barely taken five steps before Jack vaulted from the porch and launched himself at him, pinning him to the ground. Jack pulled a gun from his waistband, disengaged the safety and pressed it to the back of Mackie's head.

"You have to the count of five," Jack told him, "and then I'm going to blow your brains out through your face."

"You wouldn't, not in front of my mother," Mackie said, though he didn't sound altogether certain.

"One."

"Mom!" he called frantically, trying to dislodge Jack. "Mommy!" he squealed.

"Two."

"Go ahead and shoot him," Mackie's mother said, shooting Jack a wink that her son couldn't see. "But do me a favor and drag him around back. I don't want a mess in the front yard."

"Mom! No, please. Mom!"

"Three."

"I didn't know!" Mackie screamed frantically. "The two jackasses took it upon themselves! I didn't tell them to do it!"

"Four."

"He's in the trunk of my car!" Mackie wailed. "I didn't know what to do— I needed to be able to think— I—"

White-hot anger burst through Jack and he flipped him over and planted his fist into Mackie's nose, then reached down and withdrew his car keys from his pocket.

Mackie's mother's face was stark white. "You've put an old man into your trunk and brought him here? He's been in your car the whole time?" She took her shoe off and proceeded to pummel the hell out of him right there on the front lawn, Mackie rolling and writhing beneath the blows, trying to get away from her.

Heart pounding so hard he felt nauseous, Jack hurried around back and hit the truck release button on the keyless remote. It popped, but didn't open completely. A flannel-covered arm popped up and pushed at it.

"Audwin!" Jack hollered. "Are you all right?"

Audwin glared up at him. "I was better until you rammed the back of his car."

Jack grabbed the older man's hand and helped him awkwardly out of the trunk. "Did they hurt you?"

"No," he said. "Just got the jump on me was all," he told him, clearly embarrassed. "Nasty characters, though," he said. "I'll admit I was worried there for a while. Those big bastards thought their boss would be happy that they'd nabbed me. But you'd gotten a hold of him first and put the fear into him. He didn't know what to do with me, so he had those assholes throw me into the back of his car."

"But you're not hurt?"

"Only my pride, boy, and I reckon that'll survive." He looked up sharply. "How's Bobby Ray?"
He shook his head. "If he'd only told me what was
going on, I could have helped the boy. I'd have
given him the money to pay them off," he said. "He
wouldn't have had to take those damned coins."

Jack blinked. "You knew about the coins?"

"Not until I heard them talking about it. They
were planning on going back and tearing my place
apart to look for them." His lips twisted. "They
weren't going to tell their boss about that, either."

"He's gone to get the coins out of hock," Jack told
him. "And Mariette found the other one in a block
of butter she'd taken up to her apartment. You'll get
them all back, Audwin." He paused. "I'd appreciate
if you'd cut the boy some slack on this. He's spent
so long between a rock and a hard place he doesn't
know what a soft one feels like."

Audwin scowled at him. "You think I don't know
that?" He shook his head. "I don't know why he
thought they were valuable," he said. "I'm not an
official collector. Those are just pieces that have
been given to me by family members—my dad and
grandfather, mostly. I've always had a knack for
finding pennies after losing people, you know. Everyone thinks that's an old wives' tale, but I'm here
to tell you that it's not. I've been finding them since
I was a boy. I found several after my daddy died.
It's supposed to be their way of letting you know

they're okay, you know? That you can let them go. I've found half a dozen since Martha died, two of them right there on her headstone."

Jack had never heard that before, but was never one to doubt or question the unexplained.

"You mean you didn't know some of the coins were valuable?"

He shook his head, clearly puzzled. "I had no idea. They were keepsakes, not cash."

Bobby Ray had gotten extremely lucky. "Come on," Jack told him. "I'll take you home."

He called Mariette first. "I've got him and he's fine. Tell Charlie so she can call everyone else off."

"I will," she said. He heard her relay the news to Bobby Ray and the boy's sigh of relief was loud enough that he heard it over the line.

"And you took care of the other?"

"I did. He has them and is going to leave here right now and go put them back where they came from."

Jack darted a look at Audwin from the corner of his eye. "He knows," he said. "But I don't think he's going to let on."

"Good," Mariette said. "I think that would be for the best." She paused. "I'll see you soon."

It was almost, but not quite, a question, and he suddenly realized that she must think that because this case was closed, they were finished, as well. That he would just pack up his things and move on with his life as though she'd been a mere distraction, a fun little excursion on this assignment.

Nothing could be further from the truth.

And no one was more surprised by that than Jackson Oak Martin.

"You will," he promised.

CHARLIE HUGGED MARIETTE'S neck and gave her a squeeze. "I'll see you soon," she said. "I've enjoyed being down here with you. As far as assignments go, short of the one where I met my husband, this one has been the best."

Mariette grinned at her. "I'm glad to hear it."

Charlie hesitated. "He's crazy about you, you know."

Mariette's gaze flew to hers. "What? Who?"

"Don't play coy," she said. "You think I didn't know what was going on from the moment the two of you laid eyes on each other?"

Mariette blushed. "Charlie, I—"

"See?" she said, laughing softly. "I can't even bring him up without your face turning six shades of red. And Livvie's got it right. You do look gooey. She told me so earlier today."

"Gooey?"

"Like the middle part of the brownie," Charlie told her. "Warm and gooey and good."

She certainly felt like the middle part of the brownie when she was with Jack, that was for damned sure. Except for when she wasn't wound tight with desire, a desperate throbbing nerve of need.

She'd never felt this way before, Mariette thought. She never needed, admired or craved a man the way she did Jack Martin. Was he handsome? Certainly. Hot? Most definitely. But he was so much more than that. He was a man who cared enough about the happiness of a less-fortunate boy that he'd done everything he could possibly do to pave an easier way for him. That took character, it took heart, it took…a real man.

Charlie gave her another squeeze. "I'd better go," she said, her eyes twinkling. "I'd hate to delay your spanking."

And with that parting comment, she turned and walked away.

Mariette looked around her suddenly empty shop and felt an odd pang. For the first time in her life she wasn't quite sure what to do with herself.

Thankfully, she didn't have an opportunity to dwell on that, because Jack chose that moment to stroll into the shop. The bell above the door jingled, signaling his arrival and there was something almost providential in the ring this time. Something that made her smile.

He strolled determinedly to her, then wrapped her in his arms and kissed her. He breathed her in, savored her mouth, tangled his tongue around hers as though somehow the act seemed to trigger a reset button, a way to get back to who they were.

"I have some bad news," Jack told her, pulling back to stare into her face. His gaze was soft and tender, his blue eyes rife with an emotion she hadn't seen in a long, long time.

"What's that?"

"I'm not going to be run off as easily as Nathaniel," he said. "In the first place, you'd have to find somebody bigger and, short of the real Jolly Green Giant, I don't think that's going to happen. In the second place, I'm not as easily intimidated and have a thicker head than anyone you've likely ever gotten involved with before."

Mariette blinked up at him and smiled. "What gave you the idea I wanted to get rid of you?"

"Nothing yet," he told her. "I'm just making a pre-emptive strike. Letting you know where I stand." He paused. "Where do *I* stand, Mariette?"

On the threshold of her heart, Mariette thought. And she had no doubt that he would knock and pummel and batter the door down until she let him in.

"With me," she said simply. "I don't know what this is," she admitted. "And don't have the experience to know what should happen next. All I know is that I want to be with you. As much as possible, whenever possible."

He nuzzled the side of her neck. "That can certainly be arranged."

"Your sister knows about us," Mariette told him.

He chuckled. "I never doubted it. That's why she filled your ears full. She didn't want you toying with my affections."

She blinked up at him. "What?"

"Charlie's protective," he said. He swallowed. "And I wasn't myself when I came home. I... I lost a couple of men. In Baghdad. I'm sure she told you that."

Mariette squeezed him. "She did. I'm so sorry, Jack."

His gaze turned inward, reliving a nightmare she couldn't see. "It was hell," he said. "But there was this one guy, Johnson... I really liked him. He was young and smart." He released a breath. "Bobby Ray actually reminds me of him. They have that same spirit of goodness, you know?"

She nodded.

"Anyway, when the blast hit he'd been talking about what he wanted out of a woman," Jack told her. He shook his head. "One of the other guys had just made some jackass comment about—" He blinked. "Never mind what it was about. But Johnson's reply was wholesome, innocent. He just wanted a woman who knew how to cook." His gaze tangled with hers. "And then I found you."

"Oh, Jack," she said, her heart crowding into her throat.

"He died in my arms, Mariette, and as horrible as that was, he kept trying to tell me something before he died. He was shouting it. He grabbed me and shook me and repeated himself until he couldn't anymore. And I couldn't hear him."

Oh, Lord...

Because of his ear. No doubt the force of the blast had rendered him temporarily deaf and... She swallowed, held him closer.

"I can see his face, every move of his lips—everything about that few minutes—plain as day. But I still haven't been able to figure out what he was trying to tell me. And it was important, Mariette. He spent his last breath trying to share it with me." He paused again, looked down and his tortured gaze tangled with hers. "I've been taking lip-reading lessons trying to learn the technique so that I can figure it out."

She blinked, astonished. "You have?"

"It was important to him, whatever it was. I need to pass the message along."

So simple and yet so profound. Sweet heaven, had there ever been a better man? "Have you made any headway on it yet?"

"Just a little." He glanced down at her. "It's much more difficult than I'd anticipated. For instance, 'I love you' could easily be mistaken for 'olive juice' or 'elephant shoes.' See, give it a go. I'll mouth it and you try to guess which one of those phrases I said."

She nodded. "Okay."

She watched his lips, her heart beating strangely in her chest. He did it and she stared at him, completely at a loss. He was right. He could have said any one of those lines. "Olive juice," she guessed.

"No," he told her, dragging her closer to him. "I said 'I love you.'"

"Oh."

"On purpose, Mariette," he said. "You think I'm insane, don't you?"

Mariette didn't know that this much happiness could occupy a single body, let alone hers. She flushed with joy, felt it permeate every cell, making her glow inside.

"Then I'm going crazy with you," she said, lifting up on tiptoe to give him a kiss. She drew back once more, framed his dear face and slid her thumb along his jaw. "It wasn't your fault, Jack," she said.

He frowned at her, a line wrinkling his brow.

"Baghdad." It might not be her place, but dammit, he needed to hear it. "It wasn't your fault."

He went chalk white and staggered back against the display case.

"Jack?"

"Say that again," he said, his gaze fastening on her mouth.

"It's not your fault, Jack."

Jack passed a hand over his face, his big body trembling. A dry bark of laugher erupted from his throat and he shook his head, but he wasn't amused. She didn't know exactly what he was, but...

"That's what he said," Jack murmured. "All this time I've been worried about making sure his message was delivered and it was for me," he said, his voice cracking. "'It's not your fault, Oak,'" he'd said. He glanced up at her. "That's what they called me. Mighty Oak, actually. It's my middle name."

Tears burned the backs of her lids and blurred her vision. "I know. Your sister told me."

He rolled his eyes, snorted. "Of course she did. The little blabbermouth."

She rained gentle kisses on his face. "Yes, but you olive juice her."

He chuckled weakly. "I do," he said. "And I olive juice you, too." He threaded his fingers through hers and then tugged her toward the staircase. "Come on," he told her. "I believe I owe you a spanking."

That he did, Mariette thought. And she'd happily take her punishment for as long as he'd dole it out.

And she hoped that was forever.

Epilogue

One month later...

THE SURGEON WALKED INTO the waiting room and said, "Bishop family," in carrying tones.

Five former Army Rangers, a pregnant security agent, a dairy farmer, a girl with Down syndrome decked out in Hello Kitty attire and a pastry chef all stood.

The surgeon's eyes widened at the imposing, eclectic group.

Audwin stepped forward. "How's my son?"

The surgeon smiled. "He came through with flying colors, sir. I'm confident that this surgery will smooth out those scars and make him feel much more confident in his appearance. He's in recovery now and will be moved to a room—"

"A private room," Payne interjected. "On my wing."

Payne's wing was actually labor and delivery, but the surgeon knew better than to argue with him, Mariette thought, smiling as she and Jack shared a look.

"As you wish, Mr. Payne," he said. "It'll probably be a little while before he's awake. I'll have someone notify you when we move him."

Everyone breathed a collective sigh of relief. It hadn't taken much to convince Bobby Ray to have the corrective surgery to repair his face. What he'd balked at was the cost, but Audwin had insisted that he couldn't think of a better way to spend his money. He'd sold every coin worth any value, had only kept the ones he'd found on Martha's headstone.

Bobby Ray had moved in with Audwin and the change in the boy since being taken under the older man's wing—and that of all the rest of them—was nothing short of phenomenal. He planned to start taking college classes in the fall, once he'd finished healing.

Jack, meanwhile, had moved in with Mariette and home had never felt so right. She went to bed with him snuggled up to her back and woke up in the same fashion. She felt cherished and appreciated and generally adored, and there was nothing quite so wonderful than being unconditionally loved.

She squeezed his hand, looked up at him and smiled. "Olive juice," she said, saying it for the first time so that he could hear her. The emotions were there, but for whatever reason, the words had been more difficult to say.

But she needed to say them and, more importantly, he needed to hear them.

He grinned, bent down and pressed a kiss to her lips. "Olive juice you, too, sweetheart."

Charlie shot them both a perplexed look and rolled her eyes. "The inside jokes are getting a little old," she said. "Olive juice? What does that even mean?"

Jack tugged Mariette up against his side and gave her a squeeze. "It means we're happy."

Yes, Mariette thought. That, and so much more.

* * * * *

Special Offers

Every month we put together collections and longer reads written by your favourite authors.

Here are some of next month's highlights— and don't miss our fabulous discount online!

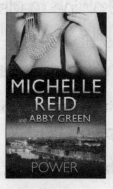

On sale 20th April   On sale 20th April   On sale 20th April

Save 20%
on all Special Releases

The World of Mills & Boon®

There's a Mills & Boon® series that's perfect for you. We publish ten series and with new titles every month, you never have to wait long for your favourite to come along.

Blaze® — Scorching hot, sexy reads

By Request — Relive the romance with the best of the best

Cherish™ — Romance to melt the heart every time

Desire™ — Passionate and dramatic love stories

Have Your Say

You've just finished your book.
So what did you think?

We'd love to hear your thoughts on our
'Have your say' online panel
www.millsandboon.co.uk/haveyoursay

- ❧ Easy to use
- ❧ Short questionnaire
- ❧ Chance to win Mills & Boon® goodies

Visit us Online

Tell us what you thought of this book now at
www.millsandboon.co.uk/haveyoursay

YOUR_SAY